D1456911

Hidden Within

the Stones

Also by Robin Martinez Rice

Imperfecta

Sisters in Pieces

Tales of the Elemental Goddesses

Hidden Within
the Stones

by

Robin Martinez Rice

Robin Martinez Rice

❋

RLMR

Note: Three Ravens Coffeehouse truly exists in Tierra
Amarilla. I have fictionalized it for this story, but if you are
ever in town be sure to stop in for a great breakfast
sandwich, coffee and, if you're lucky, some music.

ISBN-13: 978-0692316955
ISBN-10: 0692316957

To all families and their hidden heritage.

Martínez

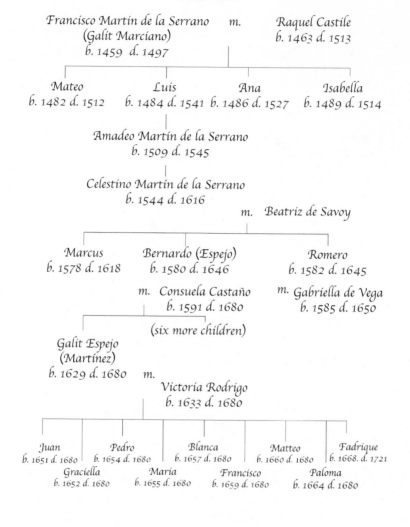

Francisco Martín de la Serrano   m.   Raquel Castile
(Galit Marciano)   b. 1463 d. 1513
b. 1459 d. 1497

Mateo   Luis   Ana   Isabella
b. 1482 d. 1512   b. 1484 d. 1541   b. 1486 d. 1527   b. 1489 d. 1514

Amadeo Martín de la Serrano
b. 1509 d. 1545

Celestino Martín de la Serrano
b. 1544 d. 1616
                                    m.   Beatriz de Savoy

Marcus   Bernardo (Espejo)   Romero
b. 1578 d. 1618   b. 1580 d. 1646   b. 1582 d. 1645

                   m. Consuela Castaño   m. Gabriella de Vega
                       b. 1591 d. 1680   b. 1585 d. 1650

                   (six more children)

Galit Espejo
(Martínez)
b. 1629 d. 1680   m.
                   Victoria Rodrigo
                   b. 1633 d. 1680

Juan   Pedro   Blanca   Matteo   Fadrique
b. 1651 d. 1680 b. 1654 d. 1680 b. 1657 d. 1680 b. 1660 d. 1680 b. 1668. d. 1721
    Graciella   María   Francisco   Paloma
    b. 1652 d. 1680 b. 1655 d. 1680 b. 1659 d. 1680 b. 1664 d. 1680

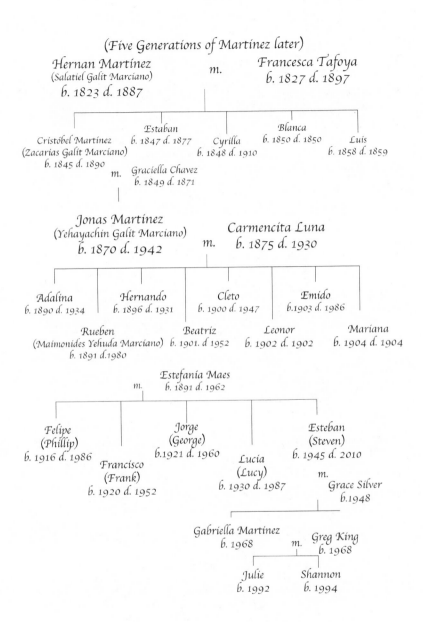

(Five Generations of Martinez later)

Hernan Martínez
(Salatiel Galit Marciano)
b. 1823 d. 1887

m.

Francesca Tafoya
b. 1827 d. 1897

Cristóbel Martínez
(Zacarias Galit Marciano)
b. 1845 d. 1890

Estaban
b. 1847 d. 1877

Cyrilla
b. 1848 d. 1910

Blanca
b. 1850 d. 1850

Luis
b. 1858 d. 1859

m.   Graciella Chavez
b. 1849 d. 1871

Jonas Martínez
(Yehayachin Galit Marciano)
b. 1870 d. 1942

m.

Carmencita Luna
b. 1875 d. 1930

Adalina
b. 1890 d. 1934

Hernando
b. 1896 d. 1931

Cleto
b. 1900 d. 1947

Emido
b.1903 d. 1986

Rueben
(Maimonides Yehuda Marciano)
b. 1891 d.1980

Beatriz
b. 1901. d 1952

Leonor
b. 1902 d. 1902

Mariana
b. 1904 d. 1904

m.

Estefania Maes
b. 1891 d. 1962

Felipe
(Phillip)
b. 1916 d. 1986

Francisco
(Frank)
b. 1920 d. 1952

Jorge
(George)
b.1921 d. 1960

Lucia
(Lucy)
b. 1930 d. 1987

Esteban
(Steven)
b. 1945 d. 2010

m.

Grace Silver
b.1948

Gabriella Martinez
b. 1968

m.

Greg King
b. 1968

Julie
b. 1992

Shannon
b. 1994

Rodrigo

Alejandro Antonio Rodrigo
b.1823 d. 1898

m. Sophia Martina Chavez
b.1827 d. 1884

Alfonso Alejandro Rodrigo
b. 1851 d.1901

María Sanchez
b. 1858 d. 1927

m.

Vincente Ramoldo Rodrigo
b. 1881 d. 1935

m. Aloisa Sophia Serrano
b. 1891 d. 1949

Rachel García María de la Rodrigo y Rivas
b. 1925

m.

Clemente Pancho Rivas
b. 1923 d. 1979

Alejandro Jorge Rivas
b. 1945 d. 1967

m. Helen Grace Luna
b. 1947

Alfredo Rodrigo Rivas
b. 1965

Patton

Joseph Patton
b. 1840 d. 1886

Joseph Patton Jr.
b. 1862 d. 1935
m.　Mary James
b.1868 d. 1941

Raymond　　　　　Benjamin
b.1888 d. 1978　　b. 1906 d. 1957

m.　Marcia Graves
b.1900 d. 1980

Richard
b.1925 d. 2012
m.　Cynthia Parker
b.1929

James　　　　Christopher　　　Andrea
b.1950　　　　b. 1955　　　　b. 1960

m.　Rebecca Connors
b.1955 d. 2010
　　　　　　　　　　　　　Raymundo Cruz
　　　　　　　　　　　　　b. 1984

Grace
b. 1990　　Jack Smith
　　m.　b. 1987

Maura
b. 2010

Before

The old man finished his prayer and raised his trembling hand to the shawl draped over his head. His gaze flitted quickly from the table near the window, the old black stove, and the painted cupboards. This was the last time he would pray under the comfort of the ancient cloth. From now on he must rely on the memories reflected in this room to guide him through his talks with God.

He drew in a breath and closed his eyes. Decisions had been made, and he had no choice. He pulled the yellowed linen cloth from his head and smoothed it.

Worn with time, the pine darkened from the oil of many hands, the wooden box on the table waited. He twisted the clasp, opened the lid, and placed the folded prayer shawl on top of the other items. After closing it, he leaned and pressed his lips against the wood before he knelt and slid it into the space he had opened in the stone wall.

He began to fill the hole, rebuilding what he had taken apart earlier that day. He placed each stone with care, accepting or rejecting it based on the fit and the color of the neighboring rocks and what each added to the beauty and strength of the wall.

When he finished, he reached for the heavy stick he used as a cane, pulled himself up from his kneeling position, then stepped back to view his work.

No one would guess this spot was newer than the rest of the wall.

He piled firewood for the small stove in front of the repaired section. He had put the hiding place close to the heat, hoping to keep mildew and damp from the box.

The old man looked down at his shaking hands. Was he making the right choice? To hide this secret from his sons?

He remembered his grandfather's hands, wrinkled as his were now, holding up each of the objects in the box as he explained the rituals.

"Touch them and you will know the story of our people," his grandfather had whispered.

The old man's grandsons would not touch these things.

They would not know their story.

One

Gabriella Martinez

Oakland, California

Sunday, March 30, 2014

She-Who-Is-Unprepared, that's who I was now.

My mother had started a trend, giving everyone special names —Indian names we called them. No longer politically correct, but still funny. You had to earn your name, and it was seldom complimentary. I earned my first name at eight years old.

"Come on, Little-She-Who-Pee. Use the bathroom before we leave." Mom had tired of the frequent stops required during every car trip.

What would my mother say about my abrupt decision to take this road trip? I hadn't called her yet but I could hear her agreeing that She-Who-Is-Unprepared was the perfect name for me, earned in the true family tradition.

Everyone encouraged me to get on with life, take a chance, see the best in things, and crawling out from my spot under the rock of numbness for just a few minutes, it seemed I had followed their advice.

But I hadn't. I fled. Away from all the prying questions, the offers of blind dates and the endless phone calls. Ran away from a son-of-a-bitch husband who'd blindsided me with his passive betrayal. I needed to escape and wallow in my self-pity unmolested.

Twenty-seven days ago my marriage had dissolved. One minute it was there, and when I wasn't looking, it all washed away.

It was a pleasant evening, the windows thrown open wide to let the first signs of spring drift through the kitchen. Greg had finished his last bite of pork chop and carried his plate to the sink. Then my partner of twenty-five years turned to me.

"Ella, I'm moving out on Saturday."

I stopped chewing. Two icy hands reached into my chest and grabbed my heart, squeezing it. I couldn't breathe. I couldn't figure out if I should swallow or spit out the mouthful of half-chewed green beans.

Greg didn't wait for me to say anything. He simply rinsed his plate, slid it into the dishwasher, turned and left the room.

His decision shocked me. I knew our life had settled into a boring rhythm. Greg constantly tried to convince me we should travel or join health clubs or go out for cocktails with this foursome or play golf with that couple. And I did these things. Sometimes. But Greg never hid his frustrated sigh when he'd ask "Wasn't that fun?" Underneath Greg's pleas I couldn't help but hear my father's commanding voice—"You'll try harder next time." I would smile at my husband, as I had at my father, with no chance of convincing either one I would ever come close to their standards.

My daughters weren't surprised when I told them their father had left me.

"Mom, that's terrible. I never thought Dad would do it." Julie looked away as she spoke, leading me to hear the "actually" she left out of her attempt at comfort.

"What do you kn—" I stopped myself. It wasn't right to draw the girls into my marital problems by trying to find out what they knew. They were barely adults, nowhere near ready to hear details of my emotional crash and burn. But Julie knew something. Had Greg talked to her?

"Oh, Mom," Shannon snorted. "Why are you surprised? You guys haven't been happy in years. I guess this means we aren't going on vacation this Easter. That's good because Jason invited me to go to Hawaii."

It felt as if my children and Greg had planned this together, although that idea was far-fetched, even in my depressed state. As if they said "Let's all divorce her at once, get away from dull Ella, live our own lives." Greg refused to talk about it. He moved into an apartment and wouldn't answer my calls. I drove to his new place and waited outside for him—ambusher, stalker, crazed abandoned spouse—catching him as he left for work.

"Ella, it's over. That's the best I can do. I really don't want to hash this over. In fact, if you want an answer, that's it." He hurried to his car, tossing the words over his shoulder.

"What about counseling?" I yelled at his retreating back. "Aren't you even willing to work on this? Am I nothing to you?" I hated myself for sobbing and whining, but I couldn't stop.

"It's too late, Ella. We both need to move on."

✡ ✡ ✡

I didn't move on. "What did he mean by that?" I asked my best-friend-since-birth, Vicki Paretti, having rushed to her house as soon as Greg drove away. "Move on? Is that all he sees, the next phase? Am I some sort of stepping stone?"

Vicki enjoyed analyzing the break up and trying to figure out what Greg was hiding. "Who's he sleeping with?"

"Have you heard something?"

"No. It's just…"

I might have laughed at her attraction to mysterious explanations, but my shock was so deep and my sorrow so great that nothing seemed funny.

I shook my head before Vicki could finish her thought. "I don't want to hear this."

"Maybe you were *too* perfect. That never works. People hold things in and then everything explodes."

Things weren't perfect, but they were certainly sustainable. An explosion would have been nice. Yelling and accusations. Something to guide me in my quest for answers. Things I could deal with, using my usual "it'll be all right" methods of straightening out my life, much like I had smoothed the clean sheets on the beds every Thursday—laundry day—for the past twenty-five years.

✡ ✡ ✡

For nearly a month I sat in our house and cried. I couldn't let reality slip away. It had happened to me once before, twice if you counted the episode when I was six, but I couldn't remember it, so I didn't count it. My mother reported a blackout and two days of confusion suffered after an incident at Sunday School. She seemed to think two girls had teased me, but I can't imagine I would have reacted to something like that with a break from reality.

"It might be a good idea if you found a job," Vicki said. "You can't just sit here for the rest of your life."

Me? A job? How? I didn't have any skills. Three years of college—as a psychology major, no less—a lot of good that would do me now. Once upon a time I had dreams of being a therapist, but obviously what little I learned hadn't even helped me run my own life. Besides, I had become Ella-Who-Sits, frozen, unable to move, yet my mind never stopping, replaying every moment of my life, over and over, trying to see what I could have done differently, where I had gone wrong.

A cream-colored envelope and two phone calls changed everything.

The letter was from Dominguez and Marconi, LLP. I didn't open it for two days, not wanting to go one more step in this whole divorce thing. I should get a lawyer, but I hadn't.

Finally, unable to escape the icy stare of the unopened envelope, I unfolded the single sheet of heavy paper and scanned the first line.

Not from Greg and not divorce paperwork. Seems I had inherited property in Tierra Amarilla, New Mexico. Property which would have gone to my father, but since he was dead, it came to me.

The thought of inheriting something from my father—indirectly or not—made me unhappy. Why did everyone think their parents owed them something? On second thought, had my father ever thought he owed me anything other than a strict upbringing? Did owning something that had belonged to your parents make you special? Move you to ecstasy? Reserve you a place in heaven?

I thought not.

The letter was vague, didn't tell me how much or what I should do now. Call Dominguez and Marconi, I guessed.

As I glanced at the clock—wasn't New Mexico in a different time zone?—the phone rang.

"Hello?"

"Ella? Gabriella Martinez?"

Who was this? Using my maiden name?

"Who is this?"

"Sorry. Ella, it's Mark. Your cousin."

Mark. How could he know I had just opened the letter? I had only met him once, when I was fourteen and he was fifteen and we had driven twenty-five miles to visit his ailing father, who was my father's cousin. That made Mark a second cousin or a once-removed cousin or something like that.

"It's a lot of property, Ella. Each of the brothers, or the heirs of the brothers, gets a portion. You get 200 acres." Mark paused.

"How much is it worth?" I quickly calculated. Didn't land sell for some high amount? Was it ten thousand or a hundred thousand an acre? I'm an idiot when it comes to decimals, but had I just become a millionaire? I caught my breath as I realized this was *my* land. Not Greg's.

"You would sell it?" Mark's voice was harsh and I'm sure he growled.

"I'm in kind of a rough spot just now." Not to mention I didn't feel any loyalty to some legacy from a family I didn't know. And I certainly didn't feel any loyalty to my father.

"I see," Mark said, not sounding like he saw at all. "You do have water rights, so that makes it a little more valuable. Land out here doesn't sell. It's really depressed, and your section is between mine and Jeff's. Not land-locked or anything, but probably not desirable to an outsider."

I didn't believe him. It was obvious he was in a snit because I wasn't making a big fuss and shouting with joy. Or maybe my cousin had called with a different thought in mind. The rich California cousin wouldn't want the land and she would give it to him.

"What about you?" I asked.

"We aren't selling."

"Not sell. Buy. Are you interested in buying my part? I mean if it's next to yours and all." Would he expect a family discount? At this point any money was welcome.

Mark didn't answer right away, and I swear I heard figures being scratched out on a scrap of paper.

"I can offer you ten thousand."

"An acre?" Ten thousand times two hundred? I fought to keep from screaming with joy.

Mark laughed. "Right. And I just won the lottery."

My instant wealth vanished. Ten thousand dollars wouldn't support me for the next twenty years.

Common sense crept into my mind, not on little cat feet, but ever so softly. After some polite mumbles to my cousin and mentioning I would get back to him, I hung up. I needed to do some research on property prices.

Ten minutes later the phone rang again.

"We have an offer on the house. It's a quick escrow. You need to sign the paperwork. They want to move in April 17th." Greg was wearing his business voice.

I started to cry. *No way Greg. You can't do this. You can't pretend everything is fine when it isn't. You can't make me raise our children and then abandon me, throw away our life without an explanation.* "What did I do wrong?" I whispered.

"Ella, you signed papers agreeing to sell. I need the money."

"I know that. But half of whatever is mine." My thoughts took a sharp left turn. Shouldn't I have been in on accepting an offer on the house? When I signed the power of attorney I thought he would keep me in the loop.

"Ella," I pictured Greg shaking his head the way he always did when he was powering up. "We refinanced, remember?"

Of course I remembered. We needed to do it when Julie picked a private university, rather than the local community college. She was smart and we both agreed it was the right thing to do.

"That's thirty-thousand dollars. We'll barely realize enough to pay it back. The market is bad now."

Was everyone singing the same song today?

"Maybe we should wait until the market isn't so bad?" *And I figure out how the hell I'm going to keep you from manipulating me one more time.*

"Maybe you should pay the mortgage."

That was a conversation stopper. In my post-trauma slump, I now avoided thinking about the future. It took all my energy to work on the puzzles of the past. Suddenly the property in New Mexico changed hue, going from black and white to Technicolor in a blinding flash of green—the color of money.

"I have to go." I ended the call and dialed Dominguez and Marconi.

I needed to sell my land. And I needed to sell it for more than ten thousand dollars.

✡ ✡ ✡

While I waited for Dominguez or Marconi to return my call, I sorted through the house full of objects. Things, so many things. Greg wouldn't help. He just wanted to walk away from the past.

"I can remember the kids, Ella. I don't need old school papers to remind me. Please don't call me about this stuff."

His words stung. As if my saving Shannon's drawings of unicorns or Julie's perfectly scripted reports about Hillary Clinton meant that I was less of a parent than he was. Didn't all parents keep the history of their children shoved in manila envelopes and cardboard boxes? Tan newsprint with pale blue lines holding first efforts of learning to write? Julie's precise letters, as if she used a ruler to keep the backbones straight, and Shannon's heavy black smudges, erased until the paper tore? Archeological signs of how these children would turn out as adults.

That was my problem, only noticing the signs of what was happening in the present when I dug through the past.

I spent the day sorting and packing and crying. Finally Mr. Dominguez called me back.

"I would advise you to come to New Mexico." he said in an official attorney-at-law tone. "I can recommend a realtor, but in my experience it's best you know what you're selling before you list it. Fred Rivas, the agent, he'll show you around so you can see some comparable properties. He'll help you decide on a realistic price."

"More than fifty dollars an acre?"

"I imagine so."

Mark had been trying to cheat me.

"I can't afford a trip out there." Hadn't I just told the guy I needed the money? Couldn't he hear the desperate tone in my voice?

"I realize it's an expense, but money well spent, in my opinion." Dominguez—what was his first name?—spoke as if time were money. I realized I was probably going to get a bill for this call.

After another set of mumbled and automatic thank yous and goodbyes, I sat and stared at the stacked boxes. Nowhere to go, nowhere to put these boxes, so neatly labeled Kitchen, Bedroom, Shannon and Julie.

Objects, not archeological treasures. Things I might be able to sell at a yard sale. I would sit outside in the sun all day while scruffy bearded men handled my daughters' old clothes and gray haired women pawed through my mother's linens and at the end the day I might have twenty-five dollars.

I phoned Julie. I hadn't told her about the letter from Dominguez and Marconi, LLP, or the land in New Mexico. My sympathetic daughter could laugh about it with me.

She didn't answer. In desperation, I called Shannon.

"Hey sweetie. I'm here at the house and there're a lot of things I think you should look through."

"Like what?"

"Oh... papers, toys, books. Some of Grandma King's things."

"Chuck it all."

"Now Shannon, you might want some of this."

"No really, Mom. I don't want it. Look, I gotta go."

I heard her mumble something to someone.

"It won't take you long to look." I would tempt her with some cookies. I just had to get her over here.

"I really gotta go, Mom. Love ya." Click.

I tried Julie again. This time she answered and I told her about the property in New Mexico.

"You're going to sell it?" Julie sounded just like Mark. "Without even seeing it?" Okay, now she sounded like Dominguez. "Isn't that where Grandpop was born?" Back to Mark.

"I need the money, sweetie. What else would I do with it? Live there?"

"What about me and Shannon? Isn't it ours too?"

"Only if I'm dead."

"I know that, Mom. I'm talking about emotionally. Maybe we'll want to live there some day. Grandpop always told me it's a beautiful place."

My father had talked to Julie about New Mexico?

"Oh, Julie." I sighed. "I really called about all these *things*. Boxes and boxes of things. I have to purge, can't you to come over and go through them with me?"

"Mom, you're overreacting. You don't have to get rid of stuff just because you're moving." She clucked like a hen. "You know, Dad isn't going to care. You aren't making him suffer by doing this. You would do us all a favor if you quit moping."

This from Julie? The only kind-hearted person left in the family?

"Mom. I'm not trying to be mean. But you're young and you're attractive. Move on with life."

Was my daughter telling me to get rid of things or not? Did she want me to move on or stay the same? And what did she mean by telling me I was young and attractive? Did she want me to date or was this just a blatant "feel good about yourself" statement?

I mumbled goodbye, hung up the phone and started to cry. Again.

I remembered my postpartum depression. It was just after Shannon was born. Withdrawal, apathy, constant tears, no appetite, skin crawling when anyone—even this new baby or the active two-year-old Julie—touched me. Everyone tried to help, but that didn't keep the black hole from opening and swallowing me.

My secret was deep. Much deeper than any of the therapists or doctors or my husband or my parents ever guessed. With two babies and a husband and magazines and friends and everyone telling me how I needed to be—no, *who* I needed to be—I faked it. Faked my way out of postpartum depression, faked my recovery, faked my acceptance of the life I had fallen into. I went to the library and checked out books, reading about inherited depression, bi-polar disorder, nervous breakdowns and medications. Just as I had studied for a biology exam, so I studied to ease the worried looks of my husband and parents.

I was good at being Fake-Ella. The whitened-teeth smile, the president of PTA, the soccer mom who glued green felt letters onto the yellow banner. No one ever knew that I constantly ran from the depression that threatened to engulf me, just a step ahead of falling into oblivion once again.

Had Greg finally seen through the camouflage of my dutiful wife and mother disguise? Was that why he left me?

Maybe he had been faking it, too.

Now, just like those post-baby months, everyone had so much advice about moving on, but no one could tell me how to make things right. I slumped to the floor and kicked at the cardboard box filled with books. Why wasn't anyone mad at Greg? He was the cause of this mess. Didn't it strike people—my mother, Julie, Vicki —that he was the one who had thrown away a good life? He was downright mean, but no one could see it. He didn't even care about the dog, let alone me.

I leaned against the cupboard and kicked the box harder, impressed by the dent my heel left in the side. In spite of everything I had done, it wasn't good enough. I kicked the box with enough force to topple the stack and send books spilling out.

"You son-of-a-bitch!" I jumped up and screamed, sweeping papers and placemats off the table. "I hate you!"

I pictured Greg's smirk, his insistence that he didn't want anything we had saved. The things he claimed to have worked so hard for. I grabbed the antique china pitcher from the center of the table, already hearing the satisfying crash the glass would make when it hit the wall. It had belonged to Greg's mother.

Arm poised, I remembered how Shannon loved this pitcher. She had even painted a picture of it when she was nine.

I set it back on the table and looked around. Dirty dishes filled the sink. Ella-Who-Sits didn't think twice about leaving things a mess. I grabbed a plate and threw it against the wall.

The crash was loud but disappointing. If I could only smash the past twenty-five years of my life. The china bits too tiny to be glued back together. But that was what had happened, wasn't it?

Bones came running, her long tail waving as if to say *Is everything under control here?* I grabbed her collar to keep her away from the shards.

Depleted, I slumped back into the kitchen chair and my dog pushed her soft nose into my trembling palm. My breath came in painful gasps, squeezing into lungs like elastic which has lost its stretch. I tried to keep the darkness from getting in, but the black hole crept up and engulfed me.

They would lock me up. Maybe that would be a relief. Some nurse taking care of me. Someone else responsible for packing up the house. I didn't have a place to go, why not a hospital?

I couldn't get enough air. I needed to get away. All this drama, all these people, even my sweet daughter telling me what to do.

Gotta go.

Could it really be that easy?

Sorry, gotta go?

I jumped up and ran to the garage, grabbed a sleeping bag, a lawn chair and the box of camping stuff: lantern, propane stove, flashlights, the red nylon tent we had bought for Julie when she was a girl scout and a tarp. There was no organization to the mess stuffed into the back of the Honda. I would camp. It wouldn't cost me much to go. To hell with Greg, I would use our credit card.

Fifteen minutes later, with my laptop, a duffle bag full of clothes and Bones perched on the seat as my co-pilot, I backed out of the garage.

With the coordinates for Tierra Amarilla, New Mexico entered into the GPS, I escaped.

Two
Francisco Martín de la Serrano
Barcelona, Spain
December 27, 1491

In spite of the cold, rivulets of sweat ran from beneath Francisco Martín de la Serrano's armpits down to his waist. No one else prowled the city this late, but the increase in guards expected in preparation for King Ferdinand's upcoming announcement regarding the fate of Jews worried him. The new year would be here in a week and in 1492 the Holy Inquisition would move forward with a vengeance. Francisco shook his head and quickened his step, although the frozen cobbles slowed him. Probably a good thing; the ice kept him from running, which would surely attract attention. The thought of an injury frightened him. He had too much to accomplish to be laid up by some crack in a leg bone.

Why would the Brothers call a last minute meeting at this hour? He adjusted the hood away from his ear, where it plagued him with its rough texture. The men knew of the King of Spain's announcement, so there must be something else they needed to discuss.

Ten minutes later Francisco approached a decrepit stone building, perched at the edge of the seawall like it was ready to dive off and end its life. This place made him feel an orchestrated sense of doom, as if one of the brothers wanted to scare the others. Weren't they frightened enough by the politics of the King and his unpredictable Queen?

Francisco lit a small candle before he ducked through the doorway, slipped the cloth mask over his face, then followed the cold hallway toward a glow up ahead. A second doorway led into a large room.

The tall man standing in front of the others began to talk as soon as Francisco tucked himself into the circle of eleven men, the last of the twelve to arrive.

The man's voice was strong. "We must thin our numbers. King Ferdinand is influenced by Torquemada. Actually, Queen Isabella is influenced, and that means he will follow. Ferdinand's announcement will be just the start."

Francisco knew this was Marcus de la Paloma speaking—the mask and hood worn by the oldest member of the Brotherhood did little to disguise who was in charge here.

"The Inquisition is taking a strong turn. If we wait, too many of our people will be discovered. We must leave Spain as soon as possible."

Francisco could not believe what he heard. The purpose of the Brotherhood was to maintain their presence on the Iberian Peninsula. He stepped forward. "I don't want to leave my home. I will stay. My place in the church is strong."

"We have no doubt, Brother." Alfonso Goméz de Tordoya's throaty growl was unmistakable. "You might stay safe, but what of the people who follow you? If they are not careful, you will all be exposed. I have heard the Queen's men have new ways of discovering our people. Many have been imprisoned. Executions are taking place already and more will follow. If we cannot stay true to our faith, cannot practice any of our basic beliefs, persecution has caught up with us once again. Exile will follow. We have balanced on this wall for many years, but now we risk tumbling off. The job of the Brotherhood is to maintain our faith, hidden but existing."

Francisco had heard the stories: men spying on people in their own homes or following them to watch their habits; payments offered to those who reported any suspicious work or eating behaviors; family members bribed to expose their relatives and escape persecution in return. The King was demanding physical examinations of male children and prisoners.

Marcus leaned toward Francisco. "What about your wife? Do you believe she will be safe? Her disguise is not so strong as yours."

Francisco's throat grew tight. He reached up and rubbed the hard knot which had formed, keeping him from speaking. He trembled at the vision of his sweet wife being dragged through the cold streets and thrown into the dank cells of the King's prison. If Raquel or he were captured what would become of their children? Mateo and Luis were old enough to be questioned, but too young to understand the outcome of their responses. Ana and Bella barely more than infants, too young to lose their mother.

He thought they were safe hiding at the convent—Raquel as a nun and the children as orphans. But last week his wife had been accosted by a novitiate. It had been a mistake for Raquel to hide the small bit of pork on her plate under her napkin. Luckily she escaped questioning by forcing herself to vomit and breaking into a fearful sweat. Her claim of illness was accepted as a valid reason for not eating the meat.

Francisco wasn't ready to leave Spain. Generations of his family had fought for the right to live here. Shaking his head, he addressed the Brothers. "We have worked so hard to build up the system. What of those who stay? Won't they need the support of the Church?"

Marcus held up his hand, palm forward. "Take a moment to think. We help no one if we are dead or imprisoned. It is better for us to go to Portugal and work from there. We won't give up the fight."

Francisco knew the old man was not a coward. Marcus was a good leader, and his decisions had been sound in the past. He dipped his chin and stepped back into the circle of men.

The Brothers discussed the details of the exodus. The first group, which included Francisco and his family, would leave by wagon as soon as the weather permitted. The trip over the mountains was rugged and snow filled the passes. Francisco felt relief at the brief respite knowing it would be several months before this journey would happen. Other men would leave by sea, but those were generally men without small children.

"El que cree y persista vive para siempre." The men parted with the code of the Brotherhood. He who believes and persists lives forever.

As Francisco walked home, he was consumed with sorrow. The twisting alleyway closed in on him, mocking the way he had chosen to live. He had dealt with abrupt turns in the past, each time thinking this would be the last change, only to turn the next corner to another demand. He could never see ahead to know what was coming.

It had all started on his thirteenth birthday—the day he was given the medallion of the Brotherhood to wear hidden around his neck.

✡ ✡ ✡

"Wake up, Cisco."

The hot breath of his younger brother warmed Francisco's cold cheeks. When he opened his eyes, he had stared straight into the gaze of Benito, the boy's eyes not two inches from his own.

"It's your birthday."

"You are correct. And one advantage to this day is that I get to sleep in." Cisco rolled his face into the straw mattress. "Go away."

"Papá said to wake you. Breakfast is ready, and he is hitching up the horses."

That's right, his father and his grandfather had a surprise planned for his special day. The day he became a man. "Today is the day I get my horse, Benito. If you do my chores, I will let you ride him."

Benito giggled. "Okay." A grin spread across his brother's face.

"What's so funny about that?"

"Mamá already told me I had to do your chores today."

Cisco punched his brother's arm, jumped from the bed and pulled on his clothes. The boys raced down the cold hallway to the warmth of the kitchen, where breakfast awaited.

"Francisco! Awake at last. I was beginning to think you would rather sleep this day away than go with us." Papá sat at the head of the table, the warm bread Glorianna, the cook, baked each morning filling a platter in front of him. His grandfather had already arrived, joining in the meal while they waited for him.

"Good morning, *Abuelo*." Cisco greeted his grandfather. It didn't take long to eat his bowl of porridge, kiss Mamá goodbye and follow the men to the wagon. He sat between Papá and *Abuelo*, gazing at the muscular flanks of the team of cart horses. If he had guessed correctly, they would pull him to Don Pablo Vega's ranch, and he would have his own horse to ride home.

As the men wound out of town into the low hills west of Seville, Cisco prayed that his birthday dream was accurate. *Please, Lord, I will be good to the horse.* Only an act of God would convince his father he was old enough for an Andalusian gelding. Most boys were happy with a Jennet, but Cisco didn't want a small horse. His father was a viceroy and that must count for something. Most of the boys did not get a horse until they were older, but Cisco had dropped so many hints, surely his father had guessed what he truly desired?

When the wagon passed the road to Vega's horse ranch without turning, Cisco slumped back onto the seat, his heart sinking to the small place inside his chest.

"Where are we going?"

"Be still, Francisco. You will find out soon enough."

The sun beat on the back of his neck as they followed the track into the hills. He rubbed at the sweat and fanned his face with his hat. Finally they reached a narrow canyon. Papá hopped from the wagon and helped *Abuelo* down. The men unhitched the horses and hid the wagon in the brush. His grandfather mounted one horse, while Cisco and Papá shared his father's black gelding.

Cisco sat with his arms tight around Papá's waist, peering at the landscape as they followed his grandfather on a narrow trail winding between towering yellow rocks. They followed this path for an hour. Cisco was soon soaked in sweat from both the heat of the horse and his father. He needed to stop for a break but didn't want to ask because Papá seemed so serious today. He pictured Mamá and Benito at home planning a special dinner to celebrate his manhood. He had asked for Gloriana's spice cake, something the old cook only made at Christmas. His mouth watered and shame filled him because he couldn't be man enough to stop thinking about food.

They reached a place without brush or trees, and the steep canyon walls closed off the view of the sky.

"We get off here." Papá slid from the horse and reached to help *Abuelo* dismount.

Five men appeared in the desolate canyon. They wore heavy robes and masks.

Cisco stood behind his father. "Papá," he whispered. "Who are these men?"

"*Fraternidad de Creyentes.*"

The Brotherhood of Believers? Who were they? What did they believe in?

His father led him into the center of the circle of men. They sat on rocks and his grandfather motioned for Cisco to sit next to him.

Abuelo rubbed his chin with his hand, as if he were worried, then spoke in a soft voice. "You are a man now, *mi nieto*. It is time for you to hear the story of our people."

Our people? Cisco couldn't believe he had been brought all these miles for a history lesson. Didn't his grandfather know that he had learned about his people already?

"Many years ago, before the world was as we know it, Abram, the son of Terach, sought the truth. He knew there was one creator and his heart was true so God came to him. He offered Abram the chance to lead a great nation, but only if he passed many tests."

Was he here with these strange men to pass tests? Cisco inched closer to his father. "*Abuelo*, I know about Abraham."

Papá held his hand up for quiet.

His grandfather continued. "Abram passed these tests and changed his life. But God had not finished. He asked Abram to sacrifice his son."

Cisco could not stop the trembling in his hands. He swallowed to relieve the knot that formed in his throat.

He felt Papá's hand on his shoulder. "Don't be scared. Just listen."

Abuelo resumed his story. "Abram, or Abraham as he came to be called, passed this test too. The Creator did not let him sacrifice Isaac. Abraham became the father of our people. But things were not meant to be easy. The tests persisted."

Cicso's trembling eased and he wondered at his grandfather's words. Our people? This story was different from the version he had learned in catechism.

"Good times and bad times filled our lives. There came a time when we were enslaved and treated as less than beasts of burden. But even that did not satisfy Pharaoh. He ordered that all male children be slain."

More talk of killing sons. Cisco was glad that Papá's hand was still on his shoulder.

"Moses was born, and God had plans for him. God came to him and told him what must be done to save our people. Moses must return to Egypt and rescue us from the burden of slavery."

"I know this story, *Abuelo*. I know that Moses led Jews out of Egypt and the sea parted. We learned this."

Papá squeezed his hand. "Yes, Cisco, you learned the story. But there is more to this tale than what you heard from the priests. Listen to your grandfather."

₀ the time of Moses the people spread out to other ₋ ₋ne earth. Some of our ancestors came to the land of Al-ıdalus, as Spain was called. We were happy for a time, in this place where we could follow our true belief." *Abuelo* slowly shook his head. "But that is not the story I am to tell, for the happiness was to end, and once more we faced the hatred of others. It was then that the great-grandfather of my great-grandfather made a decision. He would hide in plain sight."

The robed men nodded as they listened to the story. Cisco leaned forward. "Hide from what?" the boy asked.

"*Somos judíos,*" *Abuelo* said to him. "We hide from those who wish to rid the world of Jews."

These men were Jews? Cisco turned to his father.

"What your grandfather is saying is that the people decided to become what was safe and to hide what was not safe. We are Jews."

Cisco pulled away from Papá, rage filling his body. His mouth was dry as he swung his fists at his father's chest. "Why are you lying to me?"

Papá grasped his hands and restrained Cisco's punches. "I know it is hard to accept. We are here to answer your questions."

"You lie, you lie." Cisco twisted and fought his father's grasp. Images of filthy Jews swept through Cisco's head. Sobs escaped his chest and he slumped to the ground.

"You must listen, Cisco. This is not a bad thing. It is who you are."

Cisco's mind was frozen as he listened to the words. *Father, guide me to know what is good,* he silently prayed. This was not who he was.

He raised his head and looked at Papá. "What about *Cristo Jesús*? He is the one who will save us. *Los judíos,* they killed him." Jews were bad—sinners who spread evil wherever they went.

"No, *Hijo.* This is only a story that is told by others to justify the persecution of our people. The Church is our cover. It is only by hiding so deep, by many generations of men working their way into the path demanded by the Christian leaders of our land, that we have sustained our belief."

Fraternidad de Creyentes. The Brotherhood of Believers. Cisco looked at his father's face, then swung his eyes over to his grandfather. Neither man had any hint of joking in their expressions. The hooded men watched him and from what he could see of their cloaked faces, a serious mood was present in each one.

He was silent. If this was so, why had his father let him go to catechism and learn the stories?

"I know this is hard to understand, my son. But it is how things must be. You will continue to learn the ways of the church. In fact, we would like you to become a priest."

Cisco shook his head in confusion. "You would like me to be Catholic?" Images swam through his mind: Catholics fighting Jews, devils fighting men, the flames of hell surrounding his father and his grandfather.

"You are not evil, my son. You are a smart young man, ready to take your place with the Brothers. It is because you have done so well at the catechism that you are chosen for this role." Papá squeezed his shoulder. "Do not fret. It is a lot to take in all at once."

The tallest of the hooded men had a deep voice, as if God himself was asking a question. He stepped toward the boy. "Do you understand your role?"

Cisco stared at the cloaked figure. Why did he hide his face? But the voice commanded a response. "I will be a priest? Like Father Carlo?" he whispered.

"Yes. And you must be a good priest. One who is respected and can rise in the church." With those words the man stepped forward and placed a small medallion hanging from a gold chain around Cisco's neck. "This is the symbol of your commitment to our secret and your promise that you will defend our beliefs."

Cisco grabbed the medallion, ready to rip it from his neck. Something stopped him. All the men, even his father and his grandfather, pulled chains from under their robes and tunics. The medallions bore a shield, like a coat of arms. Inside the shield was a tree, covered with leaves. Feathers surrounded the edges.

Father placed a hand on Cisco's shoulder. "You cannot talk about this to anyone. Not Benito or Jose Miguel, not even Mamá. Only *Abuelo* or me. And only when you are sure we are alone."

Cisco stayed silent.

"When you need to talk, or when we need to talk to you, we will move the silver goblet, you know the one?"

Cisco nodded. The goblet was kept on the mantle in the big room, surrounded by other ornaments his mother collected.

"We will place it on the right side of the mantle. This means that you are to go to the stable after Mamá and the servants are asleep. And if you need to talk to us, you can do the same and we will be there."

The sun was disappearing behind the wall of the canyon. Father patted his shoulder. "That is enough for now. We must get home to celebrate your special day."

His grandfather nodded to the men, and they slipped away as quietly as they had arrived.

On the long ride home Cisco's mind churned and his head ached. He rubbed the surface of the medallion, his thumb tracing the engraved tree and feathers. As they passed the road to Vega's ranch, he thought about the prancing gray horse he should have been riding home tonight.

✡ ✡ ✡

The walk back to *Catedral de la Santa Creu i Santa Eulalia* seemed longer tonight. Francisco pulled his cloak tight to fight off the cold. So many years had passed since the day he followed the instructions of the Brotherhood and became a priest. He loved the Torah and the traditions of the Jews, his people, but he never abandoned the piece of his heart which held the Catholic faith. It had been years since he had been tormented by nightmares reminiscent of his first day learning he was Jewish: Jews fighting Catholics, Moors fighting Jews, even Jews fighting lions and tigers, but this feeling never ceased to hover just outside his consciousness. He kept the dreams at bay by concentrating on how important his role was to the Jewish people of Barcelona.

Tonight Francisco felt all the confusion of his thirteenth birthday. As he returned home through the deserted streets, his hands tightened on the cloth mask he carried, twisting it into a ball. For once he would like to make his own plans.

As he turned the corner of the dark alleyway, he heard voices. Too late to turn back—he quickly stuffed the mask into his sleeve.

"Halt." Two soldiers blocked the road. One of them lifted a candle to look into Francisco's face.

"Your Excellency? What are you doing out here so late?" The second soldier touched the knife strapped to his side.

Francisco felt his pulse race. "Señora Castellano's time came tonight. There is concern about *la recién nacida*." At least the soldier had recognized him and addressed him with respect. "A baptism was in order."

The soldiers glanced at each other, the eyebrows of the first arching up. "Who summoned you? *Doña* Estella or *Don* Vincenté himself?"

A trickle of sweat fell into Francisco's ear. He hoped it was covered by his hood. The soldiers were searching for Jews. "A servant came to the church. I do not know who sent him."

The soldier with the knife smirked. "Another girl you say? What is that? Five daughters? If only *Don* Vincenté Castellano would have a son, then the Queen would know the truth about him, wouldn't she?"

Ice filled Francisco's gut at the thought of what would happen if the truth were known about his friend, but he glared at the soldier with the authority of the Catholic Bishop he was. "*Don* Vincenté is a generous patron of the church. You would do well to keep your insults to yourself." Francisco knew if Castellano ever did have a son, the child would not be circumcised. The ritual had become too dangerous and most Jews made the decision to forego this instruction of God.

The first soldier stepped forward, his chin jutting out as he pushed his nose close to Francisco's face. "And you would do well to keep from insulting the Queen by speaking ill to her soldiers. Those guilty of treason share a cell with the *judíos*."

Francisco pulled himself to his full height and stared directly into the eyes of the soldier. "Are we done? I have mass at dawn and even a holy man must sleep." With a nod he stepped away from the soldiers before they replied and before they could see his quaking hands.

As Francisco walked down the road, keeping his pace even, he waited to feel the knife in his back. The city was chaotic, and the king's soldiers could use any excuse to rid themselves of a man they disliked. It wouldn't matter to them that he was a respected holy man or the son of a nobleman. With the power they now held at their sword tips, they could mumble the word *heresy* and be spared explaining their actions. They didn't need to know Francisco was a crypto-Jew for the night to take a disastrous turn.

At the end of the road he turned into the narrow alleyway which led to the back of *Catedral de la Santa Creu i Santa Eulalia* , a sigh escaping as soon as he was out of sight of the two men.

Even at this late hour, his manservant, Paulo, waited for him. He held out his hands to take Francisco's cloak. "Is everything all right, Your Excellency?"

"*Gracias*. A drink, then bed. I'm tired." Francisco tried to smile and reassure Paulo, but exhaustion kept him from any more than a twist of his lips. The manservant was pale. It wouldn't do for Francisco's late night activities to exhaust his servant to the point of illness. "You should not have waited. There is no reason for your day to be so long."

Paulo nodded and his tongue wet his lips. Without speaking he left the room. Francisco wondered what the man wanted to say, but obviously held back. He was lucky to have him and he trusted Paulo. But after the meeting tonight, he knew he could not trust anyone. When the price was their life all men could be bought.

✡ ✡ ✡

Later that night, Francisco lay awake. Could he convince Raquel to stay in Spain? And what of his mother? Since the death of his father last year, she had become feeble. Traveling would be hard on her, not to say leaving all her belongings behind. Benito was in the North. Would he also flee Spain? Perhaps Mamá could go to live with him.

Tossing and turning, Francisco realized things would happen quickly, even with a few months to plan. His mind buzzed like the flies that filled the stables, landing on one thought, only to flit quickly to another.

If they did leave, what could he take with him? The family wealth had been hidden over the years, but the officials knew where to look for secret gold coins. Riches sewn inside hems or beneath the soles of shoes were too common. Francisco wished he could take something of the old ways, something which he could use to teach his children about their true faith when the time came. He reached up and squeezed the medallion. He would travel in his role as a Bishop—that had been decided by the Brotherhood. Papers indicating he had business for the church would see him across the border and into Portugal.

But how to disguise Raquel and the children? His wife could travel as a nun. The children as orphans. But the officials at the border would not be fooled by a bunch of orphans leaving the country. Portugal didn't want parentless children.

But they would take Jews.

He stared through the darkness. Maybe the best disguise would be no disguise at all.

Three
Gabriella
Tierra Amarilla, New Mexico
Tuesday, April 1

I was here. After two days of restless catnaps, wrong turns, pit stops and ten thousand cups of coffee. Too nervous to set up the tent at any of the roadside campgrounds, I had stayed locked inside the car both nights, slumped in the seat to doze at the edge of garishly-lit parking lots.

My heart pounded as I drove into the town of Tierra Amarilla, less glamorous than the fancy carved road sign had promised. A single block of Main Street. An avenue of ancient boxy buildings with rotted wooden skeletons showing through holes in the chipped stucco, the graffiti of adolescent taggers the only paint left on the worn walls and boarded over windows. A dried up town. My doubts, tucked away in that sturdy box labeled denial, sprang forth like a whirlwind of demented fairies.

A tall Victorian style house converted into a coffee shop rested next to the courthouse, the only business on the street with a new sign and lights shining from narrow windows which stretched to the second floor. The iron ravens perched on the steep roof, along with a bright blue sign, informed me this was Three Ravens Coffeehouse. Coffee would be nice, but what if the people inside asked questions? I wanted to see the land without explaining anything to strangers. Not that I was capable of an explanation. Or ready to talk to anyone other than Bones.

Twenty minutes later I wished I had stopped. The GPS instructions had brought me to Tierra Amarilla, but now I was faced with vague road names like SR 57 and CR 23, overgrown dirt roads and left turns that went nowhere. Following the instructions, I turned off the two-lane highway onto a mud track, hoping this wasn't one of those time when GPS was way off course. Thankfully, there was a huge granite peak off to the east, a landmark to keep my bearings. The rest of the mountains blurred into a bowl of peaks and mesas which all looked the same. The road dipped into shallow arroyos and rose again, crossed a railroad-tie bridge and led me through a field of sage brush. My tires spun in the slick mud each time the road dipped down—although things looked dry, these little river beds were wet—so I crawled along, gripping the steering wheel and preparing for the worst.

I spotted an adobe house across the field. Down a road so bumpy and filled with rocks that I didn't notice the punctured tire until I parked in front of the house.

Over a thousand miles traveled and bad luck floated around me like dust motes. A flat tire and no cell service.

Wait until tomorrow to deal with it? I looked around. Not the most welcoming place to be stuck alone. I decided to walk back into town. It wasn't all that far, maybe a mile or so.

It proved to be too far for this forty-five year old woman, beyond tired and really grouchy. As Bones and I trudged down the road I swallowed to relieve the tight knot in my throat. *Don't cry again. You'll never stop.*

Hopefully the coffee shop was still open. The dark metal roof of the courthouse marking the center of town was still a long way off and it was already four o'clock.

By the time we made it to the railroad-tie bridge over the canal I realized my mistake. Running away? All the way to New Mexico? Stupid, stupid, stupid.

She-Who-Is-Unprepared and An-Idiot.

The sun moved to the far end of the valley. No streetlights out here and, of course, no flashlight tucked into my pocket. I pulled out my phone. Two bars. And six new messages.

I needed help. But who could I call? Welcome to New Mexico, Ella. Land of no cell service, no phone booths, and no friends to dial up in an emergency. Bones waved her tail and gave me a doggy grin as I punched in 9-1-1.

A sweet voice answered. "Hello?" She was very cheerful for an emergency operator.

My phone hissed. "It's not an emergency. I need a tow truck."

"Where are you?"

"At the Martinez property." Hopefully she would know where that was. I didn't have an exact address.

"Which one?"

A loud crackle on the line interrupted my distracted thoughts. I better get to the point before the tiny bit of contact disappeared. "Just south of town."

"Hmm. Not sure where you mean," Cheerful-Woman mumbled.

"Past the courthouse, toward that highway that goes to Taos." Damn. My notes were back in the car. "Road 37? You turn by the goats, just before the river. You have to drive through someone's property."

"By the goats?" She paused, then sucked in her breath. "You must mean the Gravelle's place. Phil and Margie. The churro sheep? Funny double horns?"

Okay. "I'm out by the old adobe house. After you cross the little bridge over the ditch."

"Ditch? You mean the acequia?" Her voice had tightened and she sounded impatient.

"Right." *Did it really matter what I called it?* I didn't speak much Spanish, in spite of my heritage.

She asked my name.

"Ella King, I mean, Martinez. Gabriella Martinez." Now Not-So-Cheerful-Woman would really think I was crazy. Or lying. "It's a new name." That sounded even worse. "What I mean is, I got divorced and changed it back to my maiden name. A while ago," Might as well be someone else right away, even if I was lying about actually being divorced.

She promised the tow truck would be out within the hour.

I glanced at my phone and the six unplayed messages, then held the power button to quiet the nagging voices of those left behind.

As I started back toward my car I thought about Julie and Shannon. How angry I was when they didn't let me know where they were or why they were late. Or when they didn't return my calls. Turning back, I walked to the bridge and the two bars of service. I could at least listen to their messages.

"Mom. I just wanted to talk. I know I hurt your feelings and I didn't mean to. Call me." Sweet Julie. Worried as always. And bossy.

"Hey, I know you said no dates, but there is this guy. I think you would at least have fun. Friday. I'm out of here, so text me." Vicki, the best and the worst friend a person could have.

It wasn't until the third message, this one was from Shannon —"Mom. I didn't see you last night, but I'm staying at Jason's for a few days. Just 'cause things are so messed up. Talk to ya later."— that I realized they didn't know I was gone.

I had run away from home and no one missed me.

The walk back to the house seemed shorter than my trek to the bridge. The land looked different; no demon bushes reaching for me and no wild animals ready to pounce. I could see now that when I crossed the bridge I had driven over a man-made thing, the edges sharply cut out and lined with rocks. On the south side of the property there was a creek and I could see that the two did not meet as I had thought. An as-key-a, or whatever the operator had called it must be some sort of water supply for irrigation.

I noticed the hint of buds on the tips of each dried stem. I admired the surrounding bluffs and distant mesas—peaks covered with snow and the bright turquoise sky contrasting with the yellows and reds of the earth. The endless expanse of sky, complete with the puffy white clouds—the place where heaven exists—diluted my problems and my lungs released from the tight cramp, which I hadn't noticed until I relaxed.

A flat tire—what difference did that make? So no one missed me, didn't that mean I shouldn't worry?

I laughed and the first smile I felt in days—or was it months?—took over. I was here and not on a schedule anymore. Unpack now, or unpack an hour from now, Bones didn't care. No deadlines, no alarms, no rush. New-Ella could handle a little bump in the road because it would all be worth it. New-Ella was free from the horror of the past month.

I took a deep breath and listened. There were no man-made sounds here, just the sounds of nature. The world was still, something left over from the creation of earth itself, something I could inhale along with the tang of the sage from the thin air and taste as vibrations from a long ago power.

I liked this place.

I might be unsettled, nervous, and anxious, but California was no different from New Mexico when it came to dealing with my problems. Face it, I didn't *have* to listen to anyone anymore. Not Greg, not Vicki, not my daughters, not my mother. And not Old-Ella with her dire warnings and her black cloud of sadness.

My walk to the house was more than a walk up a dirt road. It was a walk to my future. The adobe house pulled me forward.

I had expected to stay in the house, but a closer look at the adobe told me it might not be habitable.

Three rusty cars hunched off to one side of the building, mean-looking plants thrust out of the open hoods and shattered windows. An old trailer perched on the edge of the creek; the weathered shell leaned forward as if thirsty for the tiny trickle of water.

The house was made up of a patchwork of additions and repairs: a wooden lean-to on one side, a stone room on the other, three porches, one in front, one in back, which held an old claw foot tub, and one oddly attached to the side of the house, with no door or window near it. I imagined an old couple, he rocking away on the front porch and she here, on this strange, isolated wooden view point. She refused to sit near him after the big fight, but wanted her chance to watch the river and the sunset. Maybe she didn't like his cigar smoke.

I had thought the adobe was the original house, but now I saw that the stone room had probably come first, with the adobe built around it.

My father was born here. Imagine living in this tiny house surrounded by the vast open fields and big sky as my grandparents had—four children, growing their own food and hauling water from the ditch.

The door to the stone room no longer guarded whoever might have lived within, as it hung from only one hinge. Could this be repaired? I didn't really want to spend any money replacing things. I pulled the door open, propping it to one side.

This was the kitchen, complete with a dirt floor. Dishes filled the sink, crusty with age. A metal sauce pan covered with dirt perched atop a plate black with grime. The cupboard doors sagged open, paint faded and peeling. Shriveled rodent droppings covered the counters; even the mice had moved out a long time ago.

Safely through the kitchen, I leaned on the edge of the doorway. Two steps led up to the next room, which had a wooden floor. This was where the stone house ended and the adobe started. I could see why the stone kitchen didn't have a floor. With its low ceiling, even I would have trouble standing. A house for a hobbit. The roof line on this part, probably the new part, was higher.

My trespass into the silent house raised ancient dust and a sneeze tickled the back of my nose. This room was a large rectangle, which stretched to the front of the house. Hazy sunlight filtered through two windows on the west side, enough illumination to see the two closed doors on one side and the front door leading out toward the creek. The roof was better here and the windows dirty, but intact. With a little work I might be able to stay in this part of the house.

Tugging a handkerchief from my pocket, I wiped my nose and opened the first of the small doors. A bedroom—the old mattress pushed into the corner told me that and I shivered, thinking what critters might inhabit the stuffing bulging out through holes chewed by tiny pointed teeth. The box springs leaning against the wall, rather than under the mattress, made me wonder who had slept here.

The granite peak, the beacon which had kept me oriented on my drive in, was framed by the window and transformed into a portrait of an ancestor with a fierce scowl, a guardian standing strong at the edge of the land.

"You will keep me safe, Grandfather." The words slipped out and a tingling sense filled me. Was my Grandfather sending me a message?

The second room was identical to the first, but the window looked out on sage, cholla, and a hill rising off in the distance. Better to sleep in the room with the view of the mountain. After I hauled out the old bed.

An occasional raven scolded from down by the creek, but other than that I heard nothing. The sun had made its way down to the top of the distant mesa and the light was fading. I really was alone out here.

Was I wise to have called a tow truck? This wasn't the city. There wouldn't be cars driving by, spectators watching as some strange man changed my tire.

Old-Ella pushed New-Ella's optimism aside as easily as my girls spilled their milk. How could I have forgotten all that my mother taught me? I was twelve when the lessons started.

"You are a woman now, Ella. And a woman needs to know how to take care of herself." My mother hadn't turned from the sink as she lectured. I continued to set the table, embarrassed that I was going to hear a sex talk while preparing for dinner. But that wasn't what my mother had in mind.

"Men are savage. You never know when they might turn. The best way to stay safe is to never put yourself in an unsafe position. No walking home alone at dusk anymore. You call me and I'll come and pick you up."

The warnings had continued through my teen years, never stopping, even when I was married.

"You shouldn't be driving alone in that neighborhood at night. Can't Greg take you down there? Isn't there another dance studio?"

And so out here in the middle of the New Mexico badlands, I couldn't help but imagine a burly gorilla of a tow-truck driver forcing me to give him all my money. Or worse. I wondered who had scared my mother, made her so overly cautious. A caution she had made sure I inherited?

Bones sniffed the air and tilted her head. A rumbling growl filled her chest and through the murky window I saw a yellow truck bumping up the rocky road.

Four

Francisco Martín de la Serrano
Barcelona, 1492 to 1498

Francisco adjusted his hat. He had stitched gold coins under the edge and the weight pulled it to one side.

Hand on the heavy knob of the door, he turned for one final look. Even though he dreaded this day, his wife had not been able to hide her enthusiasm for leaving. He might have resisted the continued admonishments of Marcus and Alfonso but for the tremble he felt in Raquel's hand when they talked of living in a land where they would no longer have to hide who they were.

But who was he?

Bishop Francisco Martín de la Serrano. Catholic leader of *Catedral de la Santa Creu i Santa Eulalia* .

Born Galit Marciano. A secret name, one he himself had not known for the first thirteen years of his life.

Judío.

He was thirty-three years old. He had lived more of his life as a Catholic than he had as anything else. He performed all the duties of the church with love and compassion. Was he still a *judío* or was he a *converso*? Had he left Judaism behind in his quest to pose as something he was not?

He thought about his secret duties. He performed "special" ceremonies on the children of *anusim*, those forced to convert—or those who hid as his family had for generations. A tiny cut serving as a circumcision, plain water instead of the Holy water used in the true baptism, special prayers woven into the lengthy Latin mumblings at Mass. At times he was the perfect Catholic priest, but there was always a soul that waged war with the *judío* man inside.

A knock interrupted his thoughts.

"Yes?"

The door creaked open and Paulo poked his head through the crack. "Your Holiness, may I enter?"

"Of course."

The manservant looked over his shoulder, then slipped into the room, closing the door behind him. He dropped to his knees and grabbed Francisco's hand.

"*Por favor*, Your Holiness. I know it's much to ask, but please take me with you." Paulo pressed his cheek to the Bishop's hand.

Francisco held his breath. If his manservant knew what was going on, who else knew? He had worked hard to keep this a secret.

"What are you talking about, my son?"

"I dare not say." Paulo pressed his forehead against Francisco's hand, then lifted his eyes. "I *am* your son."

"Yes, you are like a son to me. We have been together a long time."

Paulo kissed his hand. Tears flowed from his eyes. "Please. If I am left here, I will die."

Francisco pulled his hand away and knelt next to Paulo. He put his palms on the man's shoulders and squeezed. "Forgive me."

Paulo's head dropped.

Francisco stood, pulled his cloak tight and picked up his bag.

As he neared the heavy wooden door, Francisco turned back. Paulo leaned against the wall. His face was white and his hands shook.

The Brotherhood had always used the utmost care in selecting members. At meetings they were cloaked and hooded, protecting identity even among themselves.

But Francisco knew that all of the members were wealthy men —Dons and viceroys and other men of title. All holding on to the riches of their Jewish grandfathers under the mask of the Catholic religion they despised. What of the poor Jews who couldn't afford the elaborate charade? Those who had been forced to give up what little they possessed, all in the name of a King and Queen so easily influenced by greed? Could Paulo truly be one of his people?

If Francisco were to believe this and Paulo turned out to be a spy, he was risking the lives of his family.

He squeezed the grip of his bag and looked down at Paulo. The manservant looked up and Francisco saw a brief moment of hope flash in his eyes, like the last ray of sun before the crimson orb falls below the horizon. In that single glance, God—the god of all men— appeared to him. Francisco knew that Paulo spoke the truth.

He looked away, then looked back. "A Bishop cannot be expected to travel without his man. How will I dress myself? Remember to eat?"

Paulo dropped to his knees and kissed Francisco's hand. *"Gracias, Eminencia."*

Francisco turned and strode rapidly to the outer door.

Paulo grabbed a small rucksack and followed him.

Francisco shook his head, unsure of his decision. His people were without a home once more. Why did Paulo look so happy at the prospect?

✡ ✡ ✡

Ten days later, weary from fear rather than travel, Francisco stood at the border of Portugal next to the wagon, which, although filled with furniture and belongings, contained a very small portion of his father's wealth. The group of travelers had been stopped for inspection.

"For the orphanage," Francisco told the guards when they questioned the items. "I am taking these children to the orphanage in Porto and the church offers these things as their support." Francisco clenched his teeth as one of the rough soldiers stepped forward and grasped Ana's tiny chin in his hand, forcing the girl to look into his grizzled face.

The second guard looked through the documents Francisco presented for their passing. "These children are Jews." The soldier pushed the tiny girl back and glared at Francisco.

Francisco heard Mateo gasp, and silenced the boy with a look. "Orphans." He dared not look at Raquel, fearing his wife would be driven to protect her children from the filthy hands of these men.

The rough soldier turned and lifted Ana out of the wagon. "What is one more or less? I like the looks of this one."

Raquel cried out, then pressed the tiny Bella to her chest and the sound of her whispered prayers could be heard over Ana's sobs.

It took everything in Francisco's power to control his anger. He drew up his chin and looked to the second guard, the one holding their papers. "One soul, more or less, to the church and King Ferdinand, means a lot. Do not let this man frighten the child." As he spoke, with as much authority as he could muster, he felt perspiration gather beneath his robes.

The guard snorted and returned the documents to the Bishop. "Put her back," he said to the soldier. "Let these pious subjects of the great king of Spain bring their discards to our land."

As the soldier hoisted Ana back into the wagon, Francisco felt the medallion hidden deep under his cassock throb like a cold orb against his chest. The pulsations were as if the firm finger of God pressed into his heart, keeping his throat from pulling air into his rigid lungs. Trying to hide his fear from the soldiers, he climbed back into the wagon. With a barely perceptible nod of his chin he signaled Paulo to drive on, to move his children away from these men.

Raquel had not lifted her face from her hands and her prayers didn't stop until the oxen had pulled the wagon well beyond the view of the Portuguese guards. She hadn't even looked at Ana, who was wrapped in Mateo's arms. Francisco looked back, the road a steep curve that took them away from the troublesome border. Once he was reassured they were not in view of the guards he reached for his wife.

"Francisco, I was so scared. What if,"— her sobs kept her from speaking—"if they had taken Ana?"

He did not know how to answer. The same thoughts filled his heart. But the medallion still hung cold against his chest and he pressed it with his hand. "I think that God is protecting us, Raquel. That is all we can ask for. He has kept us safe so far."

But as the wagon rolled slowly down the road, Paulo focused on guiding the large animals, the children huddled quietly among the belongings, and Rachel still trembling beside him, Francisco asked himself, *Whose God?*

He failed to notice the look on Mateo's face.

✡ ✡ ✡

Francisco was grateful when Porto was finally within a day's journey. It had been a long trip over the mountains, although they hadn't had any more heart-wrenching experiences. Just tired children and the worries of what awaited them.

They went straight to the home of Leon Milano, as instructed by the Brotherhood. *Señora* Milano took Raquel and the children to see their quarters and rest, while Milano led Francisco to the plush sitting room which adorned the palace-like house. It was obvious Leon had no trouble bringing his wealth out of Spain.

"We have a place for you in Santo Alifon. Raquel and the children will stay with us for the time being."

"I was hoping I could be with them."

Milano's eyebrows came together on his forehead in a severe arch. "That is not realistic. I was told you are a bishop."

"A crypto-Jew, *Don* Leon. I am waiting the chance to shed the secrets and lead a normal life."

"Your wait is far from over, my friend. Portugal will not stay safe for Jews. You will see. Your wife and children will be Catholic, particularly if she is to pass as my wife's cousin."

Francisco didn't speak. He knew he had fooled himself and not looked at the reality of this world when he dreamed of a place where he could be free.

And so it was that he was separated from his family once again. It was somewhat easier to visit them, as they were able to secure a small room near the church. But he had argued with all his heart when Raquel opposed his idea that Paulo masquerade as her husband.

"No. It is not proper for him to be here with me. One room, Francisco! It is much too intimate."

"We will hang a tapestry across to make him his own room. Easily taken down when visitors are here. Raquel, you need to understand, it is not safe for you to live here alone. You can see that Paulo is a good man and the children have grown to love him. It is better to masquerade as a married woman so that my visits are above suspicion."

"He must find his own place."

Francisco didn't want Rachel to be scared and he didn't want to give cause for anyone to question his actions. He should have made arrangements for Paulo at the church. But there were already servants of the parish and no room for another in the service of Santo Alifon. Given the opportunity to be the extra Bishop as a favor to *Don* Pedro Begaso, one of the wealthiest men in Porto and a strong member of the Brotherhood, Francisco couldn't push his luck any further. This was not like having his own church, one in which he had built his way up and the parish was filled with his own people. He was responsible for Paulo now and knew this man would protect Raquel and the children.

✡ ✡ ✡

The days spent in the routine of church, parish duties, and clandestine visits to his family stretched into months. Francisco wished they could move to the place he felt God had promised—the land where Jews could keep the covenant without fear. Each night as he locked himself in his room and recited the Sh'ma, he felt further from the place of his heart. Could anyone hear his nightly prayers, whispered so softly that they were nearly non-existent?

Porto didn't have the feel of home and he didn't have his brother or his uncles, or even the members of the Brotherhood to provide the sense of belonging. The identity of the members of the Brotherhood in Porto had been kept secret from him. He hadn't been invited to the inner council meetings, with only the privileges of a fringe member. How could this be, when he was a Bishop?

He had won his battle with Raquel, and Paulo lived in the room with his wife and children, but now he realized his mistake. The image of Raquel and Paulo, together, kept him awake at night.

Even the most miserable man can get through his days. And soon the months had turned to years and the family settled into their life in Porto. The children grew, and it wasn't long before three years had passed and Francisco had something new to worry about.

Mateo would soon be thirteen years old. It was time for his mitzvah.

Five

Gabriella

Tuesday, April 1 - Wednesday April 2

As I listened to the truck stop outside, Old-Ella's fear—or maybe it was my mother's fear— swept over me. I searched the dim room for some kind of a weapon. The remains of a wooden chair sat in the corner. I yanked off the leg. A splintered sword would have to do.

Don't be ridiculous. The guy is here to help me. This place was no different than any other town. Tow-truck drivers change tires, jump dead batteries, and get keys out of locked cars. They don't attack their customers. In spite of my rational thoughts, a ball of emotion twisted into knots inside my stomach. No amount of frantic pulling could unravel the complex mess of feelings and maternal warnings and fatigue.

"Heel," I whispered to Bones. "But feel free to ignore me when he attacks."

She wagged her tail and a horn tooted.

"Hello? Ms. Martinez?" He didn't sound particularly fierce.

He was walking around my car. The truck lights were on, illuminating the yard. He knelt and examined my flat tire.

Inspection completed, he walked toward me. Tattoos covered his arms and more, visible because he wore a leather vest. That was it. No shirt. He had long dark hair, pulled into a pony tail. A cow skull was inked into the skin of his abdomen, half covered—make that uncovered—near his belly button.

"Tattooed-Buck," I named him, sliding my weapon down to my side, hoping he wouldn't notice the silly stick.

As he came closer I saw his eyes were green, his face tanned and his dark hair peppered with gray.

"What are you doing way out here?"

I stepped back and put my hand on Bones' head. She sat quietly, ready for my signal. I felt protected by my dog, but it wasn't like she was attack trained. She only knew I wanted her to sit.

"Your tires are in bad shape. You probably shouldn't drive these dirt roads."

I nodded. *Tell me about it.*

He tipped his head toward the car and raised his eyebrows. "I can put the spare on for you. You do have a spare, right?"

Sure did. In the back hatch, under all my stuff. "I'll show you." Moving toward the car, I kept Bones at my side and veered in a crazy wide loop around him, ashamed of my fear, but unable to let it go.

It wasn't easy to keep an eye on him while unloading my life from the back of the vehicle. I spread the tarp and piled everything haphazardly while clutching the wooden sword in one hand.

"Let me do that." He stepped up beside me and reached for my ice chest.

"No!" The word burst out like a gunshot as I whirled to face him. I swung the chair leg in a wide arc and back pedaled away, stumbling on the rocks.

He raised his hands in front of his chest and stepped back. "Hey, it's cool. No problems, okay? I'll just wait over here." He stepped back toward his truck.

Face burning, I set the stick on the bumper and finished tossing everything onto the tarp. What a fool I was. No doubt this guy had given me an Indian name too—Crazy-Woman.

Twenty minutes later Tattooed-Buck brushed off his hands, the spare installed. "I'll follow you back into town. Where are you staying?"

I looked at the huge pile on the tarp. I didn't want to tell him, but it seemed pretty obvious.

"I'm fine. You don't have to wait."

"Do you think it's a good idea to stay out here? You seem"—to my surprise, he blushed— "a little jumpy."

No, I didn't think it was a good idea at all. Not now that he knew I would be here alone. But my choices were limited. Limited to one choice, in fact. "I'm not staying here. I just want to take my time packing this stuff back in the car."

He was silent, as if considering *my* options.

"You sure I can't help?" he said, reaching for a folded camp chair.

The moisture was sucked out of my mouth, leaving my tongue sticky. What was he doing? Why didn't he leave?

The car sat like a fortress, with heavy windows and locking doors. Keeping my eyes away from his gaze and his crazy tattoos, I picked up the stick from where it still lay on the bumper. "I'll get my card. You take auto club, right?"

He set the chair back on the pile and nodded, then bent and patted Bones.

Christ, Ella. Quit being ridiculous. Just give him the card and he'll leave. Do it now, before he completely makes friends with your dog and you have no protection left at all.

I grabbed the door handle, keeping the stick down, as if Tatooed-Buck couldn't see it and I was somehow going to use it to find my purse. The dashboard was covered with things—maps, sticky notes, my toothbrush. Leaning into the car felt vulnerable, my back to Tattooed-Buck, so I slid all the way in. My purse was stuffed between the console and the seat, upside down, and I had to reach down and grope under the seat, finally finding the bulky leather of my overstuffed wallet. I kept my hand on the door handle and held out my auto club card without turning my head to look at the tow-truck driver.

He stepped forward and took the card from me. This man, who had done nothing more than appear in my complicated life, carefully copied down the numbers on a carbon receipt, then reached out to return the card without coming closer. He must have detected the primitive odor of fear steaming off my body.

"Have a nice day."

A business card nested against my auto club card.

Tattooed-Buck had a name. Andy Lloyd. As he drove off down the rocky road, I stayed in the car and watched his truck until he turned onto the highway, a mile away from my land of isolation.

There wasn't much for me to do after that. The light had faded and I was exhausted. The back of the car, empty now, made a bed of sorts. One inch taller and this wouldn't have worked. Surprisingly no images of rocks or baseball bats shattering the windows filled my tired brain. I must have used up my senseless worry on the tow-truck driver. The car was such a mess, no one would notice a woman curled around her dog, crying once again. And the doors were locked.

✿ ✿ ✿

The following morning, after a night of uncontrollable shivering, interrupted by starting the engine and heating up the car every hour, I awoke drained and groggy. I squirmed under the weight of all three of my blankets and my coat piled on top of the sleeping bag. Dog feet poked my stomach—I read that a dog can keep you from hypothermia and it hadn't taken much to convince Bones she would be warmer inside the bag with me.

My night had been filled with crazy dreams about priests and nuns, but I couldn't remember the details, only the feeling of unease. The sun peeked over the edge of the mountain and the sage was decorated with glittering ice.

Coffee.

I pulled my coat on and slipped out of the car. Clapping my hands together to bring some circulation to my fingers, I searched through the pile on the tarp and found the camp stove. Everything was covered with a layer of frost.

My water bottle was frozen. No problem, it would thaw on the flame. But the propane bottle was iced. Would it explode if I tried to light up the stove? Frustrated, I slipped my hands into my pockets.

The coffee shop wasn't really that far, if you were driving.

When I got to the bridge over the azz-key-a or whatever this ditch was called, I realized I should phone Mark before I did anything else.

"You're here? In New Mexico? Where did you—" The phone hissed and my cousin's voice faded.

"Hang on. I didn't catch that? I don't have good service."

"It's not you, it's me. Let me pull over." Static filled my ear.

"Okay." He was back.

"I was hoping to see you today. Do you live close?" What if he lived somewhere else? Santa Fe or Albuquerque?

"I live in Los Ojos, Ella. But I'm on my way to Idaho. I didn't know you were coming."

Where was Los Ojos? "It was kind of a last minute decision. When are you coming back?"

"End of the month, if things work out."

Wasn't today April 2? Fool that I had been yesterday, I did remember that this was only the beginning of the month. My heart started to pound and the breath slipped from my lungs.

A roller coaster. That cliche was just what my life was. Confidence then panic. I sucked in a deep breath of cold air and pinched my thigh. *Stop it, Ella.*

"Does Jeff live around here?"

"He lives in Soccoro."

"Is that close by?"

"South of Albuquerque." Mark sighed. "I'm sorry no one is there for you, but why did you come? I thought you weren't interested in the land."

I need money? I need to get away? I'm a flake and impulsive?

"I'm staying here. At the property. I wanted to see it."

Mark was silent and I thought we had lost our connection.

"Hello?"

"I'm still here. You can stay in the house. Use the wood burning stove. It's too cold this time of year to camp."

Tell me about it.

"Look, just let me know what you decide. I'll come see you as soon as I get back."

I wasn't about to wait a month for the cousin who had tried to cheat me.

"I can't wait that—" The cackle of dead air interrupted my protest.

Six

Francisco Martín de la Serrano
Porto, Portugal, 1495

Francisco pressed his hand to his chest. The cold of the medallion seeped into his heart, the ache like ice.

His son was thirteen. It was time to tell him the truth.

Francisco didn't feel he could rely on the Brotherhood to help explain the secret to Mateo. The men were still cautious about meeting here in Portugal. Messages were sent only when there was news of extreme importance. A boy celebrating his mitzvah was hardly considered reason to meet. How he wished his father was here. He remembered the long ride up the canyon, his arms wrapped around Papá's waist, staring at his grandfather's back. Somehow, having two generations explain the secret emphasized the tradition.

During the time since Raquel and Francisco had melted across the border into Portugal, he had watched the relationship between his children and his wife change. No longer living as nun and orphans, they blossomed. He watched Raquel's love for her children grow, standing outside the circle, as if he were a distance relative, rather than the father of these beautiful young Jews.

"No, not yet," Marcus de la Paloma had told him when he mentioned moving in with Raquel. His old friend had come to Porto a year ago, one of the last to flee Spain. "We must still live with caution. The persecution of our people will not stop."

Marcus had been right. King Jao had granted the Jews little leeway. And what he did grant, he quickly withdrew. The death of

Jao had brought a hint of relief, but the Jews were not safe. Francisco knew that Portugal would not become their home.

Raquel had been right as well. Living as a Catholic with her four Christian children just might save them from another exile.

Francisco slipped out into the narrow alley behind the church and made his way to the room which his wife and children called a home.

With Paulo masquerading as Raquel's husband.

When Francisco arrived he knocked before entering. It was important to keep up images, even though he never felt anyone was watching him. Not like in Spain.

"Cisco," Raquel was chopping vegetables at the heavy wooden table. "Will you stay to eat?"

Francisco nodded and bent to kiss her neck.

Paulo was seated on a three-legged stool near the window, Isabella in his lap.

"Hola, Francisco."

Francisco felt a surge of jealousy. Last time he visited, he had heard his daughter call Paulo *Papá*.

He walked over to her and held out his arms. Bella jumped off Paulo's lap and ran to Francisco. As he hugged her, a lump grew tight in his throat. He longed to hold his tiny daughter in his own lap every night. Walk with her and teach her colors, plants and words.

Hear her call him Papá.

Mateo and Luis knew that Francisco was their father. Bella and Ana were too young to keep the secret, so they looked upon him as a good friend of the family, the Bishop who came to call because Mamá loved the church.

Lifting his daughter onto his hip he turned back to Raquel.

"Where is Mateo?"

"School. He'll be home soon."

"I spoke with the Brothers. I have to do it on my own. It is too risky to meet here in the city and there is no reason for me to leave town now."

Raquel looked up from her knife. "Cisco, it will be fine. He is a smart boy and he loves you." She paused and then asked, "Will he have a medallion?"

Francisco shook his head. "Not yet. There is no metal smith who can be trusted."

☆ ☆ ☆

Three days later Mateo came to the church. Francisco had decided today was the day he would talk with his son. The boy sat in the small chair reserved for the scribe, the wooden desk like an island between them. His son stared down and didn't speak as Francisco gathered his thoughts.

I barely know this boy. Am I wrong in thinking he is like me? Without the guidance of a father or a grandfather can a boy grow to have the heart of a man?

Mateo had been raised by women, first the nuns and then his mother. Even Paulo spent little time with the boy; soon after they arrived in Portugal Mateo started attending school.

Alfonso de Tordoya and some other members of the Brotherhood had protested, but Francisco insisted the boy be educated. It hadn't been easy to keep up the pretense. How did a poor widow like Raquel have the means to send her son to school?

In the end Pedro Begazo had stepped in. A member of the Brotherhood, he had left Spain several years before the others and had established a business and a reputation in Porto. Mateo was introduced as his nephew, which paved the way for the boy to go to lessons at Santo Ildefenso.

Francisco looked across the big desk. His son sat very still.

"I have something important to discuss with you, Mateo. You know there have been things we cannot tell others, secrets."

Mateo nodded.

"Like the fact that I am your father, not Paulo." Francisco felt his face grow hot.

"I know that, *Padré* Serrano."

Francisco cringed at the twist of fate that allowed the boy to address him as Father, but not *Papá*.

"When I was your age, my father and grandfather took me on a journey. That is how I learned about our family. I wish I could do the same for you, but times have changed so we must make do with what we have. I am going to tell you a story today, the story of our people."

Francisco explained the story of Abraham and the chosen people, then told his son about the Brotherhood. The secret names, not known to anyone else, the duties that being a member of the Brotherhood carried: the hiding, the secrecy, the entry into the priesthood. He felt rushed, but didn't know of any way to soften the news.

Mateo dropped his chin to his chest and kept his eyes lowered.

Francisco continued. "So you see, we are Jewish. Our true name is Marciano."

Mateo sat very still. His breath was even and he seemed calm.

Why didn't the boy speak? "Do you have any questions?"

Mateo shook his head.

"None?" Francisco stood and walked around the desk. He placed his hand on Mateo's shoulder. "It is a big piece of news. Perhaps you need time to think about it?"

Without raising his eyes the boy spoke. "What if I don't want to do it? Can Luis be the one?"

Francisco was shocked. He had never anticipated refusal. This was family. The traditions were passed from a man to his eldest son. Not just those of the Brotherhood, but those of all people of Spain.

He squeezed the boy's shoulder. "I know we have not had a life like that of your friends. But this is important, Mateo. More important than anything else. This is our true faith, it is who we are. Without someone to take over for me, our family will lose the traditions. We will disappear. Fade into nothing."

Francisco could barely make out the words his son whispered. "I am not Jewish. I am Catholic."

"Haven't you listened to what I've been saying? You are not Catholic. You did not receive the holy baptism, did not go through confirmation. Each time you take the holy communion, it is without the promise to Jesus."

Moving as quick as a cat after a mouse, Mateo twisted from under Francisco's hand, jumped up and ran to the table which held the flask of holy water. He pulled the cork from the top and dashed the contents in his face. "Now I have been baptized. And I did go through confirmation. In my heart I have confirmed my faith in the Holy Father and the Catholic church." Water dripped off his face. and tears ran from his eyes to join the trails left from his self-baptism.

The boy continued. "You lied to those guards and you lie now."

"Guards? I do not know of what you speak."

"The ones that tried to take Ana. You told them we were Jews so they would give her back."

The sharp pain in his chest left Francisco feeling his heart might stop. So long ago. He had thought the eight year old Mateo too young to listen to what was being said. He remembered the horror of the soldier grabbing Ana, but nothing of what the other children were doing.

He thought of the time in Spain when family members exposed their own people to the Inquisitors. Surely Mateo was not so indoctrinated that he would deny his own father?

"What have you done?" Francisco rushed around the desk and snatched the flask from the trembling boy. "I do not—"

But his words did not have a chance to leave his lips and fall into the ears of his son, for Mateo turned and fled.

✡ ✡ ✡

Francisco trudged down the narrow alley, all the fear of his years of living a double life weighing down his legs as if a huge stone sat in his stomach. When he tried to follow his angry son he had been waylaid by Padre Garcia, anxious to discuss the upcoming Feast of All Saints. Now the boy was nowhere to be seen. Would he run home? Francisco realized he knew so little about Mateo that he had no idea where he would run for solace.

"What is it?" Raquel rushed to Francisco when he burst through the door.

"Is Mateo here?"

She shook her head. "Is he not with you?"

Francisco looked around the room. His despair left him hoping Raquel was mistaken and the boy was here. "It... things did not... where would he go?"

Ana ran to her mother's side. Bella, left alone in the corner, started to cry. Luis sat still, his eyes wide as he stared at Francisco.

"Shh." Raquel said to Bella. "Do not fret."

It was only then that Francisco realized he had burst in without knocking and his voice was loud and harsh. But even the frightened children did not stop him from pressing Raquel for an answer. "I need to find him. I fear he may do something unwise."

"Unwise? What happened, Cisco?"

"He did not take the news well. He is insisting it is not so, that he is not a Jew, but a Catholic." Francisco felt weak as the words left his lips. In a flash he realized that for all these years it had taken a tremendous amount of energy to keep the secret. If his son turned them in to the authorities, he could not fight it. He slumped into the chair next to the wall, his gaze meeting the frightened eyes of his wife. "If he goes to the wrong person, if he tells Señor Vasquez or some other teacher who is loyal to the Queen, then all is lost."

"He won't. Not Mateo." But Raquel's creased brow told him she was worried.

"He knows too much." Francisco took inventory of what Mateo did know. He knew of the brotherhood. He knew of Don Leon

Milano and of Pedro Begazo. He did not know the other men, as he had never met Tordoya or de la Paloma.

But Begazo would be a huge loss to the Brotherhood of Believers. He was the most firmly established connection in Portugal, beyond suspicion because of his close relationship with King Jao, although that had weakened now that Manuel I ruled.

And what of Raquel and his other children? Francisco looked at Luis, listening to every word. In his haste he had pulled his younger son into this mess. No one would escape persecution, not even Mateo. Although informants were led to believe this was so, it was never the case in the end.

✡ ✡ ✡

Francisco visited the house twice a day, and Paulo was set to looking for Mateo, but it was three days before the boy appeared.

Raquel sent a message that he was home, but she met Francisco at the door and slipped out into the alley.

"Paulo has taken the children for a walk. Mateo is inside, but I beg you do not allow your words to betray you, my husband. Remember he is just a boy. Confused. He does not have all that you had."

"What do you mean?"

"A father."

Raquel's words pierced him like a spear heated in the fire. Was this the price for carrying on the secret? Francisco hadn't let his own needs take precedence over that of the Jews. It had been necessary to live a life that was not the one he dreamed of as a boy, but at least he had his father, his grandfather and his brother beside him. Men who shared the secret.

But what of a boy with a bishop as a father? One who did not even know until age ten that this holy man who spent so many hours with his mother, in a convent no less, *was* his father? Mateo only knew himself as the illegitimate son of a priest who had disregarded his vows.

Subdued by these thoughts, Francisco followed Raquel into the house. Mateo was seated at the table, eating a bowl of stew. When he saw his father, he dropped his spoon and rose from his chair.

"Sit. Finish your food." Francisco waved a hand toward the bowl and sat across from his son. "We will talk about this thing as men."

But if Francisco thought his words would be comforting, the panicked expression on Mateo's face made him realize his mistake.

Francisco reached a hand across the table to comfort his son, but Mateo shrank from his touch. He pulled his hand back into his lap. "Please do not be scared. I am not angry. We just need to talk about this."

Mateo glanced toward Raquel and then looked at his father. "There is nothing to talk about. I am not a dirty Jew."

Raquel gasped and stepped forward, but Francisco waved her away. "That is what we need to talk about."

Mateo was not a dull boy. At Santa Ildefenso the students talked of politics. And he was keen to listen when men talked of religion and wealth and the world. "I know what you fear, *Padre*." This last word came out a sneer. "That I will expose your little game."

Francisco considered the boy's anger. He had practiced diplomacy in his years as a priest, but fear of outcomes was something he had used to control the behavior of others, not felt within his own soul.

Mateo picked up his bowl and slurped down the last of the stew. "I will not say anything. But not because of you. It is because Mamá and Paulo would pay the price. And your children. But you never thought about that, did you?"

With that he set his bowl down and rose. But he did not run from the room, as the boy had done three days ago. This time he walked with his chin up, picked up his coat and left the room with a firm stride, never glancing back as he shut the door behind him.

Mateo left the room as a man.

"Do you think you can convince him to see straight?" Francisco asked his wife.

Tears filled her eyes. "I do not know. He is distant from me. You know he spends all his time at school now."

"I cannot leave this to chance. If he speaks to anyone anxious to get into the good graces of the viceroy then word could easily spread."

"Surely there have been other times when men have hesitated to take on the weight of the secret?"

Raquel was probably right. But Francisco didn't know personally of any son or man who had resisted becoming a part of the Brotherhood. While his own transition had been a surprise, there had been no choice in his mind. A matter of honor, his father had explained, when he continued to question how a man could be a Catholic and a Jew.

When Francisco realized the problem was bigger than he had ever imagined, he finally made the decision that this did constitute a situation with enough urgency to contact Marcus de la Paloma.

Marcus came to confession and Francisco made sure he was the priest on the other side of the curtain.

"Forgive me, *Padre*, for I have sinned." Marcus's deep whisper comforted Francisco. At last someone to share in his troubles.

"I have a problem, Marcus. It is Mateo, my oldest son. He is thirteen years now. It is time for his mitzvah. But he has not accepted the duties."

"So I have heard."

Paloma had heard? Francisco's throat tightened and he could barely whisper his next words.

"What have you heard?'

"Mateo frequents the Moinho Velho, along with every drunken soldier in town. Apparently the father of Fernam de Nunez allows the boys to accompany him. Your son has been witnessed making threats."

"Threats? Against whom?"

"The Jews."

This was worse than Francisco had imagined.

"What—" he choked. "What do we do?"

"I have called a meeting. We will discuss it then." Someone came into the church. Marcus whispered the specifics of the meeting between mumbled prayers, then slipped away.

Francisco bent his head and pushed his face into his folded hands. His legs were shaking and wouldn't hold him if he tried to stand. And for just a moment, because he was in this holy place of the Catholic church, he clutched his rosary and prayed to the God who looked out for them all.

Seven
Gabriella
Wednesday, April 2

I stared at my cell phone, my cousin Mark's words ringing in my ears—he was gone for a month?—then looked across the fields at the town and made up my mind that a river in motion was better than a stagnant pond.

Coffee. That was still top priority.

The town was every bit as deserted as it seemed on my first trip through. Was that only yesterday?

In the gravel parking lot between the coffeehouse and the courthouse stood four cars and two trucks parked at odd angles, like people had rushed to the scene of a crime and jumped from their vehicles.

I squeezed the Honda into a tiny space under a huge tree. Shade for Bones.

But fear and anxiety are unexpected house guests, popping in for a visit whenever they feel like it. Suddenly my heart beat too hard and my lungs constricted.

What was I doing here? I imagined old men in coveralls, farmers or cowboys, hunched over their steaming cups of coffee. Heads would turn when I walked in.

New girl.

The quivers made their way from my stomach to my hands and I squeezed the steering wheel. Bones stood, her body too long for the cramped seat, slapping me across the cheek with her tail as she pressed her nose against the window and whined.

I didn't need coffee, I needed a drink. At nine in the morning.

Drive home, She-Who-Is-Unprepared whispered. *Go back.*

I couldn't go back to California. What was there to go back to? Packing up my life and moving it into a smaller container. Wasn't it time I let myself out of that box? Not that my impulsive trip had made much of a difference, because here I sat, shaking and paralyzed. *Stop it, stop it now*, I told the black whisper, even as I started the engine, ready to drive away from this town. I would go back to the old house and think.

Think? Or fret?

The house. That was it. There had to be paperwork and fees and considerations for selling the property. That's what I came here for, wasn't it?

Windows cracked for Bones, I crunched my way across the gravel to the courthouse.

✡ ✡ ✡

The tall doors of the courthouse opened into a foyer, double stone staircases on either side of me. Hallways branched off in both directions. Double doors stood at the top of the stairs—the velvet theater ropes hanging across them warning no admittance. A musty smell—old museums—filled the air.

The sounds of voices led me down the hall to the right. That feeling of being in a library or a church or somewhere that you have no business caused me to step as lightly as possible.

The hall was lined with heavy wooden doors. All closed and unlabeled, except for one near the end, propped open with a chair. A regular office, complete with a counter to protect the two women seated at desks behind it.

"I can't believe you let him get away with that. Why didn't you —can I help you?" The dark haired woman didn't pause for a breath and it took me a minute to realize she was talking to me now, not gossiping with her friend. Her eyes were so black I couldn't make out her pupils. Olive skin and a long braid, not as dark as her eyes.

"Uh... I'm trying to find out where I would talk to someone about selling some property?"

"Which property?" She glanced at the other woman. This one was older, hair a wonderful salt and pepper and clear brown eyes the color of aging oak.

"Uh..." Wait a minute. Why did it matter which property? Shouldn't she be asking me what I needed to do, not what I needed to sell? "I inherited some property. I want to find out about paperwork, you know, what it takes to sell it."

Alaura Paloma—if the brown plastic sign on the desk was correct—turned all the way around so that I couldn't see her face. "What do you think?" she asked the other woman.

Salt-and-Pepper stood and walked over to the counter. "*Hola.* I am Carmen Murch. Tell me more about what you need?"

The knots in my neck relaxed a little. But just a little.

"I'm Gabriella Martinez. I came here from California because I inherited some land. And a house. I need to sell them."

"Martinez? Jonas Martinez?"

I nodded.

More glances. This was why I had avoided the coffee house.

Carmen turned back to me. "You probably want to start with the records department. They can research the title for you."

"You really need a realtor." Alaura thumbed through a rolodex. "I have some names if you need them."

I nodded, unable to think of anything else I could say.

✡ ✡ ✡

Five minutes later I was on my way upstairs to the records department—my starting point according to Alaura and Carmen— fourth door on the left. I was armed with a list of five realtors, printed in Alaura Paloma's neat handwriting. I glanced at the list, noticing the first name was Bradley Paloma. Relative?

The doors on this level were different. Not solid wood, but old-fashion bubbled glass. Each had one of those funky windows above the door and I imagined a quick escape via the transom a la Pink Panther.

I stopped at the third door. Marconi and Dominguez, LTD stenciled in elegant gold. Everyone must be in this building. Not surprising, as I hadn't seen any other buildings with intact windows on my drive through town yesterday.

In spite of Carmen's advice, this was where I needed to start.

The attorney's office was every bit as funky historic as the rest of the building. An old desk, complete with an actual rotary phone greeted me. I expected a white haired secretary, but there was no one there. Ghost town. There was a doorway off to my right.

"Hello?" I called out.

Papers rustled and I heard the sound of a chair scraping across the wooden floor.

"I'll be right with you." More noises, unrecognizable. Clanking and grinding, like farm equipment or tools being tossed into a metal box.

"Hello. Sorry. Joel Dominguez."

He was younger than I expected, but every bit the attorney. Nice black suit, fit him well. Shiny, expensive looking watch. Red tie, white shirt and clean shave. Deep brown eyes, but a cowlick in his shiny black hair, just above his left ear, interfered with his perfect look. I smiled and took the hand he offered.

"Gabriella Martinez." He laughed. "I can't believe you came. Does Mark know you're here?"

I nodded. "I talked to him this morning."

He smiled and motioned to the office I imagined was full of farm equipment. "Come in."

Barbells. I had to step over them to reach the chair in front of his desk. Which was covered with haphazard stacks of files, pens, three coffee cups and a bottle of water. Photos of women, children, couples and dogs were propped in silver frames, facing me, which seemed peculiar. Didn't that mean he couldn't see them?

"You'll have to excuse the equipment." He pulled a file out of an oak cabinet. Antique like the rest of the place.

Mr. Dominguez explained the will. The land was divided by sections to the heirs, but there was no legal division of the 1900 acre parcel. Mark and Jeff had started the ball rolling on splitting the parcels.

"How did they decide who gets what?"

"They didn't. It was spelled out in the will, just never legally recorded."

"But why now? Didn't my grandfather die a long time ago?"

"Actually, the will was written by Hernan Martinez, but it had some strange specifications. As long as someone wanted to live there it stayed as is. Only when all the heirs agreed could it be split. That's why is was never recorded."

"Who was Hernan?"

"Grandfather of Jonas, who I believe was your great-grandfather."

So many generations, it was strange. I looked at the copy of the map Dominguez slid across the desk. "Why is it split into these narrow strips?"

"Not so narrow, it's a lot of property, but to answer your question it's for water access." He leaned forward and traced a narrow line on one edge of the map. "This is the acequia, water supply for the area. Land owners buy water."

"Buy?"

"Yes. But the rights have to be granted to you. You can't just buy it. Water is very valuable."

"Rights?" I felt like he was speaking some other language.

"Water rights and easements. That's what it all comes down to around here."

"So how do I sell it?" I held up the list from Alaura. "I have some realtors here."

"Did you talk to Fred?"

That's right. Mr. Dominguez had recommended someone as well. Probably *his* cousin.

"No."

"Well he's a good resource. He can show you around, let you see what else is on the market. Help you figure out an asking price."

Drive through these hills in an old truck with yet another strange man? "I don't think—"

"Doesn't really matter. You can't list it yet. Not until the title is clear."

What about all his advice to come here? The *professional* advice that I had impulsively followed when I was filled with rage and desperation and couldn't see any farther than the windshield of my car?

Suddenly my head was so heavy I couldn't hold it up. My chin sank to my chest and I pressed my palms over my eyes. A migraine hovered off to the right, waiting to strike. The elephant in the room had perched on my shoulders—there was no clear title to the property I had come here to sell in a hurry. Why had I thought I suddenly knew how to take care of myself? I didn't know a thing about business or titles or taxes or water rights. These things were completely unfamiliar to a housewife and mother using all her energy to be happy. Unprepared, yes, but I could fix that, couldn't I?

I stood and grabbed my purse. "Thank you for your time."

Mr. Dominguez stood as well. "Fred's office is just down the hall, how about we see if he's in?" He waved a hand toward his phone and I noticed that this one was modern. A smart one. He held out the file.

"Not right now." I took the file and walked out of his office and past the antique desk in the front office, The rotary phone wasn't really connected to anything. I had been foolish to have such a romantic first impression of this place—quaint?

Nothing but surface dressing.

✡ ✡ ✡

The sun blinded me and pierced into my throbbing brain as I stomped around the corner of the courthouse and smacked straight into someone.

"Easy does it." A voice said.

"Sorry." I squinted and put my hand to my forehead to block the glare.

Tattooed-Buck.

I jumped back. "Sorry. Sun. Couldn't see." I waved a hand upward, then headed across the parking lot to my car.

I tripped over one of those cement tire-stops. The file flew from my hand as I tried to break my fall and all those important papers scattered everywhere. Why was the tire-stop located here, as random as the cars parked every which way? It certainly was not being used as a parking guide.

Not-So-Tough-Ella burst into tears.

"Gabriella, are you okay?" Tattooed-Buck dropped to his knees and grabbed my shoulder. He remembered my name.

I remembered his too. Andy Lloyd. I had memorized it so I could report him when something bad happened out at my isolated house. Now he held my arm.

He pulled out a clean white handkerchief and handed it to me. Wasn't that a bit too much of a cliche? Mad stalker offers damsel in distress a cloth to wipe her tears?

"Gabriella?" He interrupted my wandering thoughts.

"Sorry." I pulled away and struggled to my feet, keeping my eyes down as I accepted the handkerchief. It was that or wipe my nose on my sleeve. Scrambling to gather the fallen pages I didn't look at Andy as he helped. I didn't know why he made me feel uneasy, but with a mumbled thanks, I returned the soggy cloth and limped to my car, leaving Andy Lloyd standing in the morning sun.

Eight
Francisco Martín de la Serrano
Magadouro, Portugal, 1497

Francisco stared at the masked faces. Unlike meetings in Spain, he wasn't able to identify these men by voices alone. He knew that de la Paloma was leading the meeting, but other than his old friend, he was among strangers.

"The boy must go," a robed figure nearly shouted. "Now, before it is too late."

Go where? What does he mean? Francisco stared at the cloaked figure, wishing for some sense of who this was.

"No, that does not remove the danger. There is only one way to make sure we are safe." The second man had a shrill voice and he shook his head. His tone left Francisco puzzled for a moment. Then he realized what this man was saying.

Francisco's hands clenched as he spoke. "What you are suggesting is no better than those who execute our people, simply for who we are, when no crime has been committed."

"If he cannot keep a secret, then things will happen to innocents. My own brother is gone, tortured, no doubt, before his execution. Would you have us all meet the same fate? The risk is too great." The man's voice trembled with grief.

Francisco wished he knew who spoke. He felt bad for anyone who had lost a brother, but what if this was only a story, told at the right moment to lead others into his way of thought? He waited for de la Paloma to stop these brutal comments.

But instead of stopping the talk of killing Mateo, the leader of the Brotherhood remained silent. Other men took up the cry of the shrill-voiced man. "The boy must go, send him away, send them all away."

"Stop! You are talking about my son. A Jewish boy on the cusp of manhood." Francisco sought a reason, something to convince these angry men he could guarantee their safety. "He does not know the names of any Brothers. You are not in danger."

"But he knows your name." De la Paloma faced Francisco. "And if a Catholic bishop is exposed, then all who worship at his side, all who come to him for prayers or baptism or wedding vows, they are all in danger."

Francisco's face grew hot at the words of his leader, the man he had stood by and obeyed for so many years. He felt a sense of betrayal so vast, that no words came to mind. A vision of the end of his world was all that he could see.

"Then let me take him away. I will take my family far from Porto, to some place where no one knows us." Francisco didn't add that he would convert, truly convert to the Christian faith if this would save his son.

The men mumbled to each other, then looked to de la Paloma.

"You must leave tonight."

Francisco choked and nodded, thinking of the late hour. His children would be asleep, even Raquel may have ended her day by now. Just his knock would frighten them and how would he tell her that they must gather their belongings and flee once again?

"You will go to Magadouro with the rest of the Jews. But there must be no sign that you are a bishop or in any way related to the Church, " de la Paloma instructed.

This was not how Francisco had imagined he would return to his faith. To live openly as a Jew? Now, when King Manuel had fallen in love with Isabel, the Spanish princess, and suddenly the Jews were no longer welcome in Portugal?

But King Manuel didn't really want to persecute the Jews. He conceded to Ferdinand's demands that all non-Christians convert, but he allowed them to escape the cities. The small towns nestled in cold valleys high in the mountains would not be scrutinized. This is where the Brotherhood was sending Francisco and his family.

✡ ✡ ✡

Francisco held Bella on his hip. At six years old she was too heavy to be carried, but the roads were crowded and he was afraid of losing her.

"Hold on to each other," he told the boys. Raquel clutched Ana's hand as she pushed through the dense wall of travelers. His wife's face was pale.

Luis ran ahead. The long journey to the mountains was an adventure for Francisco's youngest son. Unlike his brother, who sulked along behind them, as if distance would keep him from being mistaken for a part of the family.

"Luis! Stay with us."

Francisco and Raquel tried to make the move seem like a good thing. *We'll travel to a new home, where there is open space and plenty of food and everything is clean*, he heard his wife tell the children. Strange words when you awaken them in the middle of the night. It had been impossible to keep the real reason for this move from Mateo. Raquel convinced the boy to come with them, pulling on the strings that still attached his heart to hers.

When the family finally arrived in Mogadouro, their new home a single room, the walls covered with green moss and the floor always damp, Mateo spent all his time away. The boy could not be bothered to tell his parents where he went each day and Francisco worried that the safety of the Brothers was still at risk.

✡ ✡ ✡

Five weeks later the Martín de la Serrano family slipped into the hopeless state that many displaced people experience. Although the town was filled with Jews, and the Brotherhood had insisted they give up all pretense, Raquel and Francisco continued the charade of Catholicism. He lived as a tool maker, falling back on his early training in Spain.

And then one night Mateo failed to come home. Raquel was frantic until a message came from one of the street children who showed up to beg for handouts. Their son had joined the soldiers. He would sleep in the barracks with them. They should not try to contact him or bring him home if they wanted him to keep silent.

Francisco waited until the children were asleep to pull Raquel outside. This was the only private place to talk.

"Raquel, I've been thinking. Would it be too terrible if we were to convert? We could go back to Barcelona. Or even Sevilla." He appealed to his wife's attachment to her place of birth.

"Convert? What do you mean, Cisco?"

"I have been Catholic for so long now. It does not feel so bad to me. Different, but there are many differences in the world. If we were to be truly converted, then Mateo would—"

Raquel shook her head and her eyes filled with tears. "Think of what you say. Such a thing must make your heart cold. He will change soon, I'm sure of it."

Francisco knew his wife prayed each day that Mateo would accept the fact they were Jews and come home. He also knew her hopes were for naught. The boy was lost to them.

"What would you have us do?"

She grabbed his hand and pulled it to her heart, pressing it tightly against her chest. "Abandon this mask, be who we are. There are so many Jews here, my love. We will be just one of many, and we will be true to our hearts and to God. We can be Jewish now, don't you see that?"

"We cannot—" He choked back his words. He had never told Raquel of the brutal words of the Brothers concerning Mateo. His wife had listened to his brief explanation of the need to slink away from Porto in the night and complied, as she had always done for him. She didn't share in the knowledge that these men would have killed Mateo if they hadn't taken him away. Francisco had never told his wife about the sense of betrayal that burned in his heart. Their wealth had dwindled—he had only a few gold coins left—and to be one of the Jews now meant to be one of the destitute people who had forfeited their belongings, meager or plentiful, to a greedy aristocracy.

The letter from Benito, now a land owner outside Sevilla, had arrived last week. Even his younger brother had heard of his failure to convince his son to carry on the traditions of the Brotherhood. Benito had offered to see that Goncalo, his eldest son, trained for the priesthood. But Benito had also warned that he wanted no contact with Francisco and that his brother was not to contact Mamá. Being a member of the Brotherhood remaining in Spain was dangerous and there could be no breach of trust. *Go on with your life, my brother*, the letter had said. *Use this opportunity to live the way you have always dreamed.* His brother seemed to think Francisco had wanted to leave. Lucky Benito, able to make that choice. The second son's role in the Brotherhood—a place of power in society—a land owner, a business man, never a holy man held an appeal to him now. Francisco supposed there was risk, but at this point his brother had the better life.

But dreams and reality are not always cousins. Francisco reached into his pocket and squeezed the rosary which he kept close. He wanted to tell his wife that the two religions were not so different, that God listened to all the prayers. Francisco remembered all too well the cold look in Marcus de la Paloma's eyes when the man had nodded in agreement to the suggestions of the heartless Brothers.

Francisco reached for his wife's arm and escorted her back to the crowded room, where the soft breath of his children kept him from sleep.

✡ ✡ ✡

"Papá!"

Francisco turned to the sound of Bella's call. He was working in the small yard at the back of the stone room, sharpening the tools he had collected yesterday, so that he might bring in enough money to feed his family.

But Bella was not calling him. It was the small man who walked around the building and entered the yard that she rushed to.

Paulo.

They had left his former manservant in Porto without an explanation. Paulo had awakened when Francisco rushed home and quickly gathered their belongings.

"I will let you know where we are," he had promised. But he had not followed up on his commitment, happy that he would no longer have to share his wife and children with this man. Raquel must have contacted him.

Paulo had the grace to act as if he hadn't been deserted. He scooped Bella into his arms and kissed the girl's soft cheek. "Your Holiness," he greeted Francisco.

Francisco detected a bitterness in the greeting, but not so bitter as the feeling in his heart as he watched his daughter wrap her arms around Paulo's neck. He looked down at his rough hands, which held the tools of his new trade.

"Paulo," he returned the man's greeting, his thoughts as heavy as the whetstone on which he sharpened the axe. Did this man expect to live with them? Hadn't they done enough for him already?

To Francisco's surprise Paulo laughed. "No need for the look of execution, Cisco. I come with a message of hope."

"A message from whom?"

"Pedro Begazo."

"How is it that you carry a message from Begazo?"

"He is my employer." Paulo looked at Bella. "Go little one. Fetch Mamá." When Bella had scampered away, Paulo continued.

"Raquel needs to hear what I have to say as well."

Francisco set down the axe and wiped his hands on the leather apron he wore to protect his legs. He knew that he should invite Paulo in, offer him something to drink, but he couldn't bring himself to say the words. Something about this man's grin—maybe it was the unexpected laughter—didn't seem right. Francisco noticed that Paulo did not look as he had in the past. No longer gaunt, his mustache was smooth and he wore a tunic of blue velvet and pants of fine wool. His boots were shined and he had a knife tucked into a smooth leather belt. His former manservant stood tall and stared directly into his eyes.

The only men Francisco knew of who came into wealth were those who betrayed others.

"Paulo!" Raquel's voice held such surprise that Francisco revised his idea that she had contacted the man. "What are you doing here?"

Paulo took hold of Raquel's hand and brought it to his lips. At least he didn't embrace another man's wife.

"I have a message for you and Francisco. An offer from *Don* Pedro Begazo."

"An offer from Begazo? What would he have to do with us?" Raquel voiced the question which plagued Francisco.

"He would like me to bring Luis back to Porto. The boy will attend school at Santa Ildefenso." Paulo paused and cleared his throat, then looked straight into Francisco's eyes. "Luis will be trained as a priest."

Raquel grabbed Francisco's arm. "Did you ask for this? Are you to send this son away as well?"

He squeezed her hand. "No, never." How could she think he would repeat the mistake he had made with Mateo?

They both turned to Paulo.

"Raquel, you should not look at this opportunity with such doubt. And you should not accuse your husband of anything other than ignorance."

"What is this you are saying?" Francisco straightened his slumped shoulders and again pulled himself to the height he had carried as a Bishop. How dare this manservant speak in such a way?

"Your grandfather was friends with the grandfather of Begazo. The two were leaders of the Brotherhood. Do you think such a man as *Don* Pedro Begazo would let the Martín de Seranno family slip into oblivion? After you left the Brothers were angry. Many wanted to follow and bring Mateo back, get rid of the risk completely. Begazo stood up for you. He did not want to see the Brotherhood lose the strength and intelligence of the heirs of Serrano.

"But the men would not agree to your return. So Begazo struck a bargain. Luis would come back and be raised in his household. In this way the tradition can continue."

Francisco closed his eyes and slumped back onto the wooden stool he kept at his workbench. The sun beat down on his head and shoulders and he started to perspire. Raquel stepped away from him.

Who do I betray? he wondered. For never had he felt so torn between the two parts of his life. To be a member of the Brotherhood, each day going to the Catholic church and praying to the saints and clutching the rosary, while each night reciting the Sh'ma. Should he give up the ruse, the Christian lie and live as a poor Jew? Or turn away from the Brotherhood completely and abide by the orders of Ferdinand and Isabella, convert, once and for all and leave behind the Jewish heritage which beat in his heart? This choice, to continue the heritage of his ancestors, surely it was God's will? He wiped the sweat from his brow and looked at his wife.

The rose of her cheeks had fled, leaving her as white as the clouds that floated in the blue mountain sky.

Francisco met his wife's unblinking stare. "Where is Luis?"

With a sob, Raquel ran to the house.

✡ ✡ ✡

Weeks passed, each day a replica of the one before—look for

work, look for food, try not to notice the absence of Mateo and Luis. Then Francisco awoke in the night, a fever raging through his body. By morning he was so weak he couldn't rise from the straw mattress which was their bed.

Raquel held water to his lips. "Just try a sip. Please, my love."

Francisco shook his head, the movement barely perceptible. "Listen." He saw the fear on her face.

"Don't try to talk." Raquel placed a wet rag on his forehead.

"We must talk. This is the end."

His beloved wife tried once again to hush him, her eyes wide and somber.

"You must find Mateo, Raquel. Make him understand. I know that you can do it."

Raquel shook her head. "You will do this, Cisco. You will teach your son. And he will listen now. He is older and things are different."

He clutched her hand. "You must."

As she nodded a single tear slipped down her cheek.

He struggled to keep his eyes open. He wanted one last look at his tiny wife. Her dark hair was pulled back from her high cheekbones, so he could see those deep blue eyes. How many times had he wished she were next to him when they were forced to live apart? Now that they were together, why had God decided to separate them?

Francisco let his eyes fall shut. He thought of the promised land. Fields which would be flush with foods, towns filled with people who worked together, young couples with laughing children. Synagogues.

He would not live to see these things in this world. But if God was listening to his prayers, if God would follow through on one more thing, them maybe Luis and Bella and Ana and all the children to come would live the truth. And maybe Mateo would see the truth as well.

Nine
Gabriella
Wednesday, April 2 and Thursday, April 3

I rushed to my car, my face hot with embarrassment at giving Andy Lloyd another reason to think I was crazy. Pulling out my cell phone I punched #4.

"Hi. You have reached Vicki's phone. Please leave a—"

"I don't want Vicki's phone. Where are you?" There was no message to describe how much I needed a friend right now.

I stared at my phone. Ten messages.

Look at me. Dialing Vicki when I needed her, but ignoring her when I didn't.

"It's not fair. Not fair, not fair at all." Bones whined and stuffed her nose into my shoulder. She didn't like it when I whimpered.

It wasn't fair that my husband left me and that no one cared enough about me to notice I was gone. It wasn't fair that I took the big step of driving here and proved, once again, that I was just as stupid as everyone thought. Stupid enough to think I could just sell the property and stupid enough to think that money would make things better. But none of that was why I needed to talk to my friend.

Face it, you want to tell Vicki that a guy talked to you. That you don't know what to do about it. That you think you should be scared, but you're thrilled.

I had gotten a better look at Andy, in spite of falling and crying and running away. He was wearing a shirt, so his tattoos didn't show. His hair was in a neat pony tail and his green eyes didn't glow red or yellow. He wasn't really seven feet tall, more like six feet. In all truth, he was very nice to look at.

I pressed my head against the steering wheel.

Which turned out to be burning hot. I pulled my face away and glanced in the rear view mirror, expecting to see a red welt branding my forehead. All I saw were unplucked eyebrows, a dirt smudge on my left cheek and the steeple of a church poking out of the top of my head like a unicorn. I turned and looked out the back window.

There was a church a block or so beyond the jail. Before I could deftly field the unwelcome memory, my father's words pushed into my mind.

"You can pray, Ella. God will always help you."

What my father never realized is that I didn't believe in God and I didn't speak my real prayers out loud and God never answered me anyway.

Not even once.

I had spent my early years in rote prayer. Each night my father led me through a ritual—brush teeth, wash face, visit the bathroom one last time, slip into a clean night gown and kneel by the bed. No night time stories or songs to help me sleep. My father stood with his hand on my shoulder, waiting for me to start.

"Thank you God and Jesus for Mommy and Daddy, for taking care of Grandma and Grandpa King and other Grandma and Grandpa. Thank you for our house and our food and my teacher. God, could you please help Mew Kitty find her way home because I still really miss her."

If my performance was a good one, my father's hand would slip off my shoulder and pat me on the head. This was my cue to hop into bed and he would pull the quilt close under my chin, kiss my forehead and whisper goodnight. He would leave the door open three inches, so the hall light would chase away my nighttime fears.

But if my prayer failed—if I didn't remember to mention sick Aunt Gertie or thank God for the good grade I got on my math test or if I asked God for help with something that was my responsibility, which might be the same math test I was supposed to thank him for—my father's hand would tighten. His huge thumb would press against my shoulder blade, his finger would sink into my soft flesh and he would say "Try again."

I would start over. Maybe more than once. I learned to be very careful about what I prayed for. It wasn't often that I felt the pressure on my shoulder, the grasp of the angry God, but my father never left me to my own devices when it came to prayer. The nights his hand grew tight, those were the nights I wouldn't—*couldn't*—sleep. The nights he shut the door with a sharp click and no hall light comforted me, I curled into a tight ball, knees tucked against my chest, one arm over my head to shelter me from the dark and the nightmares that surrounded me.

Now, forty years later, I didn't want to think about it. Taking my eyes off the steeple in the distance, I turned back to the front of the car. No way, Ella. He's dead. And God was never really listening, anyway. I picked up my phone and nearly dialed Vicki once more. Instead I sent a text to Julie. *Don't worry, I'm fine. Just needed some space. Love Mom.*

I headed back to hide at the old house that wasn't my home.

✡ ✡ ✡

The next morning, after another night of drifting in and out of painful sleep and more crazy dreams, I drove to Three Ravens Coffee House again. Today I would have my coffee.

I hadn't slept in the house. Another walk through convinced me that I would have to do some cleaning before spending the night with spiders and dirt. But if I didn't do it today I would lose my fingers and toes to the cold, dog in my sleeping bag or not. I'd find a place that sold brooms and sponges after I had my coffee.

The building that housed Three Ravens was a faded majestic queen, with peeling paint and a sagging facia. Decorative boulders surrounded spiky plants at the edge of the gravel parking lot. Brightly painted tables and chairs lined the creaking wooden porch. I took a closer look at the three laughing metal ravens perched above the tall painted door. Nice.

I tied Bones to a post and went in. No old men crouched over scratched white cups at a formica counter, just the smell of cinnamon and coffee welcoming me. The high walls were covered with paintings and shelves displayed colorful pottery and jewelry. One wall was lined with native drums, from the size of a coffee can to a giant instrument equivalent to a truck tire. The stretched skin on top seemed ready for three men to play it. There were strange wooden boxes, like end tables or something, the fronts made of beautiful inlaid wood with a round hole in the middle.

In here there were more painted tables, like those on the porch, scattered around the room. Only one table was occupied—with an oldish man and a not-so-oldish, but far from young woman engaged in lively conversation. Two chattering high school girls manned the counter. A glass case housed fat muffins with nuts and shredded carrots, huge cookies coated with cinnamon, and sweet rolls drizzled with sticky toppings.

"What can I get for you?" The girl had bright white teeth and a welcoming smile.

I ordered a mocha, two shots and added one of the cookies. Although the place was rustic, it certainly had a modern flair. Hope upon hope. "Do you have wi-fi here?"

She nodded. "No password needed."

Civilization, at last. "Does it work out on the porch? I have my dog." Then I reconsidered. Maybe they would let me charge up my phone here. I glanced around for an outlet and came face to face with a tall man.

"She can come inside," he said in a rumbling voice well suited to his height.

I looked up into a face that matched the voice. Brown eyes bordering on black, a gray mustache perched atop a smooth lip and a long gray pony tail. Did all the men in this town have pony tails? Or was this man a native? Didn't Indians wear their hair long?

I heard my father's complaints. "God damn hippies. Taking over the world. They'll bankrupt us all."

Deep-Voice reached out his hand. "I'm Nathan Pierce. Welcome to Three Ravens."

I shook the offered hand. Big, warm and rough. "Ella Martinez."

"And the beautiful red lady outside?"

"Bones."

A graying shepherd walked over, his long tail waving. Nathan patted the dog. "This is Max. He owns the place."

It turned out instead that Nathan was the owner of the coffee house. He walked beside me as I carried my mocha to the table with the outlet. "Is it okay if I charge my phone?"

"No problem." He tipped his head toward the door. "You going to bring Bones in?"

"Really?"

While our dogs completed the requisite sniffing I set up my laptop. More customers came in.

"If there is anything else you need, just let me know." Nathan smiled. "Welcome to T.A."

T.A.? As he walked away, I realized he meant Tierra Amarilla.

✿ ✿ ✿

I checked my emails, nothing important—my girls only sent texts and my mother was computer illiterate. After I checked my bank balance—it hadn't magically increased—I realized that having been so thrilled to have internet access, there really wasn't much I needed to do. I searched real estate in the area. I could check out what was here before I drove around with any of the realtors.

After an hour of aimless searching—there didn't seem to be any pattern to the prices people were asking for property—I was ready for one of those sticky buns I had spied at the counter. Walking back to the table, I studied the drums along the wall.

Nathan appeared beside me. "You play?" For such a tall man he walked on soundless feet.

"No. Not me. But these are wonderful." I pointed to the wooden boxes. "What are those?"

"Cajóns." He smiled. "And my livelihood."

"You make them?"

"Yep. Out back. Have you ever heard one?"

I shook my head and he pulled one of the wooden drums out to the center of the floor. To my surprise he sat on it, legs akimbo on either side. Leaning forward, he placed his palms on the front of the box.

Bump-a-bump-a-tap-tap-tap. The deep sound of the cajón echoed off the high ceiling of the room. I smiled and tapped my foot, even though I was conscious of the other people in the room. No one else seemed fazed by the sudden concert.

I tried to ignore everything else and listen, wondering if Nathan expected me to buy a drum. Slowly I let myself enjoy his performance.

As soon as I relaxed something happened. A feeling, as strong as if a swirl of mist or energy had crept from out of the earth and surrounded me, entered the room. I felt trapped and free and confused and wise all at once. I leaned forward and pressed my palms on the table, fearing the black cloud that might come if I wasn't in charge. The sound of Nathan's drumming continued. I gasped and tried to escape whatever it was that had engulfed me. Black cloud or not, the loss of control scared me.

As I let my breath out, this strange power pulled everything out of my soul. My fear went with it and my tight shoulders dropped and released the tension that always lived there. It was as if the sound cleansed the impurities of the world. My jaw went slack and my eyes rested. I didn't know what this was, some ancient form of hypnotism, but I liked it.

The deep beat was steady. My mind didn't go anywhere at all, just settled into a immense nothingness. No need to worry about anything anymore, it said.

After some amount of time, I have no idea how long, the beat began to slow, then drifted seamlessly down to a quiet pulse and stopped. I opened my eyes. When had I shut them?

Nathan smiled at me. "Your first time?"

I blinked, blushed and smiled back, unwilling to move, but managed a slight nod. This world of quiet peace was new to me. It was so open. A vast space of swirling mist that held a secret. A secret I knew I would find, but felt in no rush to seek, the journey to its source as pleasant as what I might find there.

The peaceful feeling was interrupted by the sound of the tall door creaking open.

"Hey Nate." Andy nodded toward Nathan and smiled at me. "Gabriella."

Nathan stood and reached out a hand. "Good morning. How's life treating you, my friend?"

The two men bantered about local things for a moment and then Andy walked over to the counter.

My shoulders tightened. I didn't want to let go of the feeling that had come over me during Nathan's drumming, but Andy Lloyd was following me, I was sure of it. As he walked over with his coffee, I tried to keep my mind still and free. I was scared, but some other burrowing thought wormed its way into my gut. I had the strange sense that I was happy Andy was here, in spite of knowing it just wasn't right.

Nathan pushed the drum back to the wall and slipped away. Max struggled to his feet and followed.

Andy set his cup down and pulled out a chair. "You seem to be feeling better today."

Stand up for yourself. Tell him you don't want him to sit there, Strong-Ella told me.

Then Bones' tail thumped a greeting on the wooden floor. She stood and licked his hand.

I've never been one to humanize my dog. She is just a dog, although admittedly a special dog. It seemed pretty clear she liked Andy Lloyd. I kept silent and the worm squiggled around in my stomach.

"Nate's pretty good on those drums. I see you had a demo." Andy added a packet of sugar to the black liquid in his mug. "Maybe you'd like to go up to the Jicarilla Nation some time. The drumming events are worth seeing."

Jicarilla Nation?

Andy stirred his coffee with a bent spoon, the steady clinking filling up the silence between us. "I mean, sometime in the future, you know." He flushed and I watched his tan cheeks take on a red tone.

Contagious red, because I felt my cheeks burn when I realized he had just asked me out on a date.

Polite-Ella took over, in spite of my intention to ask him what he was talking about. "I'm sorry, I was just lost in thought for a minute."

He sipped his coffee. "The drums will do that to you."

I didn't know if it was the drums, but something had led me to total confusion and drifting thoughts. Maybe this was just part of trying to start your life over. "What is the Jicarilla Nation?"

He smiled. "Used to be called a pueblo. Reservation, maybe. But not any more. It's up in Dulce, the Apache, they're the Jicarilla tribe."

Andy's radio cackled and he pulled it out from the clip on his belt.

"Nice talking with you, Gabriella." He stood and slipped out the door, radio to his ear.

✡ ✡ ✡

That night, watching the sunset over the mesa, wrapped in a blanket and holding a cup of tea I'd made on the camp stove, I decided fear wouldn't send me back to California. An impulsive decision brought me here—I had come here to sell the land—and that is what I needed to do. Tomorrow I would go see Fred Rivas.

That problem solved, my thoughts slipped back to Andy Lloyd. Just what did he want? Warning bells, along with my mother's fearful advice, went off whenever I was around him, yet he really hadn't done anything other than help me. More than once, really. It was just so strange he kept showing up wherever I happened to be.

Ten

Bernardo Martín de Serrano
Al Norte de Nueva España, 1605

Bernardo Martín de Serrano leaned against his horse and rubbed his hands together, desperately trying to bring some warmth to his finger tips. The gelding, Esclavo, was tired of waiting too. He shifted and snorted. Bernardo slipped his hand under the bulky collar the animal wore and scratched him on the neck. The horse pushed at Bernardo with his velvet nose. The fine whiskers of his muzzle were covered with ice crystals.

The conquistadors had been standing in the cold for hours. The heavy leather armor soldiers and horses wore did little to keep the biting wind from penetrating their bones. Add the fatigue of the endless journey from Mexico City and Bernardo was an unhappy man.

In need of help right now, he whispered a prayer. "Incline Thine ear, O HaShem, and answer me; for I am poor and needy. Keep my soul, for I am godly; O Thou my God, save Thy servant that trusteth in Thee. Be gracious unto me, O Lord; for unto Thee do I cry all the day."

He stopped his prayer when Diego, the only man who had befriended him on this journey, climbed up the bank and stretched his neck to peer over the edge of the red rock.

Diego never sat still. Waiting was torture for Bernardo's friend. "What do you think is happening?" he called down.

"I do not know and I do not care. I am so frozen, even my mind is ice." Bernardo didn't think his friend had heard his mumbled prayer.

Diego, Bernardo and eight other Spanish conquistadors were gathered in the steep gully. They had been ordered to wait while the leader of the group, Alonzo de la Paloma, went ahead with two scouts.

"Do you think those Indians killed Marcus?"

Bernardo didn't like to think about what might have befallen his older brother. Marcus had been missing for two weeks. He had gone out on a scouting expedition with a small group. They were to look for the supposed riches this unexplored land of *Nueva España* held. Marcus, a priest, was along to save the souls of any heathens who might happen to be in the way. This was General Juan de Oñate's way of pretending he followed the King's orders, the stated purpose of his venture to convert the indigenous people, rather than search for gold.

After over a year of following Oñate, Bernardo was sure that nothing of value would ever be found in this wilderness. The northern part of New Spain was nothing like Mexico City or the land down south. No silver, no gold. Just some turquoise stone which was of little use to soldiers. He also had his doubts about his brother's ability to save any souls. The natives were not exactly welcoming the Catholics with open arms. Not that Marcus was a true Catholic.

Bernardo's stomach burned. The colonists hadn't been able to grow much food, even with the help of the natives. All Bernardo could think about was going home to Mexico City and feasting on Mamá's cooking.

He knew his dream was hopeless. The Brotherhood would never allow the Martín de Serrano brothers to return. The Jews had lived in the safety of New Spain for more than fifty years, but things had changed.

It was all because of that fool, Juan Goméz de Begazo. The wealthy merchant had drawn the attention of the Mexican officials to their people with his meetings and his flamboyant ways. Trying to get the Jews to live openly. Wasn't it enough that they could worship in relative secrecy without being persecuted? Juan Goméz did not have the sense of his ancestors. Bernardo's father, Celestino, had cursed the man, telling his sons that the Begazo family should have stayed in Portugal.

Juan Goméz de Begazo had been arrested.

Infiltration into the secret life of the Jews increased and thus so did the need for expansion to new land. The Brotherhood never put up with persecution. They would protect themselves, and their riches, by hiding in plain sight, while looking for a new home.

Marcus, Romero and Bernardo Martín de Serrano, as well as other sons of Brothers, had been sent north with the Spanish conquistadors and priests to look for a new land where the Jews of the Brotherhood could live. Marcus as a friar, Romero as a farmer and Bernardo as a soldier.

Bernardo thought about the day he first learned of the *Fraternidad de Creyentes*. It was soon after his father had taken thirteen-year-old Marcus away for a week. Bernardo, only eleven years old, begged to go with them, but Celestino Martín de Serrano refused.

Marcus returned with a smug smile. "I can't tell you." His brother made light of Bernardo's questions. "You'll find out someday."

Bernardo was clever—no matter what his parents thought—not the dull son they made him out to be. While Marcus collected all the praise—how smart he was, how handsome, how he would make a good priest and bring success to the family—Bernardo watched. He might not be courageous or strong, but he was passionate.

"You tell me or I'll tell Papá about Maria Consuela Tordoya." Bernardo knew his brother was sweet on this girl. Her father, Juan de Tordoya, was the *Alcalde Mayor*, a staunch man of the old ways.

The Martín de Serrano family politics were in the opposite direction. Marcus would never be allowed to court the girl.

Under threat of exposure Marcus told Bernardo about the Brotherhood, the secret of their Jewish belief, and the tradition of the first son becoming a priest.

"A priest? But that can't be right. If you are to be Jewish how can you be a priest?"

"That's just it, little brother. It started with the grandfather of our grandfather, a hundred years ago. He left Spain. His name was Francisco and he pretended to be a priest. Since that time the oldest son has been chosen to be a priest when the old one dies. That is why the secret has been safe for so long." Marcus grinned. "This means me! I have been chosen."

And now, ten years later, Bernardo realized the mistake his father had made.

Celestino had failed to see that Marcus was not holy material. He was a soldier. One had only to watch him gallop over fields and jump boulders on his sturdy black stallion. The young man's chest puffed out, his heart filled with the glory of riding fast, of throwing rocks and sticks, of learning to use the weapons of the Spanish fighters.

Bernardo, on the other hand, should have been the priest. His nose was always in a book. Inspired by the revelation of the family secret, he listened intently to the sermons, he learned Latin and he puzzled out the mysteries of the world. He memorized the stories of the Jews who had moved from Spain to Portugal, then to the mountains and finally sailed across the vast ocean to New Spain. And he could never use a weapon on another, be it man or beast.

But Papá hadn't noticed. When Bernardo reached thirteen years, Celestino told the story, but there was no special medallion for him. The second son's role was to take a place in society, but that was not to be. Times were different and Bernardo was to become a soldier and protect his brother. Celestino's youngest son, Romero, would manage the property.

So here Bernardo was, ten years later, following Fray Marcus Castaño, Franciscan friar—formerly Marcus Martín de Serrano, older brother.

Father was right. I am not good at doing my job. I have not kept my brother safe. Bernardo closed his eyes and leaned into his horse, trying to keep the image of his brother's broken body from his mind.

The sound of hoof beats interrupted Bernardo's self-depreciation. De la Paloma and the scouts were back.

Their leader pulled his horse to a stop and spoke. "The Indians are angry. They do not want any more men coming through this land. But they say they didn't kill the others. They didn't even see them."

"You believe them?" Diego was quick to ask.

Alonzo de la Paloma glared at the young man. "Mount up. We will go over the mountain. If Fray Castaño and the others did not come this way, they must have headed south."

Bernardo pressed his forehead against Esclavo's withers. His head hurt. He could not think, he could not ride, he did not want to be here anymore. But more than that, he did not want his father to know that he had failed to protect his brother.

✡ ✡ ✡

Ten days ago, when they had set out to find Marcus and the others, the weather was cold but clear. Now deep drifts made searching for the men impossible.

"I think—" Alonzo de la Paloma hesitated, as if waiting for the opinion of the rest of the men. "We should return to the pueblo."

Bernardo said nothing. He wanted to turn back, but he needed to find his brother. If Marcus was dead, what would he do? He would be hanged for deserting if he didn't follow de la Paloma's orders. If he went back to Mexico City he would have to face his father and the others, but at least he would have some guidance.

Celestino Martín de Serrano was a powerful man. He would be able to keep his son alive. Unless he was so angry he decided not to protect Bernardo.

The soldiers spoke up in agreement with de la Paloma. It was time to give up the search. When the weather cleared they could try again.

Two days later, when the conquistadors returned to the pueblo, Marcus and the scouts were there. Bernardo was happy to see his brother safe. He hadn't failed his father this time. Now if he could just keep his brother from going off again.

But life was not simple. Marcus pulled Bernardo aside.

"It was incredible, *Hermano*. There is so much to see in this land, so much to explore. There are giant canyons with dwellings in the cliffs, pueblos ten times the size of this one." His brother's eyes were as bright at the midday sun.

"Did you convert a lot of natives?" Bernardo scowled to hide his relief.

Marcus paused. "They do not want to be converted."

"Of course not. Kind of like us. But that is what you must do."

"I want to talk to you about that. But not here. Meet me at the rock after vespers."

✡ ✡ ✡

That night, in the cold and the dark and the snow, the two brothers made their way out to a large rock by the river. Sheltered from the wind, they crouched together while Marcus revealed his plan.

"Bernardo, I can't do this. We both know Papá made a mistake. You should be the one who is a holy man, not me. I am a *conquistador*. I need to be out there. Never have I felt such joy, so alive. I know with all my heart it is what I was meant to do."

"What are you saying? The Brotherhood must come first. You can't abandon your duty."

"I am a soldier, Bernardo. It is in my blood."

"How does a priest become a soldier?"

"That is where I need your help. I have asked to be assigned to a pueblo up north. We will work it so that you accompany me. On the way we change places. When we arrive, you will be the priest and I will be the soldier."

His brother's plan stunned Bernardo. What Marcus was suggesting would never work. There weren't very many settlers or soldiers in *Nueva España*. Someone would recognize that the man who used to be a priest was now a soldier. Or worse yet, that the man who used to be a soldier was now a priest.

"You are crazy."

Marcus leaned back and crossed his arms, uncrossed them and moved his face close to Bernardo's. "We will both be happy. You will no longer have to pretend to use the sword. You can trade it for this." His brother touched the medallion hanging around his neck. "You can live the life of a Jew and still do the King's work of converting the heathens."

"And when someone recognizes one of us for who we are? What then?" Bernardo shifted away from his brother, picturing himself the holy father of a tiny adobe church. He imagined the secret meetings on the Sabbath and the rituals he had memorized, but never participated in freely. He saw the people kneeling at the altar, peaceful and one with God.

Marcus leaned forward again, his breath a mist in the cold air. "We switch names. We look enough alike, and no one knows us well. They would be puzzled, perhaps, but soon decide that their memory was cloudy."

Bernardo could see this. The brothers did look alike. "What of Romero? Will he know? Will he come north with me?" They would have to include their younger brother in the plan.

"Does it matter? Romero will make his own choices." Marcus rubbed his hands together. "The timing is perfect. General Oñate has requested more men. A new group will arrive any day. There will be many unknown faces."

"I am Bernardo. How will I answer to Fray Marcus?"

"Fray Castaño. Can you answer to that? I am sure it will not matter. There will be no one who cares up north."

And with this agreement, they continued to plan the details of their deception.

✡ ✡ ✡

Although the brothers were ready to execute their plan, winter set in and they were forced to wait for spring. It was nearly four months before they were able to set out for the north. At last, on a warm April afternoon, Marcus came to Bernardo with the news. He had secured an assignment far beyond the settled area of Taos. He was to go to a small pueblo high in the San Luis range. His grin was contagious and, although worried, Bernardo could not help but smile as well.

After traveling far to the north, exhausted from the six day journey, the brothers stopped at the base of a mountain. Marcus pointed to a green valley. The river which ran down from the peaks flowed rapidly.

"Pueblo Lindo is up that way." Marcus smiled and slapped Bernardo on the shoulder. "I stop here, Brother."

Bernardo pulled nervously at the woolen robe he wore and adjusted the bag hanging over Esclavo's withers. Marcus had tried to make him leave his horse behind. Too fine for a priest, he said. But Bernardo pointed out that Marcus rode a fine horse when he was *Fray* Castaño.

The newly disguised priest drew in a breath of cold air as he pressed his hand against the medallion that Marcus had slipped around his neck when they switched clothes. In spite of his worries, Bernardo knew he was finally where he belonged.

Eleven
Gabriella
Friday, April 4

I cruised the courthouse looking for Fred Rivas's office. Hadn't Dominguez said it was just down the hall?

Three doors down. Locked and dark.

Back in the car I pulled out Alaura's list of realtors and phoned Mia White, the only female on the list. No one answered. The next two didn't answer either.

The fourth—Vernon Garcia—picked up his phone. "Y'ello."

"I'm looking for someone to list some property?"

"Where?"

"Tierra Amarilla?"

Mr. Garcia asked for a few more details. How many acres (200), how many feet of water available (no clue), was the property ever listed as land grant property (no clue), and who was the original owner (Jonas Martinez, I guessed).

"Sorry, can't help you." Mr. Garcia hung up.

I stared at the phone.

Back into the courthouse. Much as I hated to admit it, I needed Joel Dominguez.

He wasn't in his office either.

I left new messages for Joel and Fred, frowned, snorted, grumbled and went back to the adobe house.

It was time to clean up the house. If I could get the little wood stove working the fire might keep me from freezing. It was either that or go find a motel, which I couldn't afford. And I couldn't afford the gas to keep running my car at night to thaw myself—not to mention carbon monoxide poisoning.

A red bandana served as a dust mask, and thankfully some old gardening gloves Greg used to carry fire wood were mixed in with the camping gear. A folded newspaper served as my dustpan, although the small amount of dirt it carried scarcely made a dent in the huge pile I swept into the corner. I scooped all the old dishes and dirt off the sink into a garbage bag. Not expecting anything, I turned the handle of faucet.

Nothing happened, but just as I was about to turn twist it back, a distant gurgling sound came up the pipe. Air coughed from the spigot, followed by spurts of black water. I stepped back and watched.

Like a cardiologist starting a heart, I felt the house come back to life. The sputtering water became a stream, the black grime cleared, and suddenly water flowed into the sink.

Actually, it filled the sink and I jumped back and turned it off. I sponged all the dirt from the sink and the drain and turned the water on again. This time it went down the drain. I left it running and went outside. Where was it going?

Sure enough, it flowed through the pipe and out into the yard. Not exactly code, but handy. But where did the water come from? I walked around, listening, but couldn't find a pipe leading into the house.

Even if I couldn't drink it, I could use it to clean. If I cleaned out the old claw foot... my plan formed. Bathing the old fashioned way, heating and hauling water. I would find something to hang up around the tub. A little privacy, although bathing with a view of the mountain appealed to me.

I couldn't stop myself from imagining fixing the place up. The floor of the newer part was made of huge planks of wood, beams of some sort. The wood was worn and dirty, but not splintery or warped. I could sand it, throw on some heavy varnish and it would come alive.

"Don't be silly. As if," I told Bones. The thump of her long tail made me think she liked the idea of staying.

The dirt floor in the kitchen was another story. Just how did one keep dirt clean? Sweeping raised a crazy amount of dust. If someone wanted to live here they would have to put in a floor and raise the ceiling. I finally left it and hauled my cot into the bedroom with the view. As I sat and gazed at the granite cliff, my heart beat too fast, making its way up into my throat. Nerves grew into flashes of lightning. I had been so calm and happy minutes ago—why was my heart racing now?

Why was thinking about this so hard? How come every time I thought I knew what I wanted, and I got it, suddenly it didn't seem like the right thing at all? Couldn't I do anything right? Was this what having a nervous breakdown was like? That black hole again?

This is not the same thing at all. Get a grip. New-Ella had more confidence.

My focus had to be on selling this property. That would give me some money—my own money—to start fresh in California. Plenty of time later to worry about how my family could forget me so quickly.

With a shuddering breath I had another thought. How long would this title thing take? What if it took months to sell this property?

The impulse to jump back in my car and drive took over again. Maybe I should keep going east. Not back to California, but all the way to Nova Scotia. I could ditch my car and jump on a boat.

Finish what you start, that was the rule. I forced myself to head out to the car for the rest of my things. If I put everything in the house, my panic couldn't push me into another impulsive decision like the one that had got me here in the first place. In theory, anyway. It had only taken me thirty minutes to run away the last time.

When I had everything unloaded I looked at the broken hinge. It didn't take much—a screwdriver and a hammer—and I had it swinging again. Maybe not freely, but I could close it. A sense of accomplishment, well out of proportion with my repair, filled me. I could do this.

I built a fire in the ancient stove, sending up a prayer that sparks wouldn't land on the roof. The blaze caught and the smoke obediently drifted up the stovepipe. Pleased with myself, I wiped my hands on my thighs and stood. Warmth!

Calmer now, I set up my camp stove and warmed a can of soup for dinner. I ate next to the wood stove, within the three foot circle of radiated heat. Moving out of the tight arc led to a chill that crept through the cracks around the windows and doors. It was too cold to sit outside, although the sunset glowed with heavenly radiance.

The healing chicken noodle soup abated my crazy thoughts, and although they still churned inside me like bats in the attic, I felt like myself again. The panic attack had been averted.

The wall behind the stove wasn't in good shape. I leaned forward and touched the dried mud which held the stones in place.

The force of my finger turned the primitive mortar to sand, revealing something metal between the stones. It didn't take long to pull it from its hiding place.

A medallion on a gold chain. Smaller than a silver dollar, and heavy. I rubbed my thumb over the dried mud, smoothing it away from the design. It was as cold as if it had just come out of a deep freeze, and I glanced at the wall, wondering if adobe had the insulating capacity to keep things frozen. There was an emblem on the front of the medallion. A shield, a tree, and some feathers. Almost like a coat of arms. I turned it over. Writing. Some language I didn't recognize—even the letters were unfamiliar.

Suddenly a pain shot through my forehead, just above my right eye. A lightning strike zapped into my brain, forcing my eyes closed as I slumped to the floor.

Images of people walking, hiding, running swarmed through my mind. I couldn't understand what these people said. Spanish, yet not Spanish. A wave of dizziness swept over me and I pushed my head down towards my lap. Pain filled my mind.

A woman came running back to where I stood in the middle of the dusty road.

"*Vamos. Hay que apurarnos.*"

I didn't understand her words, but there was no mistaking the frantic look and the tugging on my arm. Nothing around us other than the road and the hills, yet she was scared. I followed her.

There were more people trying to hide.

We followed the horses and carts and dogs and children and chickens and cows and donkeys and more and more things I was surprised to see. My heart pounded and I was out of breath and coughing from the cloud of dust surrounding us.

The woman pulled me up a a steep path into a narrow canyon and we ducked behind jagged red boulders.

"*Toma ésto.*" She pulled a leather cord from around her neck and placed it over my head.

The medallion.

A tingling wave swept over every inch of my body at once. It was both warm and cold at the same time, as if a thick mist clung to my skin, then permeated down into my internal organs.

I saw the people again, only this time they were smiling, gathered around a fire. In this dream inside a dream, I watched myself from a distance, transported from the boulders and the woman with the necklace. An old woman handed me a bowl of stew. In this other world I could understand what they were saying, although the part of me that was watching had no idea.

The layers of my consciousness blurred and I struggled for a sense of what was happening. Seated by a fire, I stared across the glow at a handsome young man, his features hidden by the smoke and the dark of the night. He pulled out a strange-looking guitar and strummed while the woman cleaned up. When he finished playing, he turned to me.

I looked into the eyes of the guitar player and gasped. It was Andy Lloyd. *This is a dream, Ella. Wake up.* I was frantic to escape this other world, this psychotic vision which seemed so real. Opening my eyes in the first layer of the dream only took me to another place. A blue mist surrounded me.

Wake up, Ella. Wake up, I begged my dream self.

In a flash of blinding light I found myself flat on my back, lying on the packed dirt floor of the adobe house. Free from the dreams and the blue mist.

I held my hands up and wiggled my fingers. Looking down at my feet, I moved my legs. Everything seemed fine, but something had happened.

The medallion was hanging around my neck. The cool gold disc settled against my chest, and my heart beat rapidly just underneath it. I yanked the chain over my head and flung the crazy thing to the floor.

Twelve
Fray Bernardo Castaño
Pueblo Lindo, 1606

Bernardo's heart pounded as he watched Marcus. He thought his brother would come to the pueblo with him and help him adjust to his new life as a priest. But Marcus was eager to try out his new role, and didn't want to complicate things by letting people see them together.

"I have pretended to be something I am not for too long. Now it is time for me to live." Marcus spurred his horse and galloped away.

The new Fray Castaño looked at the narrow valley and the sparkling river. This pueblo was nothing like any of the others. If he hadn't been looking for the place he would have missed the small adobe and stone houses hidden among the trees. He had heard that there were great forests in the north, and now he saw this was true. How much snow covered the valley in the winter? He shivered at the thought. Born and raised in Mexico City, Bernardo had no heart for a chill in his bones.

He clucked to Esclavo and the horse trotted onward. Man and beast wound around a field of corn and squash. Not planted in the rows Bernardo was used to, these vegetables grew in strange misshapen patches between the mounds which told him the food was shared with prairie dogs. He saw more houses—at least that's what he guessed them to be. Not adobe or stone, but small buildings constructed from smooth branches leaned against each other to form walls, and grass of some sort piled on the roof. A stone-lined ditch, only twelve inches wide, led from the river to the crops, the flooding used to irrigate the low lying fields.

"Hola, Padre. ¿Es usted el nuevo?"

The voice surprised both man and animal. Neither had noticed the figure standing next to the creek.

A worn leather hat covered the boy's eyes from Bernardo's angle atop the horse. Was this a native? Speaking the Spanish tongue with such ease? At least they were expecting him, as the boy had asked if he were the new priest.

The boy removed his hat and Bernardo found himself looking at the most beautiful face he had ever seen. Not a native and not a boy.

A whirlwind of emotion swept across the small patch of grass which separated him from the girl. It shot through his body, hot and cold all at once, as if he were standing in a snow storm in the middle of the desert. He leaned forward and studied her, oblivious to the rudeness of this gesture. He took in her eyes, filled with gold flecks, smooth brows perched like dainty caterpillars on her forehead, roses in her brown cheeks, and hair that glowed in the sun now that she had removed her hat. Her mouth was a perfect blossom, smiling sweetly to reveal just a hint of her pearly teeth. She wore a tunic and leggings made of deer skin with decorative beading around the neckline. For a moment he felt much younger than his twenty-six years. He felt like a young boy who has fallen in love.

"He... hello." No other words could pass his lips. Suddenly he remembered how he looked. The brown robe of a priest, covered with the dust of many days on the trail. More than a year of living in the wilderness had changed him. He pressed his lips together, hiding his yellow teeth filled with cracks. Four were missing, including one near the front. His skin wrinkled from the relentless sun. He felt very old and ugly. Surely he would scare this beautiful creature with his awful stare. Drawing in his breath, he blinked and tried to calm himself.

"I am Fray Castaño."

"I am Consuela. May I show you the way to the church?"

Bernardo was surprised there was a church here. What of the word that these natives refused to be converted? Marcus claimed this pueblo was remote and undisturbed by Spanish priests. With a nod he slipped off his horse.

As he followed the girl up the winding path, he realized the main pueblo was ahead and the shelters he had passed were no more than outbuildings. They moved up the slope and he saw the familiar adobe dwellings lining the base of the gradual hills which led from the river. Bernardo decided that the natives who lived here hadn't seen as many conquistadors as the rest of New Spain. These people lived in moderation, and did not show signs of Spanish influence—maybe Marcus told the truth. But if that were so, why did this girl speak Spanish? Not only that, she didn't look like any of the indigenous people he had met.

With the healthy stream running next to the meadow, there was room for farming, but the crops here were like those he had seen earlier—random groups of plants. As he studied the strange fields he realized that the food was planted in those spots where exposure to the sun would give it a chance to thrive. The trees and the steep sides of the canyon shaded much of the land. The mountains pushed upward above the canyon walls, so deer, elk and other game must be available.

Bernardo tried to study the buildings and the people as he followed the girl through the pueblo, but he could not keep his eyes from Consuela. Her long hair was twisted into a braid and wrapped with a leather cord. He imagined his fingers slipping inside the cord to untwist her hair.

She stopped in front of a small doorway and called out. "Padre Ortiz. Fray Castaño has arrived."

The sweaty faced friar who burst through the door wrung his hands and cried out "At last!" He turned to Consuela. "Gracias, my dear. You may leave us now."

Bernardo smiled and put out his hand in greeting. Ortiz shook it hurriedly and glanced around. "Let me show you what you'll need."

Bernardo was tired from the journey and had hoped for some refreshment and a nap. He turned and watched as Consuela walked away. "There is a hurry? A fire somewhere, perhaps?"

Fray Ortiz wrinkled his forehead and looked down the valley. "You saw a fire? Where?"

Bernardo realized this man was anxious about something and had no sense of humor. "No, no. I jest. You seem in a hurry."

Ortiz scowled. "Good luck with converting any of these people. They smile and agree to whatever you say, then do as they have always done. I am hoping to get back to Mexico City this year. What have you heard about anyone going back?"

"Nothing. I have been isolated from the happenings in the south. Well, not like you, but far enough away so that we only get old news. I think a group did go back, and they were arrested as traitors."

The little friar frowned and shook his head. "Where are the settlers and soldiers we were promised? We should have had five times the number of colonists by this time."

Bernardo shrugged. "Where are the riches they were promised? I don't think there is much to draw people to such a remote place compared to the mines and commerce of the south."

"Be that what it may. Good luck and adios." Fray Ortiz walked toward a swayback horse dozing next to a boulder, mounted and rode off without a backwards glance.

✡ ✡ ✡

That evening Consuela came to Bernardo's tiny room at the church—which wasn't a church at all, but just a room with some stones and logs set outside for seating—carrying a bowl of warm gruel and a steaming cup of some native tea. No one else came to see him.

Bernardo approached several of the natives who passed his door, but they merely smiled and hurried on their way. Marcus had instructed him that he must celebrate the mass each day, but Bernardo wanted some time to think about his role. Tomorrow would be soon enough to lead mass. He needed time to prepare his liturgy.

"Consuela, how will the people come for Mass? I don't find a bell to ring for call to service."

She pressed her lips together and looked away.

"Will you tell me why this is a problem for you to answer?"

She turned her speckled eyes back to him. "Padre. There are not many here who will listen to a service."

"Will you be here? Do you have a mother? Father? Brothers? Can I count on them?"

She hesitated, then nodded. "Sí. They will be here."

Morning arrived and Bernardo took up his Bible and walked out to the stones and logs. Five people were seated. Consuela, two old native women, one bedraggled soldier and one native man.

"Good morning," Fray Castaño began, wondering which of the group could be the girl's family. "Thank you for coming."

The following day the same five sat in the worship area. He knew a little about them now. The two native women were sisters, unmarried and giggling. The man was a lone conquistador who had left, perhaps deserted, his position and come to live at the pueblo. The other man was an outcast of his tribe—apparently he had committed some atrocity when he was a boy. None of these people were members of Consuela's family.

Bernardo stood in front of the five. "Good morning. Today we will do something different." He did not open his bible. He did not speak in Latin. He walked over to the log and sat next to Consuela. "Today you will tell me your stories."

No one spoke. All five looked down at folded hands.

"What about you, Consuela. Will you start?"

"I don't know what to tell."

"Were you born on the pueblo?"

"Yes."

"And your mother? Where is she?"

"She is home. In our rooms."

"Was she born here also?"

Conseula shook her head.

Bernardo was surprised. He had decided that she was of mixed blood, supposing that her father was a conquistador and her mother a native.

"Where was she born?"

"She was born in Portugal."

This couldn't be right. He quickly did some adding and subtracting. Consuela was about fifteen, making her mother thirty or thirty-five or so, which meant she would have been born around 1575. How did she end up in New Spain?

"Who is your father?"

"He was born here."

Her father was a native and her mother from Portugal? None of this made sense. Women had not come to this part of New Spain.

And what of being from Portugal? The settlers who came to *Nueva España* from Portugal were Jews.

Consuela leaned forward. She stared into his eyes. "My grandfather is a conquistador. But not with Oñate. Before that. He wasn't a deserter. They ended up here, waiting to be rescued. No one ever came, so they lived in the pueblo.

"My grandfather believed that people should not be expelled from their land. He lived in peace with the First People, the ones who live here. He told me that this is how the Catholic Pope said it should be, but no one listened." Consuela continued. "More people came. They came before Fray Ortiz, with another priest. Fray Luis de Torres."

"Where are all these people you speak of?" Bernardo had seen no one but natives and a few tired soldiers living in the pueblo. Was Consuela saying her mother traveled with the conquistadors?

The girl shook her head and continued to stare directly into his eyes. "Are you cousin to the conquistador? Gaspar Castaño?"

Bernardo considered her change of subject and her question. Although he had heard about the ill-fated explorations of Gaspar Castaño—the man had explored the area before Oñate and failed to return—he didn't know why Consuela asked her question. Perhaps only because he shared the name.

"No. I do not know this man." Bernardo did not add that his name was not really Castaño.

She looked away from him, her eyes focusing on the distant mountains. "I do not know why they do not come to mass."

Bernardo stood up. "That is all for today. Worship is over." He would question Consuela away from the others. He could see that the girl held a secret, and if there was one thing he knew about, it was keeping secrets.

When the girl brought his afternoon meal, he invited her to stay. "There is a secret here, is there not?"

She blushed and bent her head low over the bowl of soup.

"Your mother? She is the secret?"

Consuela looked up and studied his face. Now it was his turn to blush under the scrutiny of this beautiful girl.

Her eyes grew soft and she smiled. "I think that it is best if I show you. I think you are ready."

Bernardo felt as if he had passed some examination and proved his worth, although as far as he could tell he had done nothing at all.

Thirteen
Gabriella
Saturday, April 5

The next morning—still no messages from Fred Rivas or Joel Dominguez—I set out for the town of Española, sixty-two miles south. Time to get some new tires. With all the driving back and forth I was sure to get another flat, and that would mean calling for a tow truck again. Calling for Andy Lloyd.

You can lie to yourself, push the truth out of sight, but it bubbles up no matter how many times you practice. I needed to get away from the adobe house and the strange events of last night, even if only for the day. Hallucinations indicated a real problem with my mental state and I didn't want to face that or any other explanation of the strange collapse and dreams.

I pressed my foot down on the accelerator, and Bones stuck her head out the window.

In spite of my plan to escape I couldn't stop thinking about the medallion and the strange visions. Funny thing was, this morning I felt normal. Better than normal. Cleansed.

Maybe they weren't visions. More likely exhaustion, fainting, and dreams.

Christ, I must be having a pre-menopausal hormone rush that clouded my judgement. I should watch my health. Dehydration could cause strange things to happen. Water, lots of water, and fresh vegetables, that's all I needed.

"Ahhhh," I groaned. Bones wrinkled her brow and wagged her tail. "Time to think about something else, wouldn't you say? Don't you have anything you want to discuss? Doggie problems regarding chasing rabbits or bland kibble?"

I cranked up the radio, opened all the windows and belted out Indigo Girl tunes for the next fifty miles.

Two hours later, new tires installed, I found the community pool and the showers. Next stop was a grocery store. There was no breeze today and the temperature was perfect. The chill of the nights gave way to pleasant days. My faithful dog placed her chin on the open window and watched me walk into the store.

Thirty minutes later I pushed the loaded cart across the parking lot. I was shocked when Bones ran toward me, tail wagging.

"What are you doing out of the car?" She hung her head and sat.

"Are you the owner of that dog?"

The shrill voice belonged to a woman, probably in her early thirties. She had bleached blond hair and bright red lips. She dug through her designer handbag for something. "How dare you leave her alone in that hot car? I'm calling the sheriff. Don't even think about trying to drive away. I'm going to write down your license number and he'll catch you if you try to leave. I don't care if your husband did let her out. She was panting and thirsty."

"My husband?" I looked toward my car. A man reclined against the back hatch. I leaned into the cart and pushed faster. Bones trotted beside me, happy she wasn't in trouble.

Blonde-Who-Minds-Everyone's-Business trotted behind me too, shuffling through her purse and yammering about dog abuse.

As I approached the Honda I recognized the figure.

Andy Lloyd.

He shook his head and rolled his eyes.

He had followed me all the way to Española? I stepped from behind the cart and faced him.

Andy shrugged. "I'm sorry. I didn't think she would run away from me."

"Why are you following me?"

Blonde-Who-Minds stopped waving her hands.

Something I couldn't read swept over Andy's face, turning his sheepish smile into a frown. "Is that what you think?"

A voice boomed across the parking lot. "Hey Margie. Come on. I don't got all day."

The young woman glanced over her shoulder, looked back at me, then shook her head. I could tell she didn't want to miss this excitement, but the loud voice was like a lasso. "I better never see that dog locked in a hot car again." She spun and tic-tic-ticked across the parking lot on her high heels. Maybe they would sink into the asphalt and she would fall. But it wasn't hot enough for that, just like it wasn't too hot for my dog.

I turned back to Andy. "Why wouldn't I think you were following me? You keep popping up out of nowhere. I don't know what you want, but you aren't going to get it."

He stepped back. "I know you're from the big city and all. I guess there are so many people living there, you don't run into folks 'round town. But here," he gestured with a flip of his hand, "we all come here to shop. And in T.A., well, everyone goes to Three Ravens, every day. If you're there, you'll see me. I guarantee it."

It was my turn to blush. What he said could be true. Or was this his way of talking himself out of a tight spot?

"Maybe running into you once would be a coincidence, and maybe in Tierra Amarilla. But here?" I threw both my hands in the air now. "There are hundreds of cars here. How do you happen to be leaning against my car?"

"Gabriella," he paused. "Why are you afraid of me?"

I paused. He was right, I'd been afraid of him from the start. That leather vest over his naked torso, covered with all those tattoos. That skull on his belly.

"Your tattoos," I blurted out. It seemed better than saying *my mother warned me about men like you.*

He raised his arms in front of his chest and turned them outward, palms up, then glanced down. Today he was wearing a green t-shirt, with the words *Nelson's Garage* stenciled across his chest. "These tattoos?"

The colorful artwork on his right arm depicted a herd of horses charging through a canyon, the same prickly desert plants that dotted my land wrapping around his elbow. His left arm had a crucifix, but so embellished with stars and flowers and other things it was hardly visible. No skeletons or knives dripping blood.

"No," Andy shook his head, "You were scared before you saw my tattoos. You came out of the house brandishing a weapon. It's okay. You're a woman alone out on that property. You should be cautious. But now? I don't know why you're still afraid of me. I'm not following you. Believe it or not, I shop in Española. I pulled up and saw some ruckus, with a familiar red hound and blue Honda at the center of everything. That woman was screaming all over the place. Trying to find out who had left a dog in the car, ready to dial 9-1-1 or the calvary or the President of the United States." He paused and rubbed his forehead, closing his eyes for a moment. He opened them and looked straight at me. "I was trying to help you."

Was my mother's voice so strong inside my head, in spite of all the years of trying to erase it? Could tattoos and a ponytail really make me fearful for no good reason?

Or was I right to be afraid because I was alone?

Andy pressed his lips together and drew in a breath. "Look. I have to tell you, there aren't many women in Tierra Amarilla. I mean, single ladies. And I'm a single man. Of course I'm interested in you—you're new to town and beautiful. But I am not stalking you. Really, truly, not." He looked away. When he looked back, I could tell he had made up his mind about something. He continued. "How about I help you load this stuff and we go somewhere for a cold soda. You can get to know me, so the next time we run into each other you'll feel comfortable, instead of trembling like I'm Charles Manson. If you really are going to stick around in T.A.

we're going to see each other, no doubt about it." A tentative smile slipped onto his face. "I know a place with a patio, so you don't have to neglect your dog anymore."

"I—" I stopped. "You—" I stopped again. Just because it was the polite thing to do I almost agreed. He really didn't seem so scary anymore and everything he said made sense. Going to have a soda might give me a chance to make up my mind about him. Better to do it here, in this crowded town, than up in the desolate and underpopulated Tierra Amarilla.

"Okay."

Ten minutes later the three of us sat at a rustic picnic table, on a cool patio next to the Rio Grande, waiting for the food we had ordered.

I jumped up. "I'm going to get her bowl out of the car so she can have some water."

When I had settled back onto the bench, my dog slurping the cool water, I tried to relax. I took another look at Andy. "Umm... so you're from around here?" *Duh, Ella.*

"My family is. Was."

"Not you?"

"My mother moved away. I was born in Colorado."

A tiny breeze blew in as we ate but I continued to sweat. I just didn't know what to think of this guy. Andy kept up a steady stream of conversation, providing a virtual tour of the whole Chama Valley: great places to eat (Penelope's trailer), where I should buy tortillas (the hardware store), shop for hardware (Harvey's Market), where to take a shower (the pool, but check the hours, they weren't open much) and other local secrets. He didn't ask me any personal questions and seemed satisfied with my "uh huh" and "nice." I didn't tell him I had already discovered the limited hours of the shower.

The comfort of tacos and icy root beer kicked in and I started to relax. He seemed pretty normal. But anyone could seem normal at first. I decided to take him up on what he suggested and find out more about him.

I leaned forward. "Why did you come back?"

The change in his face was surprising. It was like watching film footage of a flooding river—trees and buildings suddenly being swept away as the muddy bank collapses. His ruddy, tanned face turned pale and his eyes grew dark, morphing into deep pools which held a pit of fire beneath the surface. He looked away, then turned back with a smile.

"I like it here. It's hard to explain until you've felt it, but there's magic in this place."

Magic? I wanted to ask more, but something kept me quiet. Not my old fears. Not the good manners which said it's rude to probe. And not my awkward teenage ego raising its ugly head. Not disbelief that this tattooed man believed in magic or was attracted to me in a way I found confusing. No, this was a new feeling, arising from the ancient sands of this mystical land. Just as the comfort of the desert and the drums had filled my body with peace, and that crazy medallion was hot and cold at the same time, and my dreams were out of control, Andy Lloyd's words filled me with some sort of mysterious emotion so unlike anything I had ever felt before that I wasn't sure if it was fear or caution or love.

But the crazy thing, the thing that really made me agree to Andy's invitation for a cold soda, was that when I looked at this man I saw the guitar player lurking behind those green eyes.

Fourteen

Bernardo Castaño

Pueblo Lindo, 1606

"Come with me. I will show you." Consuela turned and walked up the valley, past the adobe buildings.

Bernardo hurried after the girl. "Where are we going? Is this the way to your family? Your mother, she came with Gaspar Castaño? A women traveling with the soldiers?"

The girl didn't answer. She simply motioned him to follow her up the winding path. Bernardo didn't know what to expect, but when they crested the hill and looked down on a second canyon, this one filled with adobe and stone homes, as well as many fields of squash and corn, a herd of sheep, and a band of horses, he felt as if he had fallen asleep and was dreaming.

A young man approached them. His pants were made of the smooth deer skin like those of a native, but his shirt was spun fabric, faded red. He wore soldier's boots, with soles that had cracked from many years of use. The knife strapped to his side was that of a conquistador, but his hat was woven from some sort of plant material. There was a hint of red in his neatly trimmed beard.

The man didn't smile as he stared at Bernardo. Consuela stopped, but did not speak.

"Why do you bring him here?"

"He needs to know," the girl replied.

It was then Bernardo noticed the chain around the bearded man's neck. Not a crucifix, but a medallion, nested in the folds of the red shirt. A familiar medallion, with a tree from which sprang the leaves of life.

Bernardo touched the spot where his own medallion hid next to his skin.

"*El que cree y persista vive para siempre,*" he whispered.

The man gasped and reached for his knife. "What did you say?"

Before Bernardo could speak the breath left his body. He tried to stand tall, but the ground rushed up to meet him. When he next saw the bright blue eyes of the man, they were above him and he realized he lay flat on the ground. A vise squeezed his head and everything around him seemed very far away.

Conseula knelt beside him and held a flask to his lips.

"I… you… a Brother?" Bernardo choked the words out between sips.

The young man glared down at him. "Where did you get the medallion?"

Bernardo's hand flew to his chest. His medallion was not there. He struggled to sit up. Consuela helped him. The bearded man held Bernardo's medallion in his fist.

"I got it from…" Bernardo paused. Now was not the time to explain how he was supposed to be a soldier, but had traded places with his brother to become a priest. "I got it from my father, Celestino Martín de Serrano. On the day of my thirteenth year. My first mitzvah. Along with my instructions from the Brotherhood."

The young man leaned forward. He squeezed the medallion between his fisted fingers and shook it close to Bernardo's face. "No priest would have such a medallion. Who did you kill for this?"

Bernardo held his palms up. "If you are truly one of the *Fraternidad de Creyentes,* you know that a Brother can be hidden behind the cloak of the Catholic priest."

The man shook his head. "I have never heard of such a thing." He rubbed the hilt of the knife at his side.

"I have heard of such a thing." A new voice joined in, and Bernardo turned. A white haired man stood behind Consuela. He also had a beard, neatly trimmed into a small "v" on his chin, but gray with age. His eyes sparkled as blue as the turquoise skies of *Nueva España*. The old man leaned on a wooden cane, and the priest could see that his hip was twisted.

"It was in Barcelona that such a thing took place. De la Paloma's men." Unlike the young man, this white haired one smiled.

Bernardo smiled back. "*Sí*. My father, *Don* Martín de Serrano, was friends with *Don* Demitrio de la Paloma. But you speak of the grandfathers of my grandfathers."

The young man glared once more. "A priest? To what end?"

"I am trained as a Rabbi as well as a priest. This is done so that our people can carry on with the true belief." Bernardo looked to the old man. He seemed to know that what was impossible could also be true.

Clearly the young man was not convinced that Bernardo was who he claimed to be. "And does such a priest also carry the name of my grandfather and not the name of his own father? Does he ride a fine horse covered in the leather armor of a soldier's steed?"

Bernardo realized his error. "Gaspar Castaño? He was your grandfather?"

The young man glanced at the older one. The man with the cane stepped forward and leaned toward Bernardo.

"I am Simón Castaño."

"Simón?"

"Gaspar was my brother. We traveled together."

"But Gaspar Castaño is dead. He never returned... gone..." Bernardo had heard tales of terrible cruelty about the man.

Simón nodded. "There was a time when we parted. It was after that that my brother, well, he paid a price for his actions." The old man waved a hand toward the young one. "And this, Rafael, he is my brother's grandson. With my brother gone, he is now grandson to me."

"How did you end up here?" Not only that, Bernardo thought, but how was it that no one had ever mentioned the famous explorer was a Jew? Surely the Brotherhood had known these early explorers were members of the secret clan? Or were these secrets so deep that few men knew the truth?

Simón turned to Rafael. "We have been isolated for a long time. De Serrano and de la Paloma are from Barcelona, not Madrid. Men of the Brotherhood must adapt, use ways to protect the secret. I have heard the stories of rabbis who hide as priests."

"I was called Bernardo Martín de Serrano before I took on the life of Fray Castaño, a name given by the Brotherhood." Well, not exactly, but close. He didn't tell these men that Marcus had been given the name of Fray Castaño first.

Simón's laugh was as wrinkled as his face. "It was foolish of the Brotherhood to send a priest to a place where you preach only to the natives and the Catholic soldiers. What purpose did they think you would serve?"

Bernardo tried to fit the pieces of this puzzle together. Consuela's mother from Portugal, a famous explorer and a split pueblo, half filled with natives and half filled with Spaniards. His face must have reflected his confusion because Simón waved his cane.

"Come. We will go to my home and I will tell you my story. Then you can tell us yours."

The young man turned, threw the medallion to the ground and stormed up the trail. Consuela held on to Bernardo's arm as he bent to retrieve the medallion.

"Are you steady enough, Padre?"

Although he was no longer lightheaded, he did not want the girl to take her hand away. He didn't answer, but laid his palm across his chest and held onto her arm where it crossed his. Surely she could feel the pounding of his heart as they followed Simón up the path.

The men were soon seated around a pine table, the grain of the wood showing the years of the tree. Consuela placed mugs of her native tea in front of each man. Rafael pulled a bottle from the cupboard, but Simón shook his head and he returned the liquor to the shelf.

"Like you, Padre, my father presented me with a medallion in my thirteenth year. But I was to be an explorer. It was hoped that here, in *Nueva España*, we would find a place for the people. It took many years for my brother to get the approval of the viceroy to travel."

Bernardo looked at the old man. "The story goes that there was no such approval for Gaspar Castaño."

"The story is true. We did not, and so finally we left without the King's stamp. The time had come. My father was dead and the others who had traveled across the ocean had melted away. Our branch of the Brotherhood was small and all who remained accompanied my brother on the journey."

"Is that why Consuela's mother came?"

"*Sí.* Abene is my daughter." The old man glanced at Consuela and smiled. "When you meet her you will see where my granddaughter gets her beauty. Anyway, the mission did not go as planned. The land was difficult to travel and the natives could not show us the riches we sought. Many men left, determined to make their way back to Mexico City. Unplanned, but it was soon apparent that those who remained were all Jews. Some of them *conversos*, but many of us members of the Brotherhood." Simón's voice was like gravel under a horse's hoof. "My brother, you must have heard, he could be a harsh man."

Bernardo had heard. Gaspar was a slaver who attacked and captured natives.

"We separated. Some went with him, those you see came with me. My brother was captured at Santo Domingo, while we escaped. It didn't take much to convince those of us who had left his company that we had found God's direction. God led us farther and farther north, to this valley where the natives live a simple life and didn't protest our appearance." Simón stopped and sipped his tea, looking at his adopted grandson. "Thank goodness these people were willing to listen. Rafael was just a boy."

"How is it that children and women traveled with a group of conquistadors?"

"Not many. My daughter was all I had. My wife was gone."

Bernardo needed to know the rest of the story. "And these children?" He glanced at Consuela. She was not old enough to have traveled with Gaspar Castaño. "Their fathers?"

"Padre, how you judge. Yes, the father of my granddaughter is a native. He is also my friend. When we stopped here we did not view this as the place we would stay. But the winter storms arrived and Jimuta made us welcome. He is a wise man and he knew that we would not survive the cold without his help. He also believed that I was not the same as my brother or the other Spaniards. I had no intention of taking anyone as a slave. When you get to know him, you will see that he is a man filled with more wisdom than his years."

Bernardo looked at Rafael. Nothing of this story explained the young man's suspicion.

The old explorer continued. "There is something here, in this place, a God unlike that which we know. The natives worship many things, and they are gentle in their thinking. More accepting than we are and much more accepting than the Pope. I hope, Padre, you will let yourself feel this magic."

"You do not practice our ways?"

Although Bernardo's question was not directed at him, Rafael was quick to answer. "Of course we do. This is the place God has provided to us so that we can worship without fear."

Simón held up a hand, his palm stopping the young man's words. "That is where you come in, Padre. Your role here will be as Rabbi, not priest."

Bernardo was quiet. This man was not the leader of his Brotherhood, although he claimed to be the leader of some Brotherhood. But it had been years since his father or de la Paloma had given him any direction. He could not help but feel a sense of relief when Simón Castaño took hold of the reins.

✡ ✡ ✡

Bernardo found that these Jews were full of questions, most of them unanswerable by a man such as himself. A man who acted falsely as a rabbi.

He had questions of his own. "What about Fray Ortiz? Did he know you were here?"

One man looked away as he spoke. "Yes. He was sympathetic to our cause. I do not think he would have exposed us, but others were not so sure."

He noticed several of the men shifted uneasily and glanced at Rafael. The priest could feel the rage this young man held below the surface. He nearly asked if they had killed Fray Ortiz when the man left the pueblo—with obvious urgency—but quickly decided he didn't want to know.

Bernardo had other concerns and he voiced these to the men. "I came here because the Indians were not being converted. You are in danger because you have not reported to Santa Fe. We will have to build the pretense to avoid persecution."

"You think you can make us into Catholics?" Rafael snorted and the men joined him in laughter.

"No, but you should be concerned. Jews are being exiled and imprisoned. It will not be long before the Catholics of *Nueva España* decide that execution is needed. The *custodes* have long arms." Bernardo was worried that the men of the inquisition would make their way here and discover that he was a fraud. Many *custodes* were chosen because of their love of delivering brutal punishments for sacrilegious acts.

Try as he might to convince them, it wasn't until Simón, Jimuta and Bernardo met and discussed the future of Pueblo Lindo that Bernardo was allowed to take on a role. The Jews would hide as

Catholics once more and the natives would hide too. When the *custodes* came to the pueblo, they would not find the hidden homes of the Jews in the upper canyon, and the natives would attend church. The indigenous people would learn just enough to pass as converts. In turn, Bernardo would leave them to their own practices.

Although Simón had joked about converting the natives, Bernardo offered to teach Jimuta about the laws of Moses so that he might understand the ceremonies of the men living in his pueblo. For a time he thought the chief was interested but soon found he was just being polite, so the priest focused his work on building a wall of deception that would stand up to any inspection by outsiders. Pretending to be a priest to those who pretended to listen wasn't much of a job.

It was on Fridays, when Bernardo climbed to the hidden canyon to be a rabbi, that his troubles came to find him.

Although Marcus had given him the little leather book filled with notes from his days as a priest, Bernardo had only his boyhood training to draw from for his role as a rabbi. Once the Martín de Serrano brothers had left their home in Mexico City, they were not able to practice any of their Jewish traditions. A hurried silent prayer here and there, a candle lit in secret or a careful honoring of the sabbath was all that they could manage. Now Bernardo had to convince Simón Castaño and his followers that he was competent to be their spiritual leader.

"Tonight I will be only the observer of your Shabbat." This excuse worked on the first Friday.

"And what of the individual families? May I see what they have been doing to honor the Sabbath?" That took care of the second Friday.

Now it was the third Friday. Bernardo could think of no more excuses. He had practiced all the words he recalled his father speaking so many years ago. He reached into the corners of his mind to pull out the messages Rabbi Carabajal had passed to him when he attended the hidden meetings. He whispered the blessings and the prayers, stumbling over the Hebrew words he had not spoken in such a long time.

His hands trembled as he stood at the head of the crude wooden table Simón had put together to make room for Rafael, Consuela and Abene, as well as several other men and women. Bernardo lifted the glass of some sort of liquor Consuela placed in front of him. Kosher wine? He would proceed on that assumption without asking any questions.

"It was evening and it was morning," he started, licking his lips and pressing them together to stop the trembling in his voice. "On the sixth day the heavens and the earth and all their hosts were completed."

He heard Rafael snort, but he continued. He kept his eyes focused on the cup, letting his words flow over his hands and down to the table, trying to let his spirit feel happiness because he was finally going to honor the Sabbath in the way it was meant to be.

"Blessed art Thou, O Lord, who hallowest the Sabbath."

"Amen." Bernardo recognized the voices of Consuela and Simón, but the others at the table whispered their responses.

Consuela stood and picked up a bowl of water. She walked slowly around the table, and each person scooped water over their hands, letting it flow back into the bowl.

This was different from the way Bernardo remembered. He knew that he needed to recite the blessing, but he was used to all those present washing at the same time. Should he wait until Consuela had visited each person and all had washed?

Rafael cleared his throat and rolled his eyes, then held up his dripping hands, clearly a message that Bernardo was to begin.

"Baruch Ata Adonai Eloheinu melech ha-olam asher kidshanu b'mitzvotav v'tzivanu al netilat yadayim," Bernardo intoned, looking away from Rafael as he spoke the blessing for the cleansing. He simply must ignore this thorn. The Sabbath was special to him—it had always been special. Think of Mamá and Papá. Think of Grandfather and *Tío* Carme, all sitting around the

table. On this night the warmth of family triumphed over any ailment of the week. For in spite of Celestino's strict ways, Bernardo knew his father had loved him. He looked around the table at this new family, as the memory of the other offered him comfort.

Conseula stood next to her mother with the bowl of water. Now it was the girl who glared at him. Bernardo knew he should have waited until all had washed before giving the blessing.

When everyone had dried their hands, Bernardo lifted the bread.

"Baruch Ata Adonai Eloheinu melech ha-olam ha-motzi lechem min ha-aretz." Bernardo passed the bread to Simón.

Simón repeated the blessing and passed the loaf to Rafael.

"That is not the way it is done." Rafael tossed the loaf of bread to the ground. "You are acting the priest. This is not communion."

Bernardo was silent. The prayer over the special loaf of bread was the only way he knew to do this and he could not understand Rafael's insistence that he had somehow made this into a Catholic ritual.

Consuela placed her hand on her cousin's arm. "Please, Rafe."

Rafael stood. "Can you not see this man for what he is? Do you not remember the stories of the traps set out for our people? He is an impostor, sent here to discover what he can and—"

"Silence." Simón's voice was firm. "Rafael, you have sung your chorus dry. We all know you have doubts, but I insist that you show respect on this night."

Bernardo kept his eyes away from the young man. He did not want to feed the flame that burned too hot.

But he looked up when Rafael slammed a fist on the table.

"I will not."

"Then you must leave this table."

Consuela gasped. *"Abuelo, no."*

But Rafael had already spun around and stormed out.

Fifteen
Gabriella
Monday, April 7

I woke up on Monday feeling calm, almost as if Nathan had been there drumming me into bliss throughout the night. I had slept. And dreamed.

I come from a family of dreamers. From the time I could talk I tried to tell my parents about these nightly adventures.

"Don't be foolish," my father would scold. "No one wants to hear your ridiculous stories."

But he was wrong. My mother did.

"Then the dog turned into a lion, but he wasn't mean," I would tell her when we were alone.

She would stroke my hair. "A lion?"

"Yep. A friendly lion."

On nights when my father shut the door tight, my prayers not up to par, she used my dreams to help me fall asleep. As I curled in the dark, my body tight enough to keep away the sorrow and fear, the soft whisper of the door when my mother entered was my antidote for the poison of the night.

"Remember your lion?" she whispered. "He's here to take you on an adventure."

I would fall asleep, her hand on my forehead, the friendly lion by my side.

Insomnia remained a steady companion. In high school my mother no longer came to my room, but I learned to conjure up the images on my own. The lion evolved to a handsome man, usually a doctor or a cowboy or a fireman. Someone who rescued me and then fell in love with me, prancing up on a snorting horse or accompanied by the whooping sirens of the ambulance. Even after I was married to Greg my imagination carried me through the rough nights.

But now, here in this new place, even though I didn't remember last night's dream, I was energized. I washed my face by dipping a cloth into the bucket of icy water. My hair was limp and greasy, even though I had washed it in Española on Saturday. I really needed to take another shower.

Hard to believe I had been here nearly a week already. On second thought, it was hard to believe it had only been a week. Old-Ella seemed so far away, even though New-Ella still didn't have much substance.

Get clean and go to the courthouse to find out why no one is returning your calls—a short to-do list. This would be a good day. I could feel it.

An hour later my day didn't have the same aura of success.

The courthouse was deserted. Not completely, but there were no lights on at either Joel Dominguez' office or Fred Rivas's. This really was a ghost town and county seat or not, this courthouse felt like a haunted mansion. I made my way downstairs.

"We don't really have any knowledge of the whereabouts of the tenants." Alaura and Carmen exchanged another one of those eye-rolling glances when I asked about Joel Dominguez. "He just rents office space. He's probably down in Española today."

Vicki's voice rang inside my head. "Take charge of your life, Ella. It really doesn't take much—just ask for what you need." At the time I had rolled *my* eyes at her. She was born assertive and didn't know how painful it could be for me to speak up.

I drew in a breath and smiled. "Maybe you can help me. I called those numbers you gave me? The realtors?"

"Okay." A tight lipped smile was all Alaura would give up.

"No one is returning my calls. Well, except for Vernon Garcia, and he hung up on me. Is there something I'm missing here?"

Carmen rose from her desk and joined Alaura at the counter.

"Have you tried Fred Rivas?"

What was this vortex I was caught in? Hadn't I just explained that?

"He doesn't return my calls either."

Carmen was quiet but wheels were turning. "Listen dear. You go next door for some coffee. Give me some time. I'll come get you if I can help."

Help. Such a nice word. Maybe Carmen wasn't so bad.

Three Ravens was packed. I grabbed my mocha and sweet roll and headed outside.

I set my laptop on the table, but didn't turn it on. A strange orange bird hopped around in the buckeye tree which guarded the front of the shop. Had Nathan planted this or did it come with the house? An image came to mind—an old Hispanic woman tending to a tiny tree, now grown to fifteen feet tall and spreading its wide, drooping branches like a canopy over the whole yard.

The bird had a tropical flair—not the familiar pointy beak of a robin or a jay, but a bright orange wedge of a nose. He tipped his head at me, then resumed his search for insects in the mottled bark.

Deep breath. I needed to regain this morning's optimism.

I closed my eyes. *Plan, Ella. Plan.*

Ha! This wasn't the way to calm down. I snapped my eyes open just as my phone buzzed.

Text from Julie.

Before I could talk myself out of it, I called her.

"Mom!"

"Hi honey." I started to apologize for not calling, but stopped myself. "How are you?"

"I've been so worried. Are you okay?"

"Yes. I'm fine. It's really nice out here. The house isn't exactly what I thought, but it'll work out." No sense telling her that the house was barely more than a pile of stones.

"We... I..."

I could sense my daughter deciding what approach to take with her AWOL mother.

"Look, Julie. I had to come here to work on this property thing."

"When are you coming back?"

"I don't know. There is a lot to do, paperwork and things like that."

"Are you trying to sell it?"

"Of course." My response was firm, but even as I spoke I realized that my original goal had slipped. Suddenly I could picture myself staying here.

It didn't make sense. But the idea swirled around in my head like the blue mist that surrounded me when Nathan drummed me into that peaceful place. I thought about the medallion and its strange pull. I hadn't touched it again, but it haunted me.

"Dad really needs to talk to you. Will you call him?"

Damn Greg. He obviously had no problems putting our daughters into the middle of our mess.

"I will." Just not right now, I added to myself, feeling like I should cross my fingers behind my back.

"I got my residency packet yesterday."

Happy that Julie wanted to change the subject, we spent the next twenty minutes talking about her trip to Spain. I was proud to have a daughter who was not only willing to take on the adventure of studying in another country, but one who had made all the arrangements herself. Would I have been able to do that at twenty-four?

I couldn't see Shannon taking on such a task.

"I love you, sweetie. I'll call you, but service is spotty, so I can't say when."

After we hung up I decided to get all my obligations out of the way while I waited for Carmen. I dialed my mother.

"Hello, Ella. I was just thinking about you. Mrs. Beasley asked how you were doing."

Five minutes into the conversation about Mom's friends from church and how they always asked after me, my mind started to wander.

I normally spoke to Mother twice a week. Last Wednesday I had called, but she was out and I left a message.

I interrupted her rambling on about the bake sale. "Mom. I'm in Tierra Amarilla."

"I'll bring my snickerdoodles—where?" She finally tuned in.

"New Mexico. Looking at Dad's property. I'm going to sell it." Once again the words struck me as a lie. "I drove out here."

"Well, now, that's a surprise. All by yourself?"

Yeah, Mom. Greg left me. Remember?

"Bones is with me."

She was silent. Contemplating my news? Thinking about how mad my father would have been? Trying to figure out how to scold me for my impulsive actions?

"Mom, are you still there?"

"That land is cursed."

"What?"

More silence.

"What do you mean? Cursed by who?"

"It… he… your grandmother. She was the one who told me. She could hardly wait to get away from there."

I didn't know my grandmother. I remembered an ancient woman in a convalescent hospital. She spoke Spanish when we came to visit. "When did she tell you this?"

"I was young. It was a long time ago. Couldn't you have done all this from here?"

"What do you know about this place, Mom? Have you been here?"

She was quiet for a moment and I let her think. Finally she spoke. "Steven and I were going to go back there to visit. We asked Rueben and Estefania if they wanted to go. I thought your grandparents would want to see the place. I think Rueben did want to go, but your grandmother was adamant. Something bad would happen if they went back. She talked your father out of going. We went to Yellowstone instead."

What had my grandmother been afraid of?

Mom continued. "I think life was hard back there. I know she lost a baby or two. I always thought it wasn't really cursed, just too sad for her."

That I could understand. Living out on the property with five kids would have been tough.

"I wish you had told me you were going, Ella. You shouldn't be there by yourself."

"I'm fine, Mom. I have Bones."

"That place, it... just don't go off anywhere by yourself."

"I'll be careful, I promise." I felt twelve again, then realized it had been a long time since I had been off by myself. My mother probably thought I was safe as long as I had a man to protect me.

After my mother warned me again, listing all the terrible things that could happen to a woman on her own, I reassured her *again* I was safe and hung up. I wasn't about to tell her I was being stalked and seeing things.

I glanced at my watch. Ten after one. Where was Carmen? Was she really helping me or were the two women back in the courthouse laughing at my naiveté? I would give her ten more minutes while I checked my email.

There was a message from Greg. With attachments, surprise, surprise. Things I needed to review and sign. My gaze slipped over the pages, but I didn't focus, other than to feel a sense of relief that it wasn't divorce paperwork, just things regarding the sale of the house. If I disagreed with what he was proposing what difference would it make? I wasn't about to question him. He'd get his way in the end and he knew it. Just as I closed the email my phone buzzed.

It was Greg. He must have set up an alert on the email. *She read it*, his loyal computer had beeped.

I watched the phone vibrate on the table until it switched over to message mode. Within two seconds a text came through.

I need to talk to you. I sent paperwork for you to sign. Don't mess this up or you will regret it.

Text-threat. The new wave of communication. I leaned back and closed my eyes, searching for peace, refusing to let the knot in my stomach move up to my throat. Trying to silence the voices of Julie and my mother and now, Greg, I remembered why I had run away.

As I sat in my numb state two voices drifted out onto the porch through the open window, breaking through my cloak of self pity.

"Have you seen the new woman? She's dating Andy. I think she's kind of dense. Or else she's good at the helpless charade. Nathan sure has a thing for her. Playing drums right in the middle of the shop, her moaning and rocking and going into a fake trance. She knows how to hook 'em." The woman's voice shrilled with laughter.

"Oh come on. Nathan loves being the town caretaker. You know he's solid with Casey. Let the new one have Andy. Even weirdos need love. An outsider is a good thing."

"Why would you think that?"

"This place is ten years behind everywhere else in the universe. Anyone with half a brain leaves. Some new blood will help move us into the twenty-first century."

I leaned closer to the window. The second voice was harder to hear.

"Let her find out for herself. She hasn't passed my litmus test yet. Kind of a sulker, don't you think? And that dog? It sulks too."

Now they were insulting my dog. Funny how that hurt even worse than what they said about me. But before I could knock on the window to communicate my rage, the voices moved away. I watched the door but no one came out. The two gossips must have left through the back exit.

✧ ✧ ✧

I walked to the courthouse, subdued by what I had heard. Sulking, according to my nameless accusers. And I certainly wasn't dating Andy Lloyd. I wondered if he had started that rumor.

"I'm sorry, Mrs. Martinez." Carmen shrugged. "I am trying."

"Can you at least give me a clue? What is the big secret?"

"It's that property. There have always been problems."

Mother's words. Cursed.

"What kind of problems?"

"Oh, you know. Family things. This is a small place, feuds last a long time around here. I'm afraid that Fred Rivas is your best bet."

"Do you know of any other way to get in touch with him?"

"I left a message too. I think he's gone fishing. He'll be back. He never goes for long." Carmen reached across the counter and patted my hand. "Don't worry, I'll find him."

"Thank you, Carmen."

The morning magic had turned to exhaustion. I felt like I was in the middle of a soap opera—family feuds and gossiping women. There was something odd going on behind the scenes of this property, but with my cousin Mark conveniently out of town and no one else willing to let me in on the secret, what was I to do?

When I turned off the highway onto the dirt road I glanced at the churro sheep. *Oh look, two of them have babies. How sweet.*

"Sorry, Ella. Changing the subject isn't allowed anymore. You need to figure this one out." Bones sat up and gave me a wrinkled you-talking-to-me? look. "The truth. I'm sure you know what it means, Girl. If only you would tell me." Distraction technique number two—discuss the issue with your dog.

To be honest with myself, I needed to figure out what part of me, which thoughts racing through my head, which images of the future, memories of the past, were actually the truth. My truth.

I didn't want to start a new life. All this mental garbage I had been preaching. New life, new Ella. No more problems. I kept telling myself I had been so unhappy in my old role of wife and perfect mother, and this was my chance to be something different. But it just wasn't true. Talking with Julie had brought back all the good memories.

Maybe if you fake being happy long enough, you feel happy. Pulling the car to a stop in front of the house, I turned off the engine but didn't get out. This house—with the adobe flaking, roof sagging and dust swirling around the sagging porch—was my future.

It didn't matter if I had loved my old life, hated my old life, or just put up with my old life, I didn't have it any more. My arms and legs weighed a thousand pounds each and I couldn't summon up the energy to get out of the car.

Was this depression? Like when people sit in a chair in the living room and don't go outside, don't answer the phone, don't bathe? A pale gray instead of the smothering black?

Bones shimmied close and rested her chin on my shoulder, her warm breath in my ear. I stroked her smooth head and realized that my life was in limbo and the bar had just fallen a notch. I would have to learn how to bend a little further and make my way to the other side all by myself.

There was no one to catch me if I fell.

Sixteen

Fray Bernardo Castaño
Pueblo Lindo, 1606

Bernardo walked slowly up the path to the hidden canyon. He wore the new prayer shawl Consuela made for him. She had stitched Hebrew symbols onto a piece of linen. He suspected the fabric came from one of her mother's dresses. But even the wonderful feeling of a shawl draped over his shoulders could not quell his anxiety. Would Rafael be back at the table tonight?

"Consuela, may I ask you something?"

"Of course, Padre. What is it?"

The girl did not live in the upper canyon with her grandfather and the Jews. She spent her days in the pueblo, working. Bernardo realized that she was the real connection between the two groups. The child of Jimuta and Abene, she was a mix between the two cultures. He had watched as Consuela floated from group to group: helping in the fields, baking bread, weaving cloth and, of course, taking care of him.

"Rafael is angry at me and I cannot find the reason."

Consuela stopped and turned on the path to face him. Her sweet smile went straight to his heart. "Padre, my cousin is not angry at you. He carries something deep inside that no one can cure."

"And my life is in danger because of this buried anger that is not directed at me?"

Her laughter slipped down the canyon like the song of a bird. "No, no." She shook her head and smiled. "Rafael was born before the explorers came to the mountains. He was small, but came with my mother and my grandfather."

"His father was a conquistador? What of his mother?"

"Rafael's father was Gaspar's son, but he was also Rabbi Castaño. His wife died and he chose to stay with Simón. I do not think he agreed with the politics of his father."

The priest leaned toward Consuela. "Where is he? This Rabbi?"

"Dead." Consuela's face took on a look of pity. "It was a bad thing, Padre. My cousin watched his father die. The horse was scared and jumped off the steep trail. A horrifying thing to see."

"But why is he angry at me? Does he think I try to take the place of a man long dead?"

"No. Rafael thinks you take *his* place. He should have trained as the next rabbi."

This made sense. The rabbi would have trained his son. That was the way of both the Brotherhood and of those who lived in remote areas. Suddenly the solution for escaping Rafael's constant harassment was clear to Bernardo. He would train him to be the next rabbi.

✡ ✡ ✡

"Will you help me with the lighting of the candles?" Bernardo waved a hand toward the table and smiled at Rafael.

"Woman's work? Do you not even know something as simple as that?" Rafael kicked at the dirt and shook his fist. "I don't know what my grandfather is thinking, letting you mislead the people as you do."

Why can't I think these things through? Bernardo's plan slipped away as quickly as it had blossomed. He couldn't think of an apt reply to the young man's accusations, so he simply lit the candles and opened his bible. *Peace was yet to come.* He would simply preside over the Sabbath meal as best he could.

Rafael stepped forward as if to grab the bible from Bernardo's hands. "Why do you have that here? I told you that we will not become Catholics. You say you have faith, but that is not enough. You do not live as a Jew so how can you claim to be a Jew?"

"Rafe." Simón's firm tone stopped his grandson.

But Rafael was not so easily appeased. He spun from Bernardo and rushed away from the Sabbath preparations.

Bernardo looked at Simón. He wanted help in forming a plan and needed to speak to him. But people were gathering and this was not something that should take place in front of the others.

After the meal, when Bernardo expected that he would be required to deliver a Sabbath sermon, he was not surprised when a crowd gathered in the center of the canyon. He had hoped for a small group, but it seemed everyone was here. As he adjusted his shawl and moved to the front of the crowd, Consuela took his arm.

"Over here, Padre." She led him to a log, and pushed him to sit. She sat next to him and offered him a cup of the crude wine the Jews had made from juniper and wild berries.

It was then Bernardo noticed that not only Castaño's people were here, but Jimuta and the puebloans were gathering as well.

"What is happening?" he asked Conseula.

"It will start soon."

"What will start soon?"

"The celebration." She leaned forward and turned, staring into his eyes. "The harvest is finished. Did you not listen yesterday? You were there. That was the last of the squash. The Full Corn Moon is in the sky and soon the old man winter will bring his chill to the days as well as the nights."

"But what of the—" a loud drumbeat interrupted Bernardo's question regarding the Sabbath.

Jimuta stood before the crowd, speaking in a language Bernardo did not understand. Consuela whispered the meaning of the words in his ear, her soft breath warm. "He is welcoming everyone, thanking those who are not natives for being here to celebrate."

The leader wore a cloak of feathers which made him look like a giant bird. A woven skirt hung from the leader's waist, covering his deer-hide trousers. The shawl of feathers covered his bare chest and shoulders. His face was painted with bright yellow and red designs.

Silver, turquoise and other polished stones hung from ropes around his waist. He held a drum in one hand and a stick wrapped with skin in the other, pounding rhythmically as he spoke. The crowd fell quiet.

Bernardo was transfixed as the leader blessed the earth, the Gods, the corn and the people. More men came forward. Some held drums and others were dressed as Jimuta was. A fire was lit and the men circled around. The drummers gathered outside the circle, just in front of Bernardo and Consuela.

"This is the best place to sit," she whispered.

The drummers started a slow steady beat. The men in the circle moved their feet, barely lifting them as they shuffled around the fire.

As Bernardo watched the bright feathers and the swaying beads on the skirts of the men, the drumming gathered speed. The change was nearly imperceptible, but the shuffling feet lifted an inch off the ground, then two inches. Consuela, as well as others, started to clap, matching the beat of the drums.

The silhouettes of the dancers against the fire made Bernardo nervous. He felt engulfed in an ancient ritual so strong it had tricked the Jews into abandoning the Sabbath. The sweat trickled from the faces of the dancers and the heat he felt coming from Consuela as her clapping increased, made his heart pound with desire for the girl. He felt the damp of his own sweat working its way through his clothing.

The dancers wavered before his eyes. What was wrong with his vision? He turned to look at the dark of the forest, pulling his gaze from the flames of the fire in an attempt to clear the fog that floated around him. In front of the trees he saw wavering figures. Ghosts. He clamped his eyes tight, but the shimmering figures remained.

Squeezing his hand into a fist, he pushed his fingernails into his palm. There must have been something in that wine. Something to induce these crazed visions.

"Are you all right?"

It took him a moment to separate the voice from the gauzy figures. The drumming was loud and the clapping and the chanting surrounded him. He wasn't sure he had heard a voice at all. With great effort and a prayer he opened his eyes. Consuela stopped clapping and placed her hand on his sleeve.

"I am feeling a little dizzy." He needed to stand—to get away from this frenzy.

As suddenly as it had started, the drumming stopped. All the dancers froze. A silence surrounded him, so deep it seemed a vortex had formed around the crowd. The dancers silently left the circle and the people rose and walked away. No one spoke, not even the smallest child.

Bernardo felt his arm burn where Consuela's hand touched him. He turned to the girl. His mind empty of everything, he leaned forward and pressed his mouth against her soft lips. His world stopped as he melted into the kiss.

She kissed him back, he was sure of it. But then she was gone, like she was one of the ghostly spirits floating in the forest.

He stood, looking for her, but there was no sign of anyone. Confused, he headed down the trail.

Bernardo stumbled. The full moon brightened the rocks, but the shadows were deep and the gravel rolled under his feet. His mind reeled from the heat of the dancers and the drumming, from the ghosts he had seen in the forest and from the kiss he had dared to take from an innocent girl.

Consuela. Her face filled his mind, blinding him even more than the lack of a candle. All those poems he had read, the passion described by Marcus when his older brother had told him what was to come—he thought he had forsaken this when he traded his life as a soldier for that of a holy man. A priest couldn't marry.

But a rabbi could.

Had she returned his kiss or had she run away? His mind was not yet clear and doubts took over.

"You are done here."

The voice startled Bernardo.

Rafael stood in the trail, his arms crossed over his chest and his chin thrust forward.

"What?" Bernardo tried to clear his mind and focus on what Rafael was saying.

"Leave. Make up some excuse, but I want you out of here. Tomorrow."

"Look, Rafael," Bernardo held up his hand. "I know we don't see things in the same way, but let us work this out."

"Work this out? That will never happen."

"We must have faith," Bernardo whispered, suddenly fearful of the young man. Was he talking to himself or Rafael? For had not his own mind taken a turn?

Rafael accused him of being Catholic, but Bernardo knew this was not the case. He was a good student of the Christian faith, but only as he was a good student of literature. He needed the information to be successful in his secret role. His heart, that was where the trouble lived. He had been away from his family for so long. He had grasped onto Consuela and Simón and even the other natives as his new family. He watched how they respected the earth, how in their world God lived in everything. And after tonight's celebration, he could actually see the magic of their rituals. These were not rules, not part of a covenant so distant he had let it slip from his mind.

Bernardo would tell Rafael that he was right. But before he could speak the man continued.

"Don't think for a minute that Simón will like hearing that you have taken advantage of an *almah*. My cousin is an innocent."

Rafael had seen the kiss.

"I promise you, I do not take advantage of Consuela. I... she..." Before he met the girl Bernardo had been sure he would never find love. The sting of Rafael's words brought back images of his parents, his father gentle and kind with his mother. How did he explain what he felt and reassure Rafael that there was no harm being in love?

Rafael unfolded his arms and his fist thrust forward with the speed of the rattlesnake. As it met his jaw, Bernardo was thrown backwards, off the side of the trail. His head snapped back and hit the dirt.

Before he could recover from the fall, Rafael had leaped upon him. Bernardo closed his eyes. Punches rained down on his head, his eyes, his chest. He tried to turn to the side, to curl his arms as a shield, but Rafael's weight kept him flat on his back.

"No, no, no," he sobbed, hoping to break through the rage of this wild man.

The pounding fists continued their assault. Bernardo grew weak, but still he yelled, hoping that someone would hear his cries.

Finally Rafael stood. Bernardo did not—could not—open his eyes. Curled into a tight ball he lay still, waiting for more.

No sound came.

Still, the fallen priest did not move. Time passed and his thoughts were dark. Demons came into Bernardo's heart as he wished for the strength to kill the man who had done this to him. The man who had punched away his dreams of love.

He did not know how much time passed, but finally he uncurled his arms and stretched out his legs. He slowly rose, moving his sore limbs with caution. He sat on a boulder, searching for the strength to walk.

It took most of the night for Bernardo to make his way down to the lower pueblo. He walked a few steps, sat, crawled, and lay flat on the ground to rest. He vomited, he choked, he gasped. He could only open his swollen eyes the merest of a slits, enough to see the bright moon had crossed the sky and the faint light of dawn tinged the east when he finally pulled himself through the doorway of his quarters.

Seventeen

Gabriella

Saturday, April 12 to Sunday April, 13

No disguise can keep you from knowing yourself. I wasn't insane, even if my best friend thought I was.

"It was crazy, Vicki. So real, like a dream but not a dream." The early morning sun cast faint shadows beside each of the prickly sage bushes. Climbing down the bank to the ditch, I leaned against a cottonwood tree in anticipation of a long chat with my friend. The Brazos cliffs and the big sky rose above me like a mural in a dome. I had learned to bundle up in the morning; even when the sun was shining it didn't thaw things until mid-day. "I understood these people even though they spoke some other language."

"Ummm."

Vicki wasn't buying my story and I hadn't even told her it was all caused by a magic medallion.

"I know it sounds crazy, but it's different here. Like the crust of the earth is thinner and there's more of a magnetic pull or something."

"Any other symptoms?"

"Thanks a lot. I'm not sick just because I had a weird—" a weird what? Hallucination? Vision? "—dream."

"This kind of stuff makes me worry. Are you sure you didn't fall and hit your head? It's not good, you out there alone, having… brain stuff. Are there any hospitals nearby?"

"Española. Just over sixty miles. There's a clinic here, but I don't need a doctor." Even though she was my best friend, I had

137

never told Vicki about my battle with depression, because it had to be a secret, that black cloud. I felt the thousand-mile gap between us.

I needed to talk to someone about the dreams and the medallion, but it couldn't be just anyone. Vicki's reaction reaffirmed my hesitation. The gossip in town was already leaning toward "crazy woman." No need to prove it was true.

Carmen called to tell me that Fred Rivas would be back from his trip next Tuesday.

With nothing to do but wait I spent more time at Three Ravens, hoping someone would sit at the table next to me and we could chat.

Andy Lloyd was the one person who regularly came over to my table and pulled up a chair. I couldn't give him the cold shoulder forever, and at least he was willing to talk to me. I was beginning to lose my strange anxiety about him. Seeing the Andy-like guitar playing man in my dreams made me feel like I knew him, although this was absurd. One thing was clear—I couldn't talk to *him* about my strange dreams.

Not every night, but most nights, even without putting the medallion around my neck, I traveled back to the tired group and trudged beside the two-wheeled cart. In the dreams I carried on long conversations with the people, but morning erased the content of those talks. I still didn't know who we were hiding from or where we were traveling.

I didn't want to touch that strange jewelry again. A dream was one thing, but a vision, especially one that lasted for hours, scared me. Although I had been upset with Vicki for suggesting I might be going crazy, the bizarre experience worried me. Hallucinations moved my state of mental health to a whole different level. I was not going to go there.

"Nathan." I was waiting for my daily mocha when he walked in to the shop. "Do you have time to sit today?"

"Sure. Just give me five minutes to make a phone call."

When Nathan joined me at my favorite table by the window, the one with the plug for recharging my laptop and phone, I didn't know where to start. I had planned on telling him about the dreams and showing him the medallion, but suddenly this seemed foolish. Maybe even dangerous.

"I need some friends." *Lame, Ella.*

Nathan nodded. "When I moved here there was a long period of isolation."

I hadn't moved here, but I was obligated to follow the direction of this conversation—I was the one who started it. "What did you do?"

He waved a hand around the room and smiled. "I asked the spirits. Then I bought this place. Needed help fixing it up, hired locally, and opened for business as soon as I could."

"So I need to start a business. And pay people to fix up my house. And find a job." I smirked. "Right."

"Or you could ask the spirits what is right for you. What about church?"

I hadn't been to church in years. Even then it was the neighborhood Protestant Congregational—the church of volleyball and picnics. We went as a family because Julie insisted. I lasted nine months. Silently meditating during each service, blocking my father from my mind and focusing on the stained glass windows, rather than the words the minister spoke, his voice droning on and on, no emotional intonation daring to intrude on his weekly spiritual lessons.

"Can't you just drum for me again?"

"I can do that, but what I'm saying is that Santo Niño has Sunday mass at eleven, with a coffee hour afterwards. First Sunday of the month everyone brings food to share, a potluck lunch."

"I'm not Catholic."

Nathan grinned. "Doesn't matter. Everyone goes. You and I are not the only socially starved people around here. The service is in Spanish and English, lots of music."

I grimaced and shook my head. No, not church. Too many bad memories. "I'm sorry for being so uncooperative. It's just, I don't do religion."

Nathan persisted. "Don't look so grouchy. Think spiritual, not religious. I'll go with you. Meet me here at 10:30 tomorrow."

✡ ✡ ✡

The next morning Nathan and I walked the two short blocks from Three Ravens to Santo Niño. The church was a tall blocky building, white stucco with a bell tower poking up, topped by that cross I had noticed in my rear view mirror. From the outside it was unadorned, but the sanctuary—or chapel or whatever the inside part is called in a Catholic church—was filled with bright plastic flowers, plaster statues, and quilted banners announcing Joy and Peace.

"Very Hispanic," I whispered to Nathan. I had admitted to him on the way over that I had never actually been to mass. My parents had settled for the local Presbyterian church. I went to Sunday School and the lessons of whales who swallowed people and women who turned to salt or stone or something worse, scared me almost as much as my father's tight grip.

Nathan grinned, took my hand, and pulled me up the aisle. I looked at the wall behind the altar. A twelve foot bloody Jesus on the cross stared at me. Just the thing to scare everyone into submission.

This was a mistake. The church was filled with my father's kind of religion. The kind that punished and preyed on fears and led the masses by promising them no matter how hard they tried hell was waiting just around the corner. My stomach churned.

"I don't want to sit up front," I hissed, resisting Nathan's tug.

"We won't go all the way up front, just to my family pew."

His family? I didn't even know he had a family. Only a girl friend and that was news spread through gossip and an open window. I had never seen her. "I thought you weren't Catholic?"

"I'm not. Neither are they."

Nathan introduced me to two young women sitting in his pew. Cousins. I guess I wasn't going to meet his parents or an ex-wife or four children or even the phantom girlfriend after all.

It was a lively service. Lots of singing, guitars, bongo drums and a ukelele. A mixture of Spanish and English, with the red hymnals in both languages, so I knew what the smiling priest was saying. Not fearful—joyous. Something I couldn't remember from my childhood Sunday school classes. Had there been clapping and smiling?

When we got to the part where the priest said a long prayer, and the people answered in unison I started to feel uncomfortable.

What was I doing here? These people might not all be Catholic, but they all believed in something. I felt like a fraud. Coming to church to serve my own motives—not to pray, or even talk to God, but as a social visit? This couldn't be right. There was so much power involved, so many other people or books or words of God telling you what to believe, how to act, what to say and do. Maybe some people needed that. A guide to good behavior. But it was so prescriptive, so rote. All these people were following something that wasn't real.

Not me. I knew the difference between right and wrong, kindness and cruelty, ethical and immoral, without anyone telling me what to do. I had enough experience of the oh-so-powerful-squeeze on my shoulder to last me a lifetime. Sweat soaked my armpits and my chest grew tight.

Nathan tapped me on the shoulder. I snapped out of my reverie to find everyone around us smiling, hugging, kissing and shaking hands.

"Share the peace," Nathan whispered. "Just shake hands and greet."

A small girl stood on the pew in front of me and turned. Tiny bright teeth shone from her grin—quite the toothpaste ad. I reached out a hand. "Peace."

Her mouth opened in a giggle and she shook my hand. "Peace be with you," she replied. "I'm Rosie."

Obviously Rosie felt comfortable here. No one told her she couldn't stand on the wooden bench. I could breathe again.

The woman beside her turned around and grasped my hand. It was Alaura. "Welcome and peace be with you, Gabriella. It's good to see you here."

Although Alaura and I hadn't got off to such a good start at the courthouse, she was just as happy as her daughter. I smiled.

Alaura had remembered my name.

✡ ✡ ✡

After the service concluded with a long list of public announcements—*don't forget to bring coats and sweaters for the coat drive, the flower committee was meeting on Wednesday, and let's all support the high school girls' basketball game next Friday by wearing purple*—Nathan led me across the gravel parking lot to a low building.

Long tables filled a large room, folding chairs on both sides, white butcher paper serving as tablecloths. A small stage, sagging curtains adorning the edge, filled one end of the room. Along the opposite wall stood more tables covered with trays of donuts. Silver percolators of coffee lurked like retro spacemen, waiting to dispense the soothing liquid. Sugar cubes. Powdered creamer. Things that would last from week to week.

As I stirred the coffee in the white styrofoam cup, an old woman approached me.

She didn't stop until she was two inches from me. I clutched the cup of coffee, fearing she was about to be covered in the hot liquid.

"*¿De dónde vienes?*"

I smiled and shrugged. "I'm sorry. I don't speak Spanish." Well, not enough to carry on a conversation, although I did know that *dónde* meant "where."

A man, who appeared to be about forty, very clean cut, wearing a relaxed linen jacket and wrinkled pants the color of the yellow earth, hurried over to us.

"Hi. I'm Alfred. This is my grandmother, *mi abuela*, Rachel. She wanted to meet you."

"*Me llamo Rachel García Maria de la Rodrigo y Rivas.*"

Rachel García Maria de la Rodrigo y Rivas was much smaller than her name. A thick gray braid wound around her head and she wore an orange polyester blazer straight out of the seventies over a white ruffled blouse. Her skirt was traditional Navajo, three rows of patchwork gathered at the waist, flaring out to fall just below her knees. Add black socks and Nike runners to top off the picture.

Her face was so wrinkled I could barely see her dark eyes, but that didn't seem to matter as she stared only at my chest.

She turned to Alfred and rattled off something in Spanish. Her voice was high pitched, with the lilting music of the language and she waved her hand toward me as she spoke. I expected no teeth, but she had straight white pearls which peeked out of her thin lips.

Alfred shook his head and looked at me, then shrugged. "My grandmother says you should not wear the necklace. I'm sorry, she gets confused sometimes."

I reached up and touched my neck. I wasn't wearing a necklace. My heart pounded. "It's okay."

Rachel García Maria de la Rodrigo y Rivas continued to stare. Then she started talking even more rapidly, one sentence running into the other. There was no chance I could catch a single word. I looked at Alfred.

"She say this is a very special medallion. She wants to know how you came to have it?"

The grandmother put her hand on his arm and shook her head. She turned to me and spoke slowly.

"El que cree y persista vive para siempre."

I struggled to translate. *Que cree...* to think? I knew *vive* had to do with life. *Para siempre, siempre...* for always?

I shook my head. *"Desculpame, Señora."* I didn't know what she wanted, but I remembered how to apologize.

She turned back to Alfred. *"De dónde sacó el medallón?"*

"Abuela, por favor, no seas tan entrometida." Alfred's voice held an edge of impatience as he answered his grandmother.

The old woman clutched his arm and tipped her head toward me, insistent on whatever it was she was asking.

"I apologize. My grandmother insists on knowing where you got the medallion. I really don't know what she's talking about."

I started to tremble. "Tell her... tell her I won't wear it."

Alfred rattled off something in Spanish, then grabbed his grandmother's arm. He glanced over his shoulder, as he pulled her away. "I'm so sorry. I think I should take her home now. I'll call you tomorrow, I promise."

He would call me? What had she said?

Then it hit me. Rachel García Maria de la Rodrigo y Rivas.

Alfred.

Fred Rivas. Realtor-at-large.

Eighteen
Fray Bernardo Castaño
Pueblo Lindo, 1606

"Padre?"

Bernardo heard the voice, and tried to turn his head. He winced. His eyes were swollen and crusty. The combination of dried blood and a parched throat sealed his lips. "Mmggg."

He heard her footsteps as she rushed to the bed. A gasp of shock penetrated the fog and he felt her hand on his forehead.

"What has happened? Who did this to you?"

In his mind he answered, he shook his head, he spoke to Consuela. But he could do none of these things, as his body would not respond to his thoughts.

He must have drifted off, because the next moment he was aware of warm water and soft hands cleaning his face.

It hurt, but the pain was not so strong that he wasn't comforted by Consuela's sweet touch.

"Thank you," he croaked when she held a cup to his mouth, feeding him tiny sips of water.

"What happened?"

Should he tell her the truth? Would that not be moving his burden onto her shoulders? For this was her home, her cousin, her way of life. He was the intruder.

"Fell. Coming home in the dark."

If his eyes had been able to work, he was sure he would have seen a look of doubt upon her face. He didn't sound convincing, even to himself. He was relieved when Consuela did not ask anything else.

It was four days before Bernardo was able to leave his bed. His eyes opened and the swelling had dissipated. When he touched his face he could feel the bruised skin, painful and tender. His jaw protested if he tried to open his mouth more than a crack.

Consuela stayed with him. She pulled a mat outside his door, and slept curled up in a thick bison skin. She spooned broth into his mouth and washed his wounds twice a day. She kept the fire burning and constantly asked him if he was warm enough.

With each movement she made, Bernardo felt himself falling deeper into a place he had never dreamed existed. As he gazed at her face, his lips tingled in anticipation of her kiss. When Consuela moved about the room he watched the way she held her shoulders straight, the smile that came on when Lipika, the young daughter of Lena, poked her head in the door and asked for bread, the quiet tunes she sang while she worked—each of these things felt like learning to read for the first time, like standing on the edge of the vista of a great canyon, like nothing he had ever felt.

If only he could be sure she felt the same about him. For never did she act as anything other than a caretaker. She did not speak of what had happened to him and she did not speak of the future. When she talked to him, she told stories she had learned from her father.

"And so Naiyenesgani went searching for monsters. He climbed to the top of the White Mountain and listened, hoping that Wind would guide him."

As Bernardo listened he came to understand the beliefs of the indigenous people. The respect they had for the land and the animals. These people were not warlike. This is why they nodded and accepted the words of the Spaniards. He saw now that they would always act as if they listened to the preaching of the Catholics, because it was polite. They were as comfortable with their own religion as they were with farming or weaving. It was what it was. They had no need to change.

✡ ✡ ✡

On the fourth day, although he did not want to give up these hours with Consuela, Bernardo knew he had to talk to Simón.

He wanted the old man's blessing. And if he was to be rabbi to these Jews he needed to make his peace with Rafael.

But no sooner had Bernardo set out up the canyon than he met the young man coming down the trail. He stopped and instinctively reached a hand to his sore jaw. *"Buenas días, Rafael."*

"No, Fray Martín. It is not a good day. Not for me and not for you."

Bernardo stepped back, aware of the challenge Rafael made by refusing to call him Castaño. The priest glanced up the trail and then turned to look back, hoping that someone else was walking nearby. As if to answer his silent plea for help, the sounds of horses and men drifted from below. He stepped off the trail and onto a large boulder. From this point he could see down the valley below the pueblo to the streams and vegetable patches. Rafael also turned toward the sound.

Five soldiers were headed up the valley toward the lower pueblo.

The lookout for the upper canyon must have alert Simón, because the old man came down the trail. "Can you see who they are?" he asked his nephew.

Rafael shook his head. "I cannot recognize them, but they are soldiers, not *custodes*. They wear armor."

Bernardo reached for Simón's arm. "I will go to greet them. The Indians know what to do. You and Rafael must go back." Without waiting for an answer Bernardo turned to set off down the trail.

"Wait." Simón reached out and touched Bernardo's shoulder. "What happened to you?"

Bernardo glanced toward Rafael. The young man folded his arms across his chest and glared.

"I fell. Friday night, coming home in the dark."

"If you greet these soldiers in that condition there will be questions. You must come back with us. Consuela knows what to do."

Bernardo would rather face soldiers than Rafael. He had hoped the young man would have settled down, but he felt angry eyes burning into his back as he followed Simón up the trail.

Hours went by before Consuela finally came to the upper pueblo.

"They are on their way west. I fed them and answered their questions."

"Did they have news of Mexico City?"

She shook her head. "No, but they did say that more settlers are coming soon. One of them was interested in this place so I told him how harsh the winters can be."

Simón seemed satisfied that there would be no problems, but Bernardo knew that while a visitor might be contained to the lower valley, settlers would explore the whole area.

"I fear that your hiding place may not be secure for much longer."

"What do you mean by that?" Why did Rafael feel compelled to respond when Bernardo addressed Simón?

"There is a way of things. First soldiers, then settlers, then the church. And where there is a priest there will soon be *custodes* to make sure he is doing his job. It is one thing for a single Jew to hide, but a whole pueblo full of Jews?"

Simón shook his head and smiled at Bernardo. "Padre, we have trust in you to keep us safe. Your plan will work, do not fret."

"A plan can only go so far. You have only to look at history to see that even Jews betrayed each other." Bernardo's voice got louder. "We are so far from anywhere. Men who have the urge to punish Jews may be thwarted by the law when close to Santa Fe, but here they will feel free to do as they want. We know nothing of the loyalty of the natives. We might be sold for a shiny trinket!"

"Padre? Is that really what you think of us?" Consuela's face was dark with anger.

The natives or the Jews? He had not been sensitive to the girl and he felt shame and guilt flush down his neck clear to his fingertips. What right did he have to accuse these people of ignorance?

"Please, Bernardo. Do not worry. We have ways to hide that you have not witnessed." Simón picked up his cane. "We have been sitting in our fear for too long. I am hungry."

Bernardo suddenly remembered why he had been making the trip up the canyon in the first place. But his head hurt and he felt weak. He would have to talk to Simón about Rafael some other time. Right now he had to figure out how to make Consuela forgive him for his unthoughtful words.

✡ ✡ ✡

"Padre, there are visitors for you. Do you feel well enough to talk with them?"

Bernardo looked up from his mending. "More conquistadors already?" Problems were arriving faster than he had expected.

"People from the pueblo." Consuela leaned the broom against the wall. "Aarón and Bianca."

"Certainly." He stood and moved toward the door. With only two chairs in his small quarters, he would take them out to the logs which served as pews.

A young man, about twenty-five, held on to the arm of a girl who looked a few years younger. They were dressed in the usual mix of native clothing and worn-out clothes which had come with the settlers. Castaño's group.

"*Buenos días*," Bernardo greeted them. "Let us go over here where we can sit."

"*Gracias*, Fray Martín."

All the Jews now used the name Rafael had bestowed upon him. With a sigh, he nodded to the young couple.

They sat across from him, she with her eyes cast down into her lap, where her hands were folded. He could see the white of her knuckles as she squeezed them tight. The young man licked his lips and rubbed his palms on his thighs. Bernardo waited but neither spoke.

"Yes?" he urged.

"We... we would like to..."

Bernardo realized they wanted to get married. That made sense. Isn't that what young couples do?

"That should not be a problem," Bernardo said.

"But we, well, with only a priest..." the man put an arm around the girl. Her blush grew and her head dropped lower. "We are not conversos. My wife... I mean, Bianca, she was born in Mexico, as was I. We came here when we were very young and so we learned only to be Jews."

He had called her his wife.

"So you are married?" Bernardo did not know what the man was trying to say.

"We live... we live as husband and wife. We recited our vows before the witnesses."

The young woman started to cry.

"My dear. Please do not weep." Bernardo could not fathom what was upsetting her. There was nothing wrong in what they had done.

Bianca looked up and wiped her face with the edge of her shawl. "So you will do this for us? Make us a ceremony?" Her hand dropped back to her lap and covered her abdomen.

It was then that Bernardo noticed the swell of her unborn child. It was not a marriage that this couple was after. The fact that he was not only a fake priest but a fake rabbi as well slapped him in the face once more. But the girl's pleading eyes swept his tongue into a promise he could never keep.

"Of course. Let us make a plan."

Bernardo regretted that he had not attended to Marcus's studies with more effort. He had learned to read, had read those things which Marcus was able to bring to him, but he had never been allowed to go with his brother to see the rabbi. He had studied the small leather book Marcus gave to him when they switched places, but he had never read the Torah or discussed the traditions of the Jews with the elders.

And he certainly had never performed the circumcision this young couple was requesting. He silently thanked God it did not look like the baby was imminent. He smiled and sent them on their way. Then Fray Bernardo Castaño Martín de Serrano prayed for a girl.

Word spread. Each day brought a new couple to his door. Many held babies—sons already born. The Brotherhood of the Castaños had gone the way of his own clan. They had used the tiny symbolic cut, with its few drops of blood, to replace the circumcision required by God, the scar invisible to the inquisitors who had inspected men for the last hundred years, but the ceremony of the promise had been completed.

"Yes, I can do this for you but we must wait." Bernardo held them off with excuses. Visions of blood he couldn't stop, screaming children and angry fathers filled his mind. These were not infants, but boys who ran and jumped and looked at him with solemn eyes. The last thing he wanted to do was cause the death of the sons of the Jews with his incompetence. He would have to talk to Simón.

"So, there is no mohel? Who has led the naming ceremonies?" Bernardo prayed that Simón would give him an easy solution.

Maybe these couples had only come because he was new and they wanted to test him.

"We kept to the ways of the Inquisition after Rabbi Castaño was gone. He was the only man among us who could circumcise the babies. *Señor* Vegas took care of things for the last fifteen years."

Bernardo felt the sweat growing on his forehead threaten to slip down into his eyes. No circumcision for fifteen years. Surely they would not want him to perform the cut on nearly grown men?

"I... Simón... the thing is... I have always worked with a mohel." May God forgive this lie, Bernardo thought. It is for the sake of the genitalia of a whole generation. Surely that was valid reason to speak falsely. "I am not trained to do this."

That was when Bernardo saw the wave of doubt cross behind the old man's eyes and he realized that up until this moment Simón had given no value to Rafael's accusations that the priest was not who he claimed to be. But now, with admission of this lack of knowledge, Simón Castaño had lost his faith in Bernardo.

"The people have lived a long time without a spiritual leader. It was my hope that you would renew the spirit we need to survive in this wilderness. It seems my hope was false." Simón cleared his throat. "Who are you?"

Bernardo could do nothing about the hot flush that covered his face. He looked down. Now was the time to tell the truth.

"I... it is a complex situation."

"I have time."

"The Brotherhood... my father... my brother..." Bernardo choked out the words. What would happen when the old explorer heard the truth? When all the people found out he was a fraud? He saw Consuela's face—no love would be there for a man who lied. He would leave this place in shame.

Where would he go? Not a soldier, not a rabbi, and not a priest? He was nothing. His shame and despair made his knees weak and he sank to the ground.

"Get up."

Simón's voice was that of a leader of men—one who had lost patience with the situation. Bernard's fear grew, but his reaction was only making things worse. He closed his eyes and drew in a breath, trying to pull in God, looking for strength in the fact that although untrained, he was faithful.

"It was my brother, Marcus, who was to be the priest. It was he who trained in our faith as a rabbi, as well as the duties of the Catholics. I was to be a soldier, and my younger brother, Romero, he was to be a farmer. We were sent north." Bernardo looked up at Simón. The man folded his arms across his chest and stared at the view of the canyon.

The priest pulled himself to his feet. He would look his accuser in the eye.

"I am no soldier. It was Marcus who could wield a sword with skill, who could throw a knife farther than any other man, with the accuracy of a diving eagle. I listened when he trained as a priest, and he gave me his book of notes. When no member of the Brotherhood was around to tell us what we did was wrong, we traded places."

A shadow ran through the back of Simón's eyes. His gaze shifted and penetrated Bernardo's face.

"You traded places?"

"*Sí*. My brother would be the soldier and I would be the priest." Bernardo's hands shook, but he kept his gaze on Simón.

Simón raised a hand to his forehead. "You cannot choose to ignore the words of God which don't fit into your scheme. No Jew would do such a thing. Let me think." The man turned and paced toward the trees, then spun and paced back.

Back and forth he went. The sun beat down upon them and Bernardo felt sweat build under his heavy robe. The skin of his forehead burned, but he did not move. Every so often Simón would stop pacing and tilt his face, looking up to the sky. Then he would shake his head and the walking resumed.

Finally, when Bernardo felt as if his thirst would bring him back down to the ground, the old explorer stopped in front of him.

"Can you read?"

"Yes."

"Hebrew? The Torah?"

Bernardo dipped his chin. "Hebrew, yes. A Torah, I have never seen. My grandfather was not able to bring such a thing with him."

"You will train Rafael."

The priest's chin shot up. "Rafael?"

"Yes. He was to be trained by his father. He was to be the rabbi for our people. The accident put an end to the plan. If you study with him, train him, then you will both learn what you need to know."

"Study? How am I to teach him something I do not know?"

"Come with me." Simón turned and walked up the hill.

✡ ✡ ✡

Bernardo stared at the scroll and the books. A Torah? Here in the wilderness? But it was true. Gaspar Castaño had been seeking a place to start over. He had come prepared with all that was needed. It was indeed unfortunate that Rabbi Castaño had fallen from the cliff, the knowledge needed to sustain the ceremonies and teachings dying with the man.

And now he understood Rafael's anger toward him. For the young man had been charged with the safety of the scrolls and manuscripts. The safety of the faith of the people.

Rafael and Consuela stood across from him. Bernardo was surprised to find them waiting outside Simón's house. Was this the plan before he had told the old man the truth? Had all that pacing been his attempt to decide if he would move forward with this?

The young man's arms were tense, as if prepared to snatch the ancient papers away from any harm Bernardo might bestow upon them.

"Have you been studying these?" Maybe Rafael really did know more than Bernardo.

"No." Rafael did not elaborate.

But Simón knew what was needed. "Fray Bernardo. We cannot read. You will teach Rafael. You will study together and you will train him as the rabbi." There was no tone of request or question in the leader's words. "We are so far from the Holy Land. I had hopes that my sons would fulfill the covenant. But now, now they fight the same battle fought by our grandfathers."

"What battle is that?"

Rafael moved forward, stepping between Consuela and Bernardo. He drew his hand across his eyes. "To stay true. That is all we can do."

He turned to face the girl. "Don't you see, Consuela? These men, these Martín de Serranos, they lead us to a way that is not the truth. They deceive us."

Bernardo pictured working day after day next to Rafael, with hostility thick enough to cloud the air. This punishment felt worse than exile. Another thought came to mind. He looked at Simón.

"And what of the children? The circumcisions?"

"We will tell people the truth. That you are not a mohel and have not trained in this process. But the rest of it, you will do what you have been doing." A look of disgust crossed Simón's face. "Deceiving us."

Nineteen

Gabriella

Sunday, April 13 to Monday, April 14

On Sunday evening, as I watched the sun sink over the distant mesa, I thought about the medallion. Rachel Garcia Maria de la Rodrigo y Rivas scared me. Part of me wanted to ask her how she knew about the medallion—was she some kind of witch?—while the other part figured I truly was losing my mind. I could no longer see bright skies or curious prairie dogs—only dust and grime and a lack of the most basic daily comforts. My tight chest warned of a headache caused by unshed tears, but I didn't want to cry anymore.

"Oh honey, there, there." I whispered to myself. I needed someone to wrap strong arms around me and make it all go away. But there was no one and being sarcastic didn't make it any better. I realized I had forsaken the piece of myself that accepted comfort. My mother's cool hand stroking my forehead was enmeshed with the steady squeeze of my father's hand, pressure that could promise comfort but suddenly leave an ache in my shoulder. I could not separate these two feelings. Maybe I was mad at my mother for not protecting me, but I never felt angry with her. Even if I had someone to say "there, there" and pat my back, I knew I would not be able to slip into that bubble of protective empathy.

I held the medallion and studied the figures again. The tree on the emblem was strangely modern. Graphic was the only word that came to mind. Not realistic or Roman or any of the things one would expect on an old coin. Maybe it wasn't old. Maybe someone had put it into my wall recently.

I didn't like the fact that Rachel had told me not to wear it. Magic or not, who did she think she was? Who did she think *I* was? Not special enough to wear it? I wrapped my fingers around the disc. It was warm, like it had been before, an energy pulsing from the very metal itself. As the sun slipped below the horizon and dark spread over the earth, and I settled into my cot, I slipped the chain over my head and let the medallion rest on my chest.

✡ ✡ ✡

My dream companions trudged along the rocky road. There was no wind but puffs of dust swirled off each footstep as we marched on and on. A murmur swept through the line of people. *Hay agua adelante*. Water ahead, was the whisper and the exhausted travelers picked up the pace and the small clouds of dust built into a swirling grit that stung my eyes.

After so many days of red sand and colorless plants, I saw a line of green trees ahead. Cottonwoods. The same trees that lined my creek.

It *was* a river. Not a stream or a creek, but an actual river. No one stopped at the edge—we all pushed forward and filled our mouths, dunked heads of dry twisted hair, immersed our bodies and laughed. I plunged my face into the water and rinsed my eyes.

After everyone was cooled off and the animals were chewing the green grass which grew near the edge of the river, a man I had not seen before rode up on a horse. He was dressed in a suit of armor. Well, not exactly, more like a metal vest and a helmet shaped like a rooster comb. What was a Spanish conquistador doing in my dream?

"*Nos quedaremos por siete dias, ni un dia más.*" We stay here for seven days, not one day more. His tone was a command and the people around me nodded and murmured.

"Why can't we stay here? This is a good place to settle." I heard one woman ask another. "Isn't this what we are looking for?"

"Maybe that is what Oñate told the King, but you know he is looking for more. Riches, or maybe the Seven Cities."

"The cities are just a fable. If Coronado couldn't find them a fool like Oñate can't do it."

"A fool? Why do you call him a fool? You had better watch what you say. The soldiers can easily cut your head off with one of their swords."

I wanted to hear more, but the shouts of children interrupted the conversation and the women hurried off to tend to their young. The name Oñate rang a bell, but I couldn't place it. Talk of kings and heads being chopped off made me sure my dream was some sort of ancient Spanish travelogue. I didn't know enough about Spanish geography to know what river this might be.

I stayed on a rock in the sun, letting the heat dry my wet dress. Examining my clothes I realized I had on several layers, all soaking from my dunk in the river. I peeled off the top layer, a thick linen shirt, and spread it on the rock. Then I removed my shoes, terrible for walking, with thin soles and too many laces. The leather was wet and I massaged the shoe in hope I could loosen the uncomfortable fit before it dried.

"I'll use the tallow on it tonight."

I turned to the deep voice and gasped. It was the man with Andy's eyes.

"You... you... who are you?" He didn't look exactly like Andy. His hair was very dark, tied back with a leather thong. He had a thick beard to match, glistening from his recent dip in the river. His ears stuck out, not like Andy's, which were close to his head. This man's lips were full and moist and my mouth tingled at the thought of kissing him. Even in my dream state I was shocked at this feeling.

He threw back his head and laughed. "Who am I? Did you bang your head on a rock in the river, *mi amor*? Or is it that now we are past the hard part of the journey you turn your eyes to some other man? Come on, my love. We will have plenty of time by this wonderful river. We must go and look through the cart. We need to replenish our supplies, starting with finding something for our next meal. I spoke with Gregario and Catalina. They have a little grain left. If you gather some greens and I find a rabbit who is not wise to the ways of man, we will have a feast tonight."

Gregario and Catalina? Suddenly I knew. Catalina was the woman who had helped me hide. She was my friend and she must be Man-With-Andy's-Eyes' friend too.

Catalina smiled when we walked toward her. She had two small children and a handsome, although haggard, husband.

"Romero. I am glad to see you found Gabriella. I was beginning to worry she had been swept away by the river."

His name was Romero.

Catalina stepped toward me and placed her hand on my arm. "You are pale, Gabriella. I think you should sit." She moved me toward a flat boulder.

Romero crouched in front of me. "Are you sick? I know the journey has been hard. This rest will help you, no?"

"I'm fine. I just..." I didn't know what to say to these people. Unlike the previous dreams, where we had walked in silence, this dream had so much going on.

Catalina interrupted. "Romero, go get us some meat. I will take care of your wife."

I was married to Man-With-Andy's-Eyes.

Bones barked. I jumped off the cot, trying to shake the dream from my head, awake enough to grab her collar before I opened the door. She whined and lunged, but I held on.

The moon was bright enough to make out the white tails of the deer that bounded through the sage.

"You have to stop doing that," I scolded, my heart slowly slipping back into a normal beat. I pulled the straining dog back into the house and groped around for my flashlight and water bottle. I glanced at my watch. 3:30. Way too early to be awake.

Settled back onto my cot, I tried to remember the dream. The medallion rested against my chest, but it was cool to the touch. Last night's heat had fled with the skipping deer.

What had seemed so clear just moments before flitted away like the puffs from the cottonwoods which sailed on the easy breeze. I had learned something about the man with Andy's eyes. Romeo? No, Romero. That was his name. We had a relationship, I was sure of that, but I couldn't find the answers in the haze which clouded my mind. I didn't think I would fall back to sleep, not after the adrenaline rush brought on by Bone's barking, but hours later I woke again.

This time my lips carried the tang of sweet kisses. I didn't move as I savored what I had felt in my dream world—something I hadn't felt in a long time and I was denying I wanted—lips pressed against mine, breath coming in short gasps, and a heart that beat in time to another. Now I remembered. Romero was my husband.

Pulling myself off the cot, I decided that I needed extra caffeine, not the bitter stuff I perked in my blue camp pot, but the real thing served at Three Ravens. I would check Fred Rivas's office. Maybe the mystery of the Martinez family property would be cleared up today.

I needed to get through the day so I could be with Romero tonight.

✡ ✡ ✡

I shouldn't have been surprised to see Andy at the coffeehouse —he told me he went to Three Ravens every day. What surprised me was how my lips stung with desire when I saw him. I still couldn't shake the last vestiges of my dream and the handsome Romero.

Get a grip. Andy was the only person who showed any interest in me at all, so why not just shut up and appreciate his friendship? Well, the only person other than a witch-like old women with dire warnings and owners of coffee shops who obviously felt obligated to take care of me. And five year olds. I felt better thinking about Rosie's smile.

"Hey, Gabriella." Andy nodded to the empty chair, slipping into it before I had a chance to say no-you-can't-join-me-this-morning-I-want-to-be-alone.

"Uh, hi." Bubbly, attractive Ella tried to push her way up as I realized that I really *didn't* want to be alone.

He smiled. "I hear you had an adventure at church."

I groaned over the fact that nothing was secret in a small town.

"Yes, I did. But can I ask you a question?" I didn't want to talk about Rachel and her premonitions right now.

"Sure. Shoot." He sipped his coffee.

"Do you have dreams?"

He laughed and licked his lip. "Sure. I plan to build a little house, adobe and traditional, on a wonderful rise atop a piece of land that I'll suddenly inherit from a long, lost uncle. No, wait, that's your dream, right?"

Great. Andy had decided to make fun of me. "No. I mean real dreams, the kind you have at night when you're asleep. Do you remember them?"

"Oh, *those* dreams. Well, yeah. Sometimes I remember them."

"Am I ever in them?" How stupid! That sounded like I was hitting on this guy who was following me around. Stammering through the hot flush which reached from my toes to my ears, I continued. "That didn't come out right. What I meant was, do you have dreams with people you know in them, only they're not exactly the people you know?"

"I suppose." He didn't laugh at me, but shook his head. "I guess I don't really know what you're trying to ask me."

I stared down at my cup, swirling the last bit of chocolate that had settled in the bottom. Was it time to stop thinking of Andy in terms of some-guy-who-was-confusing-the-hell-out-of-me and go to the this-guy-is-my-friend level? Did I really want to go there with *Andy*? Or was it the memory of Romero's warm lips that drove me on?

"Do you have any ancestors named Romero?"

"Whoa! What does that have to do with the price of onions?" Now Andy's face was filled with confusion.

Better get used to it, buster. New-Ella says what she wants, even if it doesn't really make any sense. "Nothing." I answered. "I was just wondering because, well… see, I had a dream and you, but not you, like maybe an ancestor of yours was in the dream and his name was Romero."

I half expected some snide remark, like *Oh, you're dreaming about me now.*

But Andy looked away. When he turned back, I was surprised by his solemn expression.

"Rachel told you not to wear the medallion, didn't she?"

Never in my wildest imagination had I thought that I would be discussing some sort of voodoo magic as if it were an everyday event. The warning from Rachel I had been able to dismiss as the senile ranting of dementia. The vivid dreams were just that, dreams. But now Andy, this man who had wormed his way into my life and into my strange dreams, was sitting here asking about something which I had kept a secret.

"How—"

"How do I know about the medallion? I'm not magic, Ella. Neither is Rachel. Nathan mentioned it."

"Nathan?" When had I told Nathan about the medallion? I racked my mind. I glanced over my shoulder to see if Nathan was anywhere in the room. No sign of him. "What do you know about the medallion?"

Now it was Andy's turn to remain silent. I recognized the look, one I had seen on Shannon's face, as my daughter worked out an elaborate response to an unwanted question.

"Can I see it?"

I touched my pocket. "I don't have it with me."

Andy stared at my pocket, now covered by my hand. He had experience in recognizing a lie too. But I wasn't ready to share this with him. Not until I understood the meaning of the dreams.

Andy looked up from my hand. I knew and he knew and one of us had to make a move.

No words came to mind and I was stuck.

"Gabriella! I was hoping to find you here. Fred is back. He's in his office right now."

Stuck until Carmen Murch saved the day.

✡ ✡ ✡

"You can't list the property until the deed is clear." Fred Rivas leaned back in his chair and crossed his arms.

"Mr. Dominguez said that shouldn't take long." Dominguez and Marconi, LTD had been locked and dark once again when I hurried to Rivas's office. No chance of an update today.

"No, I can't imagine it would. In the meantime we can visit some comparable properties that will help set a price."

"Isn't there a standard? A per acre thing or something?" Couldn't we make this simple?

"Not really. Every thing is so different, with water and road access and easements." He tapped a finger on the map he had spread in front of him. "Your parcel is locked in between the others, that will make it difficult to sell. You'll have to get an easement from Mark." He moved his fingers to the highway. "Or spend some money building an access road here. You need county approval, permits, and a culvert."

I leaned in and looked at the map. Why Mark? What about Jeff?

"I don't really know my cousins."

Fred was quiet. I could hear his breath slip in and out of his long nose, his lips pressed tight.

"I think you should visit my grandmother."

"Your grandmother?" Of course the crazy old woman was involved. I didn't know what it was about her that made the hair on the back of my neck tingle like the hackles of an angry dog.

"Yes. There isn't much we can do until the paperwork comes through and she—"

"Hold on. I'm not going to sit around and wait for paperwork. How convenient that Mark doesn't want me to sell and he leaves for a month. And Jeff? No one will even give me his phone number. Now Mr. Dominguez, LTD has flown the coop. What about Marconi? Where is he? Why can't he help me get this mystery paperwork completed?"

"I'm sorry. I would be frustrated too. But no one is against you in this, Miss Martinez. Mark had this trip planned for a year. I can give you Jeff's phone number, but he… let's just say he won't do you much good. Tends to follow Mark's lead."

"What about Mr. Marconi?"

Fred covered his mouth with his hand, but not fast enough to hide his smile.

"Mr. Marconi is a Mrs. Or I should say, was a Mrs. Mrs. Dominguez, to be exact."

"She's dead?"

"No, not dead. Divorced."

"Why is she still on the letterhead? When did this happen?"

"Ten years ago."

So much for thinking Joel Dominguez was going to be any help. This guy was stuck in the past. Not just antique desks and telephones, but a marriage he wasn't giving up.

Would I be like that?

Twenty

Fray Bernardo Castaño

Pueblo Lindo, Spring 1607

"**I** do this because Simón demands it, but don't think for a minute that I will forget about my cousin. Stay away from Consuela." Rafael shook his fist at Bernardo.

The two men had spread the scroll on the wood table. It was obvious to Bernardo that care had been taken not to let moisture or sun damage this treasure.

"You speak out of turn. I have only respect for the girl. She cooks my meals and takes care of my household. How would I stay away from someone who is close every day?" Bernardo had not approached Consuela again, although he dreamed every night of her kiss.

"You know what I mean."

Bernardo rubbed his throbbing jaw. He wanted to tell Simón— partially to make him aware of the conflict between them, but even more to gain the leader's protection. The anger Bernardo had felt on the night of the beating, when his thoughts flew to thinking of killing Rafael, had dimmed. He knew if they fought again, the same thing would happen, just as it always happened. Bernardo was not a fighter. Rafael would walk away triumphant, while he would be crushed to a whimpering heap of manure.

No, the way to fight this young man was with his brains. He had to be clever enough to make Rafael want the false priest as the husband of his cousin.

If she would have him.

"Going through the rituals, moving your hands, your tongue, your head in a certain pattern, these things have no meaning if your heart is not true. Can you say that this is so with you, Rafael? You have accused me of being false, but what part of God's instructions say that you should beat a man if he varies from your ideas?"

The young man glared. "Show me the Torah from which you speak. For yours are lessons I have not heard."

Time to move back to the real lessons. "So Sukkot is not only a time for celebration. This line tells of the harvest, much like the celebration Jimuta led." Bernardo didn't really want to bring up anything related to that night. "By this we know that the east brings us new possibilities."

Rafael would not be steered clear of the subject, now that Bernardo had brought it up. "You consider yourself just. How can you when you are a coward?"

"Can you not see that God himself has sent me to this place?"

"And I could say that God himself was responsible for my father's death. That he has sent me here as well."

"All the more reason for us to continue learning." Bernardo returned to the scroll.

And so the lessons continued. Simón insisted that the men work nearly all day, every day. When spring came he had no doubt that soldiers and settlers would seek their fortunes in the north and they must be prepared.

Rafael was a quick study. He learned to read and write with no trouble. But his interpretations of the writings were tainted by his untamed emotions. Bernardo decided it was best to overlook their disagreements—after all, he was not an expert in these matters— and try to reduce his conflict with the young man. Even if only for the sake of Consuela.

No sooner had he resolved himself to this issue than Jimuta approached him.

"We must talk. You will come sit with me."

"Of course." Bernardo followed the leader to a flat rock near the river. He didn't know the native custom for asking a man for his daughter's hand, but maybe Jimuta had some inkling of his intentions.

"What must my people do so they no longer have to become such a bad thing each week, these sinners you tell us about? We want to honor and respect this man you talk of, Jesus, but we do not understand your ways. Why is he not happy if we dance for him? Does he require a sacrifice?"

Bernardo didn't know what to say, remembering his agreement that Jimuta's people merely had to pretend to convert. The chief was trying, that much was clear. The natives had an uncomplicated life, full of love and work. It was difficult for them to survive in this land and he felt guilty asking them to worship Jesus when he himself did not. How did he explain this to Jimuta?

"Jesus will be happy if you come to mass and you bow your head and you learn the prayers. That is all he asks." Bernardo would not preach sin or confession to these people any more.

✡ ✡ ✡

The first signs of spring had come to the canyon, the river rushing as the snow melted, the sky filled with fluffy clouds, rather than the gray overcast of winter, and a green veil of tiny sprouts covered the red earth. Bernardo marveled at the minute buds bursting from even the rockiest landscape. The sagebrush bloomed a ghostly blue-green and the pines were tipped with bright needles.

Consuela was like a songbird. Bernardo heard her singing as she walked along the trail and his fingers tingled. Saliva filled his mouth and he had to lick his lips and swallow so as not to look like a gasping fish when she arrived each morning.

"Walk with me today?" he asked when they had finished the bowls of soup. "I am headed up the canyon."

"I promised Maria I would help her this morning. Three little ones! She needs me."

"I see." Bernardo wondered how other men did this. He wanted to be alone with her somewhere that would take her mind off work and maybe, just maybe, she would see him as something other than a false priest or inefficient rabbi.

She smiled at him. "How about later? After you and Rafael have finished your work? I need to go down to the lower fields and change the water. You could help."

His heart pounded. He drew in his breath and tried his best to speak, but the words came out like those of a tongue-tied boy. "Yes, I would like that."

✡ ✡ ✡

Rafael thwarted Bernardo's plans. The young man greeted him at the top of the trail.

"I have invited Tío Simón to come today. I want to show him that I am ready to take over."

"Take over?"

"Even a fool like you can see that I know more than you do. I have studied at night, while you saunter back down to your room and smoke that ugly pipe. These are my people and I am ready to lead them."

"Where do you plan on leading them?"

"Your humor is as lame as an old donkey. Lead them spiritually."

Bernardo had no answer for the pompous Rafael. The young man was correct. Both had learned at the same time. Bernardo's only advantage had been that he knew how to read and had heard the lessons once already, years ago when he sat outside the window and listened to what Marcus was learning.

"Now that I can take over, you can leave." Rafael's words pulled Bernardo from his thoughts.

"Leave? Where would I go?"

"What do I care? I just know that I want you gone."

"What of the church below? What of the Catholics? Will you also be the priest?"

"No. I would not be so cavalier about my faith. We will deal with that in some other way. Jimuta is tired of the priests as well. He no longer wishes to be host to those who do not respect his position."

"What will he do? Will he fight off the soldiers who come?"

Rafael shrugged, but Bernardo had the feeling this was the plan.

✡ ✡ ✡

"The boy will continue to learn, even as he leads. We are used to making things work."

Simón's words echoed in his head as Bernardo rolled the blanket tight around his belongings. The deer-skin moccasins, the woven prayer shawl, the leather book. He didn't leave with much more than he had when he arrived. Esclavo shifted and snorted outside the door. His horse was ready for adventure, even if Bernardo felt his heart turn into a heavy stone—one that pressed down into his body and left his stomach churning.

Both Simón and Jimuta had agreed with Rafael.

"I think you should consider traveling back to Mexico City. Carry the word of the need for more Jews to your Brothers. If we are to make progress, we need to establish a community here." Simón seemed to believe that Bernardo would be capable of completing this mission—that the priest was brave enough to battle the wilds of travel and the questioning his father would rain down upon the wrong son. He wished he knew where Marcus and Romero were. Maybe if the three traveled together they could go home.

Bernardo lifted the rolled blanket and carried it out to his horse. As he strapped it to the gelding's saddle he looked around. Consuela had delivered his breakfast and left without a word. Had he been wrong in thinking that the girl felt the same stir in her soul as he did?

No one was here to see him off. The Jews had said their goodbyes the day before, if telling him he must leave immediately could be construed in such a way. Jimuta had come by as well, presenting him with a small piece of turquoise, perfectly round and smooth. "Hold it in your hand and you will breathe easy," the chief said, as if he knew that the thought of his daughter had kept Bernardo from breathing for weeks.

"Well, *adios* and *gracias*," he said to no one. He glanced at the adobe house which had been his home for nearly a year before swinging up into the saddle. Esclavo shook his head with a jingle of the bit and bridle and the two set off down the trail.

Bernardo did not look at the trees or the irregular fields of vegetables. He did not look at the river or the sky. He stared at the gelding's soft ears, the gnats swarming already. He had not figured out where he would go, but the first part of the journey was the same. Taos or Mexico City, a man must travel south and follow the Rio Grande.

Suddenly Esclavo snorted and stopped, staring off into the trees. Bernardo tensed—was he to be attacked by a bear so soon in his journey?

But it was not a bear. The figure that slipped out of the forest was slim and light on her feet. She wore a familiar leather hat—one that covered her shining hair. She carried a deerskin pack upon her back and when she saw Bernardo looking at her, she raised a finger to her lips. Without a word she approached him. When she stood next to the horse she reached out her hand and nodded to the spot on the horses hindquarters.

In that moment, a flash as short as the sting of a bee and as long as the birth of the sun, Bernardo understood. He reached for her hand and pulled her on to the horse. She adjusted the leather pack and wrapped her arms around his waist.

Esclavo needed no signal. He started down the trail.

Twenty-one
Gabriella
Los Brazos, New Mexico
Friday, April 18

I followed the directions on the slip of yellow paper Fred had given me, heading up Highway 84 and looking for the signs. I still wasn't happy about waiting to sell the property and I wasn't happy about visiting his grandmother. But something—curiosity?—made me agree with his suggestion.

Right turn at the deserted roadhouse next to the nursery - Tierra del Sol. People drove fast on Highway 84 so slowing down to peer at each deserted building was suicidal. The third time I pulled over to let someone pass a yellow tow truck pulled up behind me.

Andy hopped out and walked to my car. The whole thing had some weird pulled-over-by-a-cop feel to it. Maybe because he had flashing yellow lights or maybe because I was anxious about seeing him. I rolled down my window.

"Hey." There was a moment when I was sure he was going to lean in and kiss me. I smelled Romero's musky odor and felt his soft touch. Instead he—Andy, not Romero—motioned to the passenger door and walked around the car. I popped the locks.

"Where's your sidekick?" He slid into the seat.

I squeezed the steering wheel, realized it was silly to be clutching it still and pushed my hands down into my lap. "She's okay staying at the house now." She seemed to think it was home, even if I was having trouble adjusting. "I'm headed to—" Why did I feel obligated to explain myself? "An appointment."

"Oh." He paused. "I won't take up your time then. I saw you sitting here and I wanted to make sure everything was okay."

As he reached for the door handle I leaned forward and touched his shoulder. He turned and looked at me.

"Ella," he whispered.

That was all it took for Brave-Ella to kiss him. A lingering kiss with lips as soft as butterflies. Then a deeper kiss that said we-need-to-figure-out-where-we're-going-with-this. I knew I wasn't kissing Andy, not by any stretch, but I couldn't stop myself. It felt just like my dreams of kissing Romero.

He pulled away. "We need to talk."

You don't even know the half of it. This was a mistake, kissing one man while pretending he was someone else. Someone who wasn't even real.

I nodded. "I know. But I'm supposed to meet Rachel—" I glanced at the clock on the dashboard, "—ten minutes ago."

He smiled. That wonderful toothy glowing look that followed the creases in his cheeks up to those green eyes. Eyes that sparkled at me. "It would not do for you to flake on Rachel García Maria de la Rodrigo y Rivas."

"I see you know her well." I stroked his cheek with the tip of my finger. What was I doing? "Can you come over tonight?"

He didn't answer, then shook his head. "Not tonight. What about tomorrow night?"

I nodded and he jumped from the car.

"Be careful with *la bruja*."

The witch? I watched as he hopped into his truck and sped up the highway. Had this just happened? Had I kissed this man? Run my finger provocatively down his cheek? My stalker? Vicki was right, I was going crazy. With lust.

Damn it all! I pounded the steering wheel. *Just turn the car around and go home.* The last thing I wanted to do was go visit a witch. I was bewitched enough as it was.

The road to Los Brazos was just up ahead, and I made the turn following Alfred's neatly printed instruction. A few minutes later I turned right and drove up the gravel road

Why was I afraid to think about Andy? I had kissed him, made a move. It was important I think about this.

I turned left. This route was narrow, but well maintained, until the third right turn. There the granite cliffs loomed overhead and the road narrowed. I turned and turned again, trees closing in, winding into the thick forest which grew at the base of the mountain. If I didn't concentrate I would get lost. *I kissed a man, I kissed a man. I invited him to my house with sex on my mind.*

I finally reached Rachel's house.

It had been built for an elf, with a tiny overgrown path leading to the front door, and a low roof. Her house had the same crazy additions as my house, rooms poking off each side, some of wood, others made of stone. The front porch was filled with cardboard boxes, chairs and an old refrigerator. Rachel leaned on a sagging screen door, waving to me the minute I drove up.

She looked different today. Her hair fell loose on her shoulders, the long waves carried the memory of the black shine of youth smudged by the gray which said wisdom rather than age. She was dressed in her long skirt, but the polyester was gone. A cotton embroidered blouse and a beaded necklace topped off her outfit.

I walked up the narrow path and a scowl covered her wrinkled face. A wave of nausea swam down to my stomach. I reached up and tapped the medallion hidden under my shirt. Not that it would be hidden from the old woman, but something drove me to wear it. In spite of my earlier reactions, I felt comfort from the thing.

"*Hola, Señora*—" I didn't know which part of her long name to address her by. Rivas or Rodrigo?

Without returning my greeting she motioned me to follow her into the house. She led me through a poorly lit room. There were couches pushed against every wall and blankets covering the windows. The smell of mildew and dust pushed up into my nose, as I followed her, peering through the dim light at all the furniture and piles of books and newspapers. The sight of a boom box on top of an old Victrola made me smile, but the whole thing was nerve racking. I couldn't get a handle on this woman. In one corner, next to an armoire that reached clear to the low ceiling, was a huge TV, the old kind with a hunched back, balanced on a heavy wooden table. Videos and DVDs were scattered around it.

Off to one side of the hulking television shelves made from planks balanced on twin towers of cement blocks were covered with photographs—ornate frames dusty with age, snapshots taped to the edges, some leaning against the adobe wall, some leaning against each other. Smiling brides, solemn grandmothers, wrinkled red newborns, children in soccer uniforms, their grins revealing missing front teeth. I thought I recognized Fred in one or two.

Rachel led me to the kitchen. White lace curtains draped the window and a wooden table nearly filled the room. Sun filtered in, making it more cheery than the living room. Stacks of magazines, books, fabric, yarn, dishes, photo albums and papers covered nearly every surface. An oversized white refrigerator awkwardly placed next to the table dominated the rest of the room. A computer was perched on a tiny desk in one corner, the screen projecting the blue glow of an email account.

She waved her hand at two delicate tea cups with matching saucers arranged on the table, two spaces cleared apparently by pushing things aside, then gestured to the chair.

"*Gracias,*" I said, as I sat. This was going to be hard. Why had I thought I could have lunch with someone who didn't speak English? How would I learn anything about the property if I couldn't even ask a simple question?

"*Que...* ?" I slipped the parcel map out of my purse and set it on the table. I should have pressured Fred into telling me more. What did his grandmother have to do with my family?

The old woman poured hot water over a mixture of what looked like bark and leaves in my cup. She set the pot on a folded towel and picked up the map. "I speak English."

My jaw dropped.

"I just keep others from knowing. Maintains my privacy."

What sort of privacy did she need maintained? I thought about Fred. "Even your own family?"

"My generation knew, but they're all gone now."

I was silent, suddenly aware that I really hadn't taken the time to find out anything about her. Endless-Name. Or maybe Private-Woman. I didn't know what her Indian name would be yet because she was a mystery.

"Give me the medallion."

Fred had set me up. This wasn't about the property at all. I squeezed my hands in my lap to keep from reaching for the medallion.

"Why are you so interested in it?"

Rachel reached inside her blouse and pulled on a thick cord. A bundle of something—one of those native leather sacks—hung from the end. She put it on the table and slowly untied the cord.

She held up a medallion. Sunlight glinted off the surface and flickered across my face, piercing my right eye before I could tell if it was like the one hidden around my neck.

I gasped and closed my eyes. This didn't feel like sunlight. It felt like a hot poker. I pressed my hand on my eye and tried to catch my breath.

"You felt pain?" I heard her chair scrape across the floor. Within seconds she was pressing a cold rag against my eye.

"I don't know what happened. It's like the sun just went straight to my brain." The cold helped ease the throbbing. I opened my eyes and looked at her medallion, sitting innocently in the center of the table. It was like mine, the same tree with the funny leaves. The surface of the gold was not shiny enough to reflect anything. Had Rachel sent the sun into my eye on purpose? "What is this? Why do you have the same medallion?"

"We will talk about it. But first we cook."

"Cook?" I found it hard to believe she was suggesting we cook after what just happened. My heart was pounding and something was telling me to leave this place, run to my car, and speed down the narrow road in a spray of gravel. Now, before something more than my eye was hurt. But I was like Gretel, stuck in the middle of a deep, dark woods, unable to resist the witch who insisted I try a piece of her candy house.

"I need you to help me. It's Friday. The day I make *pan trenzado.*"

She was just an old woman asking for help, not a witch or a shaman or capable of magic. Then I looked at her medallion again. This woman could tell me something, but somehow I didn't think I was going to get any answers without paying some sort of price.

"Bread?"

"*Sí.* You know it?" She leaned close and peered into my eyes.

She was so intense. One minute scowling, the next creeping into my personal space.

"No." I didn't add that one of my promises to myself was I would never be anyone's kitchen slave again.

"It's easy. You'll learn. It's in your blood, baking the special bread." She turned and pulled out bowls and bags of ingredients, flour, yeast, seeds.

My medallion settled against my chest and it comforted me. At least I hadn't caved to *that* demand, even if I was forsaking my self to her other requests. She wouldn't get her hands on this necklace.

Rachel measured out water, sugar and butter into a large blue bowl, threw in a pinch of salt and handed it to me. "Mix this."

While I sat and stirred she sifted flour into a second bowl, then poured liquid from a measuring cup into the middle.

She noticed my curious stare. "Yeast." She took the blue bowl from me and slowly stirred this mixture into the flour, then added some eggs.

"Now we knead." She pulled a wooden cutting board from beside the stove and set it on the table, then sprinkled it with flour.

I watched her and tried to push and pull the sticky dough just as she did. After several minutes of this she put it back in the bowl and covered it with a red gingham dishcloth.

"Now it rises."

"Can we talk about the medallion while it does that?" Surely I had paid my dues by now.

"There is more work."

I chopped vegetables and mixed the various bowls she handed me. At one point I asked her what all this food was for—tamales, enchiladas, beans—but she ignored me. The smells of roasting chili, spicy tomatoes and peppers and the yeasty bread surrounded us and I began to relax.

"How long have you lived here?" I tried to keep the conversation going.

"All my life."

She told me about Alfredo, as she called Fred. What a good grandson he was, where he went to school. I grew impatient. She might speak English, but she sure wasn't saying what I needed to hear. She instructed me in how to wrap a tamale, but she didn't tell me any of her secrets. Finally, she placed the bowl of bread dough on the table.

"Watch me, then you will try." She punched the dough lightly, removed some of it, and split it into three portions, which she pinched into long logs. Laying them side by side, she rolled them into a twisted loaf.

I had seen this before. I racked my mind, but I couldn't remember where.

Rachel pulled out another glob of dough and set it in front of me. "Now you."

It was harder than it looked, but I managed to make a lumpy braided loaf. She reached over and pinched the ends a little tighter.

"Not bad."

Soon the loaves were lined up like babies in a hospital nursery. And like babies, Rachel covered them with a cloth.

I glanced at my watch. Two fifteen. "Rachel? Do you think we could talk about the medallion now? I have to go soon. I left my dog alone at the house."

She frowned. "This cannot be rushed."

Did she mean her bread or telling me about the medallion? Or could I still hope she had something to say about the Martinez property?

I should question her, insist she tell me what I wanted to know. Needed to know. "I really need to hear—"

Suddenly I was six years old, seated at the table with my parents.

"Children should be seen and not heard." The first time my father said those words I had looked around for the children. I couldn't hear them, but hadn't he just said I could see them?

"Where are they?" I asked my mother after my father tossed his napkin onto the table and headed for the television.

"Where are who?" She picked up plates and carried them to the sink.

"Those children. The ones we can't hear. Daddy said they could be seen but I can't find them. Why won't they play with me?"

My mother set the dishes down and pulled me to her. "Oh Sweetie. Daddy just means you shouldn't interrupt when he— grownups—are talking."

"I didn't, Mommy. I waited until he took a bite of potatoes. It's not polite to talk with your mouth full."

"You ask so many questions. That's all. Maybe save them until later."

"Next time bring your dog." Rachel's words snapped me back to the present.

It hit me then. Rachel was lonely and withholding information was her way of making sure I came back. I sighed and rubbed my forehead. I couldn't ask her for what I needed.

She walked over to the tiny stove and opened the door. Coals filled its belly. She pinched off a bit of the dough and threw it into the fire.

I would politely thank this eccentric old woman and be on my way. But before I spoke she said it was time for us to eat. Just because there was no hope any information was forthcoming, that didn't mean I needed to pass on the wonderful food. I settled back while Rachel placed a warm tortilla and a bowl of beans on the table.

"Have you been back to the church?" she asked.

"No. I… I'm not really very religious." I dipped a bit of the warm tortilla into the beans as she did, using it as a scoop. Delicious. "It was nice, but I don't think I'll be going again."

"I have gone all my life. It is the thing people do in this town. But it wasn't always like that."

I reached for another tortilla.

"There used to be a school here, Presbyterian. They had a service in the schoolhouse on Sunday morning. And Bible study for adults on Wednesday nights."

"Are you Presbyterian?" I realized I had assumed all hispanic women in this area were Catholic, Rachel included.

"No, no. But I like to try new things. Are you Catholic?"

I shrugged. "My parents went to a Presbyterian church. Nathan said it was okay to go to Santo Niño even if I wasn't Catholic." Maybe she was mad I had been at Mass.

There was no way to find out just what Rachel was talking about. This woman did things on her own time. She turned to the sink and rinsed her cup, then poured more tea before turning and waving the pot toward me.

"No thanks," I covered the cup with my hand.

"It's a shame," she mumbled. "Jonas was so spiritual, he had such a good heart. Did you talk much with Rueben?"

It took me a minute to figure out who she was talking about. "Grandpa Martinez?" It occurred to me that Rachel must have known my grandfather. I stopped to figure out the ages. He would have been a hundred and eleven years old if he was still alive. It was hard to tell her age. Her wrinkles and stooped back had initially made me think she was at least ninety. She had a lot of energy and I supposed she had a sharp mind, although she hadn't talked with me enough to be sure. Maybe eighty?

"I did spend a lot of time with my grandfather when I was quite young. We would go visit and he would take me for walks. But he died when I was twelve. Did you know him?"

"There is a story—it is about Joseph."

"My great-grandfather was Jonas."

She shook her head. "No, this story is from the Bible. You know of Joseph? The favorite child of Jacob?"

"Not really. Is he the one with the coat of many colors?"

"Listen. So Joseph, he had many dreams and he could see what they meant."

She knew. Somehow she knew.

"So Pharaoh has these dreams, and he doesn't know what they mean. He calls on Joseph, who just happened to be residing in his dungeon at the time, and tells him about his dream. Seven fat cows, seven emaciated cows. Seven withered ears of corn and seven fat ears. All consuming each other. Joseph tells Pharaoh what his dream means. Pharaoh is so grateful he gives Joseph a place on his, oh, council, I guess. Time passes and something brings Joseph's brothers to the city."

She paused. "I forgot to tell you Joseph didn't get along with his brothers. Anyway, he was kind of a spoiled young thing and they didn't like him, but now he has changed and they have changed as well. They come and live near him and everything is good for awhile. Lots of crops and children and they decide maybe this is the promised land. But it wasn't. That pharaoh couldn't live forever and a new one didn't like them so much and they were exiled again."

She stopped and looked at me. I forced a smile, because I really had no clue what the point of her story might be. She seemed to be waiting for me to say something.

"That story, it's from the Bible?"

"Did your grandfather ever tell you such a story?"

"I don't remember anything like it. He didn't really talk about religion much."

She stared at me to the point that I had to turn away. Was this about my dreams or just the demented story of a crazy old woman?

"Ah!" She cried out. "The bread."

She jumped from the table. I stood to help, but she waved me back.

She pulled the twisted loaves from the oven and set the warm bread on the table.

"They're so pretty." I leaned forward and inhaled. "They smell wonderful."

I straightened and the medallion swung back to my chest and hit me like it weighed five hundred pounds, knocking the air out of my lungs. A vision flashed in my head.

I was twelve. Leslie Morganstein had invited me to dinner. It was a special dinner, Sabbath. I pictured Mrs. Morganstein coming to the table with the loaves of bread. Special Hebrew prayers. I had bowed my head and listened.

I knew what these loaves Rachel had baked—we had baked—were. "These are—"

Rachel interrupted me as she brushed her hands over her apron. "Now we are ready for the weekend."

Was Rachel Jewish? I was pretty sure she hadn't actually said she was Catholic, only that she wasn't Presbyterian. But before I could ask her to explain, she went out into the yard.

"Come." She called over her shoulder.

Long resolved to do whatever this woman asked, I followed her. She walked down a winding path to the creek which ran behind her house. The yard had been cleared to the edges of the tall ponderosa pines standing guard. Next to the creek two chairs and an old iron table perched on a flat rock. Ceramic pots with flowers circled the spot, making it feel like a sanctuary.

"Sit." Rachel took one chair and I sat in the other.

She leaned forward. "I need to know more about you before we talk. Did your grandfather ever talk to you about the family? I'm not sure he knew."

"Knew what?" I reached up and squeezed the golden disc around my neck. *Tell me what to ask.* "Was my grandfather a member of a cult?"

Laughter spilled from deep down in her chest. Tears rolled down her cheeks and she began to cough.

Finally she stopped, wiping her face with the back of her hand. "I guess some might call it a cult. It has been called many things."

"What is *it*?" I was tired of everyone beating around the bush, glancing at each other over my shoulders or behind my back, hiding something from me. Tired of holding back my questions.

"The medallion is the symbol of the *Fraternidad de Creyentes* - the Brotherhood of Believers. It is very old."

A secret brotherhood? I felt like Zorro had swept into the clearing. Maybe this was one of my crazy dreams and I had completely lost touch with reality. If you slipped into the black hole who's to say you even knew you were there. I pinched my thigh. It hurt, but did that mean I was awake? "Who are they, this Brotherhood?"

"They are a very old Brotherhood. From Spain. Probably the twelfth century. I don't know how much Spanish history you know, but Spain, it was many things. Home to the Romans, the Moors, to the Jews, to Christians and Catholics who fought the others as well as themselves. Filled with civil wars. Brothers who were kings fighting each other." She brushed imaginary crumbs from the rusty surface of the table.

"But your story, and it is my story too, begins hundreds of years ago, long before the Spanish Inquisition. That is when anyone who was not Catholic was forced to convert, but it was not the first time the Jews were in danger of losing everything. The Brotherhood was a way for the Jews to keep safe and a way for them to maintain their hard-earned wealth. They converted on the outside, but kept their beliefs in secret."

"The Jews?"

"Yes. You are Jewish, my daughter. Just like me."

I smiled. Rachel was confused. "No. My grandfather's family was Presbyterian."

Rachel reached forward and touched the medallion. "Take it off."

I slipped it from my neck, but when I held it out to her, she shook her head.

"What do you see?"

I studied the tree. It looked just as it had the hundred other times I had stared at it. A strange tree, with odd leaves. Then I saw it.

Not a tree. Not a trunk or branches. Not a shield or feathers.

A six-sided star. How could I have missed it?

"This belonged to your ancestors. You found it in the house, didn't you? Where was it?"

"It was in the wall, grouted in behind the stones."

She nodded. "The Martínez family, the Lunas, the Espinosas, Ríos, Trujillos and many more, they came to New Spain early on. Not with Columbus, but not too long after that. Many of them migrated to New Mexico when the inquisition came to New Spain. They had not run far enough. They ended up living near Taos. Still they kept their religion a secret. They pretended to be Catholic for many years."

My dream. All the people walking along the rocky road. Gregario and Katalina. They were migrating into New Mexico.

Another thought struck me. Romero was related to me, not Andy. But they looked alike, so Andy had to be related to him too.

Had I kissed my own cousin?

Rachel continued. "Somewhere along the line, I don't know if it was Jonas or even earlier than that, they switched to being Presbyterian. Easier to hide and this place was no longer strictly Catholic. Jonas was a circuit preacher all right. A circuit rabbi."

Why would my father be so fanatic about Jesus if he was Jewish? None of this made any sense at all. "But what about you? Where do you fit in?"

"My family, Rodrigo, we were also part of the Brotherhood."

"But you go to mass." I had watched her kneel and cross herself. If she was Jewish, and believed, why would she do those things?

"Yes."

"So what about God?" The words came out unplanned, bringing to mind the pressure of my father's fingers. Although I denied my emotions for years this memory had stayed twisted into one ball of confusion. God and pain and my father's displeasure. Only now, puzzling over what Rachel was telling me did I have a sense of a different God.

She looked up. "You should go now. It will be sundown soon. Jews must not drive during the Sabbath."

"But you're saying I'm Jewish and that can't be right. Someone would have known. My grandfather, he wasn't Jewish." Maybe that was why she had asked about Reuben, she knew something. "Did you know him? Was he Jewish?"

"We can talk another time." She rose from the chair and hobbled back to the house, her stiff back sending the message that I would have to save my questions for another day. I would have to be seen and not heard once more. My stomach churned, the acid moving into my throat.

I wanted to argue that I wasn't Jewish any more than I was Catholic or Presbyterian. I also had about a million more questions about this whole Brotherhood thing. Maybe she really was a witch, trying to cast some sort of spell on me by making me believe in magic medallions and Spanish Jews. Maybe she was channeling my father. In any case, she hadn't answered my question about Reuben or told me what I wanted to know. Working hard to keep the anger off my face, I silently cursed Fred Rivas and wished I had never come to see his grandmother.

There had to be someone I could ask. Maybe my cousin knew about this. But my father was a believer in Christ, that much I knew for certain.

Twenty-Two
Consuela Castaño Espejo
Taos, 1680

Galit Antonio de Espejo was not her son's real name. Years ago Bernardo, on his deathbed, had attempted to explain things to their son but his words only added to the young man's confusion.

"It was a time when the Brotherhood was not strong. They lost the intensity of keeping our secrets due to false comfort. No one thought the Holy Office of the Inquisition in Mexico would follow through with the punishments they handed out. Even when men grew wary and began to explore new places to live, they sent me away with a name which was that of a known converso.

"Martín de la Serrano." Galit had heard this part of the story before. Her husband didn't remember that his children had grown up with these tales.

Bernardo shook his head. "No. That name was for my brother. In my role as a priest, I used the name Castaño. Little did I know that I would soon meet the real Castaño, well, his brother anyway. And your mother, a real Castaño as well. When I married her we took the name Espejo."

Consuela had noticed the deep sigh move through her son's chest, but she had not guessed what Bernardo's final story would lead to.

As a young man Galit had been ready to accept his destiny. In 1649 he changed his surname back to Martín de la Serrano. Now, at fifty-one, with new fears of the uprising natives, added to the old worries from the times of the Inquisition, she knew he was not so sure. To add to his concerns, last night she had revealed yet another name. But with the way things were going, Consuela knew she would not have another chance to tell him.

"Things were very complicated in Spain. Even in the years before the Inquisition. Your many-times-great grandfather had already changed his name. Galit Marciano. That was his true name. But that was the name of a *judio*, so he became Francisco Martín de la Serrano. Father Martín de la Serrano." She pressed her hand to Galit's arm, her frail fingers barely making a dent in the light cotton of his shirt.

"Where did Papa get the name Espejo?"

"That was my idea. I liked the idea of *the mirror* as our name because we were living a dual life. The one we presented to the world, to the Catholics and the government, and the one we truly lived. When we married it seemed easy enough to change it." Consuela looked off and smiled, she always did when she thinking of Bernardo. "Your father hated the idea. He felt robbed of his true identity. When he was a young man he was angry that he couldn't be who he really was. As he grew older he decided he didn't know who he really was. He accused the Brotherhood of changing history."

"So if I am to be true to my roots, I am Galit Marciano?"

She nodded.

Her son told her that to bring the old name back now was poor timing. There was talk of an Indian revolt. The Spanish would be distracted, but they would also be looking for traitors. Martín de la Serrano seemed a better choice. Although his father had not been known by this name, his uncles had been well known and respected, Marcus, as a famous explorer and Romero as a wealthy land owner. Consuela could only hope he had made the right decision.

In late July the political pressure rose. It had been five years since the idiot Treviño had imprisoned all the medicine men. The Tewa warriors—who had stormed the governor's palace and terrified Treviño into releasing the native priests—had not disappeared. The fact that several medicine men had already been executed didn't help. The vibrant native, Popé, had suffered during his imprisonment and he would not be easily silenced. Galit questioned Consuela as she kept ties to her native cousins, but she would not reveal anything, insisting her people were not inclined to battles.

Her son had his own opinion. "We should go south. Things could get bad and we are isolated here. We will travel as colonists. Catholics."

She could not survive the journey. Now, at eighty-nine, she still walked throughout Taos, leaning on a gnarled stick and sitting often. Age did not stop her from keeping the Hebrew traditions strong. She gathered her grandchildren close, teaching them the old ways.

A choking cough kept her from sleep each night. Her lungs would not last out the year. But even these things would not have stopped her from the journey. She had never been south. Born in Pueblo Lindo, the journey to Taos was her only adventure. The thought of mingling with so many Catholics, as well as men who still hated the Jews, was more than she would be able to bear.

✡ ✡ ✡

On July 30, 1680 Galit received a message from Governor Antonia de Oermín. He was assigned to travel down to Santo Domingo as a messenger. He was too old for fighting, but the governor wanted information from this northeastern settlement. Galit suspected he had been selected because of his mother's native ties.

Consuela watched as Fadrique, his youngest son, saddled up his father's horse. "I will go with you Papa."

Galit smiled at the twelve-year old. "I wish you could, *Hijo*. But I need someone to stay here with *Madre* and *Abuela*."

"The others are here." Fadrique turned and spit. "No one listens to me anyway."

Galit studied the boy. "Come sit with me, *Hijo*."

Consuela held her tongue. She knew what her son was going to do and there was nothing she could say that would stop the explosion which would soon rain upon her and her grandson.

When Galit started to explain the history of the Brotherhood and how the family had come to live in Taos, Rique interrupted.

"I know all that Papa. *Abuela* told me."

Galit smiled, but she heard his anger surged into his throat, leaving his voice tight. "Your grandmother has told you about the medallion?"

"*Sí*. The one that she wears will come to me. I know that yours goes to Juan."

Galit glanced at her. She saw thunder gather in his brow. His oldest son, Juan, had trained as a priest. It was important to keep a foot in the door of the church. Juan would replace Galit's brother, Thomás, who currently served as Fray Espejo of Taos.

She hoped he realized that Fadrique was different. He should wear the medallion. She wanted to explain to Galit that she saw something in him. Something special.

"Then it is all the more important you stay here to protect your grandmother and your mother." Her son stood and left them without looking her way.

Thirty minutes later Galit said his goodbyes to his wife, his mother, and his children. As he rode off Consuela felt a pain in her throat. It wasn't right that a man should abandon his family when the future was filled with uncertainty.

But the future of the Jews had always been uncertain.

Twenty-three

Gabriella

Saturday, April 19 to Sunday, April 20

I was running, my heart pounded and I didn't dare look behind me. Screams everywhere, yet no familiar faces. Catalina wasn't here to save me, to lead me to a safe place. Where was Romero?

I slipped behind a boulder and tried to find him. The spear came from above, piercing my shoulder. It should have hurt more than it did. Then it struck me again.

"Arooo."

I woke up as the spear struck a third time. Deep sad eyes stared at me from three inches away.

"Arooo," Bones moaned again and pawed my shoulder.

"Uhhhhhh." I closed my eyes at the pain of a headache. The dog's mournful whine, a sound only a hound can make, was worse than the spear of my dream. I struggled off the cot and opened the door, propping it with a rock. Bones ran out and relieved her bladder.

Falling back onto the cot, I pulled the sleeping bag over my head. This time I knew I was awake, because my head throbbed.

Which was worse? The news that I was Jewish or the news I had made a pass at my own cousin?

Two hours later I woke again. The door was open. Bones!

A thumping tail answered my whistle and she strolled in from her spot on the porch.

"Good girl," I mumbled. I needed to get up.

Then again, why did I need to get up? I couldn't do anything about the property. I had followed Fred's instructions and visited his grandmother, and I sincerely hoped I never saw Andy again.

Andy! I sat up. He was supposed to come over. What happened? I looked around the room, as if I would find him lurking in a corner.

This world shared no resemblance to my old world. Nothing was familiar. No alarm clock, no automatically timed morning coffee brewing, no news anchor sharing the latest celebrity scandal. My hands tingled with the pins and needles of inactivity.

I closed my eyes and fell back into the black hole.

✡ ✡ ✡

Sunday, having spent most of Saturday on the cot, I still couldn't shake my despair. Each time I tried to talk myself into moving, talk myself out of this shallow grave for the living, my eyes slipped shut and sleep grabbed me once more. My dog was taking care of herself. I had ripped open the whole bag of kibble and filled a bucket with water. I moved the cot into the kitchen, close to the stove. The door was propped open and it was some sort of blessing that no wild animals came in at night and that Bones didn't wander off.

I had a different dream. I was traveling again, walking up a steep road with people I didn't recognize.

"Where are Gregario and Catalina?" I asked a young woman.

"Who?" She shook her head.

"What about Romero?"

"I do not know who you ask for." She shook her head again and glanced over at the young man who walked beside her.

"Romero... Martinez? Bright green eyes and ears that stick out?"

"No. Maybe one of the others?" She motioned behind us, an attempt to get rid of me, no doubt.

No one knew of the people I asked about. Not until I finally reached an old man, helped along the trail by a boy. They stopped to rest and I rushed to question them.

The old man leaned toward me. "My grandparents had friends who were called Gregario and Catalina."

At last! But this man was so old.

"And the man, Romero? I do remember him."

"Where is he?" I looked around. "Is he here?"

"Not for many years, *Hija*. He died a long time ago."

Romero was dead. My heart grew tight and heavy. "How did he die?"

"In peace. With his family near him. No different than falling asleep." He reached out and patted my hand. "Why do you wish to know of this man?"

"Was it an illness?" I pictured my husband with a grievous wound, festering, in pain. It did not matter that the old one said differently, I knew it had to be so.

"No, not an illness. Simply old age. As we all must go. My time will be sooner than yours." He smiled and turned to the boy. "I am rested now."

As I watched them walk off, I fell into that space between dream and waking. My husband was dead. I screamed in anguish at the thought I would never see him again. Why had I dreamed his death?

"Gabriella? Where are you?" The sound of heavy footsteps on wood tore me away from the dream. I opened my eyes as Andy came through the door.

"What's wrong? Are you sick?" He knelt next to the cot.

His kiss was warm and for a minute I was back in a dream. Andy reached a hand to my shoulder and we kissed again.

I started to shake and pulled back. "I... I think we might be cousins." I sat all the way up.

Andy stood. "You know I grew up here, right?"

"Here on my property?" Kissing cousins. Gross in theory, but my lips still glowed with the pleasure of a kiss I was eighty percent sure had come from Andy and not my dream. Actually, I was only about eighty percent sure I was awake.

"Just about. I spent a lot of time out here."

"You knew we were cousins."

"We are not cousins, Gabriella."

Wait a minute. Andy had told me that he didn't grow up around here. "What about Colorado?"

"We came back. Several times. But we always left again. My mother... she had a rough time with her parents." He scuffed the toe of his boot in the dirt of the kitchen floor, then looked at me with a big grin, his eyes crinkled with laughter. "Ella, you live in the haunted house. You know, like in all those movies? We would come out here and dare each other to go in, spend the night, prove our manhood."

My house? I thought about the medallion, the weird hot and cold I felt, the visions. "I know. I felt—" I looked at Andy's broad shoulders and firm chin.

"What?" he asked. His grin never stopped.

I wasn't ready to tell him all my secrets just yet. Shaking off the last of my doubts I returned his smile. "I guess I've proved my manhood."

"Come on. Let's go for a walk. There's more for you to see."

✡ ✡ ✡

He waited outside while I pulled on my jeans and sweatshirt. I followed him across the flat sage field. We walked along the ditch and he showed me where the bridge—a plank, really—made it possible to cross. Once on the other side, we wound up a steep, rocky path. The trees changed here, from scrubby piñons to tall ponderosas. We slipped into the shade and walked between the trees. The tangy smell of the woods brought back memories of camping trips and summer adventures.

We walked along the road, yellow stones rolling under our feet. I had to watch where I stepped which saved me from meeting Andy's eyes or looking at the mountains or worrying about the gathering clouds. The sounds I usually heard seemed to have entered some vortex—the raven was silent, although I spotted his dark shadow now and then—no wind, no tumbling brook, no conversation. I could hear my sharp breath from inside my body, not through my ears. It penetrated my heart.

"Well," said Andy, kicking a stone from the road, "I think you should ask her."

"Ask who what?"

"Rachel. About your family."

"She... " How did I describe the fear this old woman dealt out along with her unsolicited advice?

"You don't need to be afraid of her." Andy read my mind. Or maybe my hunched shoulders and tight lips.

"I am afraid of her. It might not make sense, but, she—well— she's like the witch my father used to talk about. The one that lived here in New Mexico. What did he call her? La Yaro?"

"*La llarona.*"

"You know about her?"

"Every kid born in this state knows about her. She's the native boogie man."

"You said Rachel was a witch too."

"I was joking. She's old, but she knows a lot."

Andy stopped and peered through the forest. "It's somewhere around here."

The trees opened and we stood at the edge of a clearing. I recognized wooden grave markers by their familiar tombstone shape—rectangles with the curved tops. Low crosses too. Brush and weeds grew thick and the markers leaned at all angles, slowly losing their fight with the elements. Rocks were piled below some of the markers, as if the ground had not been willing to hold the bodies which lay there and some weight was needed to keep the spirits at rest. Andy had brought me to a cemetery.

I stooped and ran my hand over the rough wood of the nearest marker. Carved words, but time had weathered them beyond legibility.

I walked from marker to marker, wishing I knew the story of these people. This must be the home of my ancestors, but their stories were locked behind the faded words.

It was a walk through time. I could only make out a few letters on many of the markers. *Her... Espejo Mar... nez, b.... 23 d. 1887.* There were gaps, but surely this was Martinez.

At the edge of the clearing I found markers in better condition. *Francesca Tafoya Martínez, b. 1827 d. 1897.*

Carmencita Louisa Martínez, b. 1875, d. 1930. Yehoyachin Galit Marciano, b. June 2, 1870 d. June 1942. 1942 wasn't so long ago. My father was born in 1935. He was alive when this man died. I knelt and traced my fingers over the symbol carved under the name. I could see it clearly here, the strange tree. The six pointed star with leaves. And the name. Was this man Jewish?

"It's my medallion."

Andy nodded.

Rachel had told me the truth, but I had refused to listen.

Had my father known? This family secret so huge, so hidden?

In that moment nothing in my life was real. Craziness had taken over, this was a dream, I was still in California, still in my bed on Crest Ave, not about to be divorced, not New-Ella. Or maybe locked in a psych ward, medication not yet adjusted to a level which brought me back to reality.

"Why didn't you tell me?"

A boom crashed in the sky shaking my teeth. Andy grabbed my arm. The static in the air around me and the black clouds gathering above pulled me back to earth. This was real.

"We better go. It's not good to be out here in the storm. Now that you know about this place, you can come back."

Twenty minutes later we were at the house, soaked to the skin. I changed into dry clothes, while Andy shivered on the porch. Surprised he hadn't followed me in, I returned with my sweatshirt.

"I don't have anything other than this." I held it out to him.

He shook his head. "You wear it. Is it okay if I build a fire?"

While Andy carried wood from the stack outside, I crinkled newspaper into balls and thought about the symbol on the graves and the fact that for years kids believed this house was haunted.

Another thought tugged the strings of suspicion tying up my mind.

Not all the names on the graves were Martinez. There was also Marciano. Who were they? There were crosses in the little cemetery too, so maybe these others were the Jews, not the Martinez family.

I felt uneasy about all the pieces that didn't fit together and the fact Andy knew more than he was telling me. I didn't want things doled out as he deemed fit.

Suddenly I was too tired for the truth. Too tired for company, particularly company I wasn't sure I trusted. Had it only been a few hours ago that I had kissed Andy? Been caught by his charm and his smile. I had felt better after that, but now my manic energy was morphing into exhaustion. And I still didn't know if he had been here Saturday night and I was suffering some sort of blackout about the whole thing. If he hadn't, then he'd stood me up with no apology or explanation.

This loss of memory had happened before, during those really down times. Confusion so strong I often hadn't known what day of the week it was. I had kept a calendar in my car. Maybe today really was Friday, not Saturday, or Sunday. Could I have dreamed my visit with Rachel as well?

As if reading my confusion, the medallion suddenly glowed cold against my skin. I gasped.

"Are you okay?" Andy stepped forward.

I tried to cover my surprise at the change in the medallion, while avoiding any hugging that might be about to happen. Taking a step away from him I scolded, "You're still all wet. You must be really cold. You'll get sick if you don't change into dry clothes."

His eyebrows pinched together. "You want me to go?"

I nodded. "It's just—"

"No, don't explain. I get it. It's okay, Ella. Really."

As he walked to his truck, I reached and touched the medallion. How could Andy get it when I didn't get it myself.

"What have you done?" I wasn't sure if I was talking to myself or to this necklace with its strange hold on me.

Twenty-four
Consuela Castaño Espejo,
Taos, 1680

Consuela leaned against her walking stick and tried to catch her breath. There wasn't much time, but if she collapsed her plan would fail for sure.

"*Abuela*? Are you okay?"

Good. It was Fadrique. Just the one she was looking for. At twelve-years of age, her grandson reminded her of her father, Jimuta. Wise beyond his years, Rique kept quiet and observed.

"*Sí.* I am good. But I need to talk with you. Do you know where your mother is?"

Rique took her arm as they walked to the river, where Victoria was washing clothes.

Consuela spoke as soon as they were near her daughter-in-law. "The plan has been moved forward. It is no longer safe here. We must leave now."

Victoria looked up from her work. Her face was pale. "I cannot leave until Galit returns."

Consuela continued. "Fadrique, you must listen. The people of the pueblo have grown tired of the priests and the soldiers stealing all the best food for themselves, destroying the hunting grounds and trying to make everyone believe in the Catholic way. They are planning a big attack. All the Spanish will be killed."

"Aren't we people of the pueblo?"

"No. Even though we have been here a long time, we are not indigenous."

Victoria dropped the wet clothing to the ground. "Won't they spare you, Consuela?"

"They might. Many know that my father is one of the first people. But it will be bad, confusing when the fighting begins. And I don't know if they will spare you or the rest of the family." Consuela thought about how many there were. Her own seven children had all married and had more of their own. She had thirty-five grandchildren. She needed to protect them all.

"Fadrique, go to all your uncles and aunts, all the children. Tell them to come talk to me. But not all at once, one at a time. Tell them to bring me some food for tonight so that nothing will look out of the ordinary."

For the rest of the afternoon and evening, in pairs or alone, each of her offspring came to her home. Because Bernardo had been well thought of in the Taos community, she had a house separate from the pueblo, near the home of the Spanish officers. The visits would not go unnoticed.

"You must spread the word that I am ill," Consuela told each of her children and her grandchildren. "Make it known that it is likely I won't last much longer." She shuddered at how true those words might be. "That will be the reason all my children have come to see me. Gather what you can and hide it out behind the grove. We leave before dawn. It must be dark when we slip away." The old woman was adamant, allowing for no argument. She instructed Juan to figure out how they could bring livestock. The drought had impacted Pueblo Lindo as well as the rest of *Nueva España* and sheep would be a welcome addition.

Later that night Consuela cursed the bright moon. Better to see the rocky trail, but also more likely the huge group would be spotted.

Some had not come. Her second daughter refused. She was married to a soldier who knew nothing of the secrets his wife's family kept. Maria would not leave her husband behind and it was too late to tell him. Consuela had cried and tried to convince her daughter to send one of her three children. *No,* she had said. *How would I explain a missing child?*

Victoria was the hardest to convince. She wanted to wait at the hacienda until Galit returned.

Consuela watched as Fadrique stood tall and acted like a man.

"Mama. You must come with us. Papa made me promise. He said we were to go with *Abuela,* no matter what. He knows where to find us. That is what he said. Please." His confidence dissolved and he tugged on his mother's sleeve.

At midnight the group left the pueblo, walking as quietly as was possible for thirty people.

Consuela refused to wait for the stragglers. She was certain there would be no other chance for the people of the Brotherhood to build a new life.

✡ ✡ ✡

It took most of the next day for the travelers to make it ten miles, less than a quarter of the way to Pueblo Lindo. Although the people managed to start off quiet, it wasn't long before babies were crying, dogs were barking, and even the sound of voices singing filled the air.

"Some people think this is a picnic." Consuela said to Fadrique. Her grandson never left her side, leading her old mare up the trail and offering his grandmother water and bits of bread.

"They are the ones who are young, *Abuela.* Not old enough to know yet." He smiled. "Like me."

Before Galit left for Santa Fe, he had confronted her about her decision to instruct Fadrique in the ways of the Brotherhood. "This is a father's job," he had shouted. "What right do you have to intrude? The boy isn't even thirteen yet."

Consuela told Galit her reasons. She explained there was no guarantee there would be a future, although she didn't tell him she knew this because she still met with her people. The Espejo family must live each day as if it were the last because things were about to change in the northern reaches of *Nueva España*. She hadn't wanted Galit to know, because he was a soldier. It was then she found out that her son already knew of the plans for the Popé's rebellion.

"Why did you not tell me of this?" she asked her son. "Do you think this would not have double meaning to me?"

"That is just why I didn't tell you. I do not want my mother accused of being a traitor. The Spaniards look for anyone to blame in times like this. They think it makes them strong to torture those who stand in their way."

Now Galit was gone and they were going too. She hoped she survived the journey. She was saddened by the thought that she had parted with her son on such stormy terms.

Consuela turned to the boy. "Fadrique. You must take my horse and ride to the front of the line. We are traveling much too slow." She reached into her pocket, then handed him the medallion she had hidden there. "It is time for you to wear this. You will lead the people to Pueblo Lindo, where we will be safe."

Fadrique slipped the medallion around his neck and nodded. "I don't need your horse, *Abuela*. I can run very fast."

Consuela put her hand on his shoulder. "I have one more thing for you. It is from my father. He gave it to your grandfather. Bernardo carried it with him in his pocket."

Rique took the turquoise stone and rolled it over in his hand.

"It is an old stone, used to keep worries away." Consuela took her hand away. "I think we might have need of it soon."

As soon as the boy had made his way around the curve of the hillside, Consuela slid off the horse and walked behind a tree to relieve herself. She would try to keep up with the stragglers, but she wasn't worried about falling behind. She knew the way to Pueblo Lindo. She hoped that she wasn't wrong and that her father's people would welcome them. If she wasn't there to speak up for the Jews, then Fadrique would have to rely on the medallion to speak for them.

When Consuela finished her task, she led the mare back toward the trail searching for a spot to remount the horse.

The trail was empty. She must have spent more time in the trees than she realized. She started up the path, her frail body hunched over the walking stick, the mare reaching for bites of grass and slowing her even further. Finally Consuela saw a boulder up ahead that would serve as a mounting block.

"Steady there," she told the horse as she pulled on the braided *riendas* and balanced on the rock. It was a little low, but with patience she could make it.

Just as she shifted her weight and tried to fling herself onto the fidgeting mare, the horse lifted its head and stepped forward. The ground rushed up to meet her before she could even cry out. She felt a sharp pain in her side

"Are you okay? Can I help you?"

The unfamiliar voice spoke strange words. Consuela struggled to open her eyes, then squeezed them shut as pain shot through her ribs.

"Are you alone?" The voice was so odd.

"Not…" She could barely whisper because each breath sent a fire arrow through her side. The sound of footsteps racing up the path and a voice calling out for help was reassuring. She would not die alone.

The footsteps raced back. "I can't find anyone. Where are you from? Is there a house near by? You need help."

Warm hands grasped hers.

"I think you hit your head."

Consuela managed to open her eyes. "Not my head. My ribs."

A woman stood over her. No one she knew, but strangely familiar. She was dressed in a long skirt and a red blouse. Her hair was red as well, but not braided as was the tradition of her daughters and granddaughters. She had holes in the lobes of her ears, with pieces of carved silver deforming the pink skin. Her eyes were the blue-green of a stream filled with moss. Her skin was pale and covered with soft spots—*las pecas*.

"You better stay still. Don't try to sit up. I need to go for help."

Consuela saw the angel behind the woman's shoulder. Peering at her with a bright smile. "Not yet," she whispered to the angel.

There was something about the woman, something important that hovered just outside Consuela's grasp. If she could only sit up and keep her eyes opened maybe she could figure it out.

"I'll bring you some water." The woman looked around. "Do you know where I can get some?"

When she turned back her bright blouse opened at the neck and a medallion swung forward.

"Gabriella." Consuela gasped, recognizing the woman. How was it that Romero's wife, dead for many years, had stayed so young?

Twenty-five
Gabriella
Monday, April 21 to Thursday April 24

After I sent Andy away, I slipped back into the dark hole. For days Ella-Who-Sits sat and stared at the clouds drifting past the bedroom window. Thunderstorms raced across the sky, bringing concerts of rumbling ghostly buffalo herds over the bluffs and down to the valley. I didn't wear the medallion, unwilling to try to figure out if it increased or relieved my depression.

I secretly hoped Andy would come check on me again, but no one came down the road. I secretly hoped that everything Rachel had told me was a dream and that I had imagined the symbols in the graveyard. I secretly hoped the entire last year of my life would disappear. But there are no secrets from yourself.

I probably would have sat there for a million years, my arms turned to stone and my feet slowly rooting in the yellow soil, but I ran out of dog food.

I could starve myself, live on crackers and coffee, but Bones shouldn't have to suffer from my mistakes.

Without bothering to wash my face or change out of the sweats that were now my uniform, I drove to town. Keeping my eyes down while browsing through the meager groceries at the market made me feel invisible. I headed home with six dusty cans of meaty dog food—no indication what kind of meat—some wilted lettuce and pale tomatoes, a loaf of brown-colored white bread that advertises itself as wheat, and four cans of vegetable soup tucked neatly into my canvas bag.

Three Ravens stood majestically on her corner. *Come in*, the old building said.

There is nothing worse than a woman who lets herself go. My father's holier-than-thou voice came through loud and clear. *She might as well be dead if she lets the world know how weak she is.* Not a conversation about someone who hadn't bathed or brushed her hair for a long time. Just his reaction to seeing our neighbor at the grocery store without her makeup and wearing slacks with paint stains. We had different definitions of what made women weak.

I looked down at my grubby sweats. *Screw you, Dad.* I wasn't so far gone that I hadn't remembered to grab my laptop before I drove to town.

The coffee was great and the shop deserted. Two points for me.

I turned on the computer, but I didn't log in to check my email. There was nothing I wanted to hear from anyone.

The search box on my screen begged me to figure things out. So I searched.

Hallucinations. My entry popped up thousands of answers, with banner status given to "Consult your doctor if you think you have a medical condition."

The art of finding what you want on the internet is not an exact science. I surfed around, reading various definitions and posts. Next I tried *Are visions a symptom of a mental health disorder?*

Schizophrenia popped up, big and blue and bold. Did I really want to look at this? I scrolled down a bit.

Conversion disorder, Grandiose delusions, psychiatric presentation of mental illness, bipolar disorder.

Take your pick. I was crazy. Really crazy. I closed my eyes and rubbed my head.

"Headache?" Nathan squeezed my shoulder.

Flashback. I twisted from his grasp and jumped up, the chair clattering to the floor.

"Ella, I'm sorry. I didn't mean to scare you."

"It's fine, really. I just—" I shook my head. "You just surprised me, that's all."

"How are things? I haven't seen you for awhile."

"Good. No, not good." I closed my eyes and squeezed, fighting to keep my hysteria from bursting out.

Had I always walked this close to the edge?

Nathan looked around the room. There were a few customers scattered at the tables. "Come on." He reached for my arm and this time I let him take ahold of me as he led me out the back door.

We wound along a back porch which stretched the length of the building, the mirror of the front porch with its cozy tables. But this side of the building sported stacks of wood, a barbecue, some rusting milk canisters, table saws, and what looked like a lifetime of things one can't bear to throw out. He stopped at two rusted iron chairs. I noticed an ash tray filled with butts under one of them.

Nathan caught my glance. "Not me. Chris, my helper, he smokes. This is the only place I allow it. Sorry it's not much, but we have some privacy. Now, how can I help you with whatever is causing such grief?"

Feelings of shame and stupidity overwhelmed me. It wasn't right to share my troubles with a stranger. "I'm sorry, Nathan. I don't mean to dump on you."

He nodded and stared across the flat meadow that lead down to Las Nutrias Creek, which I had learned was the name of my creek and used to be the name of the town. Tierra Amarilla was downstream from my property and the creek was wide and slow here. The back of the coffee house actually had a better view than the front, but I could see that he wouldn't have the road exposure if he had expanded in this direction.

"I haven't been here long, not compared to many. But I have been here long enough to know that people who come here from other places, from cities or lives or things, they come here to escape. Why else would someone come here? There really isn't much. No jobs, no fancy houses, no shopping malls, not even very many places to hike." He turned and nodded. "It's a good place to escape. There is something here, some sort of magic or vortex. We don't get the press of Sedona, but it's similar. I think you felt it when I drummed for you."

I thought back to that day. I had been running on adrenaline and the hope that coming here would solve all my problems. No clear picture of how, just the knowledge I needed to get away. Even though I had never believed in hocus-pocus, as my mother termed anything mystical, the drumming had swept me into another world.

"I did." I rubbed my hands on my thighs, the sticky sweats reminding me how dirty I was. "Nathan, does anyone around here ever talk about strange dreams? Like time traveling?"

"At night or during the day?"

"Both. Mostly at night, but at times, kind of like, well, losing consciousness or something. But very real, like dreaming a continuous story night after night and being a character in that story. Being able to do things or be other people. Sometimes I'm visible to others, but other times I'm like a ghost. At times I'm me, sometimes it seems I have become someone else."

"Have you heard of shamanic journeys?"

I shook my head. Wasn't a shaman like medicine man?

"I'll try to keep it basic, it's a complex thing. Many of us feel another world, another dimension, just off to the edge of what we see and feel. People gain access in different ways, like drumming or meditation. The idea of a vortex is that the barrier that keeps us separate is thinner in that spot. People come so they can increase their chances of accessing this spiritual place. One of the ways people access it is through a dream which is more than a dream. It is a journey to somewhere else, but very real. No one experiences this in the same way, but what you described could be a shamanic journey."

"Why would I have them?"

Nathan smiled and reached for my hand. "Because you are lucky. Many people try for years and never achieve what you have described. Someone out there is looking out for you, wants to teach you. I think you're scared, but really, you shouldn't be."

Someone was looking out for me. Some spirit or dead ancestor? I was comforted by Nathan's explanation, but it didn't really relieve my confusion. And I sure didn't feel lucky.

✡ ✡ ✡

Fred looked up from the files piled on his desk. "Is Mark back?"

I watched his gaze slip over me, dirty clothes and wet hair and all. I would have to make a trip home to remedy the terrible outfit, but I decided not to let it bother me too much.

"I'm not going to wait for him." I pulled up the chair and sat. "I can't stay here forever. I need to list my portion of the land."

"Ella, that can't happen until there is clear title."

"Then let's do what it takes to get clear title. Or conditionally list it or something."

"How did your visit with my grandmother go?"

Nothing like changing the subject. I guess Rachel was real.

"Fine. So I'm thinking $4,000 per acre." I had done my homework. There was land just east of Tierra Amarilla at $3,600. Weren't you supposed to start a little high so people could negotiate and feel like they were getting a deal?

Fred shook his head, obviously unimpressed with my ideas, but pulled out a yellow tablet. "What are the water rights?"

I had spent my time in Three Ravens researching all this. "I don't know if I figured it out correctly, but I think it's nine acre feet for a thousand acres. So I guess we have to divide it to figure out what is mine?"

His pen hovered over the paper. "One house or two?"

"One. But not anything to speak of. It will have to be torn down." Why did Fred think there were two houses?

"Are you sure you want to do that?"

"I'm not planning on doing it. That's up to whoever buys it."

"Didn't your grandparents build that house?"

Sentimentality had no place in business deals. Surely a realtor would know that. Didn't he want a commission?

"I really don't know."

After Fred had begrudgingly finished his notes and we had agreed to list the land for $3,500 per acre, he told me to come back in two days and he would have some ads and paperwork typed up. "But you really should go visit my grandmother again."

My determination was wearing off in a hurry, but I wasn't going to let Fred pull any more stunts. "Family is important to you, I know that. But I really didn't know my grandparents and the house just doesn't hold much meaning to me." Not only that, but accepting this inheritance felt dirty. I had hated my father. If I wasn't desperate for money it would have been great to throw it all back in his face. Even if he was dead.

"It's not that."

Drawing in all the power of New-Ella and relegating my father's voice to the back of my thoughts, I pushed. "Fred, if you know something would you please just tell me? Rachel is just too... vague for me. She wanted to show me something or tell me something, but she never did. We spent the day cooking. Then she tried to tell me I was Jewish, and my ancestors were part of a secret club, which, sorry, but that is just crazy."

I was testing him. I did believe what Rachel had told me. The headstones, with their strange names and six-pointed stars had convinced me of that. But the story had so many holes, there had to be more to it. Maybe I could glean some new information from him.

Fred tapped his pencil on the folder. Angry. "She told you?"

"Yes."

"Are you coming to the meeting?"

Whoa there, Freddy. The meeting? Wasn't this Brotherhood some ancient thing? *Play this right, Ella.*

"When?"

"Next Friday."

Okay. Magic medallions, visions, Jewish, not Presbyterian or even Catholic and now a secret Brotherhood that still existed?

"She didn't tell me about it. Can I go?"

I watched his face change. He had gone too far and he back-pedaled.

"I really think you should go see her again. Ask her about it."

✡ ✡ ✡

I don't know if Bones was happy with her by-product goulash or pleased that I had moved from my stationary position. Regardless, her long tail wagged as she ran up the trail and back, checking on me every thirty seconds.

If my ancestors were part of a secret Brotherhood, a Jewish one no less, and that Brotherhood still existed, was it wise of me to hook up with them? New Mexico had strange things going on and Tierra Amarilla was a tiny town, far from anything even close to civilization. Weren't there people in these hills who whipped themselves bloody, wore crowns of thorns, and sacrificed animals?

Ask Rachel. Fred had urged me to do just that, but I didn't feel one hundred percent certain I would get answers. My hands tingled and anxiety inched up from my fingers toward my heart. The feelings of loneliness swept through me with a force that closed my eyes. Things hadn't been great at home, but at least I had Vicki and the girls. Even my mother was better than no one. New-Ella had given me one burst of confidence, why couldn't she give me another? Why did I have to panic now?

I hurried back to the house and jumped in the car. I would phone Vicki. An ear, that's all I needed to avert this anxiety.

But when I got to the bridge and powered up my phone, I called Andy.

"Hey." He didn't commit to more than a greeting. Who could blame him?

"I... can you... I'm... "

"Yeah," his voice was soft. "I get it. Some of it, anyway."

"I'm sorry."

"I don't want you to be sorry, Ella. I want you to be happy."

I licked my lips and jumped into the turmoil of emotions. "I would be happy if you came over."

Silence. Had I misread things? Burned my bridges?

"I'll come tonight. After work. I'll bring some dinner."

Thank God for second chances.

Twenty-six
Fadrique Espejo
1680

Rique jogged up the trail, although he was tired from the long journey. If he had a horse, as some of the others did, he could ride ahead and talk to his grandmother's relations before the parade of animals and people and carts showed up. He could have used Grandmother's horse, but he did not want her to walk. Traveling was hard on her, she fell behind, even as she urged the family to move faster.

He trotted around the last bend in the trail, happy to see the fields of maize and squash. The place was as his grandmother had described: a small, but steady stream snaked down the middle of the plants. He noticed a man pushing the dirt around the tender shoots and called out.

"*Hola, Señor.*" Rique smiled and waved.

The man stood and shaded his eyes with his hand. The boy was a little disconcerted that he did not return the smile or the greeting. He walked closer.

" I am Fadrique Espejo, grandson of Consuela."

Nothing changed on the man's carved face.

"Great-grandson of Jimuta?"

A tiny nod. Then the man looked over Rique's shoulder and his face finally changed.

To a scowl.

"Why are you here?"

Rique considered his words before he spoke. His grandmother had made him practice this technique. The way of the people, she preached. *Don't be in a hurry. Time is the concept of man, not nature. Things which change slowly change for the better, while those who jump often fall.* If he told this man they were running away, would he consider them weak?

He stood straight and spoke. "There is unrest below. Our people are being persecuted, just as yours. Because my grandmother is the daughter of Jimuta we felt that this was our place." Did that sound too entitled?

Now the man turned to face him. His cold stare and closed lips showed that he too knew how to measure his words. "Boy. Go tell them to wait in the meadow. Do not come any further. Keep the animals out of the crops." The man turned and walked up the trail.

Hoping he had not messed things up, Rique ran back toward his brothers and their wives. He scanned the group for his grandmother, but did not spot her among the crowd. She should be the one to talk to her people.

As he waited, Grandmother's voice echoed in his mind, as if she knew of his conflict. "Fadrique, our people live a way of peace. They are in touch with the earth and feel that each man should have his own relationship with nature and the world around him. They do not have the rules we Jews have. No covenant in writing, but a great unspoken covenant with the mother of all, the earth. They celebrate, and when something happens they take it in stride."

"What about the drought?" Rique was only seven years old when his grandmother spoke the lessons to him. But even a seven-year-old knew that their life depended on water.

"If you have planned well, your stores will see you through. A drought is the earth's way of telling man that he must not become greedy."

"What if someone steals your food?"

Consuela had smiled at him. "Like someone stole the pie yesterday?"

The boy felt his ears burn and did not answer.

"This can happen, among any people. But the men of my pueblo would try to find out why the pie was stolen. Was the thief hungry? Was he jealous of the wife who baked the pie, his own wife a terrible cook? He would not be punished, but he would be made, no, make that *led*, to a better way. Perhaps the pie baker could teach his wife how to make a better pie. He would bring the wood and pick the apples and help to watch the children while the two wives cooked."

"The Indians make pies?"

Abuela had smiled at Rique. "*Nieto*, you make fun of my story. But the real point is the people like to solve their problems."

"But what if the man is very angry? What if he wants to fight?"

"My people do know how to fight. They have weapons and they will protect themselves. They treasure what is theirs and do not want to lose it. Over the years other tribes have tried. It was only luck that put my father in charge when Tío Simón and the Spanish first arrived. Another leader may not have let them stay." She chuckled. "Maybe he saw my mother and fell in love. Letting the soldiers stay was the only way to be assured that she would stay as well."

Rique was awakened from his memories when more native men came down the canyon.

✿ ✿ ✿

"Yes, we have heard that there was cruel treatment of the medicine men." Rique stood close, but kept quiet as his brothers spoke with the three native men.

"You understand that is not how we feel. Although we left Pueblo Lindo long ago, we have been raised in the ways of both grandfathers—Jimuta and Simón." Juan had taken over the negotiations, laughing when Rique suggested that Consuela had told him this was his duty.

Grandmother was still missing. Rique listened to his oldest brother's negotiations, glancing down the trail every few minutes. Where was she?

"We? Who is this "we"? Your grandmother left with the friar many years ago. This is not her pueblo or your pueblo. That choice was clear."

"But Simón and some others stayed. Jimuta did not turn them out."

"One old man who has been dead for many years." The chief glanced at the other men and Rique wondered what they were not saying.

He could not keep quiet. "We have nowhere else to go. We will be slaughtered, either by the Spanish or by Popé."

Juan glared.

Okuwa-T'sire, the Summer Chief, drew in a deep breath and looked up the canyon. "There is no room for you in the pueblo. The upper place is home to the first people now." He turned and looked at the crowd in the meadow. Two hours had passed since they'd been told to wait and they had settled in. Cooking fires sent up wisps of smoke. Sheep munched on the grass below the crops.

"You cannot stay. The snows will come and you will not survive."

In response to the stance of Okuwa, Juan puffed up his own chest. Rique held his breath. Nothing would be settled through confrontation. Not with the first people. Don't back any man into a corner, because he *will* get out.

Grandmother's words were so clear in his mind, but had she ever told these things to Juan? His brother spent his days with Spanish priests for as long as Rique could remember.

Rique was disturbed by the sharp tone of Juan's voice.

"We will not leave."

He knew that his brother's confrontational tone would not win the family a place in the pueblo. So he drew in a deep breath and stepped into the circle of men.

"Juan, can we please find Grandmother?"

"*Hola* Okuwa. Greetings Oyegi-a ye."

Rique had never been so happy to hear the melodic voice of his grandmother as she greeted both the Summer and the Winter chiefs.

He turned to her and was surprised to see a strange woman holding Consuela's arm. The second thing he noticed was the large purple mark on his grandmother's forehead.

"What happened?" He rushed to her and grabbed her other arm.

"Nothing, *Nieto*. Just a spill." She pulled both arms away from the stranger and him, then moved toward Okuwa. "How are you, Uncle?"

Okuwa did not smile. He let Consuela hug him, then waved a hand toward the crowd. "These people cannot stay."

Conseula nodded. "Of course, of course." Then she waved up the trail. "Will you help me to find Oyi-tsa?" I have not seen my brother in many years."

Her brother? Rique was sure his grandmother had never mentioned a brother in the pueblo.

"The one you ask for is in the upper village. These people cannot come." The native shook his head and pointed to the sheep moving toward the squash plants. "Take the animals away."

Rique felt torn in three directions. He wanted to listen to his grandmother speak with her relatives and find out if his family had a place to stay or not. He knew he should go and help his sister, Paloma, keep the sheep away from the crops. And he wanted to find out who this strange woman was. He could tell at a glance that she was not one of the people of the pueblo. Her hair was loose, the color of the red rocks that lined the rivers in the south, with a smooth shine that reflected the sunlight. Her skin was covered with soft dark spots and her eyes the same hazel as his own. She wore clothing unlike any he had ever seen, with bright patterns woven into the fabric which stretched across her body. With a flush he stared at the outline of her breasts. It was as if she had dressed in her underclothes and lost her blouse.

"Fadrique." Grandmother's voice was sharp. He suspected she had spoken his name more than once.

"I'm sorry, Grandmother. What is it?"

"Please go tell Pedro to move the sheep back down the canyon. Take my horse." She turned back to Okuwa. "I will speak with my brother and then we will do as you wish."

Rique grabbed the mare and swung up onto her smooth back. He kept his head turned and his ear ready as he rode off. The last thing he saw was his grandmother and the strange woman walking up the trail with Okuwa.

✿ ✿ ✿

A boy of any age is not known for his ability to wait with patience. Fadrique was no exception. In fact, he was more likely than most to come up with his own conclusion as to why a rule did not apply to him. But he knew enough to wait until the people, especially Juan, had finally rested their heads on the bedrolls and blankets spread around the campfires before sneaking away.

His grandmother had not returned from the upper pueblo. A young native had come and instructed Juan and the others to make camp well below the crops. Rique's brothers had stayed up late, muttering angrily about the way things were working out. Rique kept quiet, sitting off to the edge of the circle. All he needed was for Juan to take notice and send him off on some foolish woman's errand. There were plenty of girls around to fetch water or check on the horses. Rique belonged with the men.

He listened to the deep breathing around him. Many people rolled and tossed, finding it difficult to sleep outside. They'd better get used to it, Rique thought. If they couldn't stay in the pueblo there would be many nights under the trees.

Moving with extreme caution and being ever so quiet, Rique slipped from his woolen blanket and crept from the group. Once past the watchful dogs and restless horses, he walked with more ease. The moon was bright and he only stumbled a few times on the rocky trail up the canyon.

When he reached the top of the trail he could make out structures lining the walls. Adobe buildings clung to the edges of the narrow canyon and tall kiva ladders led up to caves. This pueblo was a strange mixture of new construction and ancient-cave-people homes. Rique was glad that his grandmother had described the pueblo to him in great detail.

No one was awake and he had no idea where his grandmother slept. She was likely to sleep in a place of honor, but with this mix of old and new what would that be? A new adobe dwelling would be larger and likely to provide more room for guests, but the ancient caves might be reserved for special occasions. Rique was just deciding that she would not have climbed a ladder in her condition when a whisper came from the darkness.

"You are her grandson?"

It was the strange woman.

Rique turned to where she sat on a rock. "Who are you?"

"I'm... I'm... a friend of your grandmother."

The hesitation in the woman's voice indicated she was lying, but Rique didn't know what to do about it.

"Where is my grandmother?"

"She's sleeping."

"That mark on her head? How did that come to be?"

"She fell and bruised her head. I was more worried about her ribs, but the... the medical person looked at her and gave her some tea. That's when she finally went to sleep."

"Medical person?" What did she mean?

"Um... medicine man?" This woman's forehead wrinkled, as if she was making things up.

Her language was strange.

"Fadrique, that's your name, right?"

"Yes."

The woman looked around in the moon light. "We should talk,

but let's move away so we don't wake her."

Grandmother must be directly inside this building. Rique wanted to check on her, but decided he could do so after he found out what the woman had to say. He followed her to the edge of the creek, where she sat on a flat boulder. There was room for him and she patted a spot next to her, but he stood, facing her, arms crossed at his chest. A manly pose, he thought. He wasn't ready to act like this stranger's best friend.

"I'm Gabriella."

He tipped his chin slightly and waited.

"I was listening when your grandmother spoke with the men. They don't want you—your family—to stay here. The tall one is afraid that you have led the Spanish soldiers here and the other one, with the round face, Oyegi-a ye, I think he is called, he says there is not enough food."

"You speak the native tongue?"

Once again her face slipped into a dark trance and he could watch the thoughts flicker behind her bright eyes. This one was careful with her words.

"Yes. Well, no. I can understand it a little. Anyway, Consuela, your grandmother, she tried everything, but they said you all have to leave in the morning."

"What about you?"

"Me?" She was startled by his question, as if she hadn't considered this at all. "I guess I go with you."

Now she frowned and lifted her hand toward her face. She stared at her palms as if there was some kind of answer there. Then she reached up to her tight shirt and pulled at the chain on her neck. and he saw the glint of a necklace.

He gasped. She wore a medallion.

"Where do you come from? A woman with the sign of the Brothers?" Although Rique knew his grandmother had worn the medallion, he knew this was only because his grandfather had died and they were traveling. It was usually stored in a small wooden box, along with other family treasures. She wore it only until she gave it to him. But this woman? Where was she taking this medallion?

"It's a long story. Right now I think we should focus on what you need to do." The woman went on to explain that Consuela was very worried about his family. If they couldn't stay here they would have to go back to Taos. And that was too dangerous. They would risk being executed by either the rebelling natives or the Spanish.

"Do you have any ideas of how to make these chiefs let you stay?"

Rique felt his stomach churn. He reached into his pocket and rubbed the turquoise stone. Grandmother had been right, now was a time to worry. One day ago he'd been proud to be considered a man, but now he felt caught in something he didn't understand. His grandmother and this stranger, Gabriella, they seemed to count on him to fix everything. But his brothers wouldn't let him participate in their planning and discussion. No one understood that he couldn't convince the natives without first convincing the rest of the Espejo clan.

Twenty-seven
Gabriella
Thursday, April 24 to Monday, May 5

Complaints of living without my customary comforts were slight when compared to my nights in the pueblo. The dreams were so real I awoke with my hands sore from helping the women with the work of preparing food, weaving baskets, and cleaning the dim rooms. Add caring for Consuela and my days were restful.

Andy was coming today and I rearranged my sparse belongings three times before I finally heard a truck.

I stepped out onto the porch. My smile faded when I realized it wasn't the familiar yellow tow-truck driving up the road.

The pickup was old, but in good shape, as if someone had taken the time to restore it to its original paint color of Navajo turquoise. The driver kept the speed low, wise on this road of sharp rocks and spiny arms reaching to scratch such well-kept paint. My mother's fears—who was this coming here uninvited—rose and I called Bones to the porch.

It wasn't until the truck was parked and the driver emerged that I realized it *was* Andy.

"Hey," he called, as Bones ran to greet him. Her red body wiggled and she moaned with delight as he scratched her behind the ears.

"I didn't recognize you." I stepped off the porch and walked to meet him, pointing to the truck.

"She's called Patrice."

"Did you fix her up?"

"A little. I inherited her in near mint condition. My grandfather kept her garaged and covered and polished within an inch of her life. I think shining her was his therapy. I remember him spending a lot of time with her."

This was the first time Andy had volunteered any of his history other than our meet-and-greet soda. I hardly knew the guy, other than what I had grilled out of him over tacos and root beer.

Was I about to sleep—no, be honest—have sex, with a man I barely knew? I stopped, unwilling to move toward Andy.

He didn't notice, just put his hands on my shoulders and kissed me. Funny how lips touching lips can change your perspective on life.

I found out that Patrice wasn't just Andy's truck. She was also a bed. I guess he had thought ahead about my single cot and my dusty floors, because he had a mattress and several quilts in the back of the old pickup, along with a bottle of wine, two plastic cups and green chili burritos.

"Good place to look at the stars," he said, as he rolled the quilts and pushed them against the cab, making a recliner of sorts for us.

The chill that took over when the sun went down seemed to be part of his plan. Time to cover up.

I shouldn't have worried about a man seeing my pale abdomen or my stretch marks. I had forgotten how making love works. How you start with kisses, which grow deeper and deeper and melt into hands exploring and slipping buttons from their holes, moving zippers down, clothes being slowly removed and skin touching skin and souls touching souls and more melting and more skin and it's all good.

All good… and followed by a peace of mind that seems to catch the glow of the bright moon and fill your belly and the snuggling into the warmth of each other and a dreamless sleep.

Andy had the week off. Patrice turned into my new bedroom, and other than my worry that Bones would scratch the flawless paint jumping in and out of the bed, I felt comfortable with the arrangement. It was quite warm with the three of us under the down comforter and pile of quilts he brought. Each morning we sat and drank coffee, planning our adventures for the day. Andy showed me where the water in the kitchen came from—a gravity feed from the acequia. Not good to drink anymore, but perfect for bathing. He showed me how to collect rocks, where to fish at Lake Heron, the mysterious dinosaur bones of Ghost Ranch, the cliff dwellings and we spent a day riding the steam train out of Chama. When the weekend came, we stayed in the truck, coming up for air and hikes and camp stove meals, then sinking back into the bliss of each other's arms.

Maybe my dreams had been a symptom of my loneliness, because I didn't have any night time adventures that week. Andy became Romero, or maybe Romero became Andy, but all I know is that my happiness was real.

I tucked the medallion back into the pocket of the camp chair and left it there. The strange hold it had over me faded as Andy's spell pulled me in.

✡ ✡ ✡

On Monday I went back to the courthouse. Andy had kissed me goodbye and headed to Santa Fe. The end of his week off and his weekly run for auto parts had arrived. I felt a pang of the old loneliness slip up on me. He'd asked me to go with him, but I had to take care of business. *Before pleasure*, echoed in my father's voice, although I couldn't remember him ever following up my chores with something fun.

Joel Dominguez was in.

"Why is this taking so long?" I asked him.

"In the world of documents, two weeks is nothing."

"More than two weeks. Mark should be back soon. Will *that* make a difference?" Reassurances aside, I knew Joel and my cousin played on the same team.

"It will happen, Ella."

I left his office in a storm of frustration. I was so tired of lip service. Being with Andy had distracted me for a week, but the reality was I couldn't just play at this. This was my life.

I glanced at Three Ravens, then remembered poor Bones shut inside the house. I would go home and let my dog out then drive to the bridge. A talk with Vicki, that's what I needed, although I swore I wasn't going to tell her about Andy.

Just as I crossed the parking lot, I heard footsteps behind me. I turned, expecting Andy. That's what happens when you have a stalker turned lover. You don't think anyone else will follow you. Or maybe it happens when you have a huge crush on someone and you want to see them in spite of knowing they aren't around.

It was Fred.

"Things going okay?" He didn't smile.

"What?" I looked away.

"My grandmother said you never came back."

"I did not."

"She also said she hadn't told you about the meeting."

The Brotherhood. I had forgotten all about my request to go to the meeting and I hadn't gone back to finish listing the property. Had a week really passed since I had made those demands?

I couldn't tell Fred that in the course of having a lover, the secret society of Jews and the sale of my land and everything else in the world had slipped my mind.

He glanced over his shoulder. "Sorry, I have an appointment, but we really need to talk."

"Can we make another appointment?"

Without smiling, Fred agreed to meet me the next day.

Before I drove home I checked my phone messages. One from my mother reminding me I hadn't called her for awhile, one from Julie, *Hi mom, just checking in,* and one from Andy.

Sorry Ella. I'm not going to make it back tonight. There's a problem with the parts order and I'm spending the night down here in Santa Fe. Miss you.

I stared out the window at the sky, the mountains miles away from this angle. It was so big, this place. And I was sitting in the middle of it, all alone. I dialed Vicki.

The phone call to my friend was disappointing. She didn't seem to understand or care about the hurdles I had to jump through to sell the land. She really wanted to talk about who was sleeping with whose husband and which adult children had moved back in with their parents and which new boutique had amazing hats. Somehow the old gossip didn't do it for me. I was tempted to tell her about Andy, in spite of my resolve to keep him a secret, so I faked a dying cell phone battery and drove back to the house, keeping my promise to myself that this affair wasn't public knowledge. In California, anyway. No secrets here in New Mexico, even if I had tried.

I pulled my chair to the spot overlooking the creek and reached into the pocket for the medallion. As I stared at the emblem I realized I had left Consuela ailing in the pueblo. I had deserted Rique and my plan to help him. What would happen? Romero's life had gone on after my dreams took me away from him. What was it the old man said? Romero died peacefully with his family.

How was the medallion tied into all this? If it was the symbol of a secret brotherhood, how did it come to be hidden in my wall? How was it possible for a necklace to give me strange visions and intense dreams? It had to be more than a membership badge. If what Nathan said was true, the dreams would help me. I slipped the chain over my head and felt the medallion settle against my chest with a burst of heat. The air grew cool and I left once again.

It took a moment for my eyes to adjust to the dim light inside the pueblo. I recognized the mat where Consuela lay, covered with a woven blanket.

"Have you talked to the boy?"

"Yes. But Consuela, he is so young. It's a lot to ask of him. The chiefs, surely they won't insist your family leave when they realize you can't travel."

"He is young, but his spirit is old. He is the answer." She struggled to sit. "You can learn to guide the dreams, but it takes a strength you do not have yet. The old woman will give it to you." She shook her head. "She is a bit selfish. You will have to work for her knowledge. When she shows you, then you must show Fadrique."

Twenty-eight
Fadrique Espejo
Pueblo Lindo, 1680

After his talk with the strange woman, Rique spent a near-sleepless night. Gabriella, this woman who wore the medallion, but refused to speak with him about the Brotherhood, confused him. He knew she was right to focus on the current problem, but he couldn't help but think that something well beyond his comprehension was happening. So when the woman had finished her talking and slipped back into the adobe house, he had crept around the building and leaned against the wall, just under a small window. He would listen.

The sun sent strong rays over the edge of the canyon wall to waken him from the uncomfortable sleep of one who has stayed curled in a sitting position all night. Rique rolled his head to get the kinks out of his neck, and licked his dry lips. For a moment he thought of his empty belly, but this was replaced by worry as he came fully awake and remembered where he was.

Today the family would have to move on. He stood and turned his ear to the window, listening for Grandmother, but he heard nothing.

Edging around the side of the building quietly—he didn't think his native cousins would harm him, but it didn't hurt to be careful—he looked around the village.

Women carried bowls of water, baskets, and plants. Children ran along behind their mothers, and men stacked adobe bricks to build a wall. He should have heard noise—laughter, footsteps, something—but the people were solemn and quiet. Rique slipped closer to the doorway.

Someone was crying.

He sprang from his crouched position and rushed inside. The transition from light to dark blinded him and he stopped.

"Do not cry, my brother." Grandmother's voice was a bare whisper and Rique turned toward the sound.

A still figure crouched next to the pallet where Grandmother lay. Rique stepped closer, his eyes adjusted to the dim light now. A man knelt on the dirt floor, as wrinkled as the dried fruits of the orchards, hands clasped and face tilted upward, tears streaming down his weathered cheeks. Rique had never seen such an old man before.

This must be the brother *Abuela* had mentioned yesterday— Oyi-tsa. A native relation she had never spoken of before. But when the figure turned toward him, it was not a native face that peered at him from under the heavy brow. Round blue eyes and pale. A long slender nose.

"Who are you?"

"I am Oyi."

Rique heard his grandmother draw a sharp, rattling breath and he rushed to her side.

"*Abuela.*" His heart pushed up into his throat, as thick as the clay that lined the banks of the river. He clutched her hand, hot to his touch.

"Fadrique," she whispered. "You are here." She raised her hand from his grasp and pointed to a jug of water.

Rique scooped some of the liquid. How would he give her something to drink without pouring it all over her? His hand shook as he held the dipper over her and drops spilled onto the hide that covered her.

The old man bent forward and cradled her head, lifting it so that Rique could touch the dipper to her lips. She took a sip, her tongue reaching out and smoothing the water over her cracked lips. Oyi lowered her head.

"Rafael, you must teach him."

Who was Rafael? Had grandmother stepped with one foot into the other world? Speaking to the ghosts that surrounded them?

"What you ask is not possible." The old man answered her as if he was the one called Rafael. "It has been many years since I have thought about the Torah or God. Those memories are buried under the rock slides of time."

Abuela shook her head and opened her eyes wide. "No, not the ways of the Jews." A smile crossed her lips. "I have taught him that. I speak of my father's ways. He must go to the sweat lodge. You must convince Oyegi-a ye to let my family stay."

The old man—Oyi or Rafael or whoever he was—leaned away, closing his eyes. Grandmother's hand shot forward with the speed of a snake and grasped his arm.

Rique held his breath.

"For me. You owe this to me." The burst of strength quickly weakened. "For Bernardo."

Oyi gazed at Grandmother's hand, his own fingers balling into a fist. It seemed to Rique as if the man wished to yank his arm from her grasp, but used every ounce of his soul to remain still.

"I do not owe that man anything."

"You still place your anger on one who was not deserving of such a role. When you look out to the people in the meadow do not see strange men, do not see intruders. Open your eyes and see men of your own blood. Men of the Castaño clan, men who carry on what your own father died for."

Oyi shook his head and placed his hand over Grandmother's as she continued.

"My grandson is our salvation. He must know everything. He wears the medallion, but that is not enough. So many men desire to kill the people of our blood. Do not add yourself to the list. These women and children, innocents. We are exiled, Rafael. As we have always been exiled. The Catholics fight the Natives and the Jews will become a target for anger that should fall elsewhere. You must understand this. You, who have lived through it over and over again."

Rique felt the stare of the old man's blurry eyes, but kept his head down. Oyi-Rafael pulled his hand from where it covered Grandmother's and reached for Rique's face. Fingers traced over his nose, his brow, his ears. They cupped his chin and tilted his head up.

Rique looked into this uncle's face. The white cloud that covered the eyes, he knew of this. His uncle was blind.

"Yes. For you, I will do this. This one will be a leader."

Gabriella had also told him he was to be a leader. Rique looked around the room.

"Where is that woman? Gabriella?"

Grandmother shook her head. "I don't know who you mean."

✡ ✡ ✡

For three days Grandmother lay on the pallet, her breath filled with the crackle of winter ice, although the days were warm. Each day Rafael, for Rique now knew this was the true name of this ancient man, sat at her side. Rique also refused to leave, although Juan and the native chiefs were angry. Okuwa-t'sire had convinced Oyegi-a ye that the people should be allowed to stay in the lower meadow until Consuela was able to travel. Juan held a different opinion.

"We will have to leave her here, Rique. You need to come with us. I know that you can't think ahead, but the snows will be here before we know it. We have to settle somewhere. Or... ."

His brothers were thinking of going back. Rique could hear this in Juan's voice.

"How can you think I would leave our grandmother?"

"You are not leaving her alone. These are her people. It is probably for the best, in fact, what she would want, to die here among them."

"She is not going to die." Rique hoped his words held magic, for he feared the harsh coughs that wracked his grandmother's body. After three days her confusion was apparent. She spoke of things he had never heard about. Journeys and disguises and secret meetings. She did know about the woman because she called out in her half sleep state. *Gabriella, it is up to you.* He didn't know what this meant, but it seemed Grandmother was placing some sort of responsibility on the phantom woman.

He asked Rafael about Gabriella, but the old man didn't seem to know who he was talking about. If she didn't live in the pueblo where had she come from? The first time anyone had seen her was when she came up the trail with Grandmother leaning on her arm. He was beginning to think she was a ghost.

Had she rescued Consuela or had she been the one to hurt her?

"Grandmother, I cannot find Gabriella. Where did she go?"

"You must forget about her, *Nieto*. She is no one."

"I cannot forget her. She spoke to me. She told me many things."

"What of these things she told you? They mean nothing. You must learn from Rafael, that is the only thing to think about now."

"If Rafael is Spanish, if he was a Jew, why does he take the name Oyi?"

His grandmother told him the long tale of this man, who it turned out wasn't her brother but her cousin.

"He was the strongest man of God you could ever know. But over time, he felt that God had betrayed him. Oh, Fadrique, he lost so much." Grandmother squeezed his hand. "He lost his mother and father, he lost his grandfather. Then he lost his Tío Simón, who was a true father to him, and he lost his sweet young wife. He felt he had lost the ear of God, that he could no longer hear the holy words he needed to continue as the Rabbi to our family.

"One day he heard of the strange magic of the peyote. In desperation he tried to reach God with the strong medicine." Grandmother stopped and motioned for sip of water.

Rique had heard about peyote. The plant was stronger than wine and a man who chewed it would leave his body, as if in death, but he could travel the air of the earth and not go to heaven.

"He did not hear the voice of God, but he heard the voice of the great Katchina Chakwaina."

"Katchina? Like the people of the pueblo in costumes?"

"Yes, like that. Only not a man in a costume, but the true god of my father's people. It was said that Chakwaina led the Spanish to this land. That was enough to turn Rafael away from being a Jew forever. When the rest of them left Pueblo Lindo to go to Taos, my cousin stayed behind. He supposed he would not live long, but God has chosen to keep him alive. My brother is nearing one hundred years."

And so Rique learned from Rafael, although the old man was difficult to understand. He spoke a strange tongue of Spanish and Tewa, all mixed together. Many of his lessons came with no explanation at all. His first lesson had been that Rique was never to call him Rafael. His name was Oyi-tsa. He led Rique to some plant or rock or spot in the river and sat. The boy simply sat with the man, but time stood still and he was soon bored. He explored. He examined his turquoise stone until he knew every pit and dark streak. He looked into the river to see the fish and the tiny spidery hellgrammites hiding under the rocks or pulled off the leaf of a plant and crushed it onto his tongue. Oyi-tsa sent him to spend time with the women, watching them prepare food, twist weeds into baskets and gather seeds from the flowering plants. If this was the way he was to learn of his grandmother's people it would take many years.

"When can I go to the sweat lodge?"

"There is much to learn before that time."

"Grandmother is doing better. I think we will be leaving soon."

"Then you must focus on learning."

Rique sighed and picked up the rock Oyi-tsa had set in front of him. "So this stone, it's used... for sharpening things, right? Don't you know that there is an easier way? We have a whetstone, I'll show you."

Oyi-tsa snorted. "To understand the way of the people you must understand that the Spanish way is the bad way. It leads to suspicion and greed and hatred."

How could a whetstone lead to all those things?

✡ ✡ ✡

Grandmother improved as the week passed. She could sit and drink, and was eating more of the strange foods his uncle brought to her each day. Rique was happy now, and it seemed as if Oyegi-a ye might have changed his mind about the family staying at the pueblo.

Juan and Pedro had different ideas. They sent Paloma to tell Rique their news.

"We are leaving tomorrow. They have sent a scout back to Taos and things have been settled. There is no reason for us to stay here for the winter." His sister smiled and nodded toward Grandmother. "She is well now, and if we travel slow it won't be a problem."

Relief washed over him. If they returned to Taos his father would be there to take care of things. Juan and Pedro might have their own ideas, but they would never disagree with Galit. Rique could go back to the carefree life he had left behind.

The following morning Rique woke before Grandmother or Oyi. He crept from the room and washed his face in the cool morning water of the creek. He would soon see Luisa and Pablo and he could tell his friends about the pueblo. Even the lessons he had dreaded would be a relief compared to those of Oyi-tsi. At least his teacher explained what he was supposed to learn. None of this mysterious waiting and sitting and nodding. Although yesterday, he had detected a smile at the corner of the old man's mouth when he mixed two leaves together and gave the paste to grandmother. He knew that one was for pain and the other for energy and figured the mixture might help her.

When the sun made her way over the steep canyon wall, Rique

knew it was time to prepare to leave.

"Grandmother, wake up." He shook her gently.

"Fadrique, you are full of energy this morning." She smiled and pushed herself into a sitting position. "Are you enjoying my brother's lessons?"

"Don't you remember? Today we go home. I will help you get ready for the journey." Rique vowed he would not leave her alone on this trip. She would ride her mare, but he would hold onto the reins and lead her down the trail and across the broad valleys.

Consuela's face lost the morning glow as a wave of gray swept from her forehead to her chin. "No. They must not go back there."

"It's all right. The scout has returned and the natives are calm. The Spanish—" Rique didn't really know much about what had happened. He hadn't thought to ask Paloma for details.

"Go get Juan. I must speak with him."

"But Grandmother, we will see him in just a few minutes. When we go down to the meadow."

"Help me." She reached out a hand to him.

Relief washed over him. She had decided to go.

It took a long time to get his grandmother dressed and mounted on her mare. *Don't rush, don't rush, that is how accidents happen*, he chanted inside his busy head as he led her down the trail. He peered ahead, surprised that no one had sent Paloma to hurry them along. He could see many people were mounted on horses and the tents and shelters had been packed onto the mules. The dogs and boys had gathered the sheep from the hills and were busy keeping the lively creatures in a tight herd.

Juan was waving his arms and talking with Pedro. He spotted Rique and walked to them.

"*Abuela*. I see our boy has you ready to go home."

"You cannot go."

Juan's smile faded, replaced by the look that said I-must-humor-this-old-woman.

"All is well. You should let your worries travel away with this autumn wind." Juan waved a hand to the trees.

Consuela shook her head and gripped the neck of the mare. "Whoever has given you the idea of safety, they are misinformed."

Juan's turned serious. "I didn't want to tell you this, but Popé has been found out. Treviño knows about the plan and has taken steps to stop the natives. I know these are your people and it grieves me that lives will be lost. But this time they are wrong. The Spanish are here and they bring a better life to this land."

"It is you who are misinformed. Popé is not a fool. He knows of Treviño's strategy. The Spanish will not defeat the natives."

Rique kept silent. He wanted to go home. He was tired of this adventure, worried about Grandmother and he missed his friends.

But Gabriella's words echoed through his heart. *Things will not always be easy,* she had said. *Decisions are forks in the road, once tread upon it is impossible to remove your footprints.* He reached into his pocket and rolled the stone. He must speak up.

"Can we stay here a few more days? Make sure that it is safe?"

Juan shook his head and rolled his eyes. "Fadrique, you are a boy. Keep out of a man's decisions."

Although Rique himself was struggling with the responsibility of being a man, he did not take kindly to his brother's insult. His fist tightened around the medallion and he stepped closer, raising the disc for all to see. "I am a man."

Juan's eyes narrowed and he turned back to Grandmother. "You gave him this?"

Consuela straightened to her full height, which barely brought her nose adjacent to Juan's chest. "Fadrique has been chosen."

"Chosen by whom? Does Father know about this?"

Rique pushed forward. "Yes. Father knows and he trusts me. He gave me instructions. We are to stay here until he returns."

"I'm sure Father gave you some sort of a man's task when he left. That is his way. He did it for me and Pedro, for all of us when we were boys. He thinks it will keep you out of trouble. It means nothing."

A whisper of doubt swirled into Rique's mind.

"Father could not anticipate the problems we are having here at Pueblo Lindo. He thought we would be welcomed, as it was in old times. But we are not. And now—" Juan stepped forward and waved an arm at the waiting family members "—I am in charge. I am the Patrón of the family. You have wasted enough of our time. We are leaving and you had best come with us."

Rique looked at Grandmother. Tears ran down her pale cheeks and she bit her lip. She reached for his hand. "I cannot make the choice for you, but I will stay here. I..." she stopped and looked down shaking her head back and forth, over and over as her tears flowed.

Rique turned back to Juan. "Some leader you are. Taking our family away from safety. You know that Oyegi-a ye has agreed to us staying."

Juan reached out and shoved Rique to the ground. As soon as the boy hit the earth, the older brother grabbed his arm and yanked him up again. He slapped his face and shook him. "You will show respect to me."

Rique felt the trembling start in his heart and quickly move through his arms and legs. His face grew hot and his brain felt as if it would burst through the top of his skull.

Juan grabbed the back of Rique's shirt and pulled him away from Grandmother. Rique could see the stares of Paloma and the others, but no one stepped forward to interfere. Juan struck the back of his head again and again. His brother hurled him to the ground once more. Rique hugged his abdomen to protect his body from his brother's kicks. Juan stopped and took a breath.

Rique leapt up with the speed of a bobcat and ran toward the river.

His mind raced as fast as his feet. He would hide and stay here with Grandmother. Let Juan and the others go where they want.

Rique was surprised to hear heavy footsteps behind him. He hadn't thought that Juan would follow. Soon his flight took him to the edge of the river. He whirled to face his brother.

Juan's face was red, with anger or exhaustion, Rique didn't know. He raised his fists.

But Juan didn't strike him. "You will stop this childish nonsense and come with me. If you are so eager to be a man, than act like one. You have upset Mother, and Paloma is hysterical."

Rique shook his head.

"You wear the medallion, but you do not know what that means. With membership in the Brotherhood you are committed to standing by this family. To protecting our heritage and our property."

"That is what I am trying to do."

"A man does not make decisions with emotions and love for women, he makes decisions based on facts and reason. You are not deserving of the medallion and it was foolish of Grandmother to give it to you. She does not have the right to do that." Juan pulled his own medallion from under his shirt. "See this? The true medallion, given by Father, the head of the family. That is the only way membership can be passed on. Not by a woman."

Juan sprang towards him and grabbed at his medallion. But Rique was ready. He ducked and jumped up on a large boulder. The current ran swift beneath him. He was a good swimmer, jumping was an option.

"Give that to me," Juan shouted. "Give it to me right now."

Although Rique had thought about jumping, he hadn't thought about slipping. In his attempt to dodge Juan's hand, he twisted and his feet lost their grip on the smooth rock. He landed hard on his arm and clutched at the surface of the boulder, but there was no hold for his desperate fingers. The cold water was over his head in an instance and he gasped for a breath.

The angry river did not like such disruptions. It tossed the boy around, teasing him by pulling him under and spitting him up for just long enough to fill his lungs. The boulders were not so forgiving, and Rique felt the blow to his forehead just before his world went black.

Twenty-nine
Gabriella
Tuesday, May 6

I stood on the river bank confused. Last night I had sat next to Consuela, and in spite of the difficulty she had in drawing a breath and my constant requests that she save her strength, she had told me stories. I learned of her love for Bernardo, her many children, and her lack of fear of death. But now, with only a river and trees around me I didn't know where I was or, more important, when I was.

A shout from up river caught my attention. Two men struggled and I watched as one seemed to push the other into the churning water. The one in the river fought against the current and I ran along the bank in hope that I could save him. A branch, that's what I needed. I knew jumping in was the wrong thing to do, but I glanced over my shoulder to see if the other man would jump in.

He was gone. I couldn't waste time thinking about where he might be; if he was in the water I would have to save him, too.

One would think that in a dream there could always be a happy ending. Super strength, the appearance of a suitable branch—why couldn't I conjure up those things?

As I watched the man sweep past me, no longer struggling or trying to swim, I recognized Rique. Not a man, a boy. Surely I was meant to save him? My heart jumped as if he were my own child and I ran frantically downstream after him.

The canyon walls narrowed and the path disappeared. The only way to follow was to jump in the water, but with the narrowing of the canyon, the strength of the river grew stronger. The white tumbling rapids were more than anyone could survive.

I sank to the ground and sobbed, Rique's face haunting me. "I'm sorry, I'm sorry I couldn't save you."

When I woke in the morning I couldn't remember anything after the terrible loss of Rique. These dreams were so frustrating.

I needed to go back and see Rachel. The dreams were changing, growing stronger, and I was moving in and out of them in strange ways. Asleep, not asleep. Observer or an active part of the events. The medallion made the dreams stronger, but it didn't seem to have the power I had attributed to it. I had never heard anyone talk about dreams that were a continuous story, a story in which they played an active part.

At least my dreams didn't feel like hallucinations any more. I only traveled when I was asleep and I hadn't had them when I slept with Andy in the bed of his truck, so they were definitely dreams. Even with Consuela's advice, that I could control them if I just asked for Rachel's help, some stubborn part of me felt that asking the old woman was giving in. The part of me which dealt with Fred and Joel, Mark and Greg, even Andy, all these men and my reliance and frustration and confusion. The dreams had to be signs, messages, I needed to pay attention to them. Maybe they were sent to cure me of my habit of blundering forward with my eyes closed.

✧ ✧ ✧

Tuesday afternoon, as Bones and I walked along the edge of the dry creek—she watched for prairie dogs and I watched for snakes—I heard Andy's truck bump over the wooden bridge. I hurried up to the house, hoping he was here for the night.

Andy stood in the open doorway, scanning the new and improved living quarters. "You cleaned up in here."

I could hear the unspoken part of his comment. "Yep. Doesn't seem like I'm getting out of here in a hurry, so I might as well be comfortable. Not that your truck isn't comfortable," I added.

I had gone shopping in Chama and added some luxury items: a card table, a propane lantern and several buckets. The camp stove was set on a crate turned on end so that I no longer had to stoop to stir my nightly canned soup. The cot and my suitcase were in the bedroom, although without Andy for heat I moved my makeshift bed closer to the stove each night.

My arms twitched, ready to wrap around Andy's shoulders. I waited for him to step forward with a hug and kiss, but he drew in a breath and stayed where he was.

"I want to talk about the medallion."

My hand slapped against my chest, pressing the mysterious disc into my skin. Did he know I was wearing it all the time?

Without a word, I slipped the chain over my head and handed the necklace to him, but in my heart I was handing it to Romero, not Andy. I watched as he turned to the sunlight shining through the window, and tipped the medallion so that he could examine the design. He ran the chain through the tips of his fingers and the thick links slid effortlessly through his hand. He traced the tree on the front, then flipped to the back and studied the foreign words, his lips moving slightly.

"Do you know what this means?" He didn't look at me, but continued to stare at the medallion.

"No. I don't even know what language it is."

"Why are you wearing it?"

When I hesitated, Andy turned and looked at me. As he did, I noticed him squeeze the medallion, the whole thing fit in his large hand, hidden from my view. I watched to see if he felt the heat of the disc.

"I..." I felt as if I were at the top of a sheer cliff, a vast expanse spread beneath me and above me the endless sky. *Jump*, the earth said. *You can trust him.* "I wanted to have the dreams."

"Dreams?"

"When I wear the medallion, I have these dreams."

"The ones you told me about the other day? With people you know in them?"

"Yes. But not exactly. Our ancestors, I think."

"My ancestors?"

"I'm not sure. Mine, yours, a lot of people."

"What else happens? When you wear the medallion?" He opened his hand and stared once more at the tree on the face of the disc.

"It gets hot."

"You control the weather?"

I saw a this-chick-is-crazy look sweep over Andy's face.

"The medallion gets hot. Sometimes it gets cold."

There is a point in time when one makes a decision. There is always that point, but often it is not visible until you look back. All my life I've always looked back. Even stopped the car and sat, puzzling over something that wasn't right. Was the iron on? Had I locked the dog outside? Things I had never forgotten to do had the power to haunt me, to grab hold of my thoughts and force them in a direction I didn't want to go. As I watched Andy's face, I jammed on the brakes. My words had done something to our relationship, something I couldn't take back or control by checking things one more time. I waited to see what he would do, now that I had truly stepped off the cliff. He didn't speak so finally I broke the silence.

"Do you think I'm having hallucinations? Have I lost it?"

"No-o-o..." Andy hesitated. "Not really. But the visions are a problem. There's a logical way to think about it, but we have to do something."

His soft tone made me uneasy. Why had he said *we*? When did this become his problem? "Do what?" I asked.

"I'm not sure," he continued. "Have you thought about writing things down?"

I shrugged. "What good would that do?"

"It might help form a time line." he said. "You could talk to Rachel about it."

Rachel. Of course. Her again. "Rachel confuses me."

"More than the visions?" He took hold of my wrist. "You need help with this, Ella. It's… dangerous to deal with it on your own."

I pulled my arm away. In that moment I felt I'd lost him. He did think I was crazy. He was only being kind, not saying so outright. Acting like he wanted to help. What he really wanted me to do was take my problems to someone else. Rachel.

"I'm not crazy," I whispered, feeling the anguished doubt take hold of me. "I used to be, but I'm not anymore. The visions, they're just…" My gut clenched and I felt the sudden bowel cramps of imminent diarrhea. I raced around the house, not even stopping to grab the shovel.

When I returned he had moved our chairs over to the bank, the lantern lit beside him.

"Sorry."

"Ella," he stood and touched my arm. "This is making you sick. You can't ignore it anymore."

"What do you mean?" *Why was he making such a big deal out of this?* I shouldn't have told him anything.

"The visions mean something. Until you get to the bottom of them, grasp the meaning, you won't be able to move on."

"Can we talk about something else?"

He put his hand on my cheek and gazed straight into my eyes. "Think about it. Where do visions come from? The medallion. You inherited them. I told you before—New Mexico, it's different. There are things that can't be explained here."

Tears slipped from my eyes and I pressed into his arms. The vise that had clamped my heart into a stranglehold slipped just a notch. I hated myself for letting him hug me into submission, but I couldn't stay out of his arms. The black hole was too close.

Thirty
Hernan Martínez
Taos, New Mexico 1855 to 1858

Hernan Martínez stomped from the room filled with men. He grabbed the reins of his bay mare, jumped on her back and with a sharp kick of his silver spurs sent her down the road.

He couldn't believe the decisions made tonight. Fools!

"Home so early?" His wife was seated in the kitchen. Francesca sewed under the lantern on cool nights, not admitting that she waited up for him. He threw his hat onto the table.

"We are no longer a part of the Brotherhood."

"What?" She set down her work. "What happened?"

"That fool, Naranja. He has blinded the Brothers with his fancy tales. They voted to relax the secrecy. There are even some that lean toward open worship. Thomás Naranja has them thinking that someday we will have a synagogue, right here in Taos." Hernan slammed his fist down on the table.

In 1847 the wars of the world moved to Taos. Men fought neighbors as well as the *Americanos*. The New Mexicans moved ahead with their plans and killed the governor. For five years Taos had remained untouched, but things slowly changed. As flour will gradually leak from the sack through a pin hole, so did the *Americanos* take over the pueblo. The Treaty of Guadalupe Hidalgo had opened the door to free worship. But when the Catholics brought in that Frenchman to lead, to be Apostolic Bishop, there was a wave of fear. This man wanted to change the practices of the

Hispanos. Practices the Brotherhood had worked to build so that no one looked very closely at how each man worshipped.

Now the Brothers were claiming they had hidden for too long and given up too much. Why couldn't they see they would destroy all that had been carefully constructed over the last four hundred years? Were the memories of his brothers so weak that they forgot New Mexico was denied statehood and remained a territory? Trusting *Americanos* was a huge mistake.

"They fail to look at history. For a thousand years we have been lured into complacency, only to lose our lives when the tide changes. My entire family wiped out by Popé in one fell swoop is not something I can forget. If not for Pueblo Lindo and one foolish twelve-year-old boy's resistance that would have been the end of the Martín de Serrano family."

"You think that could happen again?" Francesca's family had converted. Truly become Catholic for many generations. It was only since her marriage to Hernan that she had learned the old ways and given up her rosary beads. "Do you think my family will be in danger? Because of me? Maybe I should go back to being Catholic."

Hernan was saddened that his wife would be so quick to abandon the old faith. He also noticed her last statement was not a question. "Francesca, I think our family is safe because we are careful. If we quit using caution we are all in danger."

"So you have resigned from the Brotherhood? We will no longer have their protection?"

She spoke the truth. The Brotherhood had saved many people from exposure. But Hernan knew even intelligent men made poor decisions. He thought of his ancestor, Fadrique. There were two versions of this story. In one, Fadrique only survived the Indian revolt because he ran away and nearly drowned. In the other version, the young boy resisted the directives of the Brotherhood and stayed on the pueblo with his native relatives. In both versions the Martínez family was nearly wiped out by the revolting natives.

Hernan did not see how the Brotherhood would help in the future if they did everything Thomás Naranja was suggesting. Naming children the old Hebrew names. Keeping the Sabbath openly, rather than in a clandestine way.

He folded Francesca into his arms. "I have resigned. Do not worry." As he felt her trembling subside he knew that above all else he must keep her safe.

✡ ✡ ✡

The next day Alejandro Rodrigo rode into the Martínez courtyard. He did not dismount.

"Hernan, will you join me for a ride?"

Hernan looked at his friend. They had been like brothers for thirty years, since they were babies together. With a nod, he went to the corral for his mare.

They rode side by side toward the Rio Grande, not speaking.

It wasn't until they reached the edge of the deep canyon and looked down at the winding river that Alejandro spoke.

"Are you really going to leave the Brotherhood?"

"I am and you should too. If you want your family to be safe you should not be lured by empty promises."

"Decisions have not been made. We are still discussing things." Alejandro used his bandana to wipe sweat from his nose. "Your temper will get the best of you. We need you there to give input. Not everyone thinks as Naranja does."

"Then why did they not speak out last night?"

"They did. After you left." Alejandro snorted. "They did not yell, my friend."

Hernan was known for his quick temper. But he was also known for his sharp wit and the ability to think deeply.

"You have the Martínez blood," his *abuela* had told him when he was a boy. "It is thick and passes well from generation to generation."

Hernan shook his head now, as he thought of the old woman's stories. Fadrique had saved himself, but not the other members of the family. He wouldn't make the same selfish mistake. He turned to Alejandro.

"When is the next meeting?"

"I invite you only if you don't bring that Martínez temper with you."

☼ ☼ ☼

Hernan tried to keep his promise, but when so many of the Brothers, like cats waiting for milk, turned their faces to Thomás Naranja, he exploded.

"This will be death to us all. You discard the ways which have provided safety to our people and I cannot be a part of this. Do not come knocking at my door when the persecution closes in."

This time no one came to invite him back.

Never one to sit and gaze at the stars awaiting his fate, within two months Hernan had a plan. He would start his own branch of the Brotherhood. Secret from the rest.

He spent weeks planning, thinking, creating and discarding ideas. How would he keep the others from exposing him? Should he uproot his family and move? He must think of a way to protect them as well as his property, his belief and the promise of the Brotherhood. The original promise, not some modern idea these men had trumped up. *He who believes and persists lives forever.*

He grew thin and Francesca was worried about all the time he spent out on his horse.

It was a blustery spring morning when he rode his mare out to the grove of cottonwoods along the creek on the eastern border of his land. As he let the horse graze on the new blades of grass, he heard the pounding of hooves.

It was Alejandro Rodrigo.

Hernan had thought that his friend would leave the Brotherhood, but Alejandro stayed with the others. These men who had rejected Hernan as too worried, calling him an old woman.

The two friends had not spoken since the split.

Hernan scowled. This could only be bad news.

Rodrigo pulled his horse to a stop and spoke rapidly. "The *custodes* have come to Taos. Fray Chavez is to be excommunicated at the least. There has been talk of something as extreme as execution."

Manuel Chavez was a member of the Brotherhood.

"Executed? Not excommunicated?"

Alejandro shook his head. "This new church, it is not like the old. The charge is not Judaism, it is falsely portraying a priest. The Bishop is horrified because it means that anyone baptized, any confession heard, anyone married by Fray Chavez, all of these must be corrected."

It was what Hernan had predicted. "There is no fear that Manual Chavez will betray the others. He is strong."

Alejandro reined his restless horse into a tight circle. "His exposure has triggered a search. Men from Santa Fe have been sent to all the outlying places to examine the lists of the church, not just a glance, like before, but a true search. They are questioning all those who appear on the church rolls, all members, and verifying each one has a commitment to Catholic worship."

Alejandro steadied his horse once more. The nervous gelding reflected his anxiety. "There are many who are not as strong as Chavez. They are what we worry about. These men will trade information for a lesser punishment."

Francesca. Hernan pictured his wife's lovely face, frowning and crying. She would panic. He also feared she would trade information for the safety of her own family. His chest grew tight and his face warmed from rage. He turned to his former friend.

"And what do you want from me?"

Alejandro had the decency to look guilty before he answered. "The Brotherhood needs you. They need your guidance in this issue."

"You have Thomás Naranja for guidance. Follow his lead."

"Naranja is no longer with the Brotherhood."

"So now you turn to me?" Hernan reined his horse toward home. Just before he put his spurs to the animal he looked over his shoulder at Alejandro. "Too late, my brother. Too late."

By the time Hernan reached the house, he had made up his mind. "Francesca!" He called out as he searched the house for his wife. He found her on the patio. "Where are the children?"

"They are with Marcía. Down by the creek. What's wrong? Why are you shouting?"

"We are going on a trip. You must pack immediately. We leave in the morning."

"A trip?"

"I will explain it to you tonight. Just get the children."

Her eyebrows rose high and her lips pinched into a tight bunch, as if she had bit into a lemon. Not the tears he had imagined, but a fierce look.

"I'll do no such thing. Not until you explain this. My mother's birthday is next week and we are having a celebration here. Musicians have been hired and I have already prepared food for the party. This is spring. There is seed to be planted and the new lambs cannot be left alone."

Hernan turned to her with anger, but he quickly swallowed his emotions and calmed his tone. He had learned his lesson slowly, but he had learned it. Francesca could be like a stone wall, impossible to tumble.

"There is trouble coming to Taos. The Catholics are conducting an investigation. It is best if we are not here when they arrive."

"What do you mean an investigation? Are my parents in danger?"

"No. It won't get that far. But it might get to me." He didn't add that her parents were just what the church desired. True conversos for many, many generations. True believers of their Catholic church.

"Then you go. Run away. I will not leave my home."

"And your children? You will let them go with me? Or will you keep them here to be discovered as false conversos?"

"They are Catholic. Baptized and recorded on the rolls of the church."

Hernan took hold of her arm and put his face close to hers. Her warm cinnamon smell both calmed him and filled him with anxiety. He must protect her. "Not this time. This time those damn priests are inspecting each man."

"What do you mean? Inspecting? My children are not men."

"But they are boys," he swallowed. "They carry the sign of the covenant."

She slowly realized what he was saying. She had protested when they performed the circumcisions, but he knew it was because of the pain to her infants. She had given in to his strong need to comply with the covenant.

Now he wished he had listened to her protests. If only his sons were not circumcised, did not carry the scar that marked them as Jews.

✡ ✡ ✡

Three years for a thirty-five year old man does not feel like much time until he looks at his children. His family had hidden on the pueblo for much longer than Hernan had ever anticipated. Cristóbel had lost every bit of baby fat, stretching into a tall twelve-year-old. Estaban was nearly as tall as his brother. Cyrilla would soon be a woman and the native boys were doing everything possible to gain her attention. His children had studied with their mother, but he would like his sons to learn from an trained instructor. As the snow melted, Hernan's mind strayed to the life he once had. He didn't mind living in the pueblo. These people were his distant cousins and they had always welcomed his visits. But a time of pretending to live in this primitive way can only take a man so far. He was not a mountain man at heart; he was *Don* Hernan Martínez and he was worried about his property.

There would be a hunt today. Food supply was scarce during the long winter in Pueblo Lindo.

It had been nearly three months since he was able to get news from Taos. Soon the mountain pass would be clear and that would change.

Francesca begged him to take her back. She hated the cold clay rooms. She didn't like the food, even when Running Star helped her learn how to cook the maize and pine nuts.

"Our children grow wilder every day. I cannot teach the boys anymore and Cyrilla, I think you have noticed what is happening to your daughter. Hernan, take us back. Do not let her pass into womanhood in these mountains. Surely the inspection has been completed by now." She clung to his arm.

"We will go back when it is safe."

"But my parents, what if they are dead? Padre was sick when we left. If you don't take me then I will find someone who will."

"Threats are ill advised, my wife."

The arguments continued. Hernan did not bend. The thought of the attacks going on throughout New Mexico painted a gruesome picture in his mind. He had nightmares in which his lovely wife bled in his arms and his children were slain. These visions kept him strong enough to resist Francesca's pleas.

Hernan thought about the spring in Taos three years ago, the time when they fled. His sheep, his crops, his ranch. Would the hacienda still be there? Had Juan Gomez kept things in good shape for them? He trusted the foreman, but without news of the political sentiments in the place, he could not be sure they had a home to go back to.

✡ ✡ ✡

With spring comes new beginnings, melting snow, and clear passes. The messenger made it through in late April. Things in Taos had calmed. The church had completed the inspections which seemed to be merely a show of power and life was back to normal in their town.

Not only that, but Francesca had broken the news she would have another baby in September. Best that she travel now, before things became difficult for her. Hernan packed his belongings and his family for the journey home, the broad smile on his wife's face his reward for this decision.

Three days later Hernan stopped his horse at the border of his land. Juan Gomez rode out to greet the weary travelers.

"Don Hernan! Welcome home. Señora, you look well. Let me get you to the house. Maria has everything waiting for you."

"Gracias, Juan. It is good to be home. Let's get these women and children settled and then we ride the ranch."

"No rush. All is well."

"But that I must see for myself, no?"

Hernan and Juan rode every inch of the property, examining the sheep grazing near the house, the cattle and horses farther afield, the orchards, the oats and alfalfa just beginning to sprout, and finally stopping to look out over his favorite part of the river. The foreman had done an excellent job maintaining the hacienda in the family's absence.

"What about the town, Juan? Is all well there?"

The foreman shook his head and steadied his mare. "I fear not. Naranja has sold his land to *los Yanquis*."

"To the Americans?" Hernan looked at the man. "All of it?"

"*Sí*. He claims his wife insists on moving to Santa Fe. But..."

Apparently Juan knew more.

"But what?" Hernan demanded.

"He is now a very wealthy man. Word is he got two dollars an acre. The *Americanos* want the land badly. They will build a railroad."

"Has anyone else sold?" The land grants had been carefully constructed. Although each member of the Brotherhood had their own land, it went without saying that no one would sell without the approval of all. It wouldn't do for anyone to have a neighbor who was curious about the secret meetings.

"No. Not yet. But there is talk that many will sell."

Two days later Hernan sought out Alejandro. His friend was glad to see him, but Hernan didn't waste any time with small talk.

"What is this I hear of Naranja? Selling his land?"

"It is true, my brother. Silva, Luque and Pizarro have all sold as well. There is also the problem of the *Americano* homesteaders. They are not so careful that the land they choose does not already belong to someone."

"And the rest of the people? The land grants provide for sharing land for grazing. Do they agree to sell? What is their part of this wealth?"

Alejandro scowled, but did not answer.

"And the Brotherhood?"

"It is weak. Many are leaving the area. There are new Jews in Santa Fe and Las Vegas, men from the east. And women. They are building homes and there is talk of open worship. It may be that the Brotherhood has served its purpose."

"And you? What do you think?"

"I am not ready to abandon years of fraternity. But I do not think we need to worry so much any more. These Jews are from Europe. They have legal immigration papers for *Los Estados Unidos.*" Alejandro drummed his fingers on the heavy oak desk. "Will you be returning to us?"

Hernan shrugged. He knew that he would not give up so easily. If he came back to the Brotherhood, things must be a certain way. He needed a plan before he committed to anything.

Thirty-one
Gabriella
Wednesday, May 7 to Thursday May 8

Andy went back to work and life went back to normal. No, there wouldn't be any normal for me now, just day after dreary day of trying to figure out what I was going to do. An affair did not simplify my life, even if last week had been one long adventure.

After a frustrating morning in town, no progress on any fronts, I wasn't happy to see an unfamiliar green truck parked at the house. Maybe my frustration kept me from my usual freakout stranger anxiety, but I didn't hesitate to park my car and approach the truck.

"I'm over here." A vaguely familiar voice called from the porch.

Who would be so bold as to sit there? Had he gone in my house?

At least he had the decency to step into the yard to meet me. As soon as I saw him I knew who this was.

My cousin, Mark. He looked a lot like my father.

"You're back."

"Been here a few days. Couldn't find you. I looked at the house, but didn't see any sign of you. Figured you must have gone back to California."

No sign? What about all the clean up?

"Then I realized you might be over here." He glanced back at the adobe house. "You know, using that old stove with this roof is pretty risky."

"You told me to." Not another double speaking man. Just what I didn't need.

"I what?"

"You told me I would freeze if I didn't sleep inside with some heat."

Mark shook his head. "Why would I—oh, you're talking about our phone conversation. When I told you to sleep in the house." My cousin was good at the adolescent eye roll. "Not this house, *my* house." He pointed across the creek.

I looked at the small building I had supposed was the neighbors shed. I had actually avoided walking near it, thinking I would be trespassing. "I thought you said you lived in Los Ojos?"

"I do. But I did live here, until the well failed. I use the house for hunters. It's in better shape than this one."

"I've been fine here." I didn't know what to say. The air between us held a thick cloud of distrust. "I'd rather stay in my house, anyway."

"Your house? This isn't your house. Your parcel is over there." Again the wide sweep of the arm and the pointing finger. "I'll help you move. It's easier to get to my house anyway. It's next to the highway."

Now I was confused. He had pointed east, but wanted me to move south. "This house, it's the one Grandma and Grandpa built, right?"

"It is, but no one has lived here in years. Like I said, that roof? One spark and you'd be torched. You're crazy to stay here."

I drew in a breath. "Put that on hold for a minute. What about my land not being this part? I have maps." My visits with Fred Rivas and Joel Domingues had some value after all.

"Maps? How could you have maps? The final decision on splits hasn't been made."

"Well, something must have been decided, because I have maps."

"Who gave them to you?"

Here I was once again. What was it with this state? The Hatfields and the McCoys, but I could never figure out who was who. I kept silent, unsure of using Joel's name. Wasn't he friends with Mark? I was totally confused. Particularly by the vicious expression on my cousin's face.

I didn't really know him. Only by name. I tried to remember anything my parents might have said about him or Jeff. All I could dredge up was the fact that he had left California and moved to New Mexico. Mark worked for the water company, and he had some sort of job outdoors. He was a hunter. I remembered that because I really didn't like men who shot things for sport.

But I was learning about bullies. Back down and you were in trouble. I wouldn't be confrontational, just diplomatic.

"Whatever. It seems we have some paperwork to resolve before this inheritance thing is clear. I'm here, so let's do it." I didn't add that I had been here a month, waiting for him. "How about we arrange a meeting with Joel Dominguez?"

The dark ridge on Mark's forehead tightened, but he didn't say anything. I waited.

Finally he pulled out his cell phone and dialed, turning away from me while he talked for a mere five seconds. Pushing the phone back into his shirt pocket he looked at me. "Tomorrow at ten."

"Your phone works?"

He pointed to the top of the bluffs. "Tower. You just have to have the right kind of service."

I needed to talk to Mark about the Brotherhood. About our family being Jewish. But a feeling—call it bad vibes—told me not to trust him. I had fought with enough men for one day, so I kept the questions to myself.

✡ ✡ ✡

"Mark is back. He came and told me I don't own the house."

"What?" Andy opened two packets of sugar and dumped them into his coffee. We had our coffee at Three Ravens now that he couldn't spend every night with me.

"Said the maps I have are wrong. Joel Dominguez gave me them to me. I thought they were straight from the records office. Somewhere official." As I spoke I realized I didn't know where Joel had got them. My hackles went up. More mysteries.

"That can't be right." Andy sipped his coffee and stared across the creek. "You should research it."

He was acting weird this morning. Our talk, well, my crazy talk about the medallion, must have impacted him more than I thought. "I don't believe it, you know. That my ancestors were part of an evil cult." I reached to my chest. "The medallion isn't evil. I can feel it."

"Wait a minute. I thought you were the one who didn't believe in fairy tales."

"I don't. Or happy endings. But that's beside the point."

He didn't answer and something occurred to me. His mother was from Tierra Amarilla. A Luna, one of the names Rachel had rattled off to me.

"Do you have a medallion?"

"What? Why would I have one?"

"Fred Rivas told me he was a member of this Brotherhood. Are you telling me that you aren't?"

"I thought those were ancient brotherhoods. You're talking as if Fred goes to meetings."

I nodded. "He does." Well, now that I thought about it, no one had actually said that. Fred had mentioned a meeting though, so that must mean he went. "Andy, you keep telling me that you'll tell me things later, so I know there's some big secret. I can't... I can't..." I wanted to tell him I couldn't move forward with things. But talking about our relationship moving forward felt like jumping the gun. Lots of men and women had sex and didn't expect anything more. I didn't want to be some old fashioned geek about our week sleeping together.

"Well I don't know anything about any meetings. Seems Fred's grandmother would be the one to tell you more, and from what you say she's not talking."

Andy's tone was pissy.

"Don't lecture me about this. I'm not the one keeping secrets."

"Will you let up on the secrets Ella? I told you, it's nothing big and I'll talk about it when I'm ready."

"Are you married?"

He shook his head and pushed his cup to the middle of the table. "No, Ella, I am not married. I do not have any children, I do not have a secret life."

I raised a hand to my right eye and covered it. As soon as I made the move I knew. Headache coming. I never actually saw the aura others talked about, but my eye became sensitive to any light.

"I've got to go." I didn't wait for Andy to say goodbye.

I had read about this feeling in a novel. I don't remember the title or the author, only the remorse that hovered in my chest for weeks after I had turned the last page. Life had dealt the main character a rough hand. He had become stronger with each terrible event in his life.

Why was it that pain was supposed to make us grow? It was all a lie, a way to keep from falling into hopelessness, as far as I could see. If life was hopeless, shouldn't we feel hopeless?

The headache hit full force just before I turned off the highway onto the dirt road. I stopped for a moment and closed my eyes. My medication was back at the house and if I didn't take it soon the nausea would make it impossible for me to take without vomiting.

The medallion pulsed cool against my chest. Seeking the relief that ice could bring me at times, I pressed it against my forehead.

To my amazement it provided some relief. Enough for me to open my eyes and drive to the house. I took my medication and lay on the cot with the pillow over my eyes.

Migraines can only be tamed by complete silence, stillness and darkness. Medication dulls the pain and takes me to a place where I can drift off to sleep. Most often I awaken hours later with a hung over feeling. Not the perfect cure, but much better than the intense strikes of lightning, the vomiting and the diarrhea that can hit if I don't handle the headache.

I had the quiet and the dark, but I could not stop my racing mind. It had been one thing after another ever since I came to this place. This damn land. Crazy dreams and hidden religions. Mark and his lies, Andy and his lies, probably Rachel and Fred and Joel Dominguez and their lies. I couldn't get the truth out of anybody in this whole state.

I couldn't figure out what I could do about it. When you're an outsider, how do you fight or move forward or resolve issues?

Just before I drifted off to sleep—the medication was doing its job after all—I had a thought.

I could go back to California and hire my own attorney to sell the land. Escaping that particular headache was as easy as driving away.

Thirty-two
Francesca Tafoya Martínez
Taos, 1880

"But Hernan. For ten years these men you call brothers have made you miserable. This is a good offer." Francesca kept her voice calm, the best way to deal with her stubborn husband.

"He can try for one hundred years and he will not get my land."

"Patton plays dirty. How long before he hurts our family?" She tipped her head toward Jonas. Her grandson sat near the fire, his head stuck in a book. The boy loved to read.

It was spring of 1880 and all of her children were gone, scattered to Santa Fe, Albuquerque, and New York. When Cyrilla had married Salomón Seligman, Francesca knew her daughter was lost to her. Although her new son-in-law promised he would stay in New Mexico, when his mother became ill he insisted on taking Francesca's beloved daughter and grandchildren back to New York.

Jonas was only on temporary loan. Just with her until Cristóbel finished building his house in Texas. Poor boy. No mother and a father who couldn't find happiness. Her son moved from place to place in search of something which did not exist.

"Leave him with me," she had begged Cristóbel. "Taos is a good place to grow up."

"Not anymore," he insisted. "Things are changing."

And he was right.

Francesca imagined that she would someday be Catholic again. Maybe when Hernan died. She moved her fingertips quickly across her chest to form the sign of the cross. Why did she think such a thing? She remembered the fights she had when each of her sons were born. The ceremony her husband insisted on. But after the bad years, when they had been forced to leave Taos and go to that terrible pueblo, she had not let him use a knife on Luis.

"No," she insisted. "You can have your prayers, your belief, but you will not mark my baby. He will grow up Catholic. He will grow up safe."

To her surprise, her husband had agreed. But Luis was not safe, in spite of her decision. Her baby died of influenza when he was barely a year old.

Her beloved Taos had changed so much in the last twenty years.

So many people came from the east, the south and even the north. It wasn't long before the town wasn't so Catholic. It was filled with Methodist farmers, Presbyterian cattle ranchers and Jewish businessmen.

One by one, Brothers sold their land to the *Americanos*.

Everyone except Hernan.

Joseph Patton and the other foreign ranchers silently negotiated for the Spanish land that had been granted to the New Mexicans as a reward to conquistadors, colonists and padres. Land which belonged to groups of settlers was sold by heirs who did not love the land and had no real rights to sell it. Deception was common and many men used tricks to become rich under the noses of their own families. Documents were posted in English, not even sent directly to those involved. As if this somehow informed the Spanish colonists of the chance to fight the theft of their land.

How were people who depended upon the grazing of sheep supposed to live?

Progress, progress, progress. Francesca read the speech General William T. Sherman delivered in Santa Fe. He hoped to outlaw the adobe house. She had seen pictures of the *Americano* houses: wood that would quickly rot, sleek tin roofs that would heat a home like a furnace, especially because they were all two stories high. Some even had attics. These new leaders were so impractical. Yesterday she heard that the Denver and Rio Grande Railway had bigger plans, plans which cut directly across the Martínez hacienda.

Francesca turned back to her husband. "Why shouldn't we take the offer, Hernan? Move west."

She watched his face. He actually appeared to be considering what she said.

"You would be happy? Away from our home?"

She hesitated. "*Sí*. There is nothing here. All of my children have moved to other places."

"What of Jonas?"

"He will come. Cristó will just have to travel a little farther to get him when the time comes." Having her grandson with her would make the move to Las Nutrias easier. She didn't know anyone in that town.

The Brotherhood wanted Hernan out of this town. She knew the talk. The young men considered her husband a hindrance to the evolution of the group.

Two months ago, when he once again refused to sell to Joseph Patton, four members of the Brotherhood came to the house.

"Francesca, leave us alone. It looks like my Brothers want to ta-a-a-alk." Hernan spoke with sarcasm, stretching out the word.

As she rose to leave, Alejandro glanced at her and spoke. "Francesca. Stay. This is for you too."

Hernan shrugged and she sat back down in the armchair.

"We have an offer for you, my friend. Two thousand acres of prime land in the town of Las Nutrias. Clear deed, no land grant questions asked. This place is soon to be the county seat. It is not the middle of nowhere, like your Pueblo Lindo."

"That is how you choose to get me out of your hair? To force me to fold to the demands of *El Diablo*?"

Francesca gasped, shocked that her husband would openly label Patton as the devil.

"It is a good offer. More freedom than you have here. Something to leave to your grandson. Taos has become… " Alejandro hesitated. "Modern."

"You know the beauty of my land. You would have it destroyed?"

"Not destroyed. Developed."

Within minutes Hernan had thrown the men from the house.

Since that night things had changed. Sheep and cattle went missing, the creek was suddenly dry as water was diverted upstream, merchants ran out of important items when Francesca shopped and Alejandro did not come to visit.

Last night her husband's favorite horse had been killed.

And now, heart in her throat, Francesca waited for Hernan to reconsider the offer.

With a sigh, her husband turned to her. She felt like crying at the sight of his face. The heavy wrinkles of his forehead drew up tight, his eyelids folded down covering the blue that had faded with the years. He looked eighty years old instead of fifty-seven.

His hand trembled as he drew it to his chin. "I will think on it."

Thirty-three
Gabriella
Friday, May 9

I rolled up my sleeping bag and set it by the door, then folded up the cot. The sense of relief that followed my decision to go back to California had chased away my headache, and with a good night's sleep behind me, I was filled with energy.

The earth and the sky decided they liked energy as well. Thunder and lightning were old school to me now, but the downpour that opened just as I was about to load the car was unbelievable. It was as if every rain storm I had ever lived through came together in one big cloud.

I moved my things to a corner of the room without a leak. Amazingly, this roof which Mark had warned could go up in a flaming ball, was able to keep out most of the rain. I slipped my camp chair out of the sleeve and sat next to the window with the best view of the creek.

No one can ever tell you what a flash flood is. You can hear numbers—the water level rose eight feet in ten minutes—but those are meaningless without personally watching a meandering creek turn into raging rapids. Amazed, I watched the water pour through the valley, happy there was a wide meadow of prairie dog villages and a tall bank between the adobe house and Las Nutrias Creek. One of the huge cottonwood trees fell with a crash that shook the earth. I had to cross the acequia if I were to leave, but I couldn't see the old railroad-tie bridge from the house. There was no way of judging what was happening on the far side of the property.

Loneliness comes in many forms. As I sat and watched the storm I thought about Andy. Was I really going to leave without talking to him? In barely a month I had gone from fear of stalking to unbelievable love-making to fighting. I guess we hadn't really fought, but something was wrong. I was doomed in the relationship area if this was New-Ella's mode of operation. Sex didn't mean love, but what about how... un-lonely I felt in his arms?

Wait. Didn't I have good reason to walk away? His tone, his secrets, the confusion of the emotions I felt when with him? I didn't owe him anything and it would be really stupid to let a man tell me what I should and shouldn't do.

I sighed and rubbed my neck, feeling the headache slowly creeping back up my spine. What was it about this place that could generously fill me with some sort of spiritual rush, then quickly snatch it away? Maybe it was cursed. This land threatened me with a religion I didn't know anything about, love that confused me and a family history so far-fetched I had trouble believing it could be true. But this land also took me on journeys into a quiet peace that swept the black hole away. Even if the darkness found its way back, I was soothed for the moment.

The medallion was tucked into my cosmetic bag, packed next to my mini-shampoo and toothpaste. I had actually thought about leaving it here, but this was the key to something about my family's past that I needed to unravel. The cool disc on my forehead had staved off the worst of the headache, maybe it would work again. But the medallion never made it to my forehead, because, as I raised it, this world disappeared into the swirling rain.

I was in a building, old, but more modern than the rooms of the pueblo I had been in with Consuela. A man sat at a rough-hewn wooden table, his head cradled in his huge palms.

I kept quiet and examined the room. From the embroidered curtains, the guns—muskets, I thought—hanging on an iron rack, the spinning wheel in the corner, and the clay oven built into the wall, I guessed this was much later than any of the previous dreams.

Should I speak to him? Or would he grab one of those muskets and shoot me, a strange woman suddenly appearing in his home?

The sound of sobs came from the next room. Whatever was making the man hold his head in such despair was also making someone cry.

He rose abruptly from the table and rushed through the arched doorway to the room with the sobs. I followed and stood in the shadow near the door with a view into the next room.

Woven blankets adorned the floors and walls. Pottery was filled with flowers and set on glistening table tops. A ornately carved wooden trunk guarded one wall.

The sobs came from a beautiful woman, who slumped on a chair near the fire. The long braid which curved over her shoulder was a mixture of auburn and gray. A wide lace collar graced a muslin blouse. I could see the edge of her woolen skirt, woven in patterns similar to the rugs and blankets. I could not see her face.

"Please do not cry, *mi amor*." The man shifted back and forth, from side to side, in front of the woman. "These decisions are difficult, I know. But this is our home."

"Aren't you the one who tells the stories of the Jews finding a new home? Why is this any different?" She wiped her cheek with a lace handkerchief and looked at him.

"I tell the stories so that we can benefit from the trials of the ancient ones. So that we can have a home because of their hard work."

"This is no longer my home. Not with men creeping here in the night to harm us. I cannot sleep. If I close my eyes they will snatch you or Jonas and I will be dragged into the road and left to die."

I nearly gave away my hiding place with my gasp. Jonas? My great-grandfather?

The man spoke again. "Your imagination is far beyond the scope of what the men would do."

"No, it is not. I know this is hard for you, but think, Hernan, think about the years to come. A safe new place for Jonas to grow. We could be there."

Hernan reached for her hand. That name, where had I heard it before? It took only a second to remember the carved wooden headstones up on the hill—the partial history that had been washed away by the weather. I had seen this man's grave. These must be the Jonas's parents. My great-great grandparents.

The woman sat up straight and raised her chin. "We made so many mistakes. Our children—" she waved a hand around the room. "They are gone. They do not want this ranch. There is nothing to be inherited if the heirs do not have the desire. Can you not see that God has given us another chance? We can go and build something that is his. Jonas will be a part of it."

"Do you accuse me of not including our children in the building of this ranch?"

"I do not accuse, my love, only try to explain. Yes, I must say that you are too strong a man for our children to feel a part of things. Yanking them off to that pueblo, then moving them back again. They resented that."

"What are you saying? No word of resentment ever crossed their lips."

I saw her chin drop and she shook her head slowly. His tone scared me as well.

Her shoulders straightened and she lifted her face. "Not that you would hear. But look around you, Hernan. Where are your children?"

My great-great grandfather went pale. I watched as his eyes filled with tears and he sagged down into the wooden chair near the table. His head went back into his hands, as I had seen him when I arrived.

She rose and turned to him. Now I could see her face. It was a face I recognized. The slim nose, the arched eyebrows, the hazel eyes and the delicate chin.

It was my face.

She knelt and put her arms on his lap, crossing them and resting her chin under his slumped face.

These two people were in pain. A pain far greater than any I had ever felt. This decision—to move away from this place—it must come with a very high price. Tears gathered in my eyes. I squeezed my hands into fists, wanting to help them. She was so like me, or I was so like her, it was my pain I witnessed.

She didn't say anything more and he didn't speak either. I could only watch as the two sobbed, the soft cries blending to the point where I couldn't tell which sound belonged to which person. He grasped her hands between his and she looked up into his face. Using the edge of his shirt he wiped her tear stained cheeks.

"We cannot know the future. If I felt that moving to Las Nutrias would change everything, I would leave this place. But pain has a way of following us wherever we go."

"Do you not see, my love? The place, the Brothers, the other people, the politics of *Los Estados Unidos*, we cannot let these be what makes us happy or unhappy. We have each other, do we not? We have Jonas. Can that not be enough to bring us joy no matter where we live?"

✿ ✿ ✿

I woke with a start, clutching the medallion so tightly that my hand was white and tingling from lack of circulation. This woman, the wife of Hernan, I wished I knew her name. We were connected, not only by blood, but by decisions and choices. My heart ached with the intensity of her love for her husband. And it seemed he loved her with the same great power. I wanted to go up to the graves and figure out who she was. I wanted a name for my great-great grandmother.

The rain had stopped. I could load my car, go check out the bridge and leave. There was really nothing keeping me here, now that the storm had decided to move to the east. But I didn't get up from the chair. I didn't grab the rolled sleeping bag, or slip the medallion back into my cosmetic bag.

I stared at the necklace. This journey I had made—it was about more than selling land. It was about more than fleeing Greg and his paperwork and his lack of explanation. It certainly wasn't about falling in love or getting trapped in another relationship.

It was about my father's firm grip and dark look. It was about family secrets and cousins who probably knew a lot more than they were letting on. It was about a stranger I allowed to work his way into my life because of a dream about someone who looked like him. It was even about figuring out the black hole that threatened me at every junction of my life. I could turn back on this road, pack the car, drive for three days, find an apartment close to my mother, find a job, have a weak facsimile of my previous life.

Or I could trudge forward, like the people in the dreams.

Traveling into the unknown with hope and confidence, even when weary, homesick and hungry.

In my dreams I felt the warm glow of the love of so many people. People whose blood flowed in my veins, whose memories came to life.

But here, in this time, when I was awake, things I would have laughed about six months ago, even six weeks ago—magic medallions, messages from the past, my own role in my history—all of these things were real and happening for a reason.

Stay here, go home, stay here, go home. I tried everything I knew about making choices. Listing the good and the bad, closing my eyes and mentally picturing the future for each option, imagining I was someone else giving myself advice, everything but flipping a coin.

I couldn't make a decision.

Thirty-four
Jonas Martinez
Tierra Amarilla, 1882

Twelve-year-old Jonas Martinez walked down the dusty road to the edge of town to look at the new sign. *Tierra Amarilla, Rio Arriba County,* the carved letters read. The sign maker had boldly included *(Las Nutrias)* underneath the name, a reminder of what the town had been called.

His grandfather had slammed a fist down on the heavy wooden table last night. "Joseph Patton is behind this name change. He's here now, buying up land. There's no escaping that man."

No one paid attention to Jonas. A quiet boy, he perfected the art of listening with his nose in a book. Timing was important when it came to questioning his grandfather. Jonas always waited several days after he overheard news passed between the men and his grandfather before he questioned Hernan.

"*Abuelo,* why does Señor Patton need so much land?" Jonas rode beside his grandfather as they went to check on the sheep.

"It's all about power, *Nieto.* The *Americanos* don't have the concept of shared land. Patton wants to fence the land and control who can graze." Hernan waved a hand over the field of grass. "The people share this land so that the animals can move to the best grass. If Patton can keep the best grass for his stock, then he will sell them for more money."

"Doesn't Señor Patton have a lot of money already?"

"That's where power comes in." His grandfather stopped his horse. "There is a balance, Jonas. Money is not a bad thing. It helps when needed. But the land, that is more important."

"Will we fence our land?"

"Never. It is open to all men."

"But what if Patton's cattle eat our grass?"

His grandfather turned and grinned, the smile never reaching his bright blue eyes. "It is your job to make sure that they do not."

✡ ✡ ✡

A year later there was a fence around the Martinez property. Grandfather and the other men had fought Patton, but the man was strong and now it was up to them to protect what they owned.

Jonas rode the fence lines every day. He carried a loop of wire and the tools for repairing the breakages. The elk and cattle were responsible for most of the bent wire and fallen posts, but it wasn't unusual for Jonas to find that the wire had been cut. He suspected it was the neighbors who didn't have much land for grazing.

"*Abuelo*, I found three spots cut today. Down by the ravine."

"That bastard! This is the last time, I tell you." Hernan grabbed his hat.

"Hernan!" His grandmother looked up from her needlework. "What are you doing?"

"I'm tired of being led around by the nose, Francesca. I told you we can't let him get away with this. He pushes it farther each time. Can you not feel his hands around my neck?"

Jonas tried to speak. "*Abuelo*, I don't think it was—" His grandfather stormed through the door and stomped into the yard.

He feared Hernan was going to kill Patton, but instead there was a meeting at the house the next night.

"You go to bed." Hernan ordered Jonas.

He pretended to go up the stairs and sleep. He stuffed his jacket under the covers, climbed out the window, stepped softly on the wooden porch, and curled below the open window.

Grandfather sounded relatively calm. "We must do something about Patton. He is disturbing the natural balance of our lives."

"There is nothing he can do to us. The Brotherhood holds clear title to land. He cannot take that from us." Manuel Luna was speaking.

"We held clear title in Taos. But that didn't stop Brothers from selling when the price was right. Patton is sneaky. He uses other men to buy for him. By the time anyone realizes what he is doing, all the land will be his. He wants to be King of all of Rio Arriba County. Look at the power he has—enough to change the name of our town." Grandfather's voice was loud now.

"But he doesn't care what we believe in. Isn't that the purpose of the Brotherhood? To protect our religious freedom, not to be concerned about land ownership?" That sounded like Benjamin Chavez.

Jonas listened to the men argue. He had heard them talk about the Brotherhood many times and he had figured out who belonged to the group, most of them Hernan's friends. But he didn't have the courage to ask his grandfather what this meant.

He was startled by his grandmother's touch upon his shoulder and her soft whisper. "Jonas. You must go to bed."

"I will, *Abuela*. What is the Brotherhood?"

"Just a club. Your grandfather and the other men, thinking they are something special. It needn't concern you."

Jonas lay awake in his bed, listening as Grandfather's voice lost the calm tone and grew sharp and loud. The voices continued late into the night. Jonas knew that his grandmother didn't understand the ways of men. No matter what she said, this did concern him.

In the morning life seemed the same, although Jonas watched his grandfather for signs that something might be happening. But that afternoon all was erased from his mind.

His father rode into town. Cristóbel came when he could, which wasn't often enough for Jonas. He hadn't seen him in over a year.

Cristóbel was a cowboy. That's what Grandmother called him. Drifter and no good, was what Jonas heard about his father from others. But he loved Papa and couldn't wait to hear the tales of his latest adventures.

Papa seemed different. Unpacking his small bag and placing each item into the drawer of the old dresser, Cristóbel told Jonas that there would be no ranch in Texas. He didn't offer any explanation, but Jonas hoped this meant he was here to stay. He didn't let his father know that he had given up on moving to Texas a long time ago.

Jonas slept on the floor so Papa could have the bed; the gentle snores were like a lullaby, easing him to sleep each night. The two of them rode out to check the fences and dig a trench to bring water to a new corral. Papa helped *Abuelo* build the little house out on the land. Grandmother didn't want to move from town, but Hernan insisted they plan ahead.

"Papa, why does *Abuelo* want to move out here so far from town?"

"Persecution. A place to hide."

"From Patton? But this is not far enough. Patton could ride a horse out here in a few minutes, just as we do."

"No, Jonas. *Abuelo* doesn't hide from a single man. He hides from his ideas. From the fears inside his head. That's why your grandmother doesn't want to come. She is not afraid." His father spit out the thick wad of tobacco he held in his cheek. "She used to be the one, fearful all the time. I remember that. But something changed in her, I don't know when. Must have been when I was gone. She stands up to him now."

"Will you live with us?" Jonas was hopeful that the house outside of town would attract his father.

Cristóbel didn't answer. He stared off at the high bluffs and Jonas knew his father would be leaving soon. His heart dropped, but from past experience he knew that taking advantage of their time together was better than grieving.

"Papa, please tell me about the Brotherhood."

His father looked at him now. "The Brotherhood? What do you know about them?"

"Nothing. Grandmother says it's just a club, but I think there are more secrets."

"You are right. I'm surprised that *Abuelo* hasn't told you about it, you're thirteen now, *correcto?*"

"*Sí.*" What did thirteen have to do with it?

His father told him a tale wilder than any of the adventure stories he read each night. Jonas felt his stomach quiver at Papa's words. A secret religion? Hidden for hundreds of years? Men who were killed for the church they attended?

"What about the Methodists? Will they be killed when the enemy comes?"

"That's just it, son. No one will be killed any more. Not the Methodist, the Catholics, the Presbyterians or even the Jews. Not in these times. We are part of *Los Estado Unidos*, The United States. But your *abuelo*, he doesn't believe it. And those other men, the Brothers, they don't either. When I was a boy in Taos there were more Brothers. There was a fight between the old men and the young. That's why your grandfather moved here, to Tierra Amarilla. The Brotherhood here is a splinter, a break off from the others. I don't even know if the others still exist, I haven't been back to Taos. It holds bad memories for me."

"About Mama?" Jonas had only the slightest memory of his mother. He knew she had died of influenza when he was a baby. Grandmother told him the story of her beauty and her tragic death. Papa carried a photograph of her in his wallet.

His father reached out a hand and grasped his shoulder. "Yes, about Mama."

Thirty-five
Gabriella
Friday, May 9

The other thing I learned about flash floods is that they disappear as rapidly as they arrive. While I sat and contemplated the medallion and my future, Las Nutrias Creek returned to its meandering state. But things are not the same after a storm. Branches clogged the little stream's route, the uprooted cottonwood changed the flow of the river, and the soil turned to mud.

I decided to look at the bridge before driving that direction. My car stuck in the mud was one option not on the list.

The smell of the wet sage and cholla filled me with the peace that always comes after a rain storm. There was some chemical explanation, but I liked to think of it as Mother Nature's gift.

I picked my way down the muddy road inhaling the tangy after-the-storm smells. My feet grew thick with the yellow clay, yet I barely noticed because I was still thinking about the the intense love between Hernan and his wife. When my thoughts turned to Andy and Greg, I pushed them away, refusing to let anything intrude on a few moments of bliss.

The bridge was fine. Rocks and branches were caught on the downstream edge—the water of the acequia must have flowed right over the whole thing—but other than that it didn't look any different. There was still the question of driving through all the mud, but it seemed to be drying out even as I inspected things.

Clouds billowed off to the north and the east. I pulled out my phone and turned it on. Checking the weather before leaving would be wise, right?

Bzzz. Messages. Lots of them.

Hi Ella. I have some information for you. Call me. Andy didn't sound any different from usual. Was he one of those people who acted badly and then just ignored it? My resolve to avoid talking with him before I left faded. Information about what?

Mom, answer, why aren't you answering. I need you. Shannon sounded hysterical, but knowing her this could mean anything. She lost her favorite bracelet or she had a fight with a friend.

Ella, I don't know what's wrong with you. You need to return calls. This is ridiculous.

"Oh Greg. Sorry. I forgot." I spoke the words to the trees and the sky, as if my remorse could float through the atmosphere and get to him. He would be glad if I came back to California, just so he could track me down and shove paperwork under my nose.

Mom, please, please answer. I really need you to answer.

Mom, Julie said you don't have good service. I hope you listen to your messages some time. Please call me. I'm flying to New Mexico. I arrive in Albuquerque at 4:47, flight 238. Pick me up. I guess I'll just wait at the airport until I hear from you.

What? I looked at my phone to figure out what day Shannon had left this message and tried to remember when I had last listened to my messages.

Today. She was arriving today.

There was one more message and I pressed *listen.*

No words. Just sobs.

It was 2:30. She was probably in the air, so I texted her.

I'm on my way to pick you up. I might be a little late. Just wait for me.

Shannon in New Mexico. This changed everything. Maybe I should just pick her up and drive all the way to California, but I hadn't finished packing the car before I took off for the airport.

What had I left in the house? My sleeping bag, the cot, my camp stove. Nothing I couldn't live without.

I was past Santa Fe when Shannon called. Breaking every law, I answered while driving.

"Mom! I've been calling and calling." The sobs started and she ranted about something. "Jmba cong a bah loup jag."

"Shannon. I know you're upset, but I can't understand a word you're saying. Slow down and take a breath. Is everyone safe?"

My drama queen. Loud screams and hysteria from birth. I thought her startle reflex was overdeveloped, but the doctor insisted there was nothing wrong. *She's just sensitive*, he coached.

She choked her sobs and cleared her throat.

"He's gone. He left and I don't have enough money to pay the rent."

This was all about money. If she didn't have money to pay the rent how did she buy an airplane ticket?

Had Greg shuffled this problem onto me?

I held the phone away from my ear and sighed. Shannon knew the situation. This was her usual routine. Set me up to say no, when she knew all along whatever she was asking for was impossible. I brought the phone back to my mouth.

"Have you talked to your father?"

"How could you do that to me? That's what all divorced parents do, lob the kid over to the other parent." Her voice was shrill. "Back and forth, back and forth, with no one to stand up for ME!"

"Shannon, stop. I don't have the money. You know that. Why didn't you and Jason pay your rent? What happened to him?"

Silence.

"You are working, aren't you?" She had a job at the local grocery store. I knew she hated it—irregular hours, an unreasonable boss and low pay—but at least she had a job.

Shannon finally spoke. "Vicki said you have a boyfriend. I guess you have time for that."

Damn Vicki. I never should have talked about Andy. But I hadn't told her, had I? Only at the very beginning, when he was a stalker, not a boyfriend. Maybe Shannon was fishing.

"Shannon, I asked if you still have your job."

"I got fired."

Damn.

"Does your father know?" Was this an end run to run away from Greg's anger?

"Stop doing that. You guys are divorced. You don't get to know what he does anymore."

I spotted a black and white cruiser up ahead and stopped myself from reminding her that we weren't divorced yet. "Look, we can finish this conversation when I pick you up. I'm about an hour away still. See you then." I tossed the phone onto the seat.

I should just take her back to show her she couldn't run away from things.

Laughter burst from my lungs as I realized the ludicrousness of my thought. *Gotta go.* The motto I had stolen from Shannon when it was convenient for me. Shannon needed time away and I would let her have it. California would have to wait a little longer.

Forty-five minutes later I drove around the circular airport arrival lane twice, but didn't spot Shannon. The third loop was fruitful and I saw my daughter laughing and talking with a good looking young man. I honked, but couldn't get my grief stricken daughter's attention.

"Hey Shannon, over here," I shouted as I jumped out of the car. The security guard kept her eye on me, ready to blow her whistle. I took a step toward Shannon and waved my arms, then quickly turned back to show the guard I actually was loading a passenger. I walked around and opened the back hatch. *See, luggage coming.* I smiled at her.

"Mom!" Shannon finally noticed me. She grabbed her bag and waved goodbye to the young man.

The security guard blew her whistle and shouted at me. "Move along."

✡ ✡ ✡

"How much longer?"

Some things never change. Wasn't twenty old enough to look at a map? Check her phone?

We stopped in Santa Fe for dinner. I thought Shannon might like the plaza, but she was more interested in Starbucks than the Georgia O'Keefe museum. We hit the road again, but we wouldn't make it to Tierra Amarilla before the sun went down.

Shannon spun the radio dial, but reception was spotty and she punched it off with a snort. "So, do you have a boyfriend?"

"I… what did Vicki…" No. This wasn't the way to do it. Even in my scattered state I knew I needed to come clean to my daughter.

"Not a boyfriend, but I've had a few dates with a man. His name is Andy."

"Will Andy be there? Does he live with you?"

Did my daughter really think I would live with a guy after a few dates?

"Is your father living with someone?"

"Mom!"

"Okay, I get it. Andy has his own… place." I couldn't tell her that the only place of Andy's I had ever seen was the back of a pickup truck.

"How old is he?"

"A bit younger. But age doesn't matter when you're old." God, I swore I would never do that. I remember my grandmother calling herself old and living another fifty years. "Not that I'm old. And he's not my boyfriend."

"You are kind of old. Too old to be hanging out with young guys."

I looked over at Shannon. "How young do you think he is?"

"Thirty?"

"I'm flattered you think I could snag a thirty year old. Just to clear the air, Andy is forty." Okay, his birthday wasn't for another two weeks. But he was almost forty.

"And you're what? Forty-eight?"

I have to admit, my feelings were hurt that my daughter didn't know my age. Did she know my birthday was next month?

"Forty-five."

She was quiet for awhile. I tried to think she was satisfied with the answer, but I had the feeling she was bored.

✧ ✧ ✧

Bored she was. Within a day she was going crazy and she was driving me crazy.

I wanted to call Andy, curious about this "information" he had, but I wasn't ready for the whole Shannon-meets-Andy thing. If I could slip into town without her... *dream on, Ella.*

"Come on. We're going to town. I have some business at the courthouse."

"Finally. I want to look at stuff. Buy something for Nonna."

My heart broken daughter must be picturing the Santa Fe plaza here in T.A.

"There's no where to shop, honey. Just the courthouse and a coffee shop. I'll get you some coffee."

Andy wasn't at Three Ravens, but Nathan was. Good old Nathan. He read Shannon immediately and pulled out a strange instrument from his office. A bass made out of a metal barrel and a board, strings wound tight with crude pegs. While my daughter was engaged in Nathan and his rhythms, I went next door.

No Fred, no Dominguez, not even Carmen was around. Distracted by Andy and the bed of his truck, I had neglected my primary purpose. Selling the property had to move to the top of the list. Now that Shannon was here I needed to get this resolved so we could both head back to California. I hadn't made up my mind when we would leave, but nothing was going to happen immediately, that was clear. I scrawled a note to Joel asking for information about the property maps and slipped it under his door.

I didn't hurry back to Three Ravens. Shouldn't a mother be glad to see her daughter? On one level I truly was. Hugging her and knowing she was safe was reassuring. But my life here, my New-Ella life, was complicated without adding Shannon's drama and problems. I didn't feel mentally stable enough to be a good mother right now.

I used the courthouse bathroom, marveling at the pink tile, filled my water bottle and looked at the historic photos in the hallways.

Ten minutes. That was all the time I could really kill, so I walked back across the gravel parking lot. Laughter drifted out the open windows of the coffee house.

At least Shannon was happy now. Nathan was truly a medicine man.

But when I entered the tall door I saw that it wasn't just Nathan who was entertaining my daughter.

Shannon was singing a funny song for Andy and Nathan. Accompanied by Nathan on the honky-tonk bass, Andy straddled one of the beautiful cojóns, his tattooed arms flashing up and down as he pounded out the rhythm of my daughter's song.

The love that had moved into my heart when I dreamed about Hernan and his wife filled me as I watched Andy and Shannon, their eyes bright, their hands and feet moving as he drummed and she danced. The words of Shannon's song broke through to me.

Come on little darlin', don't you be carrin' on no more, maybe I lied, maybe you cried, but the wind done blowed that all away.

I didn't want my hidden black cloud to spring up and spread to these happy people. But hiding it for so many years hadn't made it leave. I might feel great now, but what about tomorrow? My tears welled up and spilled over. A sob followed. The sound caught Andy's attention. He looked up and I rushed for the door.

Suddenly his arms were around me and my face was buried in his chest.

I couldn't stop the tears that soaked his shirt. Shannon had paused her song and Nathan's bass was silent.

"Hey, we'll be right back," Andy called across the room, his arm tucked around me as he scooted me out the door.

Once on the porch my confusion welled up as fast as the water in Las Nutrias during the storm. Andy's hug should feel good, but I waited for it to grow tight, pinning me to some opinion other than my own. *No, Ella, that was your father, not this man. He's kind, remember?*

"I'm sorry, I'm sorry," I mumbled over and over, my face still pressed against Andy. "I want to be happy, really I do, but I'm so sad."

He didn't say anything, just held me, his breath warming my hair where he kissed the top of my head.

When the hiccups stopped, I pulled away from him. Embarrassed, I didn't look him in the eye.

"What about the news you had?"

"Ella, that can wait." He pulled me back into his arms.

I tried to bring up the feeling I had only a little while ago—the love my great-grandparents shared—but nerves and shame took over. I pulled away again. "It's... Shannon... I can't..." A shadow passed over Andy's face.

"Okay. Come here and sit down." He lead me to one of the tables on the porch. "I spent some time researching what Mark said. About the house? Your cousin is lying about the property division. Well, in a way."

"I knew it."

"There are some other things, Ella."

"What?"

"Mark and Jeff are planning to sell their parcels. But you own the parcel in between them. They are either going to try to get you to sell to them, or maybe to trade or something. But I think they have some pull. I felt something in that office when I asked for the records. I don't know... a hush came over the room when I turned in the request."

"I don't get it. Apparently I don't even have access to my part unless one of them gives me an easement or I spend a bunch of money putting in a road. I tried to sell to Mark, before I came out here."

"You did?"

I nodded. "Now that I think about it, he actually made me an offer."

"Hmm." Andy chewed on his lower lip. "I don't know what that means. All I know is what I found out yesterday. Mark and Jeff are planning on selling to a man named Patton. He's kind of a big deal around here. Used to work at Los Alamos, became a lawyer, then a judge and now he dabbles in state politics."

I thought about this. Mark had been gone for a month. Where had he really been? I had never even met Jeff. Now there was some mysterious big wig—if he was so important how come no one had mentioned him before?—who wanted the land?

Andy squeezed my hand. "I know. It doesn't make sense. There are some pieces missing. I stopped by to see Joel Dominguez, but no one seems to know where he is."

"Probably fishing." My sarcasm zipped past Andy. Of course he didn't know how many people had been *fishing* this month.

"Ah... I don't think fishing in May is very good around here, and as far as I know, Joel doesn't fish."

Thirty-six
Jonas Martinez
Tierra Amarilla, 1895-1898

Jonas Martinez swept the porch then polished the brass sign next to the door, although it already gleamed in the morning sun. *La Academia de Tierra Amarilla, Instruccíon Presbyteriana.* Est. 1895. The first students would be arriving soon. His young wife, Carmencita, was inside, spreading refreshments out a long table. Within an hour he would be instructing five young men.

"We need to spread the word, Jonas." Carmencita lectured him. "Five students is not enough to pay for the food on our table, let alone the money you borrowed." She was wise for someone of twenty years.

It had been so much work. Building the school. Even though Hernan had been dead for eight years, Jonas still respected his grandfather's wishes. As long as he could keep up on his loans he wouldn't have to do the one thing he knew would hurt Hernan—sell the land. Thank goodness for the Brotherhood, for no one else would loan money to a twenty-five-year-old new graduate. But bringing a teaching credential back to this part of the state was a rarity, and the men appreciated his dedication.

You would be proud, Abuelo.

His happy thoughts wobbled. Would his grandfather have agreed with the idea of hiding behind a new religion? Surely this was better than the old way of faking Catholic belief? The Presbyterians were liberal, allowing Bibles to be read, prayer groups outside of the confines of the church. No more snooping priests or inspection from the dioceses.

Starting the school had been Jonas's idea. The rest of the Brotherhood agreed that it would be a way to teach their sons about the traditions of the Hebrew people. Jonas had established himself as a circuit preacher, moving from town to town, ranch to ranch, to hold meetings.

Sabbath meetings.

"*Perdón, Señor Martinez?*" The boy's voice snapped Jonas from his reverie.

His first student had arrived.

✡ ✡ ✡

La Academia grew. The word of the Brotherhood was slowly moving through the area. Men who had been hiding their faith for years, as well as hiding from the Brotherhood, came to Tierra Amarilla with their sons. Soon Carmencita and Jonas had to make room for younger boys, not just the high school students they started with. They provided a place for some of the boys to live during the week, as students from as far away as Española and Ojo Caliente, even Antonito up in Colorado, appeared at their doorstep.

When they reached forty students Jonas hired two men to help. Then he heard about a brilliant young man looking for a job. Raol Garcia from Albuquerque had a degree from Columbia University, but wanted to return to the Southwest.

With the growth came unexpected problems. First, true Presbyterians brought their sons. They questioned Jonas about his training. Was he a minister? He was able to field their questions, because as part of his disguise he had carried on the traditions of the Brotherhood by training as a true Presbyterian minister, as well as learning enough about his Jewish faith to teach the students. He wasn't a true Rabbi, but pseudo-Rabbi was enough for the Brotherhood these days. He led worship when needed.

The reputation of *La Academia* continued to grow. The first boys to graduate went on to universities, with ambitions of studying to become doctors, architects, attorneys, businessmen.

Then the Catholics arrived. Could Catholic boys not have this opportunity to be well-prepared for the university?

"Carmencita. We must make a decision soon." Jonas held up the stack of applications that had arrived in this week's mail. "I can turn away the Catholics for awhile, but what of all these others?"

"I have been thinking about it, my darling. I think I have the answer." His sweet wife looked up from the book she held in her lap. "Clubs. We will start many clubs at the school. There will be a way for our boys to be members of a club. Then we use that club to teach them the Hebrew lessons."

"The Junior Brotherhood club? Is that what we call it?" Jonas saw problems with her idea.

She smiled at him and tapped her book. "No. I'm still working on that one. I think the idea will be to make the other clubs so wonderful and exciting, that no one really wants to join this club."

"Then the boys who join the junior Brotherhood will be looked upon as idiots for joining." Jonas had a certain sense of pride about the Jewish students. He was building up their personal strength through true worship. He wasn't about to risk the image he had for their success.

"That is why I am still thinking."

Carmencita was the smartest woman he had ever met. He should trust her. Jonas turned back to his stack of mail.

His wife proved to be an excellent problem solver and the Horsemanship Club a good solution. All boys could be members, but one must try out by showing skill in some form of riding. These included racing, cutting, herding, battle, and equitation. Each group then met separately, working on their own area of expertise to compete in a year-end rodeo.

By chance only certain boys could ride well enough for the racing group. Catholic boys. And lo and behold, the battle and cutting groups were comprised of those Presbyterian boys who weren't hiding anything.

All Jewish boys became a part of the herding and equitation groups. Originally Jonas had wanted the racing group for his boys, but Carmencita pointed out that many were terrible riders. Hence equitation. Even the poorest rider could fit in.

Jose Morgan and Patrick Baptiste were Jewish boys who didn't know how to ride. Patrick trembled uncontrollably when he came within ten feet of a horse.

Carmencita started the chess club.

✡ ✡ ✡

All went well until the day Jonas came home to find Mary Patton at the house.

He wasn't surprised. He had opened several requests from her. Her son was ten now, the youngest age he allowed to enter the classes. He had ignored all three letters.

"Jonas. You remember Mary." Carmencita's face was tight as she introduced the woman.

Mrs. Patton wore a beautiful green dress and her shiny blonde hair was pulled up in the latest style. Jonas hoped that Carmencita knew he found his wife much more attractive than this carefully coiffed lady. Wealth didn't impress him, especially when he knew it had shady origins.

He tipped his head. "Of course. How are you, Señora Patton?"

"I think you know why I'm here." Mary twisted her handkerchief.

Jonas remained silent.

"About the school?" She didn't look up from her fidgeting hands.

He felt cruel acting like he didn't know what she wanted. But the trouble between their grandfathers held a cold place in his heart.

He had told Carmencita parts of the story before they married. He wanted her to understand why he felt so strongly about the Brotherhood and the land.

His grandfather hadn't been able to ignore Patton. Initially the Brotherhood refused to back his grandfather in his personal war. But when things escalated, these men were willing to step up and help Hernan.

Two men fighting, not physically, but with every ounce of cunning and hatred that filled their hearts. It was a fight to the death. Not just of one man, but of both.

It had been a Thursday afternoon in November, 1886. Jonas didn't remember how many times the two men had been in court, but Hernan Martinez and Joseph Patton were battling before the judge once again. Fences, water rights, easements, who knows what this case was about. Neither Francesca nor Jonas had been there that day, although they usually made sure one or the other was in attendance to support Hernan. Jonas had to rely on the word of witnesses regarding the events of the day.

It seems that his grandfather had suspended good behavior, his anger building until he yelled out and cursed Patton right there in the courtroom. The banging of the gavel and the threats of the judge had only served to further incite his grandfather.

Both men grew purple with rage as they exchanged insults. But it was Joseph Patton who clutched his chest and collapsed, dead within minutes of a fatal heart attack.

The two families might have moved beyond the battle between the patróns. But Hernan didn't stop when Patton fell to the floor.

"God has made his choice," his grandfather had yelled before the crowded court room.

No Patton had spoken to a Martinez since that time. Not even when Hernan went to his bed two days after the death of Joseph Patton. Not even when Hernan died as well, just after the start of the new year.

And now Mary Patton wanted her son in his school.

Thirty-seven
Gabriella
Monday, May 12

I tried to get my grumpy daughter to go for walks, offered to see if we could borrow a horse from the neighbors and go riding, toured Chama and even bought beads and jewelry-making tools at the craft store up there to tempt her.

"You always wanted to do this when you were young. You got mad because I wouldn't let you."

"Right. When I was *young*. And now that I don't want to do it you'll let me. What's wrong with this picture, Mom?"

All she *wanted* to do was go to Three Ravens. I tried to explain that Nathan couldn't play with her all the time, and that I had to watch my cash flow. Lunch for two every day was taking a small, but deep bite into my savings.

"Mom, at least they have a bathroom there. This whole shovel in the wilderness thing is gross." She snorted. "How come Andy doesn't come out? Is it because I'm here?"

"No." What else could I say? I figured if it wasn't because she was here, it was because he and I were still at some sort of strange odds. I kept flashing on the look that had crossed his face when I pulled away from his comforting arms and changed the subject.

What was the matter with me? Kicking love in the face, even after my great epiphany of what a couple who grew old together could offer in hard times. But lies and secrets were not the ingredients for that kind of love.

"Shannon, you chose to come out here without talking to me. I could have told you there was nothing for you here."

"There was nothing for me there."

"What about school?"

She rolled her eyes. "That's fine for Julie, Mom. But me? Everyone knows it was a joke to pretend I was going to college."

"Why do you say that, Shannon? You're every bit as smart as Julie."

"Right. I know this speech. Everyone is different, everyone has their own strengths, each one of us is special. Give me a break, Mom. I hate school. Even you should know that by now." She tossed a chewed up sock monkey across the room for Bones. "Grandma said to tell you it's time to stop all this nonsense and come home."

Nice change of subject, but I wasn't biting. Instead I took her to see Rachel.

I told myself I had been planning on going back to see Rachel anyway and this wasn't just a crazy idea to entertain Shannon. I did want to find out about my great-great-grandparents. I also wanted to follow the dream advice of Consuela and ask Rachel about controlling the medallion, but I couldn't do that with Shannon tagging along. I would have to save that for some other time. I had left the medallion buried deep in my duffle bag. I didn't want any dreams with Shannon here.

Shannon craned her neck to look up at Brazos Peak. "Now this place, with that cliff like Yosemite? Why don't you find a house here?"

"Because I could never afford it. Well, I can't afford any house, so good thing I inherited something." Although the jury was still out on that.

Rachel met us at the door. There was a brief nod for me and then she reached out and held both Shannon's hands, as if to hold her still while she studied her.

"*Ella tiene los ojos de Rueben.*"

289

I hadn't thought about Rachel not revealing that she spoke English.

"*Gracias, señora.*"

When did my daughter learn to speak Spanish?

Rachel turned to me. "You didn't tell me she was a true *Hispana*.

"I didn't know it myself." I hid my sigh of relief that Rachel had switched to English.

"Oh Mom. You should be happy all those classes paid off. And you haven't been around Julie. She won't speak anything but Spanish ever since she got accepted to that program."

"You will go to Spain?" Rachel still grasped Shannon's hands. She raised them and squeezed, excited at the prospect.

"Not me. My sister's going to study there for a year."

"Today we learn about the old ways."

The thought of Shannon buying into cooking lessons made me laugh. Rachel glared at me. "That's funny?"

"No. It's just, I... oh never mind. Private joke." I sucked air through my nostrils and swallowed.

Shannon glared at me as she followed Rachel to the kitchen.

First things first, of course. Rachel fixed tea for everyone.

Shannon twirled her spoon in her tea and looked around. "Is there any sugar?"

Rachel reached across the table for the honey jar shaped like a tiny bee hive and scooted it over to Shannon.

"Are we going to talk about this Jewish thing, or what?"

"Shannon." I hadn't been sure Shannon was paying attention last night. She hadn't moved from her slumped position against the wall of the old house. I had explained a few things—a group of people who were Jewish and had fled Spain, the fact that Rachel believed we were related to them. I had been worried about how I would answer her questions, but she was so disgruntled she hadn't asked any. To punish me, I guess.

"Your mother has explained about the Brotherhood?"

"She told me there was a group from Spain. From the Inquisition. And that our family and your family had been members. That this meant we could be Jewish. What is the Brotherhood?" Shannon made a face as she sipped the tea. "I'm not sure I want to be Jewish."

Rachel shook her head and frowned. "It's not a matter of wanting to be Jewish. The fact of the matter is you are Jewish."

I jumped in before Shannon could practice more rudeness. "I've been meaning to ask you about that. The way I see it we have two issues here—Jewish heritage and Jewish religion."

Shannon clinked her spoon against the edge of the tea cup. "I heard about a blood test you can get. I want that before I decide."

Rachel and I both stared at Shannon.

"Blood test?"

My daughter nodded. "Yeah. DNA screening. There's a show on TV. All the stars and stuff find out who they really are."

Rachel shook her head. "Please drink the tea while it's hot."

Shannon pushed the cup away. "I don't like tea. Do you have any coffee?"

Rachel looked at me. I shrugged. Rachel finished her tea and stood.

"We will cook."

Shannon might be a pain in the ass at times, but right now she must have caught on to the fact that she shouldn't push any further. She cooperated, if not with enthusiasm, at least without hostility. She even chatted with Rachel as they measured out the flour, greased the pan and kneaded the dough.

Unlike my bread baking lessons, Rachel led Shannon outside to a clay oven. My daughter followed Rachel's instruction for building a fire in the hunched clay horno.

We were making a lot of bread. Twelve loaves.

When we carried the loaves out to the oven, Rachel put up a hand to stop us.

"*Un momento.*" She mumbled something, then took a pinch of dough from the loaf Shannon held and tossed it into the fire.

Shannon looked at me and winked, then leaned forward and spoke to Rachel. "You practice, don't you? You throw the dough into the fire and all this cooking. You keep the Sabbath."

If I was lost before, now I was adrift in the center of the ocean. What was my daughter talking about?

Rachel pulled her braid over her shoulder and tugged at it, her lips pressed together. "You know a lot about the faith?"

"Not a lot. Some. From my friends."

Shannon had Jewish friends?

"I can teach you more."

No one spoke for a few seconds.

I had seen this Shannon before. Polite up to a point and then suddenly bored or tired with the charade. Maybe it was the bit about Jewish friends, or maybe it was the fact that Rachel was ignoring her earlier statement about not wanting to be Jewish, but my daughter seemed to have run out of things to say.

I broke the silence. "Rachel, Would you tell me more about my family? Did you know anything about Hernan? His wife? What was her name?"

Rachel wiped her hands on her apron. "It is time for a break. I have some cold tea in the refrigerator. Let's go to the creek."

Shannon made a face, probably at the thought of more tea, but she helped us fill glasses and carry them to the table overlooking the flowing water.

Rachel sipped her tea. "Where did I leave off last time?"

"We were talking about Jonas being a circuit Rabbi, not Presbyterian like I thought. But I'd like to know about Hernan."

Shannon interrupted. "Jonas was my great-grandfather, right?"

"Great-great," I said, then turned to Rachel. "Hernan was his father."

"No." Rachel shook her head. "Hernan was his grandfather. Jonas's father, his name was Cristóbel."

"But I thought…" I stopped. How did I explain that I had visited these people in a dream and they spoke as if Jonas was their son? "What was his wife's name?"

"Cristóbel or Hernan? Hernan's wife was called Francesca. Jonas was raised by his grandparents. They were the first of the Martinez family to come to Tierra Amarilla."

This explained what I had overheard. The decision had not been an easy one for them. My great-great-*great* grandparents.

Shannon leaned forward and spoke just as I spoke.

"What about my grandfather?"

"What happened to Cristóbel?"

Rachel held up her hand. "One at a time. Cristóbel's wife, Jonas's mother died young. He was always trying to find his fortune and it seemed best that Jonas stay with his grandparents. And about your grandfather, he comes a lot later. Jonas was married to Carmencita. They lived in the big house, over in T.A. Next to it they built a school. Looked like an old barn because that is what it was. Classrooms downstairs and sleeping quarters upstairs.

"Of course it was only for boys. But many came from a great distance, so during the week they stayed. The school was for teaching the boys about the secret heritage. But soon everyone wanted to send their sons to the Martinez school because in those times the nuns were the only other option. They were fierce and often didn't know much. Certainly not what was being taught in other parts of the country." Rachel swirled the dregs of her tea. "*Mija*? Can you go get me some more?" She handed the glass to Shannon.

Shannon looked at Rachel. "Are you going to tell my mother something secret while I'm gone?"

Rachel laughed, the chuckle low in her throat. "No. My throat is dry. I will rest it until you come back."

True to her word, Rachel sat in silence.

Even when Shannon returned with the drinks the old woman seemed to leave us for awhile. She sat very still and her breath was nearly imperceptible. Shannon and I exchanged a glance, and just as I was about to ask her if everything was all right, Rachel spoke.

"When Jonas decided to hide the medallion, hide the fact that he was Jewish, I thought it was about what was happening to the Jews in the rest of the world. I guess things were happening right here as well, but I never saw it."

"What medallion? Is that the secret?" Shannon was paying attention now, even after Rachel's rapid change of subject.

Rachel stood up. "It's time to check the bread. That story will have to wait for another day."

Then she looked at Shannon and said something in Spanish. My daughter grew pale, then flushed.

As we walked up the path I realized that once again Rachel had stopped her story midstream. It was obvious she knew that Jonas hid the fact he was Jewish and that's why he hid the medallion. She had always known.

✡ ✡ ✡

"Shannon. I can't believe how rude you were to Rachel."

"Mom. I'm not eight. Don't scold me."

"Don't act eight." I turned out onto the highway. "Rachel is an old woman and she's my friend. Both those reasons are enough for you to show some common courtesy."

"She's weird. She gave me a total creepy feeling. And Mom?" Shannon rolled down the window, then raised her voice to talk over the sound of the wind. "You shouldn't drink her tea. Did you see those crusty old jars? She probably gathers that stuff in the woods. It could be poisonous. I think she's a witch."

Anger, frustration, disappointment, guilt. I don't know which thing made my lips burn as I pressed them together. *Don't engage with her, don't do it.*

I kept my eyes on the road. I tried to forget about Shannon, even though she sat next to me rolling her eyes and sighing. She was almost twenty-one, an adult. I wasn't going to change who she was at this point in her life. All I could do was offer what I really had, a mother's love and support. And I would try not to enable her self-destructive behavior. If she didn't keep a job or go to school or want a good life, and I could barely manage my own, well, so be it.

Shannon wasn't ready to drop the subject. "She was putting on an act, you know. Throwing the dough in the fire and making us cook all that food."

"What do you mean? Wasn't she just testing the temperature of the oven?"

Shannon shook her head. "Don't you see? Those were all Jewish traditions. Getting ready for the Sabbath. She was trying to prove to us that she is Jewish. I'm surprised she didn't make us light candles before we left."

"What did she say to you? Right before we left."

"Maybe it's better if you don't know."

"I don't want you to keep it from me."

"I don't want you to keep things from me either. You tell me about the medallion and I'll tell you what she said."

Part of me wanted to tell someone about the dreams and the magic and the medallion, but the mother part of me was strong enough to know that Shannon wasn't the one to be my confidant.

"Shannon, I need to know what she said."

"And I need to know about the medallion. AND this secret Brotherhood."

"Okay," my stomach churned as I spoke. "It's a long story. I'll tell you tomorrow, but you need to tell me what Rachel said right now."

"I didn't understand it all, but I think she said you were in danger and it was a good thing I was here to protect you. She told me I had to stay here, that I couldn't leave."

What did that mean? Danger?

"Well, I guess she can be a little far out there."

Shannon didn't have a glib answer for that. I could tell Rachel's words had scared her.

I took advantage of the fact we were approaching the gas station and pulled in, not to see Andy, although that was an added benefit, but because I needed gas and a break from this conversation.

"Can't go for ten minutes without stopping to see your boyfriend?"

"You pump the gas." I handed her my credit card and walked into the station.

"Hey." Andy wiped his hands then put them on my shoulders. He looked straight into my eyes. "Do I detect a few new wrinkles?"

"Oh yeah. Hundreds, I'm sure." We both turned and looked out at Shannon. She had plugged into her music and was dancing around the car while the gas pumped.

"She seems happy."

"Happy to torment me? Happy to make me her slave? You should have seen how rude she was to Rachel."

"You went back?" Andy shook his head. "I thought... Oh well. It's only for... how long?"

What hadn't he wanted to say about Rachel? "One way airfare. Can you believe it? I think Greg was happy to get rid of her for awhile. Plus that means I have to buy her a ticket home if I want her to leave." I didn't mention my plan to drive home to California. A plan which originally meant escaping my confusion about him.

Andy reached for my chin and looked into my eyes. "Ella, what we have is good. Really good."

I couldn't believe this guy was willing to give me so many chances. But the stress of Rachel and Shannon had left me exhausted and needy. Didn't I deserve someone? Sure there were some problems, but we would work those out, wouldn't we? *Do the right thing this time, Ella. Don't screw it up again.*

I leaned against his chest and inhaled. "Come to dinner tonight? She's mad and grouchy anyway, so what can it hurt?"

"I'll be there with my armor on. How about I bring Navajo tacos from Penelope's?"

"Sure. But mild for my darling gringo daughter. She's never been a true Martinez."

✧ ✧ ✧

Andy was still my hero. In spite of Shannon's clear decision to shun him tonight—go figure that one, didn't she love him just the other day?—he broke through her cover. By 9:00 they were deep in a poker game, piles of pennies at their elbows and piñon shells scattered everywhere. I was at the end of the table stringing beads for bracelets. If Shannon wouldn't play with the beads, I would. I'd spent money on them, after all.

When the game wound down and Andy stood up to leave they looked at my pile of colorful earrings and bracelets. Christmas presents or something. I really didn't know what I would do with all of these.

"Mom. You should sell those on the internet. I have a friend who makes a ton of money."

What was a ton to a twenty-one year old? I started to scoff at her idea. Then I remembered; I always did that to her.

"That's a great idea, Shannon. I would need your help to set it up. I don't know anything about selling on the web."

"I forgot. You don't have internet here. I guess you couldn't do it."

Andy rubbed his chin. "No reason she can't go into town to do it. She has a permanent chair at Three Ravens."

"How about tomorrow? We can go in for breakfast and you can show me what to do?" I held my breath.

The dragon turned to me and I finally saw the flash of those beautiful white teeth as a smile covered her face. "Sounds great. They have a breakfast sandwich to die for." She looked at Andy. "And a real bathroom."

Thirty-eight
Jonas Martinez
Tierra Amarilla, 1898

Mary Patton did not give up easily. Jonas had avoided her for several weeks, but now she crowded past his doorstep and was sitting in his parlor.

"Can I get you some tea?" His wife was polite, no matter what the circumstances.

"Why yes, thank you."

Undoubtedly Mrs. Patton was using Carmencita's offer to extend her time in his house. He could see that she would not be turned away at the door

"And you, my darling?"

Jonas shook his head. He wouldn't let this turn into a social event, but he was polite. He made small talk until his wife returned with the tea, setting the cup in front of Mary Patton and slipping away, although he signaled her to stay.

"Mrs. Patton, I fully appreciate your wanting your boy in our school. But I just don't think, well, with circumstances being what they are, you know... " Jonas shrugged and waved his hand. Surely this woman didn't really think it was a good idea for her child to be educated by a sworn enemy?

"Mr. Martinez, I beg you. I know we have had our differences, but you see, Raymond" —she shook her head and looked down —"nothing but trouble with those nuns."

To Jonas's surprise the woman suddenly lost her calm hold on her tea cup and it crashed to the floor. But she didn't appear to notice, for she crumpled forward onto the table, dropping her face into the crook of her elbow and breaking into horrible sobs. Gut wrenching sobs, not ladylike at all.

"Carmencita!"

His wife came rushing from the kitchen. "What happened?" She glared at him. "What did you do?"

"Me? Nothing. She's having an emotional breakdown because I suggested having her son attend the school of her mortal enemy wasn't such a good idea."

Carmencita's patting of the woman did nothing to stop the sobbing.

"You used those words? Mortal enemy?"

"No, of course I didn't." He pointed to the floor. "Watch your step."

Glass crunched beneath his wife's feet.

"My grandmother's tea cup?"

Jonas shook his head and raised his hands. "Don't look at me."

The bickering broke through to Mary Patton. She raised a blotchy face and looked at Jonas.

"I'm so sorry. It's just…"

For a moment he was sure the sobs were about to return, but she sniffed and gulped.

"The nuns are terrible teachers. They don't understand boys at all. My boy is not a bad boy, he, he just has a lot of energy. Your school, it's the only way any young man around here can ever hope to get into a good college."

Jonas shook his head. This was beyond belief. The Patton boy had obviously been in trouble at his school and now she wanted the Martinez family to take him. Grandfather must be rolling over in his grave, spitting down from the hill outside of town toward the church cemetery where Joseph Patton was twirling in his own burial site.

"I think not, Mrs. Patton. I'm sorry."

"Wait a minute." Carmencita still had one arm on Mary's shoulder. "Let's think about this, Jonas."

"What is there to think about? It won't work."

"I know there is history, bad blood and all that, but think, Jonas. Maybe this is our chance to make things right."

"Make things right? Her husband's father killed my grandfather. How can we make that right?"

Mary started to say something, but changed her mind.

"That's not the real story, Jonas. You know that. Those were two smart men, stubborn enough to stay locked in a battle until it killed them both. If you want my opinion, they were each responsible for their own death. It was a long time ago, and it had nothing to do with Mrs. Patton's son. What if it were our son who wasn't allowed an opportunity for an education? Reuben or Hernando?"

Jonas could not see the comparison. He had worked hard just so his sons could attend a good school. In fact, hadn't his whole life been preparing for just such a thing? Why was it his responsibility if others were not so conscientious?

"We can talk about this later."

Jonas didn't like the glance that passed between his wife and Mary Patton.

Their argument continued. It started over supper. Jonas had a brief respite while Carmencita cleaned up, but she started again as soon as the last dish was dried and put away.

"We are doing well, I know that, but new students are the only way for a school to survive. Junior Patton is a strong man in this town. Think of all his friends. All their sons. We need this to survive."

"We are doing fine with what we have."

"How long do you think it will be before someone builds a school in Española? People don't like to send their children away for so long. We will lose our boarders, over half of the enrollment."

Jonas was quiet. He could fight his wife on the Martinez-Patton war, but she was the financial brains behind their success. He loved to teach math, but when it came time to apply these concepts to his account books, Carmencita was in charge.

As he gazed out the window, the corner of the tall schoolhouse roof visible, he thought about how hard they had worked for the past five years. It wouldn't do to jeopardize the academy.

Yet he also remembered watching Hernan's face turn red, and his fist grow tight every time Joseph Patton's name was mentioned. Such a battle had raged between those two. He often wondered if there was more to the fight than the land issues. Such emotion over land seemed extreme.

He was not Hernan and Joe Junior was not his father. He had lost his grandfather, an old man of sixty-three, but Joe had lost his father, who was not yet fifty years old when the heart attack took him. Who had suffered the greatest grief? Was Carmencita right? Should he use young Ray Patton to clear the air between the two families?

"Papa."

He felt the tug on his sleeve and turned to look at Adalina. At eight years old his daughter was already turning into a beauty, although she didn't look like her mother. He saw his grandmother in his little girl. The same auburn hair and hazel eyes that he remembered in Francesca. The way her lip quivered when she held tight to her pride, refusing to cry no matter the pain. He felt the loss of her childhood, when he could toss her up in his arms and listen to her contagious giggle. Already she refused to sit in his lap, pointing to her brothers and telling him she was not a baby.

"What is it, my love?"

"Please don't fight with Mama anymore." She lay her cheek against his shoulder. "It makes her so sad."

He rubbed her back and held her close. His daughter should be in bed by this hour. In fact, glancing at the clock, they should all be in bed at this hour.

"Come on, my sweet. Let's go to bed. I promise your mother will be fine."

✡ ✡ ✡

Raymond Patton proved to be a handful, yet Jonas did not dislike the boy. He was smart, that was apparent, but he did not fit in with the other boys. The Americans sent their children down to Santa Fe or Albuquerque for school, so Ray did not have many childhood friends to band with.

By the second day of listening to Raymond's bragging, breaking up three fistfights, and moving his seat twice when he irritated the boy who was unlucky enough to be seated with him, Jonas was questioning his decision. Family feud or not, this boy was making his life difficult.

He could hear Carmencita without even bringing up the issue. *Give him a chance, it has only been two days, he is just a little boy.* Jonas tried to be fair, tried to think about what he would do if any other boy had been so much trouble.

But no other boy had been such trouble. Not that there weren't occasional fights. But when Raymond Patton threw a punch it was for the kill, not some childhood skirmish.

With a sigh, Jonas looked out his window at Los Brazos. The peaks often saved him from his own doubts. So strong, reigning over the whole Chama Valley. They had become a visual symbol of God, reminding him to pray and ask for guidance when he forgot that part of his life. Here he was, a man acting as a leader of the Jews and forgetting about God in the day to day rush of raising a family and running a school.

Blessed are You, Eternal One our God, Universal Ruling Presence, Who creates a variety among living beings.

Head bent in peace, feeling the presence of God with him, Jonas knew he had to give Raymond Patton another chance.

✡ ✡ ✡

"Where is my son? Where is Raymond?"

The loud voice could only come from one man—Junior Patton.

Jonas stepped outside of his office and hurried to the classroom, where Señor Garcia used his frail body to block the big man from entering.

"Raymond! You get your sorry ass out here right now."

Jonas watched as the boy ducked under his teacher's arm. Raymond seemed glad to see his father, and hurried to him.

A strong cuff to the side of his head stopped him. Jonas rushed forward as the boy leaned against the wall and pressed his hand to the spot where his father's blow had knocked him off balance.

"You! I should have known a Martinez was behind this. What do you think, Pattons are so weak that you could teach my son with your primitive ways?

"Señor Patton, please come in to my office and we can discuss this matter." Jonas held his emotions in check because eighteen sets of eyes peered through the doorway. It would not do for the students to see their headmaster lose his temper.

"There is nothing to discuss." Junior turned and grabbed Raymond by the arm. The boy flinched, but followed his father.

Well, that solves that problem, Jonas thought. But Raymond looked back over his shoulder and his eyes met Jonas's gaze. Jonas couldn't mistake the message in those eyes.

Help me.

A boy in trouble. Not something God would wish him to ignore. Jonas ran after the Pattons.

"Wait. Señor Patton, wait." To his surprise the man stopped.

"It is Mr. Patton, this is the United States, not Mexico. Speak English to me."

Jonas felt the tiniest burst of hope. The man was insulting, but showing a willingness to talk. He glanced at Raymond, but the boy stood with his eyes glued to the ground.

"I know that our families have not always been on good terms, but do you not think it is time to put all that behind us? Raymond is an excellent student and your wife has asked that he be prepared for the university." Well, maybe not an excellent student yet, but Jonas did see the potential.

"Of course my son is an excellent student. I would not expect anything less from him. Much too good for a podunk barn that thinks it can compete with a real school just by calling itself an academy. No spic can teach my son what he needs to know."

Jonas couldn't believe the insult of this man. Every word of the Brotherhood and his grandfather coursed through his brain. How the Americans would never accept the Hispanos, let alone the Jews. He could see that in Junior's anger and hatred.

Jonas clenched his fists to his sides. "Give me strength." He needed God to guide him as he turned away from this man. He felt strong as he walked back to the school, but couldn't help but wonder if Junior Patton was about to strike him from behind.

✡ ✡ ✡

"He said that?" Carmencita seemed duly sympathetic to how he was feeling, but Jonas couldn't help but hear something else in her voice. "Does he hate us so much? He doesn't even know us."

"We did grow up in the same town. But you are correct in feeling that there is some sort of hatred that goes beyond us. I think that Patton hates all of our people. Which puzzles me because he lives off our fortune."

"If he hates us so much why does he stay here? Surely his family would be happier in Santa Fe or Albuquerque?"

"There is no answer to that question, my love. But the boy, if you could have seen his face. I think his father is a very cruel man, even to his own son."

"Can't we do anything?"

"What would you have me do? Fight the strongest man in town? No one has the right to make decisions for another man's son.

Besides, after only two days with Raymond, *I* felt like striking him as well."

"I should hope not. Don't ever think of humiliating our sons, my husband. Or you shall be dealing with a mother bear."

Jonas was grateful for his wife's warm presence in their bed that night. As he held her close and stroked her smooth brow he felt the rage and emotion of the day fade away. He was a very lucky man.

✡ ✡ ✡

The fire bells awoke them not long after he had finally fallen to sleep. Fires were of great concern in this town, although the adobe buildings resisted flames more readily than those built solely of wood.

As Jonas grappled around the room for his trousers he glanced out the window, wondering how close the fire might be. He saw the flames.

"Wake up Carmencita! The school, it's the school," he shouted. He pulled on his pants as raced for the stairs, nearly falling in the process. He didn't stop for shoes or a shirt.

"No, no," he yelled.

The entire building was engulfed in flames. Men lined up and threw buckets of water on to the edge of the building and the grassy field, but they could not get close enough to his school to fight the fire.

"We must stop it," Jonas ran for the line of men and grabbed a bucket. "Save my school, please save my school!" He ran toward the fire, aware of the heat blistering his skin, but unwilling to stop. Flinging the water onto the inferno, he turned back to get more.

Manuel Luna grabbed Jonas, wrapping his thick arms around the young man from behind and pulling him away from the burning building.

"It is too late son, too late. Do not risk your life."

The students who boarded were gathered under a tree. They had escaped the fire. Luna spun Jonas around. "Look, there is your family. Go to them, they are what matters."

Carmencita and the children huddled in a mass, the glow of the fire painting their faces a sickly orange. It was as if they stood at the very edge of Hell itself. His wife clutched Hernando to her body, and he could see the tears running down her face. Adalina sobbed into her mother's arm, which she clung to like a life line. Rueben stood stoically at his mother's skirt and watched the fire.

Luna did not let go of Jonas until Carmencita stepped forward and he took her in his arms. The man obviously thought Jonas so crazed that he might rush back into the fire once more.

Jonas buried his face into his wife's neck, unable to turn back and watch as his life went up in flames.

Thirty-nine
Gabriella Martinez
Tuesday, May 13 to Thursday, May 15

My daughter slept through everything. The croaking and cawing of the ravens, me making coffee on the camp stove, and Bones jumping around the room with excitement before we set off on our morning walk.

I had skipped my walks since Shannon arrived. Shouldn't she see the property, even if I had to force feed it to her? I looked at my sleeping daughter.

I had a busy day planned: go to Three Ravens for some Internet service so that Shannon could move forward with her idea for selling bracelets, sign more of those blasted papers for Greg and find out about the deception my cousin was using to cheat me. I would track Joel Dominguez to the ends of the earth this time. Especially since Andy had disabused me of the fishing story.

I needed some time to clear my head and focus my energy. There would be plenty of time with Shannon later.

I looked down at Las Nutrias Creek, then turned and looked up the hill toward the tiny graveyard. When I had visited the cemetery with Andy I hadn't known about my family, hadn't dreamed about my great-great-grandparents and hadn't listened to Rachel's cryptic stories. I vaguely recalled seeing the name Francesca on one of the graves, and, according to Rachel, this was the woman who had filled me with such love. I headed toward the acequia.

Bones splashed across the swiftly flowing water, in spite of my whistles and warnings. It was flowing strong enough to pull her downstream, but she made it across the ten foot span and shook vigorously when she reached the other side, her tail waving as she waited for me to cross on the board. It amazed me that she didn't even shiver, because the mornings still held a chill that would not be chased away by the sun for a few hours.

It had seemed a straight forward walk when I visited the graves with Andy, but it took me thirty minutes to find the tiny cemetery sheltered by the pines. After wandering up what looked like trails, but ended abruptly in steep gullies or thick, spiny brush, I finally spotted the wooden markers.

Carmencita Louisa Martinez, b. 1875, d. 1930. Fifty-five when she died, not much older than me.

This had to be Hernan's marker, the worn letters still hinting at his name; *Hern... Espejo Mar... nez,* Shouldn't his wife be nearby?

I found her. *Francesca Tafoya Martinez, b. 1827 d. 1897.*

I sat on the ground next to Francesca's marker and traced the carved letters. I wanted to know more about her. When Consuela said I could control the medallion, did she mean I could guide my dreams to certain places?

I looked at the marker next to Francesca's. Not Hernan, as I had predicted, but one of the very Jewish sounding names, *Yehoyachin Galit Marciano.* I leaned over and ran my finger over the rough wood. The symbol of the brotherhood, the symbol on my medallion, the symbol Rachel seemed to warn me about. And that warning to Shannon yesterday? Was I in danger because of some magic or because my cousin was trying to cheat me out of my land?

Deep in thought, it took me a minute to notice that the wooden marker was growing warm beneath my finger. I drew my hand away and stared at it. Then I placed my palm over the symbol and pressed.

"I want to know Francesca."

My palm grew hot.

"Take me to her." A flash of doubt rushed through me as I thought about what might happen. I really shouldn't mess around with magic.

There was no warning, no wind, no darkness, but suddenly I was traveling. Then I was there.

I sat in the same room where I had watched Hernan and Francesca take comfort in each other arms. Sunlight poured through the window onto my lap, which held a piece of fabric. In my hand was a needle and thread.

I was embroidering a shirt. I was also wearing different clothes, the muslin blouse with the broad lace collar.

"Francesca?" a voice called from the kitchen.

I waited to hear her answer, but there was no reply to the inquiry. The sound of footsteps moved toward me.

"There you are. Didn't you hear me?"

I gasped and dropped the needle into my lap. I recognized the man who spoke. A little taller, a lot more muscular and more gray on the temples, but he was nearly Fred Rivas in duplicate. This man had to be Rachel's ancestor.

He spoke as if he knew me.

"Is Hernan here?"

I shook my head without answering, meaning to say I didn't know. But Nearly-Fred took this to mean no, because he rushed to me and pulled me into his arms. His lips were upon mine so quickly that I hadn't even drawn a breath. Without stopping to think, I kissed him back.

"Francesca, Francesca. I have missed you my love."

I tried to pull away, but his arms kept me close. I was not Francesca. And he was not her husband. Was this before she married? I looked at my hand, which was now embracing this man.

My hand was wrinkled, not that of a young woman.

Nearly-Fred gazed at me with passion I had only dreamed about. Of course, this was a dream, but all those sleepless nights of imagining rescue by a doctor or a fireman, they were here now. This was a dream, I thought. Might as well enjoy myself.

I kissed him again.

As the kisses grew, he pulled me down to the sofa that stood in front of the fireplace and I felt as if the flames had jumped from the fire into my chest. His hands worked to remove my clothing and I did nothing to stop him. Fleetingly I wondered if I was doing something that would make a difference in Francesca's life. Changing the future.

But all concerns of past or future fled as I made love to this man. I had made love to Greg, to Andy, even to the dream Romero, but it had never been like this. I wanted to inhale this man, to move him inside me, to become him. I sniffed him, I licked him, I bit him. It seemed like hours that we kissed and caressed and sent each other to ecstasy. When he finally pulled away, I couldn't move, panting beside him on the cramped sofa.

"What of Hernan? When will he be back? Is Jonas with him?"

"I don't know." I watched his deep eyes. This man truly loved me. "I am not Francesca."

"Oh, my love. Please do not feel that what we do is a sin. God cannot see wrong in such a love."

"But I am not Francesca."

"I am saddened to bring you such guilt that you do not even want to be yourself. Especially when who you are is so blessed." He sighed and pulled away. "It is getting late. You should dress. It would not do for my friend to find us here."

I sat and groped around for the scattered garments. As I reached for my skirt, my hand met with something sharp.

Just as fast as I had moved to this other world so I was back. The blood on my hand was from a splinter of wood. I used my fingernails to remove it and stuck the wound into my mouth.

My grandmother, great-great-great, was not so great after all. She was cheating on her husband. What about the love I had seen between Hernan and her, stronger than any I could imagine? Could it compare to this explosion, this volcano of emotion when making love to this other man? She must have felt very guilty about it and she must have talked it over with him, this man who had to be a Rodrigo since he was the clone of Fred. Or more accurately Fred was the clone of him.

I thought about religion. I knew about Catholic guilt, it was such a part of literature. The whole confession thing seemed to encourage people to find something to feel guilty about. But Francesca was Jewish, so what was her guilt centered around?

Duh, Ella. Anyone cheating on their husband would feel guilty. This wasn't about guilt, it was about sin. The sin preached in Sunday School, the sin my father made me feel with his glare and his tight squeeze. If being a Jew meant I had to go back to feeling sinful, well, then, never mind. I wouldn't go there.

I shook my head as Bones raced back from some adventure and licked my face. The sun had burned off all the frost and the air was warm. I didn't know how long I had been away but Shannon was probably awake and wondering where I was. As I walked back to the adobe house I realized this hadn't been a dream. Did that mean it was a hallucination? Or as Nathan said, was I lucky enough to guide myself on a psychic journey?

✡ ✡ ✡

"So, go back. I'm not sure what you just did," I tapped the computer screen to point out the area of my confusion.

"Look Mom. It might be easier if you just, I don't know, go play with Nathan for awhile and let me get the website set up. Then I'll teach you how to navigate it. If you try to understand this part, it will take us months."

I sighed. Of course. I should have known working on a project with Shannon wouldn't bring us any closer. At least she wasn't complaining. And, according to her, this whole website-to-sell-beaded-bracelets thing could all be accomplished for free. I just hoped it really was free and not some hack thing that would land my daughter—or even worse me—in jail. Oh well, it was just across the street so Andy could visit us.

"Okay. Got it. I'll go next door and check on some details about the property." This was next on my list anyway, and it would be better to tackle Joel Dominguez without Shannon and her two cents worth.

On my first visit to the courthouse I must have caught Joel on the three days of the year he was in his office, because things were dark again today. Luck had not abandoned me completely because Fred was in.

"Hi Ella." He looked up from the stack of folders on his desk.

For a moment I was speechless. I had known the man in the dream was very much like Fred, but it didn't hit me that this could actually be the same man until I stared into his dark eyes. I felt certain parts of my body grow hot.

"I—" What if Fred time traveled too? What if I had made love to him this morning? Christ! I watched his face for any signs. I wasn't related to Fred, but I felt incestuous at the thought of kissing him.

"I thought I might see you today. Andy was here, asking about the parcel maps."

Fred appeared innocent, but I couldn't keep from blushing. "Do you know anything about this buyer? Patton?"

He nodded and sighed. "It's complicated. I tried to tell you about it last week, but..."

He was polite enough not to mention I had stood him up twice.

"Why didn't Mark try to buy it from me a long time ago? I mean when I first called him from California?"

"He doesn't have the cash flow to buy it from you. Neither does Jeff. And Patton won't buy it unless he gets the whole thing."

"Still, they could have just told me. My god, they know I want to sell. Are they trying to make money off me or something?" Now that I thought about it, of course that's what they were trying to do.

Mark was probably trying to convince me that I owned some other less desirable portion of the land when he steered me away from the house. Dumb woman won't investigate it or something.

"I'm sure Mark would love to pull as much cash out of the deal as possible, but it's more than that."

"What?"

"James Patton. He—I thought my grandmother would tell you about him. You went to see her again, right? And she didn't mention James? Or maybe Joseph Patton? Or Raymond Patton?"

Holy cow. There must be as many Pattons as there were Martinezes. I shook my head.

"The Pattons and the Martinezes have been at war for years. Since the United States won New Mexico, I think."

"Patton isn't really a Spanish name, is it?"

"No. And they aren't Spanish. The first Patton came from the east to buy land, and every Patton since that one has kept that tradition alive."

This didn't make sense to me. "If we're at war, why is Mark so eager to sell to him?"

"That's just it, I'm not sure."

"Andy said that James Patton has a lot of power around here."

"As a judge with questionable ethics, yes, I would say he has more power than anyone wants him to have. But there is more, Ella." He rubbed his brow and looked out the window. "It's about the Brotherhood. James Patton is anti-Semitic, well anti-many other things too. But Mark? He doesn't know about your family being part of the Brotherhood. And he's not the only one. Lots of younger generations don't know. Because of Hitler. Men decided that their safety was at stake again and they didn't tell their children. They just went with the Catholic, or in your case, Presbyterian, thing and buried their histories."

"But you said he knows about the Patton and Martinez thing."

"He knows that your ancestors fought over land. I don't know this for a fact, but Joel seems to think Mark figures to make a bundle selling the land to Patton and that balances things. Because the land isn't worth much, but for some reason James Patton really wants that property."

"Maybe it has secret oil wells or gold mines or something?"

"Not that I know of."

I tried to work this out. Was my cousin really so greedy that he wanted to make money off me? And why would someone as shrewd as Patton was supposed to be pay more than the land was worth?

Fred continued. "There's more. I tried to find out why there has been such a delay on you getting clear title. Seems someone filed a Right-to-Title questioning the division in the maps that are already filed. An heir can do that, but I really couldn't find any evidence that either Mark or Jeff had filed. But that's not really the problem. The issue is that when a Right-to-Title is filed it goes to the desk of the corporation council to be investigated. And in Rio Arriba county that man is Chris Patton."

"Chris Patton?"

Fred nodded. "Younger brother of James."

"Okay, Fred. This just doesn't seem real. It's like a... made for TV movie or something."

"I know. Only I'm not as quick to pick up the pieces as Columbo. Ella, we need help and I only know of one source for this kind of help." Fred folded his hands, as if praying. "We need to bring in the men of the Brotherhood."

"What can they do?"

"They can do a lot. These men have connections all over the state. Whatever game Patton is playing, the Brothers will find out."

"How do we get their help?"

"We go to the meeting on Friday."

✪ ✪ ✪

I walked back to Three Ravens, deep in thought about what Fred had told me. Secrets still, and not enough information. But there was someone who might know more than she was letting on. I stopped at the car and called my mother.

"Hi Mom, how are you?"

"Ella, I'm so glad you called. Mrs. Falkner was asking how you're doing out there. I told her you should be home soon. You are coming home soon?"

"Soon, Mom. Soon. Shannon's here now."

"My Shannon?"

What other Shannon would I be talking about? "Yes, your Shannon. Look, Mom, there are some things I need to find out. About Dad's family. I know you said his parents wouldn't come visit, but did he ever talk about anything? Like family fights about the land?"

"Well, one of his uncles lived there. I think he felt everyone owed him something for taking care of the land. But your father didn't care. He didn't have any plans for the land."

"What about religion?" I decided to be direct. "Did Dad ever say anything about part of the family being Jewish?"

The line was so quiet I thought the call had been dropped.

"Mom?"

"I... no... never. I'm sure if someone were Jewish he would have told me."

Her voice sounded odd to me. "Mom, are you sure?"

"Oh dear, the doorbell's ringing. I have to go answer that, Ella. I'll talk to you later."

"I can wait, just go see who it is."

"No, no, it's probably Mrs. Falkner. She said she would drop by today She has fabric for the Linus blankets. I'll just talk to you later."

My mother hung up on me.

Forty
Jonas Martinez
Tierra Amarilla, 1940

Jonas walked slowly down the hill. He had visited Carmencita and his two daughters up at the family cemetery. His daughters had died in infancy and he had spent the years talking to their spirits and imagining the beauty of his girls as they would have grown older. He appreciated his living children, but could never shake the loss of those he had not had the chance to know.

When Carmencita left him, he felt a sharp bend in the road. He stood at the fork, unable to go straight ahead and unwilling to make the turn. The only saving grace was that she went without too much suffering.

He set the wildflowers next to the wooden headstone. "Our children have moved away, light of my heart. I am a lonely old man. I think soon we will be together."

Carmencita Louisa Martinez b. 1875 d. 1930

She had been gone for ten years.

Jonas knew he was going to die. His cough had worsened and the doctor had told him to rest and get his things in order. He had not written to his children, spread around the country as they were. He didn't want a fuss made when he joined Carmencita on the hillside. "You are the lucky one now. This world has gone crazy once more." He paused. Did he need to tell her about the latest atrocities toward the Jewish people? Wouldn't she already know?

"Why does God allow this? Can you ask him? Haven't we paid enough?"

Jonas thought about his choice not to tell his children about their heritage.

After the school had burned he would not have survived without his wife. The Brotherhood viewed Patton's move as an act of violence toward the Jews, but Jonas knew it was personal. He tried to talk the Brotherhood into rebuilding the school, but they didn't want their sons in Tierra Amarilla, because the anti-semetics had come out of hiding and were openly hostile. Mario Chavez built a school in Española, just as Carmencita had predicted and Jonas was left tutoring students in the parlor.

A poor way for a man to make a living so Jonas turned to raising cattle and sheep, thankful he had preserved his grandfather's land.

They had been blessed with more children. How happy he had been to have another daughter. But the tiny baby had not lasted out the winter, taken by chicken pox.

A year later Emido was born. A son. The Bris ceremony was well attended. The baby was held by the new mohel, but no knife was at hand. Jonas and Carmencita decided not to have their son circumcised.

"What is this you do?" Manuel Luna had asked. "My grandson must keep the covenant."

"It is not safe, Papa. We have decided that our lives are more important right now. This is how the secret will be kept." Carmencita stood up to her father, while Jonas looked down at the baby. He folded the birth certificate and tucked it into his pocket. Next week the baby would be baptized.

When each of their sons reached age thirteen, Carmencita and Jonas faced another tough choice. This was the time when young men must learn who they truly were and take their place among the men of the Brotherhood.

"It doesn't make sense to me," his father-in-law looked sadly at the boys riding through the pasture. "My grandsons should know about their faith. The time of being Catholic or Presbyterian has passed."

"The Great War may be over, but do you know what the European Jews do now?" Jonas looked at Manuel. "They flee. They leave their homes behind and get as far away as possible. It's not over, Papa Luna. Not yet."

It was not long after this that Carmencita begged Jonas to leave the Brotherhood completely. "At least stop the meetings. Just teach our boys to believe what is good, but irrelevant to which religion one belongs. To be kind to others, to be fair and honest in business, to take care of their wife and children. This is for all boys to learn."

Jonas had abided by his wife's wishes. He had not told his children about their heritage and he had stopped the meetings. The Brotherhood still met in secret, but nearly all had chosen to keep the knowledge of their heritage from their children. It had taken some work to convince Manuel Luna to keep this knowledge from his grandchildren, but the man loved his daughter and did what Carmencita asked.

✡ ✡ ✡

The day after he visited the cemetery, Jonas sat at the table, the carved box passed from grandfather to son to son open in front of him. He looked at each of the eight birth certificates. Hebrew names. This was the one thing he and his wife had done to keep tradition—using a Spanish name for the baptismal records and hiding the true name of each child. Names his children did not even know they had.

The knock on the door startled him. He closed the lid to the box and pushed it under a towel.

It was the Rodrigo girl. What was her name?

"Hola, Señor Jonas. It's me, Rachel." She held out a basket.

"Come in my dear. What brings you way out here?" He stepped out on the porch and looked around. What did bring her here? There was no horse or bicycle. Didn't the Rodrigo family live over in Ensenda?

"Dr. Swanson said you were poorly. I brought you some fruit and *biscochitos.*"

So now he was on the do-gooder list.

"*Gracias.* Did you walk all the way out here?"

"It's not far. I like the fresh air."

He waited for her to set the basket down and leave, but she breezed in and fluttered around his tiny kitchen.

"I can clean up for you. Do you want some tea with the cookies?" She grabbed his kettle.

She paced around, running a wet cloth over the counters and washing the dishes in the sink while the water heated. When she had poured the tea and sat at the table with him she drew in a deep breath.

She's after something, Jonas thought. He was an old man with many daughters and grand-daughters. He knew the signs.

"Señor Martinez. Will you tell me why our grandfathers fought? I mean, your grandfather and my great-grandfather?"

"You should ask your father."

"He doesn't know. Or he won't tell me, anyway."

Jonas looked at this girl. Dark hair and eyes as black as a starless night. Skin the nut brown of her mother, but roses in her cheeks. She held her shoulders back and her chin high. A proud young thing, not afraid to ask for what she needed.

But what did she know of the Brotherhood? He suspected that Alfonso Rodrigo had kept the fact that they were Jews from his children, just as the many of the Brothers had done. It was not his place to tell this girl any of these secrets.

"My grandfather, Hernan Martinez, he was a stubborn man. Too stubborn. I suppose you know the story of how this killed him?"

The tale of the explosive battle had taken on epic proportions over time.

She nodded.

"So you know that he always looked for a fight? He was righteous and persistent, but anxious as well. What he felt belonged to him, that was important and he watched over these things carefully.

"Your great-grandfather, Alejandro, the two of them were raised together. Like brothers, although they lived apart it was only by a short distance. The two ranches were side by side, over in Taos."

"I know this. I have been there to visit."

Jonas was surprised. "But the land? It no longer belongs to the family?"

Rachel shook her head. "No. But my father showed me where it was. He was born there."

Yes. Jonas remembered that Alejandro and his family had not moved to Tierra Amarilla at the same time as Hernan and Francesca.

"I think they fought about the land. The Americans offered everyone lots of money for their property. My grandfather did not believe anyone should sell. The Americans had different ways— fencing off ranches owned by one man. The Spanish still shared grazing land, although they no longer lived around a plaza, which is how they lived when they settled this place. "

"But what about the Brotherhood?"

Jonas felt his heart thump against the wall of his chest hard enough to knock the air from his lungs. He started to cough, covering his mouth quickly with the heavy handkerchief he kept in his pocket. His eyes watered and he bent his head low.

Either Rodrigo graced his family with the knowledge or this girl was trying to trick him into revealing something.

Rachel rushed to the sink and returned with a glass of water. She handed it to him.

"I can see you are surprised that I know the secret."

"*Sí*. It has been a long time and you are… "

"A girl. I know. But my father has no sons."

"Well, I wasn't thinking about you being a girl, but rather so young. Does your father still meet?"

"Not for a long time. I don't think there is anyone his age, and there is definitely no one my age." She sat. "Now will you tell me what really happened between Hernan and Alejandro?"

Jonas looked at her bright eyes, the serious turn of her lips, and her folded hands.

"Yes. I will tell you."

And so he told this girl, Rachel, how Hernan had become a tyrant toward the one who loved him most, Francesca. His grandmother was a saint who never hurt anyone, but Hernan was blinded by his over zealous protection of the Brotherhood, not what they had become, but what they had been. He never accepted the rules of the Americans. With no one to turn to in a town where she was a newcomer, Francesca had been happy when Alejandro Rodrigo moved his family to Tierra Amarilla. Surely she thought that her husband's best friend would comfort him.

Alejandro had not comforted Hernan, but he had comforted Francesca.

"They had an affair? But what of my great-grandmother?"

"She died shortly after the move. Your great-grandfather was alone."

"And Hernan, he found out?"

"Yes. It was bound to happen. There are not many ways for people to hide things in a town with eyes as sharp as Tierra Amarilla." Jonas didn't tell the girl he suspected the affair had started much earlier. Although he had been young when they left Taos, he remembered many visits from Alejandro Rodrigo.

☆ ☆ ☆

The girl came back. Happy to have an audience, a chance to share all the secrets he had kept since Carmencita died, Jonas looked forward to her visits, although at times he was sure Rachel tricked him into telling more than he should. He warned her many times that she could not repeat any of the stories, as his own children did not know they were Jewish.

"I think you should tell them. Write it down and I'll mail it for you. They deserve to know." Rachel persisted in her quest to make him tell his children the truth. "Why aren't they here to visit you? You are going to die soon, I can see that. Don't they want to say goodbye?" This girl did not hold back any of her thoughts.

She almost had him convinced. He had started the letters, first one to Rueben and then one to Adalina. He was trying to decide if he should let the two oldest know first, when he heard Rachel's feet pounding down the road.

Why was she running so fast? He stood and peered past her, but no enemy or wild animal chased after her.

"The war, it's so terrible… " Rachel choked and cried as she handed him the newspaper she had rolled and tucked inside her shirt. The headline leaped out and struck a blow.

Nazi Roundup of Professionals is Reported in Paris

His hands shook as he read the paper. The girl beside him sobbed into her folded arms.

Soon tears rolled down his wrinkled cheeks.

Jonas stood and picked up the letters he had started. He walked to the old stove and opened the grate.

As he watched the flames turn the paper to ash, he knew the Jews would never be safe, no matter how far they ran.

For a week Jonas stared at the terrible headline. Then he made up his mind. He carried the wooden box to the table and removed the prayer shawl. He would speak with God, ask for guidance.

Two hours later Jonas finished his prayer and raised his trembling hand to the shawl draped over his head. He looked around the small room, staring at the table near the window, the old black stove and the painted cupboards. This was the last time he would pray under the comfort of the ancient cloth. From now on he would rely on the memories reflected by this room to guide him in his talks with God.

He drew in a breath and closed his eyes. No sense putting off his decision. Rachel brought him news each day and things were getting worse. Soon the United States would be in this terrible war. Jews might be safe here now, but what if things changed?

For the Jews things always got worse. He had to hide the truth.

Resigned, he pulled the cloth from his head and folded it.

He placed the carefully folded birth certificates and baptismal records in the box. Wrapping his grandmother's silver candlessticks in a soft cloth he put them in next. Then the old prayer book. He set the folded shawl on top and closed the box.

When he finished hiding his history behind the stone wall, he walked out and sat in his rocker on the porch. Tomorrow he would tell Rachel of his decision. She wouldn't take it lightly, but he knew she would respect his choice.

It was only when Jonas stood next to the bed and pulled off his shirt that he remembered the medallion around his neck. As exhausted as he was, he lit the lantern and returned to the kitchen. He chipped away two stones, close to the edge of the doorway, and slid the medallion into the small space. He covered the golden disc with mud and mortar.

"You are as emotional as an old woman. What would Grandfather say about crying?" he chided himself out loud, but that didn't stop the tears from rolling down his cheeks. His sons would never know their story.

Forty-one
Gabriella
Tuesday, May 13 to Wednesday, May 14

"Why Twisted Bead Dreams?" I should have known better than to let Shannon make all the decisions concerning the website.

"Twistedbead.com was already taken."

"But why the twisted?"

"It will get lots of hits, Mom. You have to pick a word that's popular on web searches." She held up a bracelet. It was made of three strands of beads twisted together. "Double meaning."

"So why the dreams?"

"I don't know. It just kind of came to me and I liked the sound of it."

Was Shannon having dreams?

We spent the next fifteen minutes going through the website my daughter had so efficiently created while I was talking to Fred. She had done amazing things, setting up a special account to take credit cards and designing buttons which customers could click on. I was impressed, but a poor student. My mind kept sliding back to the story Fred had told me and my agreement to attend a secret meeting of a secret cult as the way to solve my problems.

"Are you paying attention to me?"

"Sorry, baby. I'm tired. Maybe some coffee will help."

"I'll have another mocha frap, extra whip, low fat."

"This isn't Starbucks."

"I know. But they make anything you want, believe me. When you get back you can keep your part of the deal and tell me about the medallion and the Brotherhood thing."

As we sipped our coffee, I explained what I had learned about the medallion and being Jewish.

"Why doesn't Rachel want to tell you about it?"

"I don't know. That's kind of how she is. She never really answers any of my questions, just bakes bread and serves tea. I have the feeling she wants to tell me something, but I haven't passed the test yet."

Shannon turned off the laptop and stuffed it in the case. She gulped the last of her mocha-frap-extra-whip-low-fat.

"Come on. Let's go home. I want to see it."

On the drive home I imagined Shannon holding the medallion and spinning off into another world. She was a Martinez as well as a King, and the medallion had a mind of its own. There was no way I could show it to her without letting her hold it. The mother bear part of me didn't want my daughter to experience anything dangerous or frightening.

There was a second part of me at work here. I had not been able to witness my journeys into the past. The last one had really only lasted thirty minutes or so, although I had spent the whole day in Looks-Like-Fred's arms.

Maybe what I was experiencing wasn't a shamanic journey at all. Maybe it was a break with reality and I was lucky to wake up. What if Shannon wasn't so fortunate?

Trying to shake off my mother-worries, I realized it was more likely the medallion was just an old piece of decorative metal and I was going crazy. These thoughts rattled the sides of my brain like ping pong balls.

The drive back to the adobe house was not long enough for me to clear my mind or come to any rational conclusion.

When I handed her the medallion, she was quiet. I watched her, my shoulders tight, ready to spring to her rescue if needed.

"This thing is really weird. The design, I mean. There's like this Jewish star thing going on in the middle."

"Kind of makes the whole story seem true, doesn't it?"

She turned and looked at me. "You don't think it's true?"

"I don't know. It just seems so... extreme."

"Why would Rachel lie to you?"

I shrugged. "This whole thing, I don't get it at all."

"If we are Jewish do we have to do it? I remember that time we tried to go to church. What a disaster. I'm an adult, I get to make up my own mind about things like being Jewish, don't I?"

"That's what I was trying to find out from Rachel. We can't deny our heritage, if we are descendants of Jews, then that's what we are. But I agree with you, Shannon. Religion is a personal choice."

"Well, I'm cool with visiting her again, but can we wait a week or something? I'm all tea-ed out."

"What about what she said to you?"

"Mom, don't worry. If you're in danger I'm right on it." She twirled the medallion in her hand and then slipped it around her neck.

I held my breath. But the medallion sat on her chest and I didn't see her react as if it were doing its hot or cold thing.

"Can I keep it?"

"No!" Mistake. The best way to make Shannon hold her stubborn ground was to overreact.

"Whatever. You don't have to yell at me." She pulled the medallion off and tossed it on the table. "I'm going out for awhile."

"Out? Where?"

"Oh let's see... the mall? Or maybe miniature golf?" She snapped her fingers for Bones, grabbed her sweatshirt and plowed through the door.

I followed her to the door. "Watch out for snakes," I called, but she didn't look back.

✡ ✡ ✡

The next day Shannon was sulking. I couldn't see that there was anything to trigger such a mood—she didn't really think I would just give her the medallion, did she—but I'm just the mom, so who knows? She declined my offer for a ride into Three Ravens, and mustered up enough cordiality to ask me to leave Bones with her in case she decided to go for a walk.

"Are you going to work on some of the bracelets?"

"Maybe."

"If you need me you'll have to walk to the bridge to use your phone."

"I know, you told me three times already. Don't worry, just go."

It felt like she was trying to get rid of me. Maybe I stressed her out as much as she stressed me. Once I was in the car and driving down the road I decided I needed to quit worrying about her. Maybe I could find out some more about this whole Patton thing today. At least I could see what was up with Andy.

The day went by in my usual fruitless efforts to track down people—find out they weren't in, leave messages, move on—until I caught up with Andy at the gas station. He was returning from a call when I pulled in.

"Hey," his hug triggered the memory of the moments in Francesca's body. It had been a long time since we had made love. Andy and me, that is.

"Where's your side kick?"

"Do you mean Shannon or Bones?"

"Well I meant Shannon, but I'm guessing they're together?"

I nodded. "Do you have time for lunch?"

"Let me check with Nelson."

As I watch him walk away, hair draped in a braid wrapped with a piece of purple leather today, I didn't want food. I wanted him. Of course, I didn't really want him. I wanted what Francesca had.

He poked his head into the doorway of the gas station, then turned and gave me a thumbs up as he walked toward me.

"So where should we eat? No calls at all, if we go in my truck and I take the radio we can head up to Penelope's. Or somewhere else in Chama if you want."

"How about we go to your place?" I had no idea where Andy's place was. I thought he might live in someone's garage or barn or something, because he never talked about it.

"My place?" He looked at the station. "Here? You want vending machine snacks for lunch?"

"You live here?"

"I thought you knew that."

What a joker. "In the store? Or the service bay?"

"You don't believe me, do you?" Andy grabbed my arm and turned me around. We headed to the back of the building. Restroom territory.

The building was deeper than it looked from the front. There were four doors in the back. Two were the restrooms, visible as such by the "Customers Only" signs attached to the doors. Andy led me up to the third, pulled his keys out of his pocket and unlocked the door.

"You asked for this," he said reaching in and flipping on the light, then stepping back and gesturing. "Ladies first."

It really wasn't much more than a closet. A twin bed, neatly covered with a red and black patchwork quilt, a tiny counter that held a microwave and a hot plate, a mini fridge with a box of dishes on top. Between the bed and the wall, cardboard boxes were stacked floor to ceiling. There was no table or chairs. In fact, there was barely enough room for the two of us to stand inside the room.

I took hold of his arm and pointed to the bed. "It has everything I need."

I slipped into another world, crossed the border between the reality of Andy and the seduction of Francesca and her lover. The skin I touched, the musky male smell, the rough wool blanket beneath me, these things burned my soul and I kissed Francesca's lover as if there had never been another man. Every other experience in my life melted to a poor imitation of the passion I had been promised by untold romance novels and school girl gossip. I couldn't inhale enough air to keep the kisses from stopping. I couldn't touch enough of this man to pull him deeper into me. A thunderbolt hovered ready to strike us dead in a flaming finale that took us straight to heaven without a stop in purgatory or any judgement from a deity or gatekeeper or my own moralistic thoughts.

It wasn't until I was so completely satiated, panting from the marathon I had just run, that I realized this was Andy, not Francesca's lover. I stayed very still, listening to his heavy breath, hoping that if I didn't move, didn't speak, then neither would he. What was he thinking? That I was a nymphomaniac? Crazy with all my on-again-off-again emotions? I tried to remember if in the storm of our lovemaking I had said anything. Had I called out a name? Professed my undying love?

"Ella. I... that was..." Andy propped himself up on his elbow and shook his head.

I smiled, but didn't meet his gaze.

"Is something wrong?"

This was not how life was supposed to be. I gave myself, every particle, to this man and he decided something was wrong.

But it was my fault. New-Ella had pushed the Ella Andy knew so far from her regular behavior that he noticed. Francesca's passion put Ella's love-making to shame. Truthfully, being with Andy would never match the dream lover. The reality could not compare to the fantasy.

"Everything's fine. That was really... amazing." There was no explanation I could offer that wouldn't hurt his feelings.

His radio buzzed. A call. We dressed, he kissed me sweetly and I headed for home, saved from any more questions and from trying to hide my disappointment.

✡ ✡ ✡

Shannon, with Bones trailing behind her, rushed out to meet me. I suspected she regretted staying home and was bored.

She wasn't bored at all. She had found plenty to do while I was gone.

"Mom, you have to come see. Hurry. I found something."

There was a wooden box on the kitchen table. It was about thirteen inches across and six inches high. The wood was dull and the clasp rusty, but the box had carving on it and was beautiful in spite of the dirt.

"Where did you find that?" She must have gone for a hike.

"There," Shannon pointed to the wall behind the wood stove.

Rocks had been pulled out and heaped beside the small stack of firewood. Dust and crumbled mortar covered the floor. It was near the spot where I had found the medallion.

"Wait until you see what's in it. We really are Jewish." She rubbed her hand across the top of the box. "Look, the symbol again."

Sure enough, hidden with filagree and carving, the sign of the Brotherhood.

I twisted the clasp and opened the box. Pandora. Would something evil spill into the kitchen when I lifted the lid?

"You already looked at all this?"

"Yes, but I put it back just like it was."

The box was filled. I lifted the first object, something wrapped in fabric yellow with age.

I unfolded the fabric, realized it wasn't wrapping anything, just stiff with age. The silk like material was about ten inches wide and forty inches long with embroidery on each end. A scarf of some type? A table runner?

I gently set it on the table.

I recognized the next item. "It's one of those little Jewish hats. I can't remember what they're called."

"Yarmulke."

Two silver candlesticks—even I knew that Jewish tradition included lighting candles.

A small leather book, wound with rough twine. I untied the twine and opened it.

Some other language.

"I think that's Hebrew."

"Really? How do you know what Hebrew looks like? And how did you know that was called a yarmulke?"

"I told you, Jewish friends."

I'd have to ask her more about that later. Right now I wanted to finish looking through the box.

The rest of the box was filled with old papers. I carefully unfolded one of the brittle documents.

I held it out to Shannon. "Don't tell me. Hebrew. Can you read it?"

"Very funny. But I think it's an official document of some kind. Look, it has a seal." She pointed to a spot of wax on the corner of the page.

I studied the thin page.

She couldn't keep from telling me more, in spite of her effort to let me discover all this by myself. "They're all like that. Like a set of official documents. There are some in Spanish, I think those are birth certificates. Mom, I know who could read them. Let's go now and we can get there by three. It's not too late."

"I... let me think." Shannon was right. Rachel would know what these papers said. And she probably knew a lot more than that about this box. We would just have to convince her to tell us.

Forty-Two

Rachel García Maria de la Rodrigo
Ensendada, New Mexico
June 17, 1942

"Rachel. You are seventeen years old. You can't do all that. You barely knew the man."

"Mother, I knew him better than anyone." Rachel thought about her conversations with Jonas. Deep conversations. He didn't treat her like a child. He took her seriously and answered the million questions she had. "He wouldn't have wanted a Presbyterian funeral. I know that."

"He was a Brother. They are willing to sacrifice."

Maybe her mother was right. When Rachel found the old man dead she had searched the house for his prayer shawl and the leather prayer book. She couldn't find anything at all that would hint that Jonas was Jewish.

Not one thing.

She searched and searched. She wanted to honor him by burying these things with him. Let him take his secret to the grave, as the old saying went.

"His children will fly in. Let them take care of putting him to rest." Rachel's mother shook her head. "Poor soul."

"It will take them too long to get here. He should be buried today."

"Today? That's not realistic and you know it."

Rachel ignored her mother and continued to plan the burial of her friend. She ticked off the list: shroud, cleansing, prayers, someone to dig the grave.

Jonas had taken Rachel to his family cemetery. She helped him walk up the hill to visit Carmencita and listened to stories about his wife. The old man missed her and talked of the day he would be beside her. For two years he'd been ready to die, and with that terrible cough Rachel had expected to lose him sooner than she had. She was going to make sure he rested next to Carmencita as soon as possible.

When her mother saw that she couldn't talk Rachel out of taking charge, she offered her support by driving her daughter from Ensenda to T.A. Rachel didn't mind the walk, but today she needed time to prepare.

At five o'clock that evening seven people stood on the hillside, watching Arturo Chavez shovel the yellow clay onto the shrouded body. Rachel cried shamelessly, not caring if people questioned her attachment to this old man.

Rachel came each day to sit by the grave, trying hard to recall the mourning rituals her father taught her before he died. She was pretty sure one cried for three days. On the second day she saw people down at the house and she walked the long way to the cemetery to avoid them. She wasn't ready to meet the Martinez family yet.

Rachel picked up a small stick and drew a line in the dirt on top of the grave. "Jonas. Did you decide not to tell them? For sure? I can tell them for you if you want me to."

She suspected there was another reason she wanted to tell the sons of Jonas Martinez about their Jewish heritage. She wanted some company. After her father's death last year, there was no one left. No Brotherhood.

She needed to know how Jonas felt. "Would you really have wanted the truth to die too?" But Jonas didn't send her any answers. Finally she stood and walked down to the house.

"*Hola,*" she called out as she approached.

"Hello." A man, surely one of Jonas's sons, sat in the rocker on the front porch, staring out at Las Nutrias creek.

"I'm Rachel. A friend of your father."

The man's forehead wrinkled. She could see he didn't expect his father to have a seventeen-year-old girl for a friend. "I'm Rueben, his son."

"He went peacefully in his sleep. I found him in the morning when I came with his meal."

"So that was you. I heard people were helping him out."

"I helped with the funeral too."

Reuben scowled. "What was the rush? I would have taken care of that."

Rachel considered what to tell the man. *Your father was Jewish, we only had until sundown,* she wanted to say, but something held her back. "It's what he wanted. He didn't like to be a bother to anyone and he wanted to be with your mother."

"I never understood why he thought anything we did for him was a bother. Christ, he was my father. Didn't he know that meant something?"

Rachel felt the corners of her lips raise at Reuben's choice of curses. She turned her head so he couldn't see her smile. Jonas would have laughed. She reached down into the pocket of her dress and rubbed the turquoise stone she had taken from the windowsill two days ago.

Jonas had told her about the stone. His father gave it to him on one of his rare visits, when he was a young boy. He kept it in his pocket all the time, rubbing it whenever he was lonely. While she was searching the house she had spotted it and slipped it into her own pocket.

She could talk to Jonas when she was lonely, but she couldn't tell Rueben and Hernando the truth.

✡ ✡ ✡

Rachel's hands trembled as she read the headline. *Vilna Massacre of Jews Reported.* She had heard about it three days ago, but didn't get a paper until today. Clemente Rivas brought one by this morning because he knew she wanted to read it.

"Jonas was right," Rachel whispered. The Jews would be rounded up and killed. She took a deep breath and looked out the window. How long before this world war made its way here?

There had to be members of the Brotherhood out there. They couldn't have all decided to be Catholic or Presbyterian. Although her father denied he went to meetings, she used to hear him sneak out after everyone was in bed.

Rachel stood and went into the bedroom. She heaved the heavy lid of the old chest in the corner.

Her mother kept some of her father's things in this chest. A jacket, some papers, his pipe.

She had gone through everything twice and was repacking the chest when she felt something in the pocket of the jacket.

It was what she was looking for.

She rubbed the medallion and stared at the crest. Her father's voice came to her.

El que cree y persista vive para siempre. He who believes and persists lives forever.

She believed, just as her father had taught her.

Now she would persist.

Forty-Three
Gabriella
Thursday, May 15

I had convinced Shannon to wait until morning to go see Rachel. Impulsivity was not serving me well these days and I wanted to think about the box. And the fact that my ancestors were, without a doubt, members of the Brotherhood.

We sat in Rachel's kitchen, with the standard cups of tea. She ran her hands over the carved lid.

"Jonas hid this."

Shannon stayed quiet.

"Have you seen it before?"

She nodded. "When I was a young girl."

Rachel never had told me about her relationship with my great-grandfather, although I had caught on to the fact there was one from her questions. She might have been in her twenties. Had she had an affair with an old man?

"He kept it on a shelf in the main room. When Jonas died and they came back to bury him they looked for it. No one knew what had become of it, but Jonas loved a mystery, so they figured he hid the box somewhere. Rueben said it was just some old mementos and he wasn't worried."

Rachel continued. "I never said a word to Rueben, but I knew the box had to do with the Brotherhood. Everything had gone very quiet because of the war. It was a bad time to be Jewish."

Shannon added another teaspoon of honey to her tea. "My grandpa said his father hated the land. That *his* father was obsessed and sad that none of his children would come back. But it was all tied up and grandpa couldn't sell his part."

"When did he tell you that?" First Julie and now Shannon with these mysterious relationships with my father.

She shrugged. "I don't know. Once when we were talking."

I would pursue that line later—now I was impatient to know what secrets the box held.

Rachel rubbed her hand across the lid one more time, then twisted the latch. She closed her eyes as she opened the box, drawing in a deep breath.

With eyes still closed she spoke. "It is the smell of my childhood. The smell of all those who came before us, the smell of an ancient people persecuted for all time."

I didn't have time for her mystical act, but I knew if I interrupted she might refuse to tell me anything.

Finally she opened her eyes and pulled out the shawl. "This prayer shawl belonged to Jonas, but I think it had been passed down. It was old when he used it."

The yarmulke shared the same story. She thought the candlesticks came from Francesca. I tried to picture the house in my dreams, but couldn't recall seeing them.

Rachel unfolded the first of the papers.

"Can you read it?"

"Yes. It is a birth certificate. It says that Salatiel Galit Marciano was born on July 10, 1823 at Rancho de Roja in Taos."

"Do you know who he is?"

She shook her head and reached for the next document.

"Zacarías Galit Marciona, also born at Rancho de Roja, but on May 24, 1845."

I wondered who these men were. "Are those Jewish names?"

Rachel reached for the next frail document. As she read, her eyes grew wide.

"What does that one say?"

"Yehoyachin Galit Marciano, born June 2, 1870."

"You know who that is, don't you?" I had a sudden flash of memory. "That name. He's buried on the hill."

Rachel nodded, but kept quiet.

"Who?"

"This is the birth certificate of Jonas Martinez."

Two hours later Shannon and I left the old woman. She wanted to keep the box with her, but I refused.

Rachel had gone through the rest of the birth certificates. We figured out they belonged to each of Jonas's children. Hebrew names. The whole family called Marciano, not Martinez.

Also folded in the box were Spanish baptismal certificates. Adalina, Hernando, Cleto, Beatríz, Leonor, Mariana, Rueben and Emidio. My grandfather and each of his siblings had two certificates and two names. My grandfather was Maimonides Yehuda Marciano, not Reuben Martinez.

"Mom, what does it mean? Did Grandpa know about it?" I had the same questions as Shannon and I tried to feel his spirit and find an answer. If only I had discovered this mystery before my grandparents and my father had died.

My ancestors were Jewish and they had hid it well. Not even my name was my own. Gabriella Marciano. I shook my head and cringed at the thought of what this meant.

I pictured my great-grandfather, worried about his children. I knew they had scattered. I had cousins in many states.

Except Jews were safe in the United States, weren't they? Many fled to this country from Germany and other places. Why had Jonas been scared?

Rachel knew. I was sure of it. But I couldn't get her to tell me everything. She doled it out in tiny portions, like an old time radio series I had to listen to every week, anxiously awaiting the next episode.

There was a way to find out more. I would direct my dreams. It worked when I wanted to know more about Francesca and now I needed to get in touch with Jonas.

It was dark when Shannon and I made it back to the house. I was glad she decided to pull her mat and blankets into the kitchen to be near the fire and I insisted she use the cot and let me keep the mat. I had the wooden floor.

When I heard her breath grow slow and even, I held the medallion up to my lips and whispered. "Show me the truth."

I was back with the long line of trudging people. My people, I knew now. Looking around for Romero, or even Catalina, I walked quickly toward the front of the group. No one looked at me or said a word.

We weren't by the river or in the desolate hills. We marched up a smooth trail, headed toward tree-covered mountains. It seemed I searched the crowds for hours, staring into a hundred faces, trying to find one that was familiar. The sun went down and still I searched, people gathered around fires now, cooking dinner and spreading out blankets for the night.

Exhausted, I decided to rest. I spotted a large flat boulder, hoping it held the heat of the sun, because suddenly I was very cold. I climbed to the top and curled up, hands tucked under my cheek for a pillow.

Wait. Consuela told me I had the power to see what I needed to see. Exhausted, I tried to rise to continue my search, but my head sunk back down on my folded hands.

I heard voices.

"We are not in Mexico. If decisions need to be made, we make them."

"We do not have that power. That is not the way of the Brothers."

"We are the Brothers now, do you not understand that?"

I crawled to the edge of the rock. Six men stood in a circle, their voices a whisper.

One of them was Romero. I looked at the other faces, expecting to see Gregario, but he was not there.

"Oñate suspects something. This is not the time to draw any attention from the general."

"We must remember the reasons we go north are not the same as Oñate's reasons or the King's. We go to look for a place for our people. If we find a spot and are forced to move on, then we discard a chance."

"Scouts, we are scouts. We make note of each place."

Romero was silent, but his bright eyes grew intense at the words of the men.

The first man spoke once more. "Any major decision must be approved by the council."

"How do you propose we send word to the council? A month's journey south and a month's journey back? A lone rider will never survive. We must form our own council. Those men are old, which is why they did not make this journey themselves. We are the new life of the Brotherhood and we make the decisions now. I say we go back to the big river and find a place to settle there."

Romero rubbed his beard and drew in a breath. "I am undecided on this issue of making decisions. But even if we decide to provide our own council, then we must consider the place you say we settle. Oñate and his men go north. If they settle, then the road to this place will be this very road, the one that we travel. Would it be wise for the Jews to settle in such a noticeable place? Is not the purpose to outrun Oñate and settle somewhere in our own land, somewhere away from the eye of Spain?"

A dog barked and the men all turned to the sound. All but one. Romero looked up, straight into my eyes. A wrinkle creased his brow and he shook his head, ever so slightly.

The magic must rely on the wishes of both parties because with Romero's displeasure I felt a swirl of blue mist surround me and try as I might I could not stay in my dream.

Forty-Four
Rachel García Maria de la Rodrigo y Rivas
Ensenda, New Mexico, 1950

Rachel lit the candles and started the prayer. Clemente and
Alejandro joined in. *"Barukk atah Adonai, Eloheynu Melekh ha-
olam..."*

Keeping the Sabbath traditions with a five-year-old child
proved challenging. Alejandro couldn't understand the need to sit
still on this one day. Not when his mother totally indulged him and
let him run free the rest of the week.

But his laughing eyes and bubbly giggle was irresistible to her.
Rachel couldn't discipline him for being full of joy. He was named
for her great-grandfather, but her mother said the baby was nothing
like the serious man.

"Hush. Listen to Mama." Clemente kissed his son's rosy cheek.

*"... asher kid/shanu b'mitzovotav v'tzivanu l'hadlik ner shel
Shabbat."*

Rachel was calm as she chanted the words. It was 1950 and the
world had settled down. Her heart was warm with the spiritual
blessing and she felt the true meaning of the Sabbath take over her
mind and body.

After the dinner of fried fish and *orejas de fraile*—the boy loved
the crispy fried treat and laughed that they were called Friar's Ears
—Alejandro got busy with his blocks and Rachel and Clemente sat
on the porch to gaze at the bright moon rising above the cliffs.

"I want to have a meeting, Clemente."

"With me?" Her husband turned down his lips as if he had bit a sour lemon. "What have I done now?"

She smiled. "No, not with you, my darling. You are as perfect as ever. With the Brotherhood."

Clemente rubbed his forehead. "Why?"

"Some of the scientists from Los Alamos are moving into the area. They're buying land, building retirement homes."

"That's a good thing, Rachel. The area needs an infusion of money. Things are not exactly booming around here." What Clemente said was true. Many of the young people had moved away during the war. There were jobs in California, along with houses, electricity and other modern conveniences. A second wave had departed after the war.

"Many of those scientists are Jewish."

"You want them to join the Brotherhood? They're not Spanish. Those men are all Easterners or foreigners. They've never hidden their religion."

"That's what I'm thinking. Maybe it's time for us to quit hiding too. But I cannot do it alone. I need the Brotherhood behind any decisions." Rachel thought about Jonas. The old man had warned her that there would *never* be a time when they shouldn't hide.

"I understand what's on your mind, but Rachel, please think it through." Clemente sounded tired.

Rachel knew Clemente loved her, but she also knew he had a hard time dealing with her stubborn streak. The first time this had come between them was when she refused to take his name. Custom, the law, whatever the reason, she wasn't giving up her name. She would add his to the list.

Rachel Garcia Maria de la Rodrigo y Rivas.

It was a long name, but a perfect fit for her. Her history all rolled up into one long string of words.

She admitted that sometimes she acted without thinking. But she had given this idea a lot of thought. It was time for the small group of Brothers she had gathered in the last nine years to become something more than a card playing group. It was time to regain sight of the purpose of being a Jew.

Rachel contacted the men and women. *Meet out at the old barn on the back of the deserted Chavez ranch at nine o'clock Wednesday night, two weeks from now. Come quietly and alone.*

Then she drove to Taos to speak with two old Brothers who still lived near the pueblo. Initially Abraám Santiago and Salvador Reyes were reluctant to speak to a woman. But when she told them about Jonas and all he had done and how the two of them were friends, the men agreed to share protocol and history with her.

As the night of the meeting drew close Rachel checked her list. Robes—Katarina Luna helped her make them, dark blue and hooded—and medallions—she had hers and urged the men to find those which had been handed down from father to son. Clemente carved six wooden replicas for those men and women who didn't have medallions.

Next on her list: selling point. She still didn't have one. How was she going to convince these men that the Brotherhood needed a resurrection? Most did not worship at all, or performed a Catholic-ized version of lighting candles and cooking. Would they be willing to renew their Jewish practices, in secret or maybe not even in secret? But then—as Clemente had asked—why would they need the Brotherhood?

She asked her husband for ideas, but he wasn't keen on the whole proposition and just shrugged and told her he'd think about it.

She looked through the old prayer books and researched world events to go with the history Abraám and Salvador had provided. Then she drew out these events on a large piece of cardboard, with arrows to show what the outcomes had been, not only when things were bad for the Jews, but when times were good. How the Brothers wove their way into the New Mexico government, the churches, Catholic, Presbyterian and Methodist, by keeping up the energy of the Brotherhood when things were going well.

They needed to prepare for the future. The Jews of Tierra Amarilla were no longer rich, as they had been in her great-grandfather's time. The land was overlogged, made for poor farming and the town was too far from Santa Fe. While they were able to draw elk hunters and those who wanted recreation on the lakes, this did little to support the area. Thank goodness they were still the county seat and people had to come to the courthouse.

On Friday evening Clemente came home, rushing straight into the kitchen. "I think I have your answer."

"Which question?"

"How to motivate the Brothers to come to your meeting." He took his hat off and hung it on the hook by the door. "There is another episode in the Martinez-Patton feud. That anti-semite is at it again."

"Tell me." She sat down at the table. Clemente sat across from her.

"Seems that after Jonas died his sons didn't do much with the property. None of them wanted to live here, so they didn't even bother to change the title. Yesterday the land came up for auction because no one has paid the taxes."

"Does Reuben know? We need to call him." The phone number she had was nearly ten years old, but maybe she could find him.

"I don't know. The auction is next week. If Reuben's going to keep that land, he better do something about it quick. Ray Patton sees his chance and he's ready to take it. You know old Joseph Patton wanted that land. Ray is no different. He wants any hint of Jews in this town erased." Clemente reached across the table and placed his hand over hers. "I know you think the Brothers have kept themselves a secret, but they have not."

Jonas had made sure Rachel knew the story. She knew it better than anyone else alive.

✡ ✡ ✡

The phone number Rachel had for Rueben was no longer in service. She mailed two letters the next day; one to Reuben and one to Hernando. Those were the only addresses she had.

All week everyone in Tierra Amarilla talked about the auction. There were twenty theories on what Ray Patton would do with the land. Talk was a new road would be built, straight up the pass and over to Taos. Folks would no longer have to drive the winding Los Brazos highway. Patton would take advantage of the new road and build a hotel and a restaurant for the travelers. Patton would build a new Catholic school. Patton would let the land rot.

The meeting was set for two days before the auction. Rachel had a plan. The Brotherhood would save the Martinez land. Problem was, none of them had much money. How would they bid against Ray Patton's fortune?

She had to find Rueben.

✡ ✡ ✡

Rachel tapped the gavel on the wooden table. Not really a table, just a board set between two barrels. The Brothers took their seats on the bales of straw Clemente had hauled to the deserted barn this morning. They wore the blue robes Katarina had passed out at the door. Only six men and women had shown up.

"The meeting will now come to order. Welcome *Hermandad de Creyentes*. He who believes and persists lives forever."

"He who believes and persists lives forever." At least most of the men and women knew the motto.

Rachel licked her lips and peered out from under the hood. She could see a few of the faces, but most held their heads down with the hoods shielding them from recognition. Good. That meant they were taking this seriously.

"I know it has been a long time since the Brotherhood has had a meeting. A dangerous thing has happened to us. We have become complacent. We have let laziness get in the way of our safety."

Rachel continued, looking down at the slip of paper tucked in her hand. She didn't want to leave anything out just because she was nervous.

"I wanted to talk tonight about our future, about how we can build the Brotherhood into the strong backbone of protection it has always been. But I will save that for our next meeting. Tonight we must discuss something more important.

"I'm sure most of you know Ray Patton has plans to buy the Martinez property at auction. Just two days from now, that man, who has voiced his hatred for all Hebrews, will own the entire south end of the valley. Not only could this be a problem for us, it is also a dishonor to Jonas Martinez. A man who worked hard to carry on our traditions. I know that many of your fathers attended *La Academia*, either before it was burned or when instruction took place in the home of Jonas and Carmencita Martinez. Your fathers probably wouldn't have made it to college if not for the excellent instruction they received." Okay, maybe she was laying it on a little too strong.

"We need to outbid Ray Patton. We need to buy the Martinez property."

A hooded man in the front row called out. "Where are we going to get the money to do that?" Other voices joined him. Rachel heard grumbling and accusations about her relationship with Jonas.

"Why are you in charge anyway? You're a woman and you aren't the oldest member. We came tonight to let you know that won't be tolerated." That sounded like Marcus Luna. He was the oldest member.

Rachel tapped her gavel. "Order. Okay. Let's back up. Does anyone have any ideas about how we can fix this? Make sure that Patton doesn't end up with the property?"

One of the Brothers stood up.

"I have an idea."

✡ ✡ ✡

Two days later Rachel entered the courthouse and followed the crowds to the conference room. This was where the auction would be held. She couldn't find a seat and had to squeeze through people into a spot against the wall where she could see the front of the room.

There was Ray Patton. Next to him sat his son, Richard, and a young woman.

Rachel saw the tax collector speaking with the auctioneer. It was only a moment before he addressed the crowd.

"This is the auction for parcel 1785962, as described in the title and deed. A reminder, the 1900 acres are bid as a per acre figure and the bids cannot be split. The bidding starts at three hundred dollars per acre."

"Three hundred." The voice came from the back of the room. Rachel twisted to see who it was, but a second bid followed on the heels of the first. This one from a stranger wearing a blue hat, seated across the room. She looked at Patton. He sat with his arms folded across his chest, a confident smirk on his lips. The bidding rose, but he never made a move.

"Four twenty-five."

"Four fifty."

The price crept higher. Already more than the Brotherhood could have paid.

After ten minutes the bids slowed. It was down to blue hat and the man in back of room.

"Seven hundred twenty."

"Seven twenty-five."

"Seven fifty." Patton joined the bidding.

Where was Clemente? Time was running out. Finally Rachel felt, rather than heard, the crowd stir. Someone was pushing through to the front of the room.

It was Mario Chavez, a clerk from the tax office. He handed an envelope to the auctioneer.

"I'm sorry gentlemen. But this land has been removed from the auction."

"What?" Ray Patton jumped from his seat, the smug look replaced with anger. "You can't do that."

"I'm sorry sir. If you have questions you'll have to take them up with Judge Luna."

✡ ✡ ✡

Late that night Rachel snuggled up to Clemente. She felt the muscles in her shoulders loosen for the first time in two weeks.

"Thank God Rueben called in time."

"I know. I didn't think there would be such a problem with paying the taxes."

"It wouldn't have worked if the deed hadn't been all messed up. Imagine, the whole thing in Carmencita's name. I wonder why Jonas left it like that?"

"I still don't think it would have worked out if Mario hadn't known about the highway coming through. Pure genius donating that easement so the county would forgive the taxes. And stop the auction." Her husband kissed her neck. "And finding Reuben through that old girlfriend."

She clutched Clemente's arm. "I'll sleep happy for a year just picturing the look on Ray Patton's face."

Forty-Five
Gabriella
Friday, May 16

Andy agreed to distract Shannon on Friday. There was an event in Dulce—music, drumming and dancing. I definitely would have rather gone with them. I didn't tell Andy where I was going, making up an excuse of a meeting with Fred and Joel. The wave of guilt which swept over me for lying to him was brief. I rationalized the falsehood by telling myself I now fit in with the rest of the people in this town. Since he didn't question my excuse, he was either very good at faking things, or he really didn't know about the Brotherhood meetings.

We headed up Highway 84. Rachel sat in front, her eyes straight ahead. She hadn't said anything other than giving me a brief Spanish greeting.

Fred turned onto a road I had passed many times but never driven down.

The road quickly changed from a two-lane, poorly-paved route, to a single-lane gravel track. After bumping along on this for ten minutes we came to a gate. Fred jumped out and twirled the combination lock, drove through, got out again and locked it behind us. I figured we must be close to our meeting place.

But we weren't. This road was barely a road. The Subaru bounced and pounded over huge rocks, and I swear for a while we drove up an old riverbed. Branches closed in as we moved up the mountain, scraping the sides of the truck.

"I guess this really is a secret," I joked, but no one laughed.

I prayed it wouldn't rain. Dark clouds had hovered on the horizon all day. I imagined the dried creek bed we drove up filling like Las Nutrias Creek had during the storm. A raging torrent sweeping us away.

Finally we drove into a clearing. There were seven or eight vehicles parked in front of an old barn.

"*Ponte esto.*" Rachel handed me a blue velvet robe.

"What? Maybe you better teach me the secret handshake now, before we go in."

"*Mija*, I know you are nervous. But this is not a night for joking. Put the robe on."

Rachel spoke to me in English. In front of Fred. Add that to the list of lies. The very long list.

The blue robe was scary, scary, scary. Like Klu Klux Klan scary.

Fred and Rachel pulled the hoods over their heads and tipped their chins forward. The sleeves of the robe were long and belled out at the cuffs so that their hands were hidden among the folds.

Rachel stepped forward and pulled my hood under the chain around my neck, tugging it up over my head and then down past my forehead, low over my face. She straightened the medallion, which made the thick blue velvet scrunch uncomfortably around my neck.

"What did you do to it?"

It took me a second to realize she meant the medallion.

"I fixed the chain and cleaned it." I looked at her medallion which hung way down, clear below her small breasts. "I wanted it to hang right so I shortened the chain."

Rachel sighed and tried once more to get things to fall smoothly around my neck. "There is a reason for all things in this world," she whispered.

Then she stepped back and spoke directly to me. "Don't speak when we enter. You may be asked some questions, but I will answer for you. Only speak if I tell you to speak."

I nodded, my throat dry and my breath caught in my chest. This wasn't exactly the men's business meeting I had imagined.

As we approached the barn I could hear voices, but when Fred opened the door and we entered, all talking stopped. The smell of hay and cows lingered, but this was no barn. The room had a concrete floor, overhead florescent lights and folding chairs were set in rows. I was surprised by the lights, then spotted long orange extension cords. Electricity way out here? Where were we? I wondered if Fred had circled back and we were close to some town. Not out in the middle of nowhere at all.

Some of the people in blue robes were seated, but most stood talking around the edges of the room. There must have been forty. One of them approached us.

"*El que cree y persista vive para siempre.*"

Rachel answered. "*El que cree y persista vive para siempre.*"

I recognized the motto or whatever it was called.

"*¿La trajiste?*"

I could tell this was a question. Failed-Monk. I couldn't help it, the name of the figure who spoke just popped into my head. These robes were ridiculous, but his looked worse than the rest, dirty and wrinkled. It was obvious Rachel and this guy knew each other.

"*¿Qué no tienes respeto para el secreto?*" Rachel responded, then turned to Fred, shaking her head and waving her arms as she continued to speak in rapid Spanish. He spoke in Spanish to Failed-Monk. Then he pointed at me and talked some more.

Failed-Monk nodded and turned back to the room. The people who had grown silent during Rachel's angry exchange, started their conversations again. I could hear Spanish and English, but voices were soft and I couldn't make out what anyone was saying.

Fred led me to a chair. "You can sit here. I'll be beside you, but my grandmother sits up front. Things will start soon."

"What was that guy saying? Why was Rachel mad?"

"He was asking questions about you. Rachel reminded him that this is a secret meeting and no one should question who a robed Brother might be."

My stomach burned and my bladder tensed. The temptation to look around was too strong, and I turned my head, trying to sneak glances out the sides of the flopping hood.

Most of the people in the room were men, I could tell by the beards just visible under the hoods, the broad shoulders, and the deep voices. Many had their hoods pulled down to hide their faces, but not all. One tall man, with a very bushy black beard had his hood draped high on his forehead so that his face was easily viewed. I didn't recognize him as anyone I had ever met.

I looked around the room, scanning the figures and feeling my body temperature rise. This barn had no windows. The only door was the one we had come through. There was a loft, and I could see the wide hay doors but no ladder.

My gaze stopped on a small hooded figure. Was this person a woman? She, he, it, stood near the wall, hood pulled well over her face.

I knew she was staring at me. I reached up and tugged my hood so my face would stay in shadows. Her gaze never wavered, although I couldn't really see her eyes. I expected orange orbs to glow from beneath the hood and burn straight into me, like one of Shannon's horror movies.

Sweat engulfed me. Not just underarm perspiration, but rivers of hot fluid dripping from all parts of my body. My clothes felt as if I had just stepped out of the rain and the robe acted as a giant humidifier.

My lungs wouldn't respond to my efforts to take a deep breath and calm down. Hands shaking, I stood and moved toward the door and some fresh air. Then a gavel struck the table up front and everyone took their seats.

When I turned to go back to the seat Fred had assigned me someone else was sitting there. I quickly sat in the nearest chair, grateful really, because it was closer to the back of the room. I saw the person I thought was a woman take a chair at the other end of the row. Five people were seated between us.

The sweating hadn't stopped and my breathing was even more erratic.

"The meeting will now come to order." The black bearded man stood in the front of the room.

The woman in my row immediately stood. "Brother, before we begin, I think we need the fans."

"So approved."

Immediately three robed figures went to the back of the room and came forward with fans.

The robed woman pointed to our row. "One here."

Once again I tried to see her face, but she was well shrouded. Maybe she was more my guardian then my enemy. Cloaked-Angel.

The cool wind generated by the fan helped, but my hands trembled in my lap.

The bearded man spoke once more. "Please stand."

I stood along with everyone else. When they started to chant in Spanish I felt my knees tremble. It was a deep, low sound, like Buddhist monks. The minor tones amped my fear tenfold. I didn't know what was scaring me, but any curiosity that still swirled around in the back of my mind fled and the fear ballooned, crowding out all my other emotions.

Cold, biting, unnamed fear.

Rachel spoke. "*Siéntate.*" She continued speaking Spanish, but everyone sat, so I sat. I caught a few words—brother, God, blood.

When Rachel finished men stood and asked questions. Most in Spanish, occasionally in English.

"Shouldn't we respect what he wanted? If he hid the medallion there was a reason."

They must be talking about Jonas.

I turned, forgetting that Fred was not sitting beside me, and whispered "Are they talking about Jonas Martinez?"

"Shh." The figure next to me hissed.

"She will have to go through the usual steps. Application and initiation."

Oh God. Now I knew they were talking about me. I didn't want to be a part of this group, this club with rules I didn't understand and probably didn't want to follow. I nearly stood and announced this to the crowd. Then I remembered Rachel's warning and stayed silent.

"I disagree. I don't think she wants to join, but I think it's our duty to help her with this problem. That *puta* Patton needs to be put in his place. We have grown lax the past few years."

"Are we ready for first vote?" This from Black-Beard.

"What are we voting on? Membership or help without?" It was the man I called Failed-Monk. His voice slid down my spine like something oily. He didn't like me.

I was a passive observer. Listening to things while answering in my mind. Regretting I didn't have the gumption to stand up and say what I felt.

I reached up and wrapped my fingers around the medallion. It went from cold to warm in my hand. A series of visions slammed into my mind, barely sequential, somehow I saw them all at once. I saw men standing tall before other cloaked figures, all wearing medallions. I heard voices calling out, defending what they believed. I saw Rique, shaking his head and refusing to change his mind. I saw the strong figure of Hernan, his bright blue eyes looking directly at me. I heard him say to me—or Jonas or someone —"The Brothers stick together." And then I saw Romero, glaring at me as I listened from the top of the rock. Where were the women in these visions? Where were Francesca and Consuela? Carmencita? The medallion heated, sending its power into me, telling me I had to act.

This was about me and I should have some input.

I stood and pulled the hood from my head.

Several men grumbled. "What the hell does she think she's doing?" I heard a deep voice ask.

"I am Gabriella Martinez. Since this is me—my future—we are talking about, I would like to be part of the discussion." My voice came out loud and clear, although I felt the tremble in my chest work its way toward my throat. I looked at the front table. Rachel was shaking her head.

She wouldn't stop me. Not this time. "It is only very recently that I learned about the Brotherhood, of which I still know very little. I want to learn more. I want to find out why my great-grandfather took this medallion," I held it up, "and hid it from his family.

"But I am not asking to join your group. I don't know enough about it to make that decision."

Rachel struggled to stand. The blue hooded figure sitting next to her pulled her back down.

"If you can do something, anything, to help me with the obvious delay to clear title to my land, I would be grateful. I don't know why or who has decided that they should stop me from selling or even owning this land, but it's all I have. I appreciate that the Brotherhood is considering helping me.

"But I don't want to be outside the loop and I don't want to be lied to. I have spent my life being surprised by what happens around me. I want to change that. I want to be in control of my destiny."

Okay, time to stop. I was starting to sound demented.

"So, if you do decide to help me, I want to know what's going on. That's all and thank you." I sat with a thump. My heart pounded against the wall of my chest like a caged felon.

Forty-Six
Rachel García Maria de la Rodrigo y Rivas
Ensenda, New Mexico, 1967

"*Deja eso.*" Rachel reached for two-year old Alfredo's hand as he raised the dirt to his lips. By this age her grandson shouldn't be putting things in his mouth, but the boy wanted to explore everything. "*Papi llegará pronto,*" she crooned as she pulled Alfredo away from the garden. She knew his parents wanted the boy to speak English, but telling him his father would be home soon in the native tongue was a daily ritual.

When Alejandro married Helen Luna, Rachel was concerned. She was a nice girl, but her family was modern. Rachel feared that her grandson would not learn the old traditions, including the language he would need to communicate with her.

Of course that wasn't really true, but Rachel had decided to keep her knowledge of English a secret. Clemente hadn't learned much of the new language. Her husband was kind and compassionate but she detected frustration at times. He didn't like that she had her nose in everything. If he knew she was working to improve her English he would want to know why this was necessary.

Clemente was blind to the changes going on around here. Blind to the need to make sure the Brotherhood sustained. Rachel knew how precarious their position had become.

It was all because of that rebel, Tijerina. Getting the whole state in an uproar about the land. Didn't he know there was a better way to settle things than barging in head first and causing a mess? Besides that, he was an outsider. A crazy man from Texas who just wanted attention.

Rachel agreed with some of Tijerina's ideas. It was true the Americans had snatched up the land from the colonists. But that was nearly a hundred years ago. How did he propose to repair history?

She feared his antics would uncover the land purchases made by the Brotherhood. The American cattlemen weren't the only ones taking advantage of the confusion in 1880.

Jonas had told her the story. She thought about that day so many years ago, aching for Jonas as she always did when she remembered the man who had befriended a young girl.

"The Brotherhood planned ahead," Jonas said. "When things were heating up in Taos, arguments grew among the men because some wanted to sell their land and some feared the upsurge in persecution of the Jews. You would think when those Jews came over to Las Vegas—they even built a synagogue there—that we would have joined up with them. But they didn't regard the Spanish as real Jews. Said we had been away from it too long, didn't do things right. Claimed Americans did it better, even though most of them were from Europe. Anyway, the Brotherhood had split. My grandfather, Hernan on one side, and your great-grandfather, Alejandro on the other, although the two were best friends.

"My grandfather had a temper. He never stayed calm, but the Brothers knew that this time he was wrong. Wrong for them, anyway." Jonas had smiled as he told Rachel the story, almost as if he had been there, although he was a very small child at the time. "They managed to get land in Tierra Amarilla. With legal deeds. There were Brothers in high places even then. Maybe even more so than now. Then they sent the stubborn old men and their families here. Away from Taos."

The young Rachel had been fascinated. "Are you saying the deeds weren't legitimate?"

Jonas shrugged and smiled that deep grin which curved up into the wrinkles around his eyes, still bright blue even as an old man.

Now, twenty years after Jonas had told Rachel this story, she wished she had asked for more details. There was no one left to explain to her what had really happened.

There were some older men in the Brotherhood, but not old enough to have lived during those times. Perhaps they had heard stories from their fathers.

Rachel feared Tijerina's call for investigation into the original Spanish grants would uncover something more than corrupt American ranchers. Something which needed to stay hidden.

✡ ✡ ✡

"Mama, what do you know about the Martinez family? Weren't you friends with them?" Alejandro sat across the table, jiggling the smiling Alfredo on his knee.

"That was so many years ago. I was a young girl."

"Right. But Jonas? All that land on the edge of town? Two thousand acres. I heard you were involved in saving it for his family."

She wanted that story to stay buried. Apparently she was naïve to think that the gossip of this valley would not catch up with her.

"Why do you need to know?" She watched her son's face. "Are you involved with this nonsense?"

"Not nonsense. It's important." Alejandro licked his lips and met her gaze. "When something is important you fight for it. That's what you taught me, Mama. You have spent your life going after what you believe in. Now it is my turn."

"What do the land grants have to do with you? We have our land. Clear title. No *Americanos* stole it from us."

"Not us, but so many others. Did you know that only twenty percent of this land is owned by Indo-hispanos?" Her son looked away.

"Indo-hispanos? Who are they?"

"Us, Mama. That is who we are."

"Add that to the list of everything else we have been labeled. It means nothing to me. I am the same person, no matter what others call me." She suspected the term had been coined by the group of rebels. They preached about equality, but used labels. How did that make all men equal?

Her son was determined. "You know the history. We came here first."

"What about the Indians? Weren't they here first? Didn't we take the land from them?" *And I should feel guilty about that, not just use it when it's convenient.*

"I agree. We should return what belongs to them, while we get what belongs to us."

"But what if it all belongs to them?" Rachel knew she was misdirecting her fear. Returning land to the Indians was not her concern, she only cared about the Brotherhood.

"Why must you argue with me?" Alejandro's voice sharpened and she watched his face grow red. "This is more important than your silly Brotherhood. Jews still hiding after hundreds of years. There's a synagogue in Santa Fe. Jews walk to it every day."

Rachel gathered her breath to scold her son, but the baby wailed and Helen walked through the door.

"What are you doing to my son?" Helen asked, scooping the boy out of her husband's arms.

Rachel and Alejandro were silent. She knew this conversation would end as every conversation with her son ended. One of them would storm out the door. Best to change the subject.

A week later Rachel was sorry she hadn't crossed that bridge with Alejandro. A fight in the kitchen would have been better than what was happening now. She would have convinced her son to stay away from the rebels, no matter what it had taken.

Ten minutes ago Helen had rushed through the door, Alfredo hooked over her hip. The baby's face was red, streaks of tears ran through the dirt on his cheeks.

"What is it?" Rachel grabbed her daughter-in-law. "Where is Alejandro?"

"They shot up the courthouse. I don't know where he is." Helen burst into tears. "He's fishing, I think."

Rachel squeezed Helen's arm. If Alejandro was fishing, why was Helen crying so hard? "Was he involved in this? Why would they shoot up the courthouse?"

Clemente came through the door. "What's going on?"

Helen sobbed and the baby screeched louder.

Rachel pulled Clemente out to the porch. "I don't know. We need to find out. It's the rebels. They've done something, shot up the courthouse. Alejandro might be with them. Can you get that radio to work?"

Her husband nodded and rushed into the house.

After three minutes of Clemente's fiddling and fussing, the radio let out a crackled broadcast. But there was no news.

"We should drive to town." Crazed with worry, Rachel wasn't willing to wait.

"It could be dangerous, if they're shooting." Clemente was so timid.

"Still? I doubt it. Come on. We'll take Helen's car."

A small crowd was gathered on the edge of town. Martin Paloma reported what was happening.

"They're holed up in there. Gun shots, but no one knows what's going on."

"Is it Tijerina?"

"Yes. And many others."

"Who are the others?" Rachel didn't want to mention Alejandro's name. No sense putting that idea into anyone's head. Maybe her son wasn't involved. So attracted to those rebels, all because he was a young man, tired of living in Tierra Amarilla, but with no way to escape now that he had married and had a child. Why must men always seek adventure?

Martin shook his head. "*No se.* Some of that rebel's men were locked up a couple of days ago. He wasn't happy about that."

Forty-five minutes later—after what seemed like hours of waiting—the sheriff pulled his patrol car to a stop near the crowd. They surged forward with questions.

He held up his hands to silence the people. "Let me talk," he ordered. "Tijerina raided the courthouse. There were injuries, but I can't announce who. We have recovered control, so there is no need to worry. You should all go home."

"Why can't you tell us who was injured?" Rachel's lungs ached from holding her breath. *Please, not Alejandro, not her son. He was fishing. He had to be fishing.*

"Next of kin will be notified." He looked at her. "Don't worry Rachel, it wasn't Alejandro."

Her whole body shuddered as she took in the news. Her son was safe.

"Was he there?"

The sheriff shook his head. "I don't know. There were a lot of men. They fled to the south, but we'll find them. We have called in extra police."

Clemente took hold of Rachel's arm, while Helen sobbed with relief. "Let's go home. He'll come there."

✡ ✡ ✡

The sun was setting, but Rachel didn't move from her spot on the front porch. Helen sat beside her while Clemente put Alfredo to bed. His voice drifted through the open window as he sang softly to his grandson.

"He's not coming. He went fishing. Sometimes he stays out all night. He went fishing." Helen mumbled over and over again. "I need Laura."

"You shouldn't go to your sister's house. Stay here. This is Alejandro's home, he will come here." Rachel didn't think Helen could cry more tears, but her daughter-in-law wept once more.

"If there is something else, you must tell me." Fear had kept Rachel from asking Helen this question earlier, but now she wanted to know.

"He was meeting with them. He felt so strong, Rachel. About the land and about doing the right thing, giving it back to the Spanish, erasing all the wrongs of the past. Last night Tijerina told them that Sánchez broke the law by arresting the protestors, his men. He said the District Attorney must stand trial for what he did." Helen wiped her face with her sleeve. "Alejandro told me he wouldn't do anything dangerous, if things got bad he would leave, come here. He promised. He said he was going fishing."

Both women turned and looked down the road.

After a few minutes Clemente came out to the porch. "I'm going to drive into town. You are not going with me."

Rachel looked at her husband. He must be afraid of what he would find out. But he was right. She shouldn't leave Helen alone.

No sooner had his tail lights disappeared than a car came down the road.

It was Martin Paloma.

"Clemente here?"

"No. He went to town. You just missed him. What do you know?" Rachel knew that Martin wanted to speak to the man of the house, but he had to tell her what he knew.

"There is word that Alejandro was with Tijerina today. They fled south. One man was shot. Wounded, but not killed. Everyone is looking for them. National Guard, Jicarilla, and a bunch of men wanting to play cowboy."

Rachel felt Helen start to tremble. She willed herself not to react to the news. "Do you know who was shot?"

Martin shook his head. He raised his eyebrows toward Helen. Rachel knew what he was asking. She shook her head slightly.

Martin was a Brother. He wanted to know if Helen knew about the Brotherhood before he talked openly. The Lunas were members, but Helen didn't know that. Her father had chosen to tell his daughters about their Hebrew heritage openly, but kept them out of the loop of the Brotherhood. Laura and Helen drove down to the synagogue in Santa Fe every few months and the Luna family kept Sabbath at home.

Rachel needed to find out what Martin knew. "How about a cup of coffee?"

When the two were in the kitchen Martin spoke in a gruff whisper. "If he comes home, send him to my place. This will all die down and we can prove he wasn't with them."

Rachel knew that in the past the Brotherhood may have been able to help. But things had changed. The older members who had worked in the police and court system were all retired. The young men were like Alejandro—they didn't see the need for the Brotherhood to continue. This was why she feared exposure of the questionable land grants.

She shook her head and stared at Martin. "How?"

"I spoke with Frank Lopez and Mario Chavez. They aren't active in the Brotherhood, but they are willing to help. Blood is still thick in these parts, Rachel. Even if you can't see it."

✡ ✡ ✡

The next morning, Martin Paloma returned with news. Tijerina had given himself up to the authorities. His men were locked up in the Albuquerque jail. Alejandro wasn't among them.

Clemente frowned at the news. "Thank you, Martin."

"You're welcome." Martin didn't add what was on all of their minds.

Where was Alejandro?

Forty-seven
Gabriella
Wednesday, May 21 to Monday, May 26

My bank account teetered dangerously low and I hadn't even started to think about how I would make money, other than selling the property. There hadn't been any orders on twistedbeaddreams, although Shannon wasn't discouraged. I had to figure out what to do with my daughter, because I couldn't afford to support both of us.

In spite of my lack of funds, I ordered a book for $3 on Amazon and paid the extra $7 for fast shipping. *Like New*. Interesting concept. The word "used" no longer described a secondhand book. What about me? Could I be like new? I had it shipped to Three Ravens, Nathan willing to help out. It arrived overnight, as promised.

How to Become a Jew. Sweet title. There were lots of books to choose from but this one seemed straightforward and it was affordable.

"Mom, are you really thinking of doing it?"

"Not really, but it doesn't hurt to know what people are talking about."

"Have you told Grandma?"

"Hmm…" I was reading the chapter explaining who was a Jew and what it was that made them a Jew. The first thing to know, the book said, was that Judaism wasn't ethnicity or culture. It wasn't a race and it wasn't a religion. I was trying to get to the part that told me just what it was, but Shannon kept interrupting.

"You should. She's old so it would be bad to suddenly surprise her with something like this." She held up an imaginary phone. "Yes, Mother. You heard me right. I'm Jewish. So was your husband."

"Shannon, I'm just reading a book, okay?"

"Well, be sure to read the part about how being Jewish is only passed through your mother. And how you can't skip a generation—that messes everything up—so no matter what you decide, it doesn't mean I'm Jewish."

"I thought you were excited about being Jewish? When you found that box, it seemed like you could hardly wait to rush to a synagogue."

"That was history I was excited about. Not my life now."

I wish it were as simple for me. Being Jewish was only one part of deciding who I was. New-Ella could be Jewish. And she could be a sex maniac. And she could be a mother who didn't enable her children. But Old-Ella was still holding on tight, no more rote religions, even if embedded in my DNA.

"Can you take me to town?"

I closed the book. "Sure." Both Old-Ella and New-Ella agreed that a gooey cinnamon roll might be just what we needed.

✡ ✡ ✡

Andy pushed crumbs around the table and watched his fingers as if the final crumb-soccer goal would make or break the game.

"So Fred and Joel, who is back in town now, jeez that guy is hard to find, anyway, we have to meet again because this whole Patton thing is so mysterious."

"Uh huh." Push, push, push, pinch. He picked up a large crumb and dropped it into his half empty coffee cup. Was he going to drink that now?

"Is something wrong?"

Andy pushed his cup to the center of the table and looked up. "Not wrong, no. I just need to talk to you about something."

Crap. Those words never, ever, ever meant good news.

He pressed his lips together, licked them, wiped them with the back of his hand, opened his mouth to speak, shut it again and sighed. "The thing is, I've had long term relationships. Too many of them, to be honest. But nothing official."

"Too many? What does that mean?"

"I fall for people. I get serious. I move in. Five years later things go downhill. I move out."

That was pretty straightforward. Puzzled, I tried to clarify what he said. "Do we have a permanent relationship? I've only known you a few weeks."

"Seven weeks, one day." He looked out the window.

You can make up your mind to change by making lists, setting your alarm for seven-thiry instead of six, parting your hair down the middle instead of on the left, but you will continue to be married to those traits hiding deep within you. I had left California determined to take action but my years of inaction took hold and now Andy was telling me seven weeks had passed, days flipping like the rapidly changing calendar in an old movie. It was nearly the end of May and I was no closer to anything than I had been as an April fool when I arrived in New Mexico.

I stared at his lips. I liked to kiss those lips. I liked those arms, the comfort they provided when they were around me. I liked this man who made me feel safe, loved, and warm. I liked the part of him that made me laugh, talked about serious things, was interested in the world, in nature, took time to entertain my kid.

When I made love to Andy I felt good. But when I—make that Francesca—made love to Nearly-Fred Rivas, I was on fire. I was filled with passion and heat. I was breathless. Something I had never felt with Greg, and I did not feel with Andy.

I didn't want a permanent relationship and I sure didn't want to think about getting married to anyone ever again, but I needed

Andy. Without him I didn't really have anyone. Loneliness flooded into me and like a spring rain, it made me watery. I tried to stop the tears, but they filled the corners of my eyes.

Andy took my hand, threading it between the half filled coffee cup and the crumpled napkin and covered it with both of his. "What I'm trying to say, Ella... I think I do want a permanent relationship with you, but you're going to leave, aren't you? This isn't your home. You'll go back to California, so I just can't fall in love with you."

Can't fall in love? Did a person have a choice in the matter? I couldn't gather my thoughts. I couldn't respond to whatever it was he wanted from me. It was my turn to look out the window.

Seven weeks. What had happened in those seven weeks? I had been stalked, courted, made love to, lied to, led on weird excursions, protected, helped, and fed.

I felt his hands tighten.

"I don't know what to say. I thought we were just friends, you know. Just having a good time."

"Is that all this is?"

I shook my head. "I'm new at this. I don't know, Andy, I really don't know."

He pulled his hands away from mine, but I reached up and grabbed them back. "Can't we just keep on being friends? Take some more time to have fun? Maybe things will work out."

"Are you thinking of staying here?"

The last thoughts I had were to run back to California, but Shannon had put a crimp in that plan. I hadn't felt guilty about running away from Andy two weeks ago.

"I don't have any money. I have to sell that property."

"That's not the only place to live around here."

Really? I hadn't spotted any rentals and living in a closet in the back of a gas station seemed pretty depressing. "What do you mean?"

"There are places to rent, Ella. If someone really wanted to stay."

I shook my head again. There was no way I could commit to anything. "Can't we think about this?"

"No. I can't." He pulled his hands away. "I mean, I have thought about it, it's all I think about."

"So, this is it?"

He nodded.

✿ ✿ ✿

Driving on autopilot I headed home, but when I got to CR 37 my car refused to turn toward the house.

I made it up to the top of the pass on the road to Taos before pulling into a turnout and staring at the valley. From up here you could see all of the Martinez property, stretching across the highway and up into the bluffs. The plan was to sit and think about my options, my life, my next move.

There is no amount of mental energy that can make you think about logical information when your heart is squeezing the breath out of you. I started to cry.

Something big came over me. Something so strong and powerful that there was no resisting it. I cried and cried, curling tight and flopping across the console, my neck bent at a crazy angle and the gear shift poking into my side. When I turned to press my face into the seat, the medallion pushed against my chest.

I was wearing it again. Maybe to keep it safe from Shannon's prying eyes, I didn't really know. Grasping it tight, I made a wish.

Please, please save me from this.

Nothing happened. When the crazy hiccups of post sobbing died down, I sat up and squeezed the medallion tighter.

Take me back to Francesca, back to that great love, away from all this heartbreak.

✡ ✡ ✡

The group around me was quiet, eyes downcast. I could hear the sound of people weeping and I turned to look.

Six men in suits carried a pine box.

I looked at the faces, trying not to stand out from the crowd, but I didn't recognize anyone. The clothes were different than my last dream, more modern, I suspected. Several of them had black ribbons pinned to their coats or blouses.

I was in Tierra Amarilla, on my property, walking up the dusty road to the cemetery on the hill. Obviously I had not been strong enough to guide the medallion to Francesca, but I was here now so I needed to fit in.

The grave at the top of the hill had a pile of yellow earth heaped beside it. The markers I expected to see were missing. Whoever was inside the pine box was the first to be buried here.

The men used ropes to lower the box into the ground, then stepped back and bowed their heads. After several minutes of silence, one of them stepped forward. I couldn't stop my gasp.

It was the man from the dream, Francesca's lover. Nearly-Fred. He picked up the shovel. Holding it awkwardly he used the back of the tool to push some the yellow clay into the grave. He turned and handed it to a young man. Tears ran down his cheeks as he took the shovel and pushed dirt as well.

Several others participated in this strange ritual, finally handing off the shovel to a man who filled the grave, shovel turned in its more functional angle.

"Yitgadal v'yitkadash sh'may raba, b'alma dee v'ra..."

I thought about the birth certificates and the familiar grave markers from my time. This was a Jewish funeral, I was sure of it. That meant it had to be someone before Jonas.

A woman stepped forward and shifted the veil from her face to wipe her tears with a lace handkerchief. She knelt and stared at the dirt covering the box.

It was Francesca. Weeping over the grave. Could it be that of her husband? Did she love him or was this all an act? Her lover stood off to the side, watching her, while I watched him. She stood and came to him and he took her arm.

"Alejandro, this didn't have to happen. Why has he done this?"

His name was Alejandro.

He didn't seem to care that all of the others would see him fold her into his arms. Thoughts raced through my mind. Had she left Hernan? Married her lover?

"Do not grieve him too much, my darling. He could never be completely happy, don't you see? Death will bring him peace."

A young man approached the two. "*Abuela*, we should walk back now." He held out his arm.

"*Si*, Jonas, my love. I am ready." She let go of Alejandro, and took hold of the young man's elbow.

"Señor Rodrigo, you will come back with us?"

"Yes, of course."

I stood still, watching as Rachel's ancestor walked down the hill with my great-great-great grandmother and my great-grandfather.

✡ ✡ ✡

It was dark when I woke up, deep in that moment of confusion between sleep and consciousness.

Headlights flashed through the windshield and I remembered.

How long had I been gone? I pulled myself out of my slumped position and rubbed my ribs. It was 9:00. I had been gone for ten hours. Shannon would be livid.

Shannon! Suddenly I realized I had driven away from Three Ravens without her. Fled Andy without remembering I had a daughter.

I sped down the curves, nearly losing control on the tight turns. My phone sat on the console, but no messages flashed any news. I thought back to the times when Shannon stayed out late. I would lie awake and wait for the sound of her footsteps in the hall. My racing thoughts were accompanied by Greg's snores, the rhythmic music of someone untroubled by parental anxiety. Thoughts of car accidents and kidnapping didn't faze him. "It's after twelve," I whispered, knowing he wouldn't wake up. "Aren't you worried. Don't you care about them?" I squeezed my eyes tight. "Don't you care about me?" In retrospect I realized that speaking the truth to your husband while he is asleep isn't very effective. What if I had voiced my fears out loud? Could it have been any worse than this?

Highway 64 cut through the Martinez property, passing Mark's house. I looked for lights across Las Nutrias Creek, knowing the dull glow of a lantern wouldn't show up from this far away.

Town or home? Which place should I look first?

Town was dark, no lights at Three Ravens, although I thought Nathan lived upstairs. The police station had only an orange tinged porch light and a sign in the window, *Please call 9-1-1 after hours.* I needed to check the adobe house before I called the police.

Two minutes later, just across the bridge, I could see a glow from the windows of the old adobe. *Thank goodness.* Bones met me on the porch, happy to see me as always. The same could not be said about my daughter.

"Where the hell were you?" Her face was blotchy.

"I'm so sorry, I… it was Andy… we… he—"

"I had to walk home. Look at my feet!" She held up a blistered heel. "Are you saying that you suddenly rushed off with your BOYFRIEND and forgot all about me?"

"No. Look Shannon, Andy and I broke up. I drove out to think and I fell asleep."

"For twelve hours?"

"It wasn't that long."

"It was long, Mom. Very, very long. I stayed in town so I could use my phone, I thought you would call. It was DARK before I came home and there wasn't anyone to bring me." She screamed her frustration and pounded her fists on the table. "I hate you. You are such a bitch, can't you do anything right?"

"Shannon, please calm down. I'm sorry. I don't know what else I can say."

✡ ✡ ✡

I slept in the next morning. Shannon banged around a bit, but I kept my eyes closed and my head buried under the sleeping bag, because I still wasn't ready to face her anger.

Anyone who has ever been sad or worried or confused knows that attempting to not think about something is a lost cause. My thoughts rolled up and down the arroyos of this land, leading me to burrow deeper into the sleeping bag. Magic medallions didn't exist —they couldn't exist. The world was a green, tangible, laws-of-physics kind of place that didn't include nocturnal journeys into the past.

Unless nothing was as it seemed. Husbands fell out of love, Catholics became Jews, daughters faced you and screamed their hatred like an automatic weapon firing armor piercing bullets straight into your heart—

"Mom. Can you please get up? I need you to take me to town."

"Later."

"Now. I'm meeting some friends."

"Friends?"

"Yes, Mother. I do have friends here. Not that you would know it because you disappear without a trace."

When I dropped her off at Three Ravens, there was no tow truck in the parking lot warning me off, but I didn't go in. My cot was calling me. Fred Rivas was probably expecting to hear from me, but he could wait too.

"When should I pick you up?"

"Don't bother. I'll find a ride." She slammed the door, nearly knocking poor Bones in the nose.

Forty-Eight
Rachel García Maria de la Rodrigo y Rivas
Los Brazos, 1990

"Where is Alejandro?"

Rachel gasped as she woke from the dream. She turned to tell Clemente about the horrible nightmare.

"Clem. Are you awake?"

The moment she spoke she remembered. Her husband had been gone for over ten years. Every morning for the last twenty-three years she awoke with the same question on her mind.

Where was her son?

She groaned and pulled her legs up close to her chest. Her sixty-five year old knees creaked a little, but she was still flexible.

"Today is Sunday." She worked to bring her mind into working order, where it needed to be to get her through the day.

Her dream of Alejandro continued to haunt her. She still saw him everywhere she went. She couldn't help but make up stories in her head to explain why he had disappeared.

Clemente had always been adamant. "He's dead, Rachel. You have to accept that. You can't move on if you are always looking for him."

She knew her husband had been right. Alejandro would never have deserted Helen and Alfredo. But if he was dead, where was his body?

The whole town had helped them look. Not just the Brotherhood, although they kept searching long after the others had given up. They looked in all the spots a man might go fishing.

Tijerina insisted that Alejandro had not been with him at the courthouse raid.

Rachel didn't believe him. "My son was there, I know it. He tried to stop that crazy rebel and they killed him. Murdered him and hid his body so that no one would know what they did." Rachel had tried to get the sheriff to question all the men again. One of them would fold.

"Rachel, we have questioned the men, the Albuquerque police have questioned the men, even a representative of the governor has questioned the men. There is no answer there."

While she waited for the water to heat—tea would help get her going—she stood in front of the refrigerator and stared at the photos held by magnets. Here was her grandson at age ten, his step-father holding a baseball while Alfredo admired a new mitt. Helen's new husband was a good man, a father to the boy who was not his own.

This photo showed Alfredo graduating from University of New Mexico. The shiny flat hat threw a shadow on his eyes. Such a proud day.

But this photo was her favorite. Alfredo stood in front of a red cliff; he had been visiting one of those desert parks in Utah. He grinned at the camera and held up a spiny lizard. He looked so much like his father, the smile crinkling the edges of his dark eyes, his lips slightly parted as if he needed to let something out.

With a sigh, Rachel poured the hot water into her cup.

Soon Martin Paloma would pick her up and take her to the town picnic to dedicate the new swimming pool. She needed to cook some vegetables to take with her. It was a potluck.

The party was in full swing when Rachel squeezed underneath one of those pop-up shade contraptions, the younger people making room for an old lady.

"It is time for you to heal. The wound is so old that it no longer festers. It is wrinkled and dried, like an Egyptian Mummy."

Rachel turned. The old woman next to her looked straight ahead. Her face was as wrinkled as the Egyptian Mummy she referred to.

"Are you talking to me?" Rachel asked.

"Of course." The woman smiled, but still didn't look at Rachel. "Please come see me tomorrow. No, Tuesday would be better. Just ask for Onawa and someone in Dulce will show you to my house."

That is all the woman said.

✡ ✡ ✡

Rachel drove to Dulce on Tuesday, although she seldom drove that far by herself anymore.

A healer. That is what Onawa called herself. It was difficult to determine her age, but Rachel felt it was close to hers. Solely based on the fact that both of them had gray streaks in their dark hair and the grunting sound both made upon rising after sitting too long.

Onawa wore her hair long, pulled back in a thick braid. She dressed the part of native healer; long patchwork skirt, laced moccasins that reached her knees, tiny beaded leather bags hanging around her neck, filled with medicines for all ailments.

She didn't say much. Just jumped right in teaching Rachel about herbs and teas.

"This one is good for healing the heart. It is the first one you must learn." Onawa pinched the dried leaves between her fingers, letting them fall back into the old coffee can.

The healer's house was filled with many such cans. Folgers, Maxwell House, Sanka. None of which held coffee.

"What's in it?"

"Aniseed, lavender, chamomile, catnip, and eyebright. I will teach you the proportions. We'll drink some now. It must be brewed with care. I'll teach you that too."

Rachel spent the next few months visiting Onawa whenever the woman would allow it. The relationship moved according to the healer's terms. Rachel and Onawa never discussed anything other than the herbs and teas.

At first Rachel imagined going out on walks with Onawa— being led to the isolated spots where the healing plants grew. But by the end of the first month Onawa let her in on a secret.

Mail order.

That was how she got her herbs. "They come from all over the world. Around here? I could find some of them, but it is too much work for an old woman."

"Did you gather when you were young?" Rachel was curious. Was healing something passed down through the generations?

For the first time the woman cracked a smile. "I am young."

Maybe it was the tea, maybe it was the opportunity to focus on learning something new, but Rachel felt the change in her heart. In the weeks that followed when she woke up, she no longer asked where Alejandro had gone.

"Yesterday I learned about skin rashes." She spoke to the sunlight streaming through the trees. Alfredo had helped her move an old iron table and some chairs down to a spot near the creek the last time he visited, even though he had protested when she sold the house in Ensenda and bought this one. *Too far from town*, he scolded. *You should be moving closer, not farther.* This house helped her build new memories and the small size eliminated so much dusting and cleaning. Her life was different now.

She sat by the creek each morning and talked with her missing son. "Teas to drink and poultices. Different when you drink it than when you rub it on your skin. I figured out that some of what Onawa adds is for flavor, not healing power."

Alejandro's answer was in the blossoms nodding back and forth as a breeze blew through the ponderosa pines.

Forty-nine
Gabriella
Monday, May 26

My web business woke up. We had twenty orders, overnight it seemed. Then I realized it had been three days since I checked the website and I didn't know if Shannon had checked it at all.

Filling the orders helped keep me out of the black hole. I asked Shannon to help me make the bracelets and earrings, along with running the website. To my surprise, she was willing.

As long as I let her borrow the car.

On Thursday she stayed out all night.

"Are you trying to prove something?" Wearing the shoes of the one waiting at home now, I hadn't slept a wink, and my face was certainly as blotchy as hers had been when I didn't come home.

"I was out with friends. Don't worry. I would have called if I could have. I probably won't come home tonight either."

"I need the car."

She shrugged. "No big deal. My friends will pick me up."

By the following week I only saw my daughter when she flew down the road to deliver a bag of bracelets and take her share of the profits. But I heard about her. I heard from Carmen and Alaura when I stopped by to check on the status of my deed. I heard from Marcia, the barista when I ventured into Three Ravens—after checking for Andy's truck—and from Nathan when I picked up my mail.

Everyone said the same thing; Shannon was seen snug on the back of a Harley, arms wrapped tight around Raymundo Cruz.

Marcia set my mocha in front of me. "They're causing a lot of trouble. Last week the whole lot of them went into the store at once and spread out. Harvey was sure they were taking things, but he couldn't watch them all. They didn't buy anything. Just snooped around and left, probably with their pockets full."

Alaura had more to tell. "There's been an increase in burglaries out at the lake. A lot of those summer homes are still locked up for the season. Some people noticed another broken window yesterday. The whole place was trashed. John McDaniel thinks they might have been living there for awhile."

"Who is John McDaniel?"

Alaura shook her head. "Lucky you. You don't know the sheriff yet."

✧ ✧ ✧

Friday, when I heard a motorcycle whining its way to the house, I lifted my eyes to the sky. *Be strong. You have to talk to her.*

She pushed through the door. Whoever had brought her left, because I heard the bike heading out.

My daughter looked like she hadn't bathed in a month. Her once shiny brown hair was matted and dull. Her clothes had stains and I could smell her from across the room. Although it was a warm day, she wore a turtleneck shirt. I thought I detected the edge of a bruise on her neck.

She unfolded the top of the brown bag and poured bracelets out onto the table. Two of the strands sprang loose and tiny beads spilled onto the floor.

"Do you have my money?"

I picked up a bracelet. The knot of this one sprang loose too, sending more beads across the table.

I needed to tell my daughter I loved her. I needed to tell her I was worried and I would help her to get out of whatever mess she had gotten herself in to.

"I can't take these. This work is terrible."

"What?" My daughter's voice was the screech of a banshee.

"Shannon, look at them, they're falling apart already. This isn't what I sell."

"So some of my knots are a little loose. Like you've never had a knot failure."

I shook my head. "I'll pay you for what you brought last week, but I'm not taking anymore."

"That's not fair. Without me you wouldn't even have a business. Maybe I should charge for that. Two thousand for setting up your stinking web site."

Damn. Why did I do this wrong every time? "Shannon. Can we talk?"

"That's what we're doing, isn't it?"

"Please. Sit down. Do you want something to eat?" She looked thin. "I have some stew from yesterday. How about I heat it up for you?"

She looked around the room, as if searching for something. "Okay, but it has to be quick."

I bit back my questions and went to heat up the lunch.

She tore into the food as soon as I set it in front of her. I slipped a glass of ice tea next to her plate.

"What's that?"

"Ice tea. It's good, a new flavor that Three Ravens is selling." Okay, that was a lie, but all for a good reason, right? She didn't need to know it was Rachel's special brew.

"Do you want to take a bath?" Although it was possible to heat water on the camp stove, taking a shower at the pool was much easier then filling the old tub. But she needed it now. Her clothes need washing too, but I was still dependent on the laundromat up in Chama.

She gulped the ice tea and shook her head. "No time. I want my share of the money."

I nodded. The number of bracelet orders was not quite like my fantasy, but they had been steady and I was making a decent amount of money. I wrote her a check for one-hundred fifty-two dollars and eighty-seven cents.

"A check? I need cash. What do you expect me to do with a check?"

"I can give you cash, but you'll have to wait until I go to the bank."

"Go now."

I waited for her to pull out a pistol and point it at my head. When had she switched from whining and drama to Bonnie and Clyde? I pictured Raymundo as tattooed and grizzled, the leader of the gang. My daughter his bitch.

"Shannon. I want you to come stay at home." A lie. I wanted her to go back to California. Briefly I wondered what her fight with Jason had been about. Was reconciliation in the picture? Such a nice young man.

She snorted. "Right. I'm sure that's what you want."

"Why are you so angry at me? I thought..." *Breathe, breathe. Feel the blue mist of Nathan's drumming.* "I thought things were going well."

"Mom. I know what you're trying to do. Just have my cash here when I get back." She headed toward the door.

"When are you coming back?"

She whipped back toward me. "Stop it. I have a life and you need to stay out of it."

Babies had to have been mixed up at the hospital. How could this be my daughter? Hideous words coming out of a twisted mouth, fists clenched as if ready to strike me?

But she was my daughter. Only a fool would miss the slim nose that flared down to wide spaced nostrils, a jaw that jutted out when she was mad—always to the left—and that widow's peak. She sprang from my loins. I stepped back from her and worked hard to keep from screaming.

When I didn't answer, she shrugged and stomped out.

I stood on the porch and watched her kick her way down the road to town. She hadn't even asked me for a ride.

✡ ✡ ✡

Fred found me in my usual spot at Three Ravens. He didn't bother with niceties, just sat, leaned toward me and launched into what he had come for.

"I need to talk to you about your daughter. You know who Raymundo Cruz is, right?"

"I haven't had the pleasure of meeting him yet."

"He's Patton's nephew."

"*The* Patton?"

Fred nodded. "You know Shannon is down in Española every night? Staying with him?"

I felt my cheeks burn. No. I didn't know. Terrible mother that I am, it was easier to let her be than to confront her.

"He's not a nice person, Ella. She shouldn't be with him."

"Not nice in what way?"

"Drugs, for a start. Probably theft. Not nice to women."

This time the red in my face was from anger as I remembered her turtleneck. What was my daughter thinking?

"I'll talk to her." Then I remembered he had said this guy was Patton's nephew. "Do you think Patton is behind this?'

Fred shook his head. "He hates Raymundo. Hated him since birth. Patton's sister married an Apache and James disowned her. But that hasn't stopped him from granting favors when her kids are in trouble. If Shannon is caught with Raymundo doing anything illegal, you can bet she'll take the fall, not that scum bastard."

Chapter Fifty
Rachel García Maria de la Rodrigo y Rivas
Los Brazos, New Mexico, 2010

Rachel looked around the crowded room. No other women, she was sure, although with hoods drawn over faces it was hard to tell. Some of the members didn't really hide who they were. The hoods seemed ceremonial, rather than functional.

"I haven't been to a meeting in a long time," she whispered to Alfredo. "Feels like the Elks club."

Her grandson nodded.

She watched him from the corner of her eye as he listened to John McDaniel speak. A warm glow spread through her tired chest. Alfredo was beautiful. He reminded her of Alejandro, but he also brought to mind her gentle Clemente.

Her grandson told her he was going to stay in New Mexico for awhile. His job with University of Arizona had ended and he needed some time off. He had renewed his realtor license and had money saved.

"I have a place in town, *Abuela.*" Alfredo reached for her hand when he told her.

"Nonsense. Why waste money on a place in town when there's room for you here?"

"It's better for me in town. I rented office space at the courthouse and I want to be close."

Maybe he had a woman? That would make her so happy, to see him married before she died. Alfredo was forty-five years old and still no wife. Almost too old to have babies. He wouldn't talk to her about it—in fact, he was silent whenever she brought up the subject. Maybe some Arizona lady had broken his heart.

At least he had agreed to come to the meeting. Rachel patted the pocket of her sweater. Tonight she planned a special surprise.

McDaniel finally reached the part of the meeting she had been waiting for.

The end.

All of the hooded men stood and reached for the medallions which hung around their necks. Each man clasped the golden disc and held it in front of his face.

Rachel pulled her medallion out of her pocket. She curled the chain into her palm and reached for Alfredo's hand.

"For you. It is time for you to take my place." She pressed it into his hand.

"*Abuela?*" Alfredo looked at her. "No. Not yet."

"*El que cree y persista vive para siempre.*" The men around them spoke in unison.

"*Sí.* It is too hard for me to stay up this late. There is no place for me at the meetings anymore."

He slipped the medallion back into her pocket. "We'll talk about it later."

Weeks passed and each time she tried to get Alfredo to talk about the Brotherhood he had some excuse. She grew impatient with him. "Just tell me why you won't make the time for this conversation. At least tell me that much."

"Okay. Let's have the conversation now." He pulled out a chair and sat at the table. "Why do you want to do this?"

"I am eighty-five years old. I don't have a son to take my place at the meetings so I have gone on far too long. The men are young and the ideas are too modern for me. Every time I listen to the changes my heart beats fast in my chest. It's not healthy for me to go."

Alfredo nodded, but didn't speak.

"You are back, Freddie. Back here in Tierra Amarilla and the valley. It's your time." She didn't add that she was worried about what would happen next. Alfredo was the last of the Rodrigo family. There was no one else.

"I know it's important to you, *Abuela*. But for reasons I can't explain, I don't fit in."

Reasons he couldn't explain?

"You mean…" She could barely get the words out. "You have given up the faith?"

"No. Although I have to admit I don't think about it much. It's not that. I grew up with those guys. I didn't fit in then and I don't fit in now."

"But you moved away from here when you were ten years old. How could those men have impacted you?"

"For three years I was an outsider, *Abuela*. And every summer when I came to stay with you. No one talked about it then, but they have a name for it now. Bullying. I was the favorite target."

"Because your father was missing?"

"That was one thing. But there were others."

"What?"

"Look. It was a long time ago. I don't want to talk about it in detail. Let's just keep it simple. I don't feel comfortable in the Brotherhood."

Rachel knew there was more. But she could see the wall build up behind his eyes, just like Alejandro. It wouldn't do to press him.

☆ ☆ ☆

All week Rachel mulled over Alfredo's story. How had she missed all this when he was a child? She knew he liked to be alone, like to collect bugs and lizards. She always felt that was why he went into the field of entomology. She thought he kept away from those sports teams because he was embarrassed not to have a father.

Having a problem to solve felt good. She realized that her pain and lack of energy might have been boredom. Now she had two problems to work on: getting Alfredo into the Brotherhood and getting her grandson a wife.

On Thursday she came up with a plan.

"Alfredo, I need your help. I want to have a party here." She didn't tell him she had already designed the invitations. Her computer classes at the adult school had been worth the hassle of finding a ride every week.

"What are we celebrating?" He spread butter on the nutty bread he brought from the bakery in Chama.

"Sabbath."

The knife stopped. "What?"

"You were the one that said it. We have slipped away from our faith. I don't even keep Sabbath regularly now. Only because I never cook much anyway. But if we all came together, did it here, it would be easy. People can bring campers, sleeping bags and stay the night. The children will learn the true meaning of keeping the Sabbath. The celebration of family, of support."

Alfredo agreed to help her. Little did he know that half the guest list was made up of every unmarried woman from age seventeen to sixty for miles around. Every *Jewish* single woman.

The Sabbath celebration was a hit. Everyone came. Kids raced around the forest, their happy laughter floating through the trees and filling Rachel with joy. Martin Paloma, leaning heavy on a carved wooden cane, led the service.

"Welcome friends. I'm happy so many of you have decided to join in the tradition of renewal. What better place than this?" He waved a hand up to the tall pines and the great cliff.

As Rachel listened to his voice she felt young again. She closed her eyes. The peace of the mountain, interrupted only by the whispering of children and the murmur of those who knew the Hebrew words, was the perfect backdrop for Martin's blessing. She felt the magic of the land surround her. She felt Clemente's spirit standing next to her, his hand clasping hers. She felt Alejandro and Jonas. She felt her mother and father. All those she had loved came to be with her during this special celebration.

And so she continued to host the Sabbath. People couldn't come every week, but they agreed to come once a month. Some of the younger women took over the planning; Rachel didn't have to do a thing. Just provide the sacred space.

The only disappointment was that Alfredo seemed to have no interest in the women she sent his way.

Rachel emailed Onawa. Was there a tea which helped with love in older people? She didn't like to think of Alfredo as old, but he wasn't young. She had fed him the potions which helped with love and sex. There had been an increased sparkle in his eye, she was sure of it, but no flirtations with Mary Garcia or Jean Brown, the two most likely prospects.

Onawa's reply was not what she wanted, and Rachel was puzzled by the healer's advice.

Accept the man for who he is. Don't try any more tricks.

Fifty-one
Gabriella
Saturday, May 31 to Wednesday, June 4

"Alaura has some questions. Can you go to church tomorrow?"

Fred's request threw me. Church? Alaura? "I guess. What is this about?"

"She has an idea. But she needs some information."

"About my deed? Is Alaura part of the Brotherhood?"

Fred nodded, as if unwilling to speak a secret out loud.

"What do you know? Why is this taking so long?"

"Not much. We've had a hard time breaking into Chris Patton's office."

"Breaking in? Hold on, you never said anything about doing something illegal. That's not the kind of help I want."

Fred held up his hand. "Whoa. Not literally, figuratively. I meant finding a way to influence the Right-to-Title which keeps moving to the bottom of his to do stack. As I said, Alaura has an idea."

✿ ✿ ✿

The following day I went to church. I got there early, hoping for a seat in the back, but there must have been some special event because the place was packed. Or maybe I had the time wrong. Needless to say, I finally found a half filled pew and scooted to the outer edge. I couldn't spot Alaura, so I sat and stared at the stained glass behind the altar. Maybe if I concentrated on the spirits someone out there would smile at me again.

The music started and everyone stood. I scrambled to find the right page in the hymnal, moving my lips along with the harmonizing voices. Just as the priest said "Please be seated," I felt someone squeeze in next to me.

It was Andy.

I drew in my breath and turned my gaze back to the front of the church. Was this Fred's plan? Did he think I was the one who had broken off the relationship? I should have learned not to trust Fred by now.

Seated next to Andy, I realized it had been exactly two months since I first came to New Mexico. Tomorrow was June 1.

I was still waiting for something. An *aha* moment in my life, when everything made sense. Regular days, with a schedule, like taking the girls to ballet or soccer, picking up Greg's shirts from the cleaners, meeting Vicki for lunch or book club. A calendar without surprises.

That's your old life. This one will never be like that. This life is about making some money, selling the property, taking Bones and Shannon back to California. Since Fred had told me about Raymundo Cruz, I had spent lots of time trying to figure out what to do about Shannon. Taking her away from here seemed the only answer.

What was Andy doing next to me? Suddenly I felt vacant. Like there was no self to be found. Once again, Shannon had intruded to grab all my energy for herself. I breathed deeply through my nose and closed my eyes. I was tired and lost.

Andy reached over and clasped my hand. I opened my eyes and looked into his face. His eyebrows met in a question mark and a tentative smile creased the corners of his mouth.

Comfort. That is what a warm hand provides. The "there, there, Ella" I had been searching for. If I allowed it, would it pulse life back into my tired spirit? This man was my white knight, after all.

But as fast as I went up, I crashed down. Was he? What was our relationship anyway? Friends with benefits? Did this warm hand come with expectations? Didn't they all?

The congregation stood, then sat, in response to the drone of the priest. I followed along, still lost in my thoughts, never letting go of Andy's hand. Maybe religion was like childbirth. You talked with other mothers about the pain, the distress, the full bladders, but you laughed while you talked because the pain was only a distant memory. The end result shadowed the misery, covered it so well that within a few years you were ready to go through it again. When you heard the ministers and the priests demand you be a certain way, there was pain and confusion, but if you stuck it out would the reward comfort you? Did rabbis do the same thing?

We were interrupted by the sound of the doors being thrown open with such force they hit the walls. All eyes turned to the back of the church.

Two men walked up the center aisle toward the priest. Several others split off and came up the side aisles. They all wore black leather pants and heavy boots. One of them grabbed a purse off the shoulder of an old woman. She let out a cry, then choked it back. Murmurs filled the room

"Did you all offer up to the Lord yet?" Everyone went silent.

This man had long tangled black hair. He wore a bandana tied around his forehead. Tattoos covered every visible part of his body, but they weren't the beautiful colored pictures of Andy's artist. These tattoos looked like they were carved with a blade and filled with dark ink from a ball point pen. I had seen these on the hands of fifteen-year olds, wanna-be-gang tattoos, but I had never seen someone covered with them. A huge knife was tucked into a sheath on his belt. He rested his hand on it.

The priest broke the silence that engulfed the room. "Raymundo, I am happy you have decided to join our service today. We are just ready for communion. Maybe you and your friends would like to go first?"

I turned to Andy and whispered. "Raymundo Cruz?"

He nodded.

"Why, thank you Father, but we already had breakfast." Raymundo stepped forward and took up the two baskets used for the collection. He turned to the congregation. "My boys are going to help out today. But when you offer up to the Lord, don't bother to take the money out of your wallet. Just put the whole thing right here in this little basket and we'll take care of the rest."

I looked at Andy and then at the aisle. We weren't far from the side door. I pointed.

"No," he whispered. "I'm sure they have someone outside."

"Has this happened before?" I watched as people dutifully placed their wallets into the collection basket. I slipped mine from my purse and flipped it open, removing my license and credit card and sliding them into my pocket.

"Now, now. None of that." The gruff voice came from behind me.

Raymundo was standing there. He had seen me. Andy pulled out his wallet and handed it to the tattooed man, shifted his weight and put his body in front of mine.

"Do you know who I am?" I asked.

Raymundo leaned around Andy and grinned. I smelled the putrid odor of rotten teeth. The thought of my daughter kissing this mouth made me gag.

He pushed his face close to mine. "That is not the question, fair lady. The question is do you know who I am?"

Andy squeezed my hand again and shook his head.

"I'm Ella Martinez. I'm Shannon's mother."

Raymundo threw back his head and laughed, spittle flying from that awful mouth.

"*Hola, Mamacita.* It's so nice to finally meet you."

The sound of an approaching siren filtered through an open window.

Raymundo tilted his head and listened, like a terrier awaiting a mouse. "I'd love to stay and catch up on family matters, but you see, I have to go." He plucked my wallet from my hand.

Although the siren grew close, Raymundo and the others didn't seem to rush. They sauntered out the back and the growl of motorcycles turned into a roar. Seconds later three deputies rushed in, guns drawn. Someone started crying, which set off a chain of sobs.

After they had calmed everyone, the police wanted to question us. Remain seated, they ordered and they would call us out individually.

"Don't tell them about Shannon," Andy warned. "She might have been outside."

"Why is she doing this?"

"I don't know, Ella. I really don't know."

✡ ✡ ✡

I left ten messages for Shannon, frantically punching my phone every few seconds. Andy convinced me to let him come home with me. Neither one of us brought up the subject of our last conversation and we parked the truck at the bridge so I could hear my phone. We shared the quilts in the back of Patrice with Bones curled between us. She was the only one who slept. I was glad Andy seemed to realize I couldn't deal with anything other than my daughter.

The next day we drove to Three Ravens to find out what had happened.

Marcia was full of news. "They disappeared. McDaniel and two other cop cars were on their way to the church, should have seen them. But they didn't. They'll get them today, though."

I nodded. "Were there more people outside?" I nearly said gangsters, but remembered that Shannon was probably one of them.

"Yeah. The whole gang. I just hope they dumped the wallets somewhere and we get our stuff back. All my pictures," Marcia moaned. "Not to mention my credit cards."

"Hmm." I wasn't worried about that since I had rescued my driver's license and credit card. Raymundo had been so amused by my introduction and the interruption of the sirens he had never asked for them.

The only missing thing I wished for was my daughter. At one-thirty my wish came true. She called.

"Mom, I need five hundred dollars." Shannon's voice sounded as if she were speaking to me from a dungeon.

I closed my eyes. *Don't say it, don't say it. She wants you to explode, to deny her. It's a test, that's what it is.*

What was I supposed to do? I didn't have training for this—my girls had been well behaved in high school. I thought of the horror stories. Kids caught with pot, truant, shoplifting.

Money for bail.

I should ask Shannon for details. What she had been charged with, who else was in jail, was she okay. I didn't want to know. I slipped into shut down mode. My mind quit working, my hands trembled and I was suddenly very thirsty. As if controlled by some beast who had sneaked into my mind, I tapped the red button—call ended.

I didn't have five hundred dollars I was willing to risk on someone I didn't know any more. What if she jumped bail?

My phone chirped again. The new birdsong tune Shannon had programmed in so I would know it was my youngest child calling. Peep, peep, peep. I let it chirp and walked out to the porch, and slumped into a chair. That's were Andy found me, sitting with my back rigid, staring at nothing. Deep in thought, he might have guessed, but he would be wrong. My mind was still numb. I couldn't guide my thoughts anywhere. I couldn't problem solve, couldn't think of the next step.

"Ella?" He bent so his face was level with mine.

"I have a headache. A bad headache. Could you help me home and get me an ice pack?" I couldn't drive with the white shimmering aura filling the right side of my field of vision.

Once again my white knight did what he could. He didn't ask any questions, just took me home, slid me into bed and chipped some ice from my cooler. I heard him settle into the camp chair in the kitchen, heard Bones circle three times to lay on her blanket and then I drifted off to sleep.

✡ ✡ ✡

The sound of voices pulled me from an intense dream. At least it felt intense, my jaw was clenched, but I forgot what it was about as soon as my brain entered the waking world. I listened.

"She hung up on me. I want to know why she did that."

"You need to wake her up. My plane takes off at eight. I want to talk to her before I leave."

Greg?

I pulled the blanket over my head. It only took about three seconds for me to realize I had to get up and face them.

Andy rushed over as soon as I stumbled from the bedroom.

I looked at my ex-husband and my daughter. "Give me a minute."

At the sink I ran the water until it was clear and washed my face. It didn't do much for the state I was in. Was this still Monday? How did Greg get here so quick? Maybe it was Tuesday? How long had I been sleeping?

As soon as I sat facing the two formidable challengers the blinding white flame took up its spot over my right eye again. I still had the headache.

"Mom, what's wrong with you? I can't believe you left me there, in that jail. It was terrible."

I looked at Andy. "Is it Tuesday?"

He nodded.

Shannon didn't pay attention to my sidebar; nothing stopped her when she was on a roll. "Thank God Dad came or I would still be in there."

I looked at Greg.

"I caught a flight as soon as she called." Greg snorted like an angry bull. "Ella, what's going on here?"

"I don't know. I think you have to ask your daughter." I rubbed my forehead. Had this been my life? Sitting accused whenever anything went wrong? Greg projecting responsibility and blame all rolled into one neat package? Why hadn't I ever noticed it before?

It was definitely déjà vu—that tone of his as he continued.

"You don't know? What's that supposed to mean?"

Poor-Misunderstood-Father-of-the-Criminal.

I glimpsed Andy's posture out of the corner of my eye. Stiff and leaning forward. He was too far away for me to put my hand on him so I tried to send him a psychic message. *Down boy.*

I looked at Greg, still waiting for me to answer his ridiculous question. "It means Shannon doesn't live here anymore. It means I was robbed at church. It means she has chosen to get herself into a giant mess."

Shannon wrinkled her nose and her lips parted. Then her eyes pinched shut and those lips turned down and quivered. She turned to Greg. "I didn't know, Daddy. They said we were going to church. I didn't go in. All I know is they were in there for awhile and then they came out and we went out for a ride."

Good. Let her try her charm on her father. He was going to have to come up with the cash for a lawyer.

Greg turned to Andy. "Do you know any lawyers?"

My former husband and I were still on the same wavelength. Damn.

"Tom Barton is probably a good choice. He knows Judge Souza and he's on decent terms with James Patton. Barton's a strong man, I don't think he'll cave to any pressure from Patton."

"Who's James Patton?"

Greg was going to have to be brought up to speed. I waved a hand to Andy. "Can you tell him? My head is still killing me."

"Of course. A headache." Greg smirked. "The usual excuse."

For a moment I almost argued with him. Then I remembered. He was divorcing me, or so he said. I could ignore him.

Nice.

Andy explained the connection between Raymundo and Judge Patton and the Martinez family.

Shannon's hearing was scheduled for the following Wednesday. Greg planned on flying home and coming back, but Shannon's hysterics convinced him I wasn't competent enough to handle her alone. Thanks.

That part was okay with me. It was the next part that sucked.

My ex-husband looked around the room. "I'll stay here, then. It seems like my daughter needs me."

I suspected Andy would have stayed for the evening, although probably not for the night, but just then his radio buzzed. Accident up by Chama and he had to leave.

Shannon walked into the kitchen and opened the ice chest. "What's for dinner?"

My head was still foggy from the headache and the medication. "I don't know. I wasn't really expecting company."

"Andy was here." She sounded six years old.

"Listen here, Shannon. You better just back off. You're in a heap of trouble and I am not sure where I stand on this." New-Ella rose to the surface, although she was slightly more hysterical than I wanted.

Greg jumped in. "Ella, calm down."

"There are motels in Chama. I think it would be much better if both of you went there tonight."

Greg reached toward me, then changed his mind. "We need to plan for this as a family."

My lips parted with a reply but Shannon beat me to it.

"Dad, let's go. She's not my family anymore. Isn't that obvious to you? She didn't bail me out and now she doesn't want us here."

Something stopped me from yelling out that she was right, we weren't a family anymore, thanks to Greg, but the medallion around my neck started to throb.

Not warm or cold. Instead it seemed to oscillate between the two, like an electric pulse. Images filled my mind. Tiny Shannon, two years old, smiling up at me as I read her a story. Eleven-year old Shannon, asking me to help her lace up the back of her dance recital costume. Fifteen-year old Shannon, sulky, but serving me a gourmet Mother's Day breakfast.

Look past the dirty young woman standing in your kitchen, the medallion seemed to say. *This is your daughter, your flesh and blood.*

Suddenly the pain in my head jabbed as sharply as a tribal spear. I winced, closed my eyes and leaned forward. Rubbing at the spot, I spoke without looking up. "You'll have to excuse me. I'm going back to bed."

In the morning I called Andy twice, but he didn't return my calls. Had I read things wrong again? Weren't we back on? I wanted to run things by him, get his sound advice and unbiased point of view. I wanted to ask him to go with me to the meeting with the attorney, because Greg insisted this was a family matter and I needed to show him he wasn't my family anymore. Without Andy I was on my own.

Thomas Barton Esquire had different ideas.

The attorney was dressed in black denim Levis, his pale blue shirt enhanced his almond skin. I'm sure Greg wasn't impressed with the silver bolo tie, but I thought the guy a perfect New Mexico lawyer.

Barton was clear. "Shannon, I know you want your mother here, but she is a victim of the crime you are accused of committing. I think it would be best if we had our discussion without her.

"She's not going to testify against me. She didn't even see me." Shannon looked at Greg, but wouldn't meet my eyes.

The attorney shook his head. "But she did see Raymundo. And that might be important." Greg looked at his watch as I left the office.

I checked Three Ravens for Andy, but he wasn't there. Nathan rushed over as I ordered my usual.

"Ella, are you okay? I heard what happened." He looked down, but Bones had stayed at the house. "Your daughter? Is she—?"

"Next door, meeting with Barton. Is he any good?"

"I haven't heard anything bad about him, but I've never hired a criminal attorney. Joel takes care of everything for me."

"Have you seen Andy?"

"No, sorry. Listen, if there's anything I can do, you let me know." I was surprised when Nathan stepped forward and gave me a tight hug. "You're one of us now, you know that, right?"

"Thanks, Nathan." I turned away before he could see me cry.

Fifty-Two

Rachel García Maria de la Rodrigo y Rivas
Tierra Amarilla, 2013

The cemetery was suffering. No one ever visited, except those kids who played in the old house. Rachel straightened two fallen markers and pulled some weeds.

"Jonas, how are things? I'm getting old. I visit the dead more often than I visit the living." She scraped some white bird droppings from the wood. It was good the raven came to visit, but did he have to crap here as well?

The sun felt nice on her shoulders. It was a long walk up the hill, even resting every few steps. She knew this might be her last trip.

"You know I moved. Alejandro and Clemente visit me there— it's a nice place. There's a creek. Maybe you could come down that way once in awhile.

"I need some advice. Alfredo, you remember, he's my grandson? He is not willing to take over for me. I give him the medallion and he gives it back. I even went so far as to hide it in that place of his—you know, he lives in town, just as well now that I moved, my place is small and quite a way out there—anyway, I hid it in his desk, but he's a trickster and I found it this morning. Hanging from the hook on my door, under my gray sweater. What am I to do? Is this a message? Is it time to end the Rodrigo family?"

Rachel used the marker to pull herself up. She should start back because the walk down would take every bit as long as the walk up.

This was a good spot for a cemetery. Jonas could watch over his land, the land that had been fought over and now stood abandoned. She regretted that she would lie next to the Catholics, but Clemente was there so she had no choice. She wouldn't give up being with her love.

"I have no grandchildren, but you have many, my old friend. Your secret stayed safe. Perhaps you can send me one of yours? Surely there is one who wants to be Jewish?"

Fifty-three
Gabriella
Wednesday, June 4 to Thursday June 5

I had no idea how long the meeting with Barton would take and it was clear no one wanted me in on anything, so it didn't make sense to wait here for Shannon and Greg. Without Andy to commiserate with I was lost. I held up the medallion and stared at the strange symbols. Family, that was what those symbols meant. Call it a Jewish Brotherhood, call it preservation of the tribe, call it a covenant, didn't all those things come down to one thing? I knew what I had to do.

Without a thought as to whether she might be home or not, I drove out to see Rachel.

"*Hola.*" Rachel greeted me at the door, then peered over my shoulder.

"She's not with me."

Wrinkled faces show guilt just like any other. Rachel couldn't hide feeling relieved Shannon wasn't with me. "Are you here for lessons?"

What was she talking about?

"You should know more about being Jewish. To make a decision."

With a sigh I followed her into the house.

Rachel led me to the table, fixed me the usual tea and arranged some cookies on a plate. She pulled out a small book, its cover battered and faded, and opened it to a spot marked with a sticky note.

"You can only enter into the covenant of Abraham if you *understand* what it means to enter into the covenant. This requires that you start from the very beginning."

"I'm not ready for this, Rachel. Even if my ancestors were Jewish or secret Jews or whatever you say they were, I have no desire to be Jewish."

Rachel closed the book.

I leaned forward and wiped away some crumbs. "I want to talk to you about my dreams."

Rachel carried the cups to the sink. She placed her hands on the edge and leaned forward, peering out the window. I wasn't going to get an answer.

Patience, Ella. Patience.

Too much silence and avoidance. I needed answers. "It's the medallion, that's where the dreams come from. Do you have them?"

"No."

"But you know about mine, don't you?"

She turned to me. "You dreams are stronger than anyone I have ever known. And I have known medicine women and Wiccans and all kinds of powerful people. I'm not sure it's good for me to fill in the blanks. The dreams tell you what you need to know. If I add things I might disturb the energy."

"I don't believe in your magic. Something strange is going on, but I probably heard these stories before and all of the stuff with the house is just bringing it back to me." I didn't believe what I was saying, but I needed more from her. The medallion and the visions, —they were something I couldn't face. The choice was to believe in something as crazy as magic or accept the fact I was having hallucinations. I had teetered on the edge for so long it seemed only a matter of time before I slid right off into the deep end.

I was tired of people holding out on me. Again and again. Like it was a motto—Chama Valley—Home of the Sealed Lips. This place caught me up in all the deception, apparent by the fact that I now felt justified lying too.

Rachel spit out her reply. "You shouldn't let your girl influence you. She is foolish. Only bad things will come if you listen to her."

Shannon?

"Don't talk about my daughter like that. I realize she was rude to you, but this has nothing to do with her. I'm tired of you deciding what I should and shouldn't know. I'm an adult. I have a right to know. To make my own mistakes, without you manipulating me. Stop butting into my life." I clamped my lips together. Did I really just say that?

Rachel's face was pale and I could see her hands shaking. But a mother's blood is strong and I didn't care if she was upset.

"Do you know Consuela?"

"Consuela? That name is not familiar."

"She told me to come to you, that you have the answers for me. You can teach me to guide the dreams or visions or whatever they are. She warned me you were selfish, and it's true."

To my surprise, Rachel crumpled into her chair and covered her face.

I waited.

"This Consuela, she is someone you met in a dream?" Rachel's voice was muffled by her hands.

"Yes. I think she lived a long time ago. In a pueblo that was built in a canyon. There were cliff dwellings, like some newer tribe had made their home in an ancient spot."

She uncovered her face and looked at me. "I do not know of this woman, but I do know about the medallion. It has power over me as well."

Rachel's description sounded as if the medallion was in control. But hadn't I felt that way too? "You *do* have dreams."

"No. No dreams. But the medallion—the Brotherhood—has driven me to make decisions I regret. Jonas warned me, in his way. I tried to keep the Brotherhood alive, even when it was not in my best interest. This led," she choked a sob, "it led to my son's death. I'm sure of it. But even that didn't keep me from putting the Brothers first."

"I'm sorry. I didn't know your son died."

"For many years I did not know this either. I still hope that some day I will hear a car and look out and Alejandro will be coming up the walk."

Alejandro.

"Was he named for... someone in your family?"

"He was named for my great-grandfather."

"And Jonas? He was mixed up in this?"

Her eyes widened. "What do you know of this? Did you have a dream?"

I told her about the funeral.

"It was true then, what Jonas told me about Francesca and Alejandro, they were lovers."

I closed my eyes and drew a deep breath through my nose, holding my mouth tight. I wet my lips with my tongue and plunged in. "Rachel, I think it's time we really talk."

To my surprise she agreed and we spent the next three hours carefully comparing notes. I learned what Jonas had told her and I told her about my dreams. She told me about her son disappearing, and for a moment we were both silent. My throat closed at the thought of never knowing where my child had gone. Shannon might be in trouble, but I knew where she was and I was here for her, even if she didn't think so. Greg was the nice parent right now.

We talked about Hernan, we talked about Francesca, we talked about Alejandro and Rachel's father and her husband. We talked about Julie and Shannon and Greg. We talked about how being sad can become a habit. Rachel told me how she still woke up every morning, sure that her son was not dead. I told her about the postpartum depression and how I faked it. She told me that faking it was the same as working through it and I thought about that for a while, a comfortable silence sitting between us. I told her about my mother, but I kept my father's cruelty a secret, halfway comfortable now with Rachel, but unwilling to speak the words that would bring him back.

We talked about so much, but Rachel couldn't offer any advice about controlling the medallion.

Biology is a funny thing. It guides us to choose a mate for life, and like geese we primp and preen and pair up. This is good, because it pushes us to want offspring and to care for them. Babies and goslings are fragile. I had picked my mate and had my chicks. No matter how I felt about Greg now, I could not have raised the girls alone. When Greg chose to leave our marriage, I'm sure he felt our children were grown. When I decided to leave California my girls were independent. I thought Shannon would probably marry Jason—she had picked her mate and was no longer under my wing. I knew that Julie was set in adulthood. Her independent spirit had a strong responsibility component thrown in.

What I didn't know was that adult children come with their own set of issues. Shannon's backslide, her impulsive behavior—was this her reaction to the dissolution of her safe family?

Greg and Shannon never came out to the house that day. Or if they did it was before I came home from visiting Rachel. There were no messages and I didn't call them. I let the dog out and went to bed. The sleep that had eluded me for days came quickly.

Dust swirled around me. I covered my eyes with my hands and felt myself lifted.

I was in a kitchen. Cooking. A baby chortled from a high chair in the corner. I heard a truck and looked out the window.

It was Alejandro Rivas. I recognized him from Rachel's photos.

"Hey, what's cookin', good lookin'?" He lifted the lid off the pot and kissed my cheek.

I hoped I was his wife.

"Beans."

"How's my little Freddy bear?" He pulled the baby from the high chair and swung him in the air. The baby laughed and squealed at his father's antics.

Unlike some of my dreams, this one seemed to move forward in regular time. I finished cooking dinner and set the table, glad that Alejandro was so engaged with the baby he didn't notice I had to search all the cupboards for the dishes.

"Da!" the baby bounced in his chair. Funny to think this was Fred.

"Your mother called." How in the world did I know that? Suddenly I wasn't Gabriella in a strange dream. I was some one else and I didn't even know her name.

"What'd she want?"

"To remind you that there's a meeting tomorrow night."

"Damn. I'm not going."

"Al, you need to. You didn't go last month."

"I've got something else on the burner for tomorrow."

"Not with that man. You promised."

He blushed, and set his spoon next to his empty bowl. "His name is Tijerina. His work is important, Helen."

"Your mother said this meeting is important. The Brothers are going to talk about him. Maybe you should go and give your side of the story."

"She just wants me to stay away from him because those old Jews stole land too."

"Alejandro! How can you say such a disrespectful thing?" I was incensed, but I couldn't help but think Alejandro might be right. I didn't get to voice my opinion, however, because this woman was obviously still in charge of her own body. I felt like a hitchhiker of the mind. Well, not of the mind, because I didn't know what she was thinking or what she was going to say next.

Alejandro paced across the kitchen and back, then turned and paced some more. "Look, I joined because she forced me into it.

But I'm not one of them and I never will be. Silly old men, thinking the whole thing is a secret. Like I don't know your father is there when he parks his truck right out front." He stopped and looked at me. "You're the hypocrite, pretending you don't know anything about the Brotherhood."

"I keep my father happy, which is more than you can say. You promised me you would stay away from that rebel and now you have some mysterious thing for tomorrow? Don't lie to me, Al."

"I'm not lying. I'm going fishing tomorrow. I promise."

"Laura says that something is going down at the courthouse tomorrow. You're not involved, are you?"

"No." He shook his head. "I'm going fishing out at a spot Marco told me about."

"Where?" I looked at him, trying to read the lie in his face.

"Way out beyond Heron. Gotta four-wheel it back into the mountains. Fact, I might take off now, get out there for an early start."

"Good. I'm glad you won't be with those men. Laura said they have guns."

"How come your sister knows so much about it?"

"Chapa's husband is involved. He tells Chapa everything and she tells Laura."

I watched Alejandro pack up his fishing gear. He kissed baby Fred and headed out to his truck.

I was inside the house, watching him go, and then I wasn't. A dizzy burst, a tiny moment of darkness, and I was in the truck with Alejandro. He didn't seem to notice me.

The highway hadn't changed much since the '60s. We drove past Harvey's store, and the post office. Suddenly Alejandro jerked the wheel to the right and pulled off the road.

"Damn, damn, damn." He pounded the steering wheel and then dropped his head on his folded arms.

He was involved with Tijerina, I was sure of it.

"Make the right choice," I said. But my voice didn't break through to him.

Or maybe it did, in some mystical way, because he threw the truck into gear and floored it, jerking the steering wheel all the way to the left and made a fast u-turn. He sped down the road, slammed on the brakes and turned west.

This was the road to Lake Heron. I had driven out to the lake with Andy and I had driven out here to look at vacation homes when I was trying to figure out how much my property was worth. All of which must have been built later, because whatever year I was in, there were no lights on this road, no driveways off to the sides. Just dark pastures and a road full of potholes.

We drove past the lake and Alejandro didn't slow down when the road changed from badly paved to not paved at all. I held onto the door handle as he skidded through the curves, the sound of scattering gravel following us.

"Slow down," I screamed. "Do you want to kill us?"

He turned off the road, and for a moment I thought he was sending us over a cliff. But we were on a path, or some sort of four-wheel-drive road straight up the mountain. I lurched to the side and hit my head on the window.

"Please stop, Alejandro. If you kill yourself that's breaking your promise. Your wife didn't want you hurt, don't you get that?" I tried with all my power to make him hear.

A ghost can't really make a human do much of anything. This was a dream. I couldn't get hurt, could I?

I soon discovered that a ghost can scream when a doe jumps from the brush and the truck swerves and loses tractions and slips off the road and tumbles over and over to the bottom of an endless gorge.

I tried to sit up, but fell back onto the pillow from the effort. The pillow. Not the cab of a truck. I was panting and covered with sweat. My throat hurt, as if the scream had been real.

I remembered the last thing I had seen, just before I woke up.

Alejandro Rodrigo Rivas had looked me straight in the eye and spoken to me.

"Tell them I love them."

✡ ✡ ✡

I cursed myself for not finding out what motel Greg and Shannon were staying in. Chama is a small place, but in the heart of elk hunting country there are lots of lodges and motels. Lucky for me they were all on Highway 84, making it easier to drive the stretch and look for Greg's rental car.

Trouble was I hadn't really paid much attention to the car. Silver sedan, mid-sized. My mind was just like a rental contract, vague. There were a lot of silver mid-sized sedans staying at motels this week. I even went so far as to go into the office of several places and ask if Greg King was staying. Surprisingly no one thought my request suspicious and they readily checked for me. But the answers had all been negative.

I finally drove back to T.A., slowing as I passed Nelson's Garage and looking at the yellow tow truck parked in front.

Where was I with Andy? We had been so on-again, off-again that I didn't know. If our relationship was this confusing should I just call it off for good?

I turned left into the lot and pulled around to the back. Patrice was parked at the edge of the gravel lot, shining in the morning sun. The sight of the turquoise truck made me think of all the nights spent in the comfort of Andy's arms. He slept wrapped around me, not like Greg who had turned his back to me each night.

Everyone I had ever known fell in love and lived happily ever after. Or pretended to. If they weren't really happy no one in my little clique of soccer mothers and Girl Scout leaders had ever run away and slept with a stranger and told me about it. My resources for relationship advice were limited to Vicki, my mother, made-for-television movies and bumper stickers. *If it feels good, do it.*

Being with Andy did feel good. Most of the time. Except when he was secretive or disappeared. What should I do? What the *hell* should I do?

"Ella?"

Bones put her paws on the edge of the window and wagged her tail at Andy. He leaned through the passenger window, open for the dog.

"Is everything okay?"

Why, oh why, did he have to ask that?

Thirty minutes later, crying cured by sex, sex stopped by crying, crying stopped by kisses, I lay under the quilt in the claustrophobic room Andy called home.

"Do you want to talk about it?"

"Not really."

Didn't he know that "not really" meant I want you to pull it out of me, fix it, and send me on my merry way? Apparently not, because he just lay there without speaking.

I sat up. "I came because I'm trying to figure out if we are on again?"

He ran a finger down my cheek. "Damn Ella. I don't like it one bit, this confusion."

"I—"

He put his finger on my lips. "Shhh. I can't stay away from you. I want you to stay, but if you can't do it, then… that's that. But, yes, for now, I think we are on again."

"No secrets?"

He pressed his lips on mine and his hand slipped down to my breast. "Hmmmm."

I grabbed his wrist, pushed his hand away, and pulled back from his kiss. "No secrets?"

"No secrets," he said as he kissed me again.

This time was almost as good as Francesca and Alejandro.

Almost.

Fifty-Four
Rachel García Maria de la Rodrigo y Rivas
Thursday, June 5, 2014

Rachel woke early but did not pull herself out of bed. A bad day, she thought. This is going to be a very bad day.

Each day added a new pain to her body. A knee, an elbow, today it was her ear. How could an ear hurt? There were no joints for arthritis to freeze, no bones to ache. Just rubbery skin which throbbed when she slept with that side down.

As she made her morning tea, carefully mixing the herbs for pain, memory, and health, her attention drifted to the back of the highest shelf. The orange powder Onawa had given to her three years ago hid behind dried lavendar. *Only for a single use. You must keep it safe.* Her friend was gone. Dead no doubt, although Rachel didn't know for sure. One day she was there in her government house in Dulce and the next time Rachel went to see her, a young couple with three kids had moved in.

"She might have died. Or gone to live with family down in Albuquerque." The young woman hadn't been very helpful.

Was it to be Rachel's fate that everyone in her life simply disappeared?

Stop thinking like a silly old woman. Catastrophizing, that's what Alfredo called it. Think positive, he would say. Of course not everyone disappeared. Her parents were buried next to the church, side by side, and Clemente was nearby. Her spot waited beside him.

It wouldn't be long now. She could feel it.

She sat at the table with her tea. It was time to think about what had happened on Tuesday. Not that she hadn't been thinking about it ever since Gabriella visited, but she had to plan.

Rachel had made a mistake never discussing things with Rueben or the others and now Jonas was giving her one last chance to make things right. He had sent his great-grand-daughter.

The woman was resisting. Even that obnoxious daughter of hers was resisting. Rachel had expected joy, maybe even excitement, at her announcement that they were Jewish. All she got was rolling eyes and scientific excuses. DNA testing, how ridiculous.

She had fixed tea for Gabriella, using the time to get a sense of the woman's purpose. Something was on her mind. Rachel had heard the girl was in jail, no surprise there, but that wasn't it. There was something else.

Then Gabriella told her about the dreams. Caused by the medallion, she seemed to think. Rachel knew this was not so.

It was Jonas. His powerful spirit, good in every way, regretting his choice to hide his heritage. The medallion was just a symbol for his great-grand-daughter to hold. When she didn't catch on he sent the box. How could anyone doubt being Jewish with a prayer shawl, candlesticks and Hebrew birth certificates?

Gabriella had told stories of a heritage Rachel knew, but the details were incredible. She was pleased that her great-great grandfather had found love with Francesca. She thought about the strong spirit of Consuela, happy that this woman still lived in dreams.

Melancholy haunted Rachel as it always did when she thought about Alejandro. Telling the woman about her missing son had not provided relief from the pain in her heart, that extra chamber filled with grief.

"What do I do next, Jonas? I try to teach her, but she does not want to learn." Rachel swirled the leaves in the bottom of her cup. She had asked Onawa once about reading leaves and the healer had laughed. "Isn't it enough to drink them? Must you have more?"

Now the leaves seemed to have a message. Rachel recalled what she had revealed to Gabriella about the Brotherhood. That it had led and she had followed, never stopping to consider she might do something different.

She would quit. And she would convince Alfredo to quit. He would think this ridiculous, after she had spent so many years dragging him to meetings and insisting he take an active role in the group. There was a meeting Friday night. The men would have to listen to her one more time.

Fifty-five
Gabriella
Thursday, June 5 to Friday, June 6

Refreshed from my tryst with Andy and the fact we were on again, I went to see Joel. I'd never had a front row seat to an arrest before and needed to be clued in. Maybe he could enlighten me on how these things worked.

"Ella!" Joel lowered the barbell and pushed it into the corner, then picked up the stack of books from the chair and set them in the corner as well.

"I caught you in."

"Right. It's Thursday. I'm always here on Thursdays."

Was that true? Hadn't I tried to find him on a Thursday before?

"You seem to have very limited hours."

He lifted a business card from the wooden holder on his desk and held it out to me. "Mondays Albuquerque., Tuesday and Wednesday Española, Thursday, Tierra Amarilla and Friday, Santa Fe. Except when I'm in court, then all bets are off."

This wasn't the first business card he had handed me, but the other one was tucked in my wallet and I had never looked at it. His number was on my phone. Once more Stupid-Ella reared her ugly face. All those wasted visits confronting a dark office.

"I talked to Fred. He said you listed the land. After you missed the appointment with Mark—I don't know—what happened, Ella? You know you can't sell the land without clear title."

Mark. I had pushed my cousin on to the back burner after finding out he was trying to cheat me, completely forgetting about the meeting.

I sat in the chair Joel had cleared and closed my eyes. Maybe I needed to ask Nathan for more drumming, to soothe my spirit and clear my mind. I was living so many lives right now, no wonder I couldn't focus on any single thing.

"Are you okay?"

My eyes snapped open. It wouldn't do for word to get back to Mark that I was losing it. "Of course. I'm not here about the property. I'm here about my daughter."

"I heard. I'm not a criminal lawyer. Didn't you hire Thomas Barton?"

"She did, her father did. But, as you probably know, I was one of the victims of Raymundo's crime." I wasn't about to include Shannon on the list of criminals. "Barton advised that I not be a part of her defense." I stopped. What if Barton had heard what a flake I was? A bad mother who left her daughter in town and let her ride around with a gang in spite of everyone warning me? Maybe that was the real reason he asked me to leave.

"Anyway, I just wondered if you could explain the process to me. I know Shannon has to go to court on Wednesday, but I'm not sure what happens then."

"On Wednesday, things will be short. You'll find out if charges are going to be filed against her and if they are, she'll be remanded or released on bail. I'm sure it will be bail because Judge Patton seldom keeps anyone in jail. Too expensive."

"How do you know which Judge it will be?"

"We only have two. Sanchez is in Wyoming visiting his brother."

I wanted to ask about conflict of interest. If Patton wanted to buy my land should he be presiding over my daughter? How much did Joel know? Did I want him to ask me questions about Patton?

"What happens after that, if there are charges?"

"Then he sets a trial date. Usually a couple of months because the attorneys have to prepare the case."

"So Shannon couldn't go back to California?"

"No. She would have to stay here in Rio Arriba county."

"What if she doesn't have anywhere to stay? This isn't her residence. When the land sells, I'm leaving."

"You ask for special circumstance. The judge would require a huge bond and she would have to come back for the trial. But he might decide that she's a risk and keep her in jail the whole time."

My choices had just narrowed. Stay in New Mexico or sentence my daughter to months in jail.

I thanked Joel and stumbled out of his office. Glancing down the hall I noticed Fred's door was open. Shocked by Joel's revelations I didn't really want to talk to Fred about the property, but maybe I should tell him about my dream.

✡ ✡ ✡

"Alejandro was my father, but I don't remember him. I was raised by my step-father. My mother and I moved away from T.A." Fred rhythmically tapped his fingers on the blotter, like a trotting horse.

I stared at his hand. This must make him nervous. "You're so close to Rachel. I thought you had grown up spending time with her."

"Summers. After my grandfather died I was the only one, so I came here whenever I could. I love her, but this place doesn't hold good memories for me."

"Because of your father?"

Fred shook his head and bent a paper clip open. He poked at his blotter, pressing the tip deep into the leather. "No, just some bad childhood memories. I was ten when we moved."

"So, what I have to say, I know it sounds crazy, but promise you'll listen with an open mind. I've been having dreams, dreams about the past. After your grandmother told me about your father, well I had one of those dreams."

"A dream?"

I nodded. "It's weird, I know. But the dream was very real. Your father didn't go with Tijerina that night. He was going to, but your mother made him promise not to get involved. He did go fishing, just like he told her."

Fred's face didn't reveal anything.

"He went out past Heron, onto a dirt road, a steep road into the mountains. A deer jumped in front of him and he went over the edge. I'm sorry, Fred, but he died out there. He thought about you before he died, he loved you."

"Look Ella. I appreciate that you want to give my grandmother some closure. But this story, a dream? They searched for him out there. They searched everywhere. The Brotherhood didn't give up, my grandmother was important to them. They would have found him if he had been there."

"It was way out there, kind of overland. A really steep canyon. I think I could find it."

"No. My grandmother has made her peace. I don't want you to get her all worked up again. She might not look it, but she's frail. If you make her think my father can be found and nothing comes of it, it's just not a good idea."

"But—"

"Really, Ella. It was only a dream. Please don't do this."

I slumped back in the chair. Why had I thought Fred would believe such a crazy story? He was right. Rachel was frail, but didn't she deserve to know the truth?

"Knock, knock?" Alaura knocked and spoke through the open door. "I thought I saw you come in."

As soon as I saw her I remembered that I had gone to church to hear Alaura's idea and that sure hadn't happened. Raymundo's big adventure made all thought of following up with her slip my mind.

"I had a phone call." She looked at Fred. "There has been some progress finding out about the Right-to-Title. It's based on an old document, a lien against the land. A handwritten thing. The issue is the authenticity of the document."

Fred leaned forward. "Did you find out who filed?"

Alaura nodded and glanced at me again, then looked out the window. "Yes. I did."

"Who was it?" Why was she dragging this out?

"It was Andy Lloyd."

I felt a hot surge of vomit and lunged for Fred's trash can. Andy had filed the Right-to-Title. Andy had stopped me from selling my land. Andy, loving, white knight, Andy was a fraud.

"No, no, no, no." The words flowed from my lips like hot lava in the wake of the bitter vomit residue on my tongue. "No, no, no."

Why, why, why?

"Come on, let's go get you cleaned up." Alaura wrapped an arm around me and pulled me from my kneeling position.

I felt her lead me down the hall to the pink tiled restroom, but my mind was not in the building. Flashing thoughts and scenes of every moment with Andy blinded me: every good deed that was a lie, every kiss a bribe for information, every minute of our time together a scheme. Why in the world would he be involved in filing paperwork to thwart me?

Alaura pulled a wad of paper towels and wet it. I grabbed it and scrubbed my face, rubbing as hard as I could.

"Hey, easy,"

"He, he..." I choked and coughed, "... kissed me... this morning."

"Oh, Ella. I'm so sorry." Alaura grabbed my hand. "Do you know why he did this?"

"No, I don't know..." my words were still fighting sobs. "Everyone... lies... even..." I stopped.

The Brotherhood. This was all about the Brotherhood. They were the ones after my land, not some judge named Patton who I had never met. Fred and Andy, they had played me. Even Joel Dominguez had to be in on this. Rachel, pretending she magically knew about my dreams when all along Andy had probably been reporting to her.

And Nathan. All that crap about how I was one of them—*come to me if you need anything, Ella*. It was all right there in front of my eyes the whole time. Andy suddenly knowing about the medallion, telling me that Nathan knew. I had been right—I never told him.

The medallion. They probably planted it in the wall and waited for me to find it. When that didn't work they hid the box. My land must have a secret all right—one that made it valuable, like oil or gold or a new freeway. So valuable everyone wanted it.

"Ella?" Alaura squeezed my arm. "It'll be okay. Fred will help you with this."

Fred! One of the biggest liars of all. And then I remembered.

Alaura was one of them too.

☆ ☆ ☆

Tears can blind you, but that doesn't mean you have sense enough not to drive. Well, I didn't, anyway. The urge to escape that courthouse, that town, these people was overwhelming. If I hadn't needed to get Bones and my things, I would have driven straight back to California.

The sight of Greg's rental car parked in front of the adobe house greeted me. I wiped my face before I got out of the car.

"Where have you been?" Greg acted like I was the one out of contact.

I shrugged.

"Shannon has to be in court next Wednesday and something has come up. I know I said I would stay, but I can't. I have to fly home tonight."

"What about the whole no-mother-allowed thing?"

"I'll be back." He looked at Shannon. "I promise, sweetie. I'll do everything I can to make it back."

Not exactly a promise.

"She needs to stay here. She can't leave town. Just bring her to the courthouse at 1:00 on Wednesday. Barton will be there, he'll take care of everything."

Everything. Patton, Barton, Rodrigo. Other people taking care of everything. I had believed in it all. And now? The wave swept over once more. Greg and Shannon stood there and expected me to do what they said. My daughter and the man, another man, who had walked all over me, smashed my emotions to bits and STILL expected me to answer to him.

I bolted up the hill, over the canal, past the graves and into the forest. My chest burned, and yet, I ran. I was lost now, traveling a trail I had never seen, pushing through the trees in spite of the branches scratching my face. I didn't care. I kept running. The forest thinned and the trail headed down a hill. Manzanita or something much more rigid with branches that tore at my clothes. I closed my eyes against them, but didn't stop, feeling my way through the mess. Another rise and I was back in the pine trees. Then everything went black.

I must have stepped into a hole because when I came to pine needles pressed against my cheek, my forehead throbbed, and my ankle burned with pain.

Oh God. Why this, why this? What did I do? I never sinned, never. Damn him, damn my father for making me believe I could escape pain if I did everything right. Damn his stupid prayers and his stupid lessons and his stupid rules. So foolish, stupid, ignorant. Why did I think I was good? Deserved something nice? I didn't, no one did. This world was evil, evil, evil. Just like he said it was. What did he know? He was a terrible parent. I curled up and let the black cloud take over.

✡ ✡ ✡

"Mom? Where are you?" Shannon's shouts came through to me, but I didn't move. The sun angled through the trees and I could feel the change in temperature, which meant it was after four. Bones sat beside me, her chin resting on my hip.

"Ella, damn it. I don't have time for this." Greg's voice was close. He grabbed my arm and jerked me to my feet. "Christ, Ella. Grow up. You need to take care of things. This is our daughter, her life. Do you *want* her to go to jail?"

"My ankle," I sank down, but he jerked me back up. "I think I sprained my ankle."

Shannon ran up the hill. "Where did you go? Why did you run away?" She was crying.

Greg didn't let go of my arm. "Look, Shannon, we have to get her to the house. I need to catch that plane. You take that side. Ella, put your arms over us, we'll carry you as best we can."

I followed Greg's instructions, because I knew he wouldn't let me lie here in the woods, which was all I wanted to do. As soon as we made it back to the house he instructed Shannon to wrap my ankle, and take me to the clinic in the morning. He drove off in a cloud of dust.

Shannon paced the room. Bones tried to follow her. "Lie down, you stupid dog." Bones slunk away from Shannon's misplaced anger.

"Why did you do that, Mom? Why did you run away? You hate me now, don't you?"

I couldn't answer her, couldn't comfort my angry daughter. I couldn't even look at her.

As I dropped onto my cot and curled up, the thought that she was scared rather than angry came to mind, but even that didn't pull me out of the place I had gone to hide from all these problems. In this spot, eyes closed, head under the edge of the sleeping bag, it was every man for himself.

✡ ✡ ✡

Andy came the next morning. I heard the truck and jumped from the cot, crying out with pain when I landed on my sore ankle.

"Don't let him come in here."

Shannon looked scared at my harsh demand. "Why not?"

"Just don't do it, Shannon. I mean it."

She stepped out on the porch. "Hey," she called out.

"Shannon! You're back. Where's your mom?"

"She's not feeling well."

"Headache?"

"Yeah, I guess."

His voice was louder now. He must be on the porch.

"Uh, she's asleep. Maybe you can come back later."

"Do you need ice? I can run into town and get some. I know that really helps her headaches."

"Sure."

"Let me see if she wants anything else."

I heard the screen door open.

"No, really, Andy. She had a rough night. Let her sleep. She doesn't like it when you wake her up."

"Well, okay. Is there anything you need from town?"

"Some chips? Maybe some soda?"

"You got it."

Shannon must have stood to watch him go because she didn't come back in until the sound of his truck faded.

"What's going on? You have to tell me."

"Just don't talk to him, Shannon. Don't tell him anything."

"Mom! Stop with the secrets. You have to tell me why. Is it something to do with my case? Is he coming on Wednesday? Oh God, he's going to testify against me, isn't he?"

"He's not what you think, Shannon. He's not—" I choked and started crying. "He's not what anyone thinks. Please, just let me sleep."

She didn't leave the room right away. I listened to her breath change, rapid huffs transformed to a huge sigh. Her footsteps pounded across the floor, the earthquake of her frustration shaking the cot and reminding me what a bad mother feels like.

Fifty-Six
Rachel García Maria de la Rodrigo y Rivas
Los Brazos, June 7

The raven squawked and gargled his displeasure. He was used to Rachel appearing at dawn, scattering vegetables and old bread. Where was his breakfast?

It wasn't his loud protest that drew Rachel out of bed. She was curled as tight as a kitten because her discomfort had caught up with her this morning. Her attempts to move—uncurling an arm and extending it under the thick quilt, flexing her foot to the side—were met with such sharp pain that tears soaked her pillow.

She had forgotten to drink her evening tea. Her mind absorbed with planning for the next meeting, she had fallen asleep in her rocker. In the deep of the night she crawled to her bed. Now she paid the price for missing the herbs that kept her moving. Her bladder was filled and if she did not make her way out soon then her day would be spent washing rather than planning.

"Ahgg," she moaned, pushing both legs straight and turning to her side. She grabbed her cane and leaned on it. Ten minutes later she made it outside.

"Craw, grabble." The raven knew she was in the outhouse and he called to her through the cracks between the boards.

Two hours and three cups of tea later, Rachel gathered paper and pencil. She could type things out on the computer, but for something as important as this she preferred her own writing. Flexing her fingers to oil her last stiff joint, she started to write.

Fifty-seven
Gabriella
Saturday June 7

I'm not sure what happened when Andy came back with the ice, because I was asleep and never heard a thing. Hopefully Shannon hadn't confronted him about her case, because that was a good place for her suspicions to stay—far way from me. She warmed some soup for dinner and didn't ask me anything other than if I wanted to go to the clinic. My foot hurt, but what can a doctor do for a sprain? I used Andy's ice for my ankle and took ibuprofen and slept through the night.

Saturday dawned, as the days will surely do, not matter how hard you squeeze your eyes shut and pretend that morning has not arrived.

"Shannon, I need to go to the bridge to make a phone call. Can you take me?"

"Okay. I need to check my email anyway."

I hopped across the room and looked in my purse for my phone. It wasn't there. "Have you seen my phone?"

"No. But don't worry, Mom. Watch." She whistled and slapped her thigh. Bones jumped up and ran to her. "Find Mom's phone, girl. Find Mom's phone."

Bones ran around the room, nose to the ground and tail waving. She threaded her way into the bedroom, around the big room and circled the dirt floor of the kitchen, tiny puffs of dust bursting from beneath her nose. She let out a sharp bark and pushed her nose into Shannon's jacket.

Shannon reached into her pocket and pulled out her phone. "No girl, not my phone. Find Mom's phone."

Nose to the floor once more, Bones moved to the screen door and let out a "woof." Shannon opened the door and Bones sniffed her way to my car. I hobbled after them.

"It must be in here." Shannon opened the car door and Bones jumped inside, sniffed and hopped back out. She circled the yard, then headed up the hill.

"You stay, I'll go with her. Maybe you dropped it when you—" my daughter shrugged. "—Had that fit and ran away."

I sat on the porch and watched them go. They were still in sight when my dog let out a joyous bark and pounced into the underbrush. Shannon leaned down and took something from her.

Bones had found my phone.

While curled in my ball of misery I had realized that I was stuck in New Mexico. Hopefully Shannon's charges would be dropped and we could go home. In the meantime, I wanted to talk to Mark. Maybe my cousin wasn't the bad guy, or maybe he was. I had to find out.

"I'm glad you called, Ella. I'll be right over. There's a lot we need to talk about."

Mark ended the call before I could protest. Shannon took me back to the house and helped me clean up, wrap my ankle and make the best of the fifteen minutes before we heard the sound of his truck.

"I don't think we've met?" He put a hand out to Shannon.

"Uh, hi." She shook his hand and glanced over at me. I had coached her on sitting and listening—I wanted a witness to this conversation.

Mark opened the leather case he carried and spread papers across the card table. "Joel said you had been in. I know you listed the property, Ella. Can I just show you some things?"

"Sure." That's why he was here, right?

The map he spread out was better than the one I had. The two roads, Las Nutrias Creek, and the acequia were clearly drawn. Blue dotted lines marked the long skinny divisions of the parcels. To my surprise, dark squares marked two houses on the land. Both fell within the same skinny strip.

"Two houses?"

"Yes. Mine and this one."

"Where is my part?"

He tapped the parcel to the east of the houses.

"So I don't have a house?"

Mark shook his head. "But that's not what I wanted to talk about. I want to talk about Patton."

I almost interrupted him to tell him about Andy, but reconsidered. Let him talk first.

"I don't know what all you've heard about the Pattons and the Martinez', but this family feud goes back years. I learned about it from my father. He was adamant I stay away from Tierra Amarilla. Cursed, he said. Nothing good would come from living here."

Cursed. Just like my mother's version of my grandmother's words.

"He said that every time there was a fight between the two families, something terrible happened. His grandfather, Cristóbel, wouldn't even stay here. He moved to Texas. His great-grandfather died from stress because of the place. His mother died of a broken heart. I'm sure you know about the school burning down? That was a Patton as well."

"What school?" Shannon clapped a hand over her mouth. "Sorry, Mom."

Mark turned to her. "The school which belonged to my great-grandfather. Your mom's too."

"I didn't know it burned." Rachel had conveniently left that out of her story.

"My wife hated this place. She left me and went back to Santa Fe. I had to leave, go after her."

"But you live here, right? Los Ojos?"

"Things didn't work out." He didn't offer more detail about his missing wife. "This place is cursed in the sense that nothing good has ever happened for our family here. That thing between your parents, there was a big hullaballoo about that."

"What thing? My parents were here?"

"When they were young. Uncle George said your mother freaked out about something and your father blamed your grandfather. They had a fight, I guess."

Did this explain my mother's refusal to talk about the land?

Mark continued. "James Patton wants to buy this land and I say let the Pattons have it and move on. I wanted to live here, but I don't now. "

"Why did you act so shocked when I told you I wanted to sell? You said you weren't going to."

"Patton hadn't made an offer. I've come to think differently."

I looked at the map. My strip crossed the creek and the acequia. I must have water rights, just no house. If the house had to be torn down, what did it matter where it was anyway?

"He'll only buy it if he can have it all." Mark swiped a finger across the entire piece of land and stopped on the last strip. "I tried to negotiate for part of it. Jeff's strip is here, on the end. I thought if he and you could trade, Patton could have all this, and you could keep this portion." He traced the lines as he spoke. This plan would give me the strip farthest to the west. Closest to town. The strip I had unknowingly been driving over each time I left the house. "Jeff was willing, but Patton said no. He wants it all."

"What about Andy Lloyd?"

"Andy? What does he have to do with this?"

"He filed a Right-to-Title."

"What? Where did you hear this? Why the hell would he be entitled to this land?"

"A—" I stopped. "Let me ask you something. What do you know about this Brotherhood? The Jewish one?"

"I see Rachel Rivas has gotten to you. I wondered why you chose Fred to be your realtor."

"So you know about it?"

"Of course. Everyone does. A bunch of men in cloaks, thinking no one knows their secret. They get together on Sabbath, out there at Rachel's place and they drive up to the Chavez ranch for their mystical meetings. The town laughs at them, Ella. Like anyone cares if they're Jewish."

"But they want this land."

"They want this land?" He rubbed his chin, then snorted and looked up. "Damn it. It's because of the whole Patton thing. They did this once before. Saved the land when the taxes were due. It's not the land they want, Ella. It's revenge against Patton."

"But if we're part of the Brotherhood then why are they trying to deceive us? Why did Andy Lloyd—" my throat froze and I swallowed—"why did he use me?"

"Wait a minute." Mark leaned forward and pressed his palm down on the table, his face close to mine. "One: we're not part of the Brotherhood. Two: What do you mean by Andy using you?"

Shannon moved over and put an arm around me. "Mom, I'm sorry."

"He... we... slept together and it was all so he could get information. I told him everything and he acted like it was good and we had something and then he, he filed that Right-to-Title, and all along he was working for the Brotherhood to block the sale and so are Fred and Alaura and I thought maybe you were too." I took a shuddering breath and looked at Mark. He leaned back and shook his head, but I wasn't finished. "The Martinez family *is* part of the Brotherhood. Our ancestors were Jewish."

"Wait a minute. Don't you think I would know if we were part of that group? My father would have told me. He's Presbyterian, not Jewish." Mark looked away. When he turned back I saw doubt in his eyes. "There was something Jeff told me once. His grandfather, Hernando, lived here for awhile. He tried to find out who the Marcianos were. The markers—you've seen the cemetery?"

I nodded.

"All those unusual names, they seemed Jewish. So Jeff asked his grandfather and he said the Marcionos lived here, on our property. They had a wooden house up above the acequia and it burned. I think that's where the confusion comes in. I wanted to be sure so I asked Emido, my grandfather. He thought the whole thing crazy, but he told me some story about how his parents never cooked meat with dairy, that's the only thing that made him suspicious."

Mark continued. "But what does it matter? All that was a long time ago. I don't know about you, but I'm not Catholic, I'm not Presbyterian and I'm not Jewish."

My cousin didn't think separating meat from dairy suspicious? He was ignoring what stared us in the face. "They didn't know. My father didn't know either. Jonas, he was the last one to know. He didn't think it was safe so he hid the medallion."

"What medallion?"

I reached up and tugged on the chain, pulling the medallion from under my shirt.

"This medallion."

Mark leaned forward again, so I slipped the chain over my neck and handed him the necklace. He studied it, then handed it back. "It's the symbol at the cemetery, the Marciano symbol."

"It's the sign of the Brotherhood of the Believers. Our ancestors were members. *Jewish* members. Marciano? It's our name too, they hid behind the name Martinez. "

"Ella, you can't believe everything you hear. Especially if it comes from that old woman. She's crazy, you know. Her son went missing back in the '60s and she never recovered. Just look at how she acts. Thinking she's a healer, trying to find a wife for her gay grandson, dressing like a Navajo?"

My mind reeled. Of course, Fred was gay. That made sense now. But that wasn't important at the moment. How did I explain to Mark that I knew without a doubt our family was Jewish? If he thought Rachel was crazy, what would he think if I told him I had psychic visions?

He glanced at his watch. "Look, we have a lot more to talk about but I want to get to the courthouse to see about this Right-to-Title. I thought you were the one who filed it. I thought—" He stopped.

"You thought what?"

"I thought you were trying to change things so you got this house. I mean, it's obvious you like it and want to live here."

"I didn't know it wasn't mine. I thought—" Was Mark a good guy? "I thought you were lying to me."

Fifty-Eight

Rachel García Maria de la Rodrigo y Rivas
Monday, June 9

"_Hola, Abuela._"

Rachel was happy to see Alfredo. She needed to discuss her decision with him before she went to the meeting. After so many years of convincing her grandson he must be a part of the Brotherhood, he would want some explanation why she had suddenly changed her mind.

It was anything but sudden. As soon as she made her decision to stand without them, she realized that the Brotherhood had been a poor substitute for her grief. When Alejandro disappeared she had blamed Tijerina, but now she could see that her obsession with hiding had impacted her son. Why else would he have joined up with those rebels? He knew that he was not a descendant of one of the original land grant owners. The fight was not his.

Her mind had wandered and Alfredo touched her arm to get her attention before he spoke. "Grandmother, I know you have gotten to know the Martinez woman, Gabriella. There's something strange going on, something between her and Andy Lloyd. We discovered he's the one who filed the Right-to-Title." Alfredo took her hands and looked her in the face. "Why would he do this?"

Andy Lloyd? Rachel thought about Mary Luna, his mother. The Luna's were loosely related to the Martinez clan, just as they were related to the Rivas clan, by marriage only. Carmencita had been a Luna. Alejandro's wife, Helen, was a cousin of some sort.

"I don't think he knows about the Brotherhood. His mother left, a scandal really. She was pregnant. When she came home she had the baby, but no husband. Then out of nowhere a man, he was the father and they were getting married and going back to Colorado."

"Could Andy have something, some document or agreement, maybe between Jonas and Manuel Luna?"

Rachel thought about Manuel. He had died in 1947, not long after Jonas. Mary Luna's father, Benicio, must have been just a boy. The Brotherhood would have discussed the future of the Luna family at the old man's passing, but Rachel was too young to have been included.

"Unless Benicio or his father gave something to Mary, I don't know. She was gone, I think. It was a scandal, you know, having a baby so young. Girls were sent away."

Alfredo glanced at his watch. "I can't stay, I have an appointment, but if you hear anything—maybe you can ask some of the others?—call me, okay?"

Rachel turned her cheek for his kiss and sighed. She would have to wait until tomorrow to talk to him about the Brotherhood. Maybe she could find out something about this Andy Lloyd and coax Alfredo back with the news.

Fifty-nine
Gabriella
Wednesday, June 10

"Mom?" Shannon interrupted my pleasant day dream, no journey to the past, no fickle men, and no problems to solve. The sun on the porch had invited me to close my eyes for a while and I wasn't ready to open them.

"What?"

"It's after eleven. Shouldn't Dad be here by now? Can I go to the bridge and call him?"

Parenting is a team process. Those left to do it alone shouldn't have to witness the heart-breaking moment when their child is disappointed by the missing team member. We drove down to the bridge.

Sorry, baby. I can't get there by one. The plane was delayed, but I'm heading up right now. I'll be there, I promise.

Tears leaked from the corners of Shannon's eyes when she listened to Greg's message, but she never said a word.

I pulled the car into the gravel lot at the courthouse at 12:30. "Shannon, I'm coming in. You can't be in there alone."

"Thanks Mom."

Her whispered words were such an unexpected blessing that I reached over and took her hand. "It'll be okay."

She jerked her hand away. "No, Mom. It won't. You should be prepared for what will happen and it won't all be nice and pretty."

Thomas Barton didn't look happy to see me beside Shannon, but the man apparently knew how to pick his battles.

"This will be short. Remember, you don't say anything other than "not guilty" when the judge asks you how you plead."

Shannon's skin took on a gray hue. She chewed on her lower lip and I was reminded of the time when someone had stolen the prize bag from the second grade classroom. Shannon was suspected and we spent several hours in the principal's office. She wouldn't say a word, chewing her lip raw throughout the interrogation. *I never saw, I don't know*, she kept repeating.

Shannon hadn't stolen the prizes, but it turned out she knew who had done it. Protecting the culprit was a strong principle in my daughter's mind. My stomach churned at the idea that today she would protect Raymundo Cruz.

Gray can turn to green. When we went into the courtroom and Shannon saw Raymundo and three others seated at the front, I feared my daughter would vomit all over Thomas Barton's shiny shoes.

I closed my eyes, waiting. When the bailiff spoke, I forced myself to open them.

"All rise. The Honorable James Patton."

Patton was older than I had imagined. His gray hair was cut short, white on the temples. His skin reflected years in the sun. Wrinkles radiated out from his eyes, bright blue, although his eyelids sagged down and covered the upper half. He didn't wear a black robe, just a green sport shirt and a bolo tie, the turquoise stone a round target in the center of his chest. A huge silver belt buckle lay against a flat stomach. No beer belly on this man.

"Sit." The judge's mumbled command was soft, but carried across the crowded room.

The process was extremely quick. Patton zipped through the docket—no extra information dared to sneak its way into his efficient courtroom. Raymundo and the others were quickly remanded to the jail. Their attorney's requests for bail were denied without a second glance. The stench of my sweating armpits seemed strong enough to fill the courtroom. If he could send his own nephew to jail Shannon didn't stand a chance.

But when it was my daughter's turn to stand before him, her "not guilty" whispered in response to his "how do you plead?" James Patton looked up.

"What are you doing in New Mexico?"

"I... I..." Shannon glanced at Thomas Barton and he nodded. "I'm here to visit family."

"Which family is that?"

"Umm... my mother, Ella King."

Patton's gaze swung past Shannon and scanned the bench behind her, landing on me.

Was I supposed to nod? Stand up? Acknowledge who I was?

I settled on nodding and he turned his gaze back to Shannon.

"You are not to leave the county. I am sending you home with a monitoring device. This device will ensure that you remain on the premises until such time as you will appear before this court. You will need permission to leave your house. The deputy will explain this to you in detail. Do you understand?"

Shannon nodded and whispered "Yes."

Patton lifted the gavel and brought it down with a hollow thump.

Thomas Barton grinned and took hold of Shannon's arm. He pulled her down the aisle and out of the courtroom. I followed, once again the forgotten mother.

Barton jabbered so manically, I had to believe he never thought Shannon would be let out on bail. "This is fantastic. I don't know why the judge took pity on her, but he must have heard that she wasn't really involved."

An officer approached my daughter. "Please come with me, Miss King."

Shannon's eyes darted around the hallway and toward the front of the building. "Is Dad here?"

"No sweetie. Not yet. Don't worry. He'll be here." God, it burned to stick up for him.

Greg arrived just as we were led into a back office by the officer. After apologies and a brief nod to me, Greg took over.

"So she wears this for how long? What about showering?" For someone who had missed everything, he was full of questions.

I sat in a chair in the corner, silently thinking about James Patton's decision. A tit for tat? My daughter for my signature? It was clear to me he knew who we were, but did he know that I was aware of his bid for the property?

"Ella! Are you paying attention?" Greg's bark snapped me out of my contemplation.

Shannon pointed to a black plastic device, like a personal cell phone booster. "Mom, this thing needs electricity."

Oh Christ, tell me this wasn't true.

I shook my head. "There is no electricity out there." I looked at Greg. "A motel?"

"What about that pole? Can't you have the power turned on?"

What pole?

Caw, caw. The raven came to mind. I saw him perched on a wire and realized that there was a power pole next to the hulking wreck of a trailer on the bank of Las Nutrias Creek.

Two hours and five phone calls later I found out that I could have had power all along. The pole even sported a rusted box that, when opened, held two outlets. The power company was cooperative once I explained the situation, and sent a man out immediately. Add two very long heavy duty extension cords and the Martinez adobe was live.

"When do we find out her court date?"

"Barton said we should hear something in a few days. Probably some time in late June or early July." Greg moved toward the door.

He would fly home tomorrow, leaving Shannon and her ankle monitor behind. My daughter might have escaped jail, but I was surely imprisoned.

Sixty

Rachel García Maria de la Rodrigo y Rivas
Friday, June 13

"**R**eady?" Alfredo arrived at 7:00 on the dot. He held the door open, and Rachel stepped outside.

No, she wasn't ready. All week she had prepared and still her heart was unsettled. It pounded against her frail ribs as if to escape the cage that kept her from knowing what to do.

Eighty-five years and still a novice. This was why she needed to get away from the Brotherhood. Such a hold over her.

When they arrived at the Chavez barn, Alfredo held her arm to navigate the rough surface of the path into the barn. There were four trucks parked out front—not many for what she had planned. When they entered the barn Rachel was shocked to see seven men playing cards. No robes, although John McDaniel was wearing his medallion. The last meeting had been so crowded, everyone cloaked. It must have been because they heard she was bringing Gabriella. Without the fervor of a new issue, Brothers stayed home and men played poker.

"Hey Fred," Carl Trujillo called. "What are you doing here?"

Then he noticed Rachel and sprang from his chair.

"Señora Rivas. We weren't expecting you."

"I can see that."

Alfredo squeezed her arm and led her to a chair. "My grandmother wishes to speak to the Brothers about an issue."

"What issue?" The question was addressed to Fred.

Rachel fumbled in her pocket for the folded paper, scolding herself for not being more prepared. The last thing she wanted was to look like a senile old woman.

The men had turned from their cards, but the awkward arrangement didn't feel right. Rachel had expected to stand before a crowd of men with attention focused toward the front, not a sidebar to a card game.

She picked up the chair and moved it to the table.

"I see you wanted in on the poker." Carl grinned and the men laughed.

"Not a bad idea," Rachel smiled. "But, no, that's not what I'm here for."

She reached in her pocket and removed the medallion, setting it on the table amidst the cards and poker chips. "I'm here to resign from the Brotherhood."

"Resign?" The Luna boy, she couldn't remember which one he was, tapped his cards on the table. "You don't have to resign, Mrs. Rivas. The only way out of this club is death." He blushed, as he realized mentioning dying to an eighty-five year old woman wasn't tactful.

"I am resigning because I no longer believe the Brotherhood to have the best interest of the Jewish people at heart. There was a time for hiding, yes, during the Inquisition. For years, over a hundred years, many generations, has that been the truth?"

John shook his head. "The truth is we haven't been hiding. Everyone knows about the Brotherhood, and they know about the parties at your house."

"Sabbath. Not parties." Rachel couldn't stop herself from correcting him and immediately wished she hadn't veered off the subject. "No matter, by hiding or pretending to hide, we are limiting ourselves. We need a more active presence, like building a synagogue in Española. We need to stop pretending we are persecuted in a place where there is no persecution."

"No persecution? Maybe not in New Mexico, but don't you watch the news?" Carl pulled out his phone and tapped away. He turned it to her and she squinted at the tiny screen.

Dormant Anti-Semitism Rears Its Head.

"Four people were killed at the Jewish Museum in Brussels. A synagogue was firebombed." Carl picked up the phone and tapped again, then turned it to her.

She pulled the phone closer to look at the picture. A crowd was gathered, holding signs. "I can't see this, you'll have to tell me what it says."

Carl made a strange motion on the screen with his fingers, as if unpinching something. The photo enlarged. "These are from two days ago."

Gas the Jews, one sign read. *Hitler was right.*

Tears leaked from her eyes. This couldn't be true.

In that instant Rachel traveled back to her time with Jonas. She thought about his sorrow, how he shook his head when he told her "Jews will never be safe."

"Don't get me wrong," Carl spoke. "I think you're right that the Brotherhood has changed. But I think we need to go back, not forward. We need to remember our ancestors, how hard they worked, how many sacrifices they made to keep things a secret. We need to rebuild, rethink, figure out how to follow the creed— sustain. Do we need to hide to sustain? To worship? I think not."

"Where is this happening? Where are the people with the signs?"

"Europe, for the most part. Not here, but that's probably only a matter of time."

"Do you have a plan? Have we, the Brothers, been talking about this?"

The men glanced at each other.

"No," John said. "We haven't. But this is a good reminder that we should be."

Rachel was silent. She had come with two items on her list.

"I... I need to ask for one more favor."

"Of course, Mrs. Rivas. What is it?"

"The new woman, Gabriella. We are helping her with this title issue. I need you to help her with one more thing."

John McDaniel nodded. "The girl?"

"Yes, it would mean a lot to me."

"Because of Patton?"

Rachel shook her head. "Not this time. Because she is our heritage. Jonas was wrong, I know that now. Hiding is one thing, but we won't persist if we turn away from our belief completely. The young people must continue what has always been. No more pretending to be Catholic, but to stand up as Jews. From what you just showed me this is more important now than ever."

It was a nice speech, but Rachel couldn't help but hear Jonas's fear and his advice that Jews would always need to hide.

Sixty-one
Gabriella
Saturday, June 14

"**I**'m going for a walk." I caught myself before asking Shannon if she wanted to go with me. She couldn't even go to the bridge to use her phone, which dismayed her nearly as much as if she had actually been in a jail cell. I felt guilty leaving her alone and going to town yesterday, but I had to get away from her. A walk would have to do for today. My ankle still ached a little, but seemed to have healed. I wasn't going to let a tiny twinge stop me.

"Mom, leave Bones. I don't want to be here alone."

I set off down the road at the base of the slope, the flat part of the property. Checking my messages wasn't on my list first thing this morning. Andy had called and called. I didn't want to hear any more of his messages. Clearing my head was top priority.

Several minutes later I came to a fence. I looked for a pass-through—spots in the fence where the wire was wrapped around a pole and could be unwrapped and pulled back—and found one just north of the creek bed.

I hadn't been this far before. This was someone else's land. I had noticed it on the parcel map—owned by someone named Smith.

Without shade the morning sun made me sweat. Using my hat as a fan, I wet my kerchief from my water bottle, and tied it around my neck. The road curled just below the acequia, and old tire tracks gave me a spot to walk without the weeds grabbing my socks. A few minutes later I spotted a barn up ahead. Curious, I walked up on the hill for a better view.

It was a new barn, obviously not accessed by this old road. Horses stood in corrals made from log fences. A shiny horse trailer stood next to the building. I walked farther and spotted the house.

Maybe not a house, but a resort. Why hadn't anyone told me I had rich neighbors? Turning back—I was trespassing—a faint cry came on the breeze.

"Maura! Maura, where are you?"

Someone ran toward me, a cloud of dust kicked up by the frantic pace. I hurried toward her.

"Help! Help me!" The young woman's face was bright red and sweat soaked the armpits of her shirt.

"What is it?" I looked behind her to see if she was being chased. What a day to leave my dog behind!

"Have you seen a little girl? She's wearing a purple shirt and green pants. Four years old. I can't find her. Please help me find her."

She filled me in on details between sobs. She had fallen asleep and when she woke the door was open and her daughter was gone. An hour, maybe a little longer.

I thought about rattlesnakes and coyotes and the dark thunderheads hovering over the bluffs. "We'll find her. She can't be far. Where have you looked?"

She had searched by the road and then come back to the barn.

"Have you called the police?"

She shook her head and cried some more. "My phone is dead. I told Jack we needed a land line. I told him and told him."

"Look, you stay here, close to the house, in case she comes back. I live just over there," I waved a hand. "I'll get help."

She nodded and I ran down the road, ignoring the sharp pain, which had returned to my ankle.

✿ ✿ ✿

"Shannon!" She looked up from her magazine and Bones jumped up from the floor. "There's a little girl missing, next door, I have to go back. You need to drive to town and get the police."

"What? I can't drive to town." She held up her foot, the anklet blinking green.

"Then drive to the bridge and call the police, I don't know. We need help. Tell them to go to the Smith property on Highway 64." Hopefully that was the right name and the entrance was over there by Mark's house. "Their little girl is missing."

Shannon started crying. "They'll put me in jail, Mom. I can't."

Bones ran to lick Shannon's face and—I swear—that dog glared at me. "Don't argue, just do it. We'll work things out later. No one's going to make you go to jail for helping a lost child."

"I can't! They'll kill me in jail! I know they will." Her shoulders shook.

"Then go tell Nathan—have him do it."

"He's not here. He went to Malibu for a drum sale."

Didn't she realize how serious this was? If I sent her to the courthouse she would freak. Too close to the jail. Finally, out of options, I grabbed her arm. "Just go. Get help. I don't care how. Go to Nelson's garage and get Andy."

I called Bones and we raced up the road. Make that she raced and I followed at a limping run.

I could hear the young woman's voice calling as I rushed toward the barn. She was up by the acequia. I hadn't even thought about the child falling in the ditch, but once the image was in my mind I couldn't shake it. Why hadn't this mother taken care of her child? If someone chose to live out here, where there was not only water to drown in and wild animals, but a highway and gangs running lose, then they should be more careful with their children.

When I got to her and saw the panic in her eyes my thinking adjusted. Hadn't I let my daughter fall prey to those dangers?

She looked at Bones. "You brought a search dog?"

"She's just a pet."

But wasn't Bones more than just a pet? She was a hound and Shannon had proved just how good a nose my dog had.

"Do you have something of Maura's? My dog isn't trained, but we can try."

We rushed back to the house and the young woman, Mrs. Smith, I guess, although I still didn't know her name, found a teddy bear. I held it out to my dog.

"Find Maura, girl. Find Maura."

Bones sniffed the bear and wiggled, her tail wagging at the game. She jumped backwards and yipped, waiting for me to throw the bear, which was very close in size and shape to her own stuffed toy.

"Get me something else. Clothes or something. Not a toy."

Mrs. Smith ran back into the house.

This time Bones settled down and sniffed the sweater. Really sniffed it, then gazed up at me.

"Find her, girl. Find." I turned back to the worried mother. "Which door do you think she went out?"

We ran around to the back of the house and I tried again. Holding the sweater under Bones' nose, I repeated my command.

Bones put her nose to the ground and started to circle. She made it to the edge of the yard and looked back at me.

"Find her." *Please God, I know I never pray, but this is important. Listen to me, please listen to me.*

Nose to the ground my dog ran toward the barn. She glanced at the horses in the corral and put her nose down again. Something caught her attention and she barked.

"She's doing it," Mrs. Smith called out and ran after my dog.

The hound's tail waved and she started up the hill, the two of us running behind her. By the time we were next to the acequia we were both out of breath.

"Look," I gasped. "I think you should go back to the house and wait. She's not a trained dog. This could all be just a game to her.

For all I know she's tracking you or me or some animal that came down to your place last night. My daughter went to town for help. They should get here soon and you need to tell them what happened."

I watched the young mother's emotions swirl up and take hold of her. Torn, as anyone would be, she made the decision to follow my advice.

Bones was definitely on the scent of something. I struggled across the acequia and up the deer trail she followed. A dog can run low through manzanita and scratchy brush, not so a human. Hadn't I learned the dangers of flight through here a couple days ago? I slowed down and watched where I was going. It wouldn't help the little girl if I fell again.

Bones waited for me every now and then. But will power and fear were not enough to keep me going. My ankle gave out and I fell into a fresh cow pie.

"Damn it," I screamed, wiping the manure from my arm. At least it was just one side, and not my face. I closed my eyes and breathed deep through my nose. I needed to get a handle on this. I couldn't just stop and rest while a little girl was out there.

Come on, God or Allah or Buddha or Jesus. Mother Theresa or Mother Nature. Anyone listening? Please help me get up and keep looking. I grabbed the medallion around my neck and squeezed. *You're magic, help me now.*

I heard sobs, but not from a child. There was someone else out here and she was crying. I grabbed hold of a branch and pulled myself up. Voices filtered through the trees.

"Hey, lady. We like your freckles. Aren't you worried out here in the hot sun?"

"Please, please, just leave me alone."

I edged up the trail. Whoever was out here wasn't having a good time. I picked up a rock.

Another voice joined in. "I know who she is. She's the wife of that stuck up guy. The one prancing around town? A Martinez."

I could see them now. One woman and three men. She was crying and they circled her like a pack of wolves. I slipped behind a pine tree.

"Please, just please let me go." The young woman lifted her head, desperately searching for help and I saw her face, but she didn't see me.

In that split second I realized what had happened. The medallion had taken me away. I wasn't on the hillside on a June afternoon looking for a lost child. I was back in time. And I knew just how far back because I recognized the young woman.

It was my mother.

"Leave her alone," I screamed, rushing forward with the rock held high.

No heads turned, no eyes met mine.

"I wonder if she's a dirty Jew like her husband? Hey, *chicka*, are you a dirty bitch Jew?" One of the men stepped forward and grabbed my mother.

I rushed at him and struck him in the head with the rock. I saw him blink, but he shook his head and turned back to my mother.

"It doesn't really matter out here does it? Jew, Catholic, or even some punk like me? We're all the same when it comes to this." He hooked his fingers over the neck of her blouse and tore it from her body.

"Please, God, please help me." She curled her arms over her breasts, although he hadn't ripped her bra.

"Time to shut up." The second man stepped forward and hit my mother across the face.

"No, no, no," I screamed and ran at the man. I prayed along with my mother, who was now crying hysterically. I punched and hit and hurled rocks and sticks and bashed the men over and over. Something had to work. There had to be a way to break through and stop them.

Nothing I did kept the three men from raping my mother.

She curled tighter and was silent, her eyes shut. I didn't stop trying to fight them off. I squeezed the medallion and asked it to give me substance, just a little substance. Finally I sank down beside my mother and wrapped my arms around her. Maybe I could comfort her with my spirit.

We all heard it at the same time. A voice, calling from down the hill.

"Grace? Where are you?"

"Come on. I don't want to deal with that Jew boy right now. Let's go. We got what we wanted." The men ran through the trees just as my father made his way into the clearing.

"Dad, over here," I called out, forgetting he couldn't hear me.

He spotted my mother and ran up the hill. "Grace, oh Grace, what happened?"

"I didn't get it right, I didn't get it right."

My father sank to the ground and pulled her into his arms.

"I didn't get it right. Why didn't I get it right." She kept her eyes closed and rocked back and forth.

"What, Grace? What didn't you get right?"

"I prayed and I prayed and I prayed, but I didn't get it right."

"What happened? Tell me what happened."

She shook her head and he pulled out his handkerchief and wiped her face. Her eyes were swollen and I could see the bruises starting on her cheeks and forehead. He dabbed at her wounds, slowly taking in the torn clothing. He looked around, as if searching for clues, and saw her underwear, torn and discarded.

"Oh my God, Grace, what happened? Just tell me what happened?" He grabbed her shoulders and shook her.

"Stop it, Dad. Don't do that to her." I cried and pulled at his arms. I tried to get between them, to save her from his interrogation.

Finally, she opened her eyes and looked at him. "Steven, they called me a dirty Jew. Why would they call me that?"

His face turned red, then purple. He clenched his jaw and I heard the grinding clack of enamel. His breath came in sharp snorts.

"Who called you that? Where are they?" He looked around as if the rapists might be waiting behind a tree. Then he stood and pulled her to her feet. "Come on, Grace."

"Why would they call me that? I'm not a Jew."

"It's not true, Grace. Don't worry about that, we just need to go get you cleaned up."

But I saw his lips, as he turned down the path, propping my mother on his shoulder, and I heard the words he whispered, words she wasn't to hear.

"They'll never call us that again."

✡ ✡ ✡

"Baa-oo." A mournful call echoed down the mountain and my parents faded from sight. Bones let out another bay and barked directly in my ear. Scrambling to my feet, I ran after her.

As I ran I tried to focus on the lost child, but my mother had been raped. I had watched and not been able to save her, just like I couldn't save Rique and I couldn't save Alejandro. What good was a trip to the past if only to witness these horrible things? Shouldn't I be able to do something? I had helped Consuela and I had felt Francesca's passion, but the important things—my mother—why was she left to suffer?

My father had known. Known we were Jewish, known bad things could happen, known other people would break through his wall of careful plans and hurt him.

I turned when Bones reached the top of the ridge, the Smith ranch a tiny speck at the bottom of the hill. My dog must be tracking something else, a four year old could not have made it this far.

Suddenly Bones barked, sharp and steady. She stood at the edge of a culvert, her tail wagging. I watched as she paced for a moment, then jumped down the steep grade.

I ran to the edge and peered down into the thick brush. "Maura?"

I heard a tiny voice. "Doggy."

"Maura!" I called, as I slid down the edge of the culvert.

"Momma?"

"Honey, no, I'm Ella. Are you okay?" I saw her now, the purple sweater bright among the dusty green brush. Bones wiggled beside her, tail wagging and tongue working overtime on the tear stained, dirty cheeks.

I didn't lift her right away. If she had fallen down the culvert there might be injuries. But she stood and wrapped her arms around my dog, smiling.

"I went for a walk?" I recognized the sound of a child who thinks she might be in trouble, the tentative are-you-mad question hidden within the simple statement.

"Yes you did. A long walk." I scooped her into my arms. "How about we go see your mommy?"

☆ ☆ ☆

As I rushed toward the ranch I wished there was a way to call Mrs. Smith and tell her Maura was safe. I couldn't run on the steep downgrade, but I kept a steady pace in spite of how heavy this little girl had become and the intense throbbing in my ankle. She fell asleep slumped over my shoulder, no doubt exhausted and relieved. Bones trotted along beside us, her tail still wagging. She liked this game.

I couldn't stop thinking about my mother being attacked. My father's face as she told him her prayers had not been up to par. I realized then that nothing stays the same, not even for a moment, not who we are. There is no permanence. The person I am changes into the next version with each bit of knowledge gained. Who I am now I will not be tomorrow and I am not who I was yesterday. My father had changed but I hadn't been there to see it, I was stuck on the man who squeezed my shoulder every night.

I carried a lost child, a child my dog had found because she picked up a scent and stayed with it. Her direction was forward. She never varied from where she knew she must go. Since leaving California I had changed direction so many times. Every bit of information—Was I strong? Was I depressed? Was I Jewish? Was I crazy?—sent me off on a tangent. I had trusted people, so many people, thinking that the natural way of things was to have everyone's best interest at heart. What a mistake that had been.

I shifted the warm child onto my other hip. I would make decisions or I would fail. There was no other choice.

✡ ✡ ✡

As soon as I saw the volunteer searcher I called out. "I have her. She's fine." The woman smiled and held up a radio. I nodded. A mother would know that her daughter was safe. The searcher noticed my limp and carried the sleeping Maura the rest of the way home.

When we made it back to the house, dozens of people were there. I saw Andy standing with Mrs. Smith, his arm around her shoulders. Both of them ran to me.

"Mommy." Maura woke up when she heard her mother.

"Baby, oh baby." She kissed her child over and over, tears of joy and relief streaming down her cheeks.

I stepped away and bumped into Andy.

"You found her!"

I bit my lip and looked around. "Is Shannon here?"

"No. She came to get me at the station, but she was freaked about the monitor. I think she went home."

I was exhausted, but I needed to find my daughter. For all I knew the police had responded to the alarm of her leaving and she had been hauled off to jail. I would have to ask Andy for a ride home.

"Ella, she told me you know."

I turned away. This was not something I wanted to deal with right now. Or ever.

"Please let me explain." Andy grabbed my arm.

I whirled out of his grasp. "Don't touch me. Don't ever touch me again."

"Please, if you just let me—"

"Shut up. I mean it. Don't talk to me." I hurried toward the barn and the road behind it. It didn't matter how tired I was or how much my ankle hurt, I wasn't asking Andy for a ride.

Sixty-two
Rachel García Maria de la Rodrigo y Rivas
Saturday, June 14

Rachel didn't get out of bed. She pulled the quilt over her head and moaned. Alfredo had dropped her off close to midnight, after she insisted they stay with the men and discuss what would happen next. The poker game had been pushed aside and Carl Trujillo made notes in a little book. She should have been happy that the Brothers were moving forward, but the image of the horrible signs haunted her. Nightmares had kept her tossing and her head hurt.

She asked God for advice. Why did history repeat itself once more? What had Jonas foreseen that made him turn completely away? Annihilation? Torture?

There were Jews who tried to go back, but she hadn't paid much attention to the Israel issues. What did this have to do with her? She was happy here and had no heirs once Alfredo was gone.

Don't go back to putting the Brotherhood first. The time for worrying about everyone else is gone. Think about yourself.

Her thoughts grew louder and pounded inside her head. She got up—tea might help.

Hawthorne, rose, and motherwort. Not her favorite combination, so she reached for the lemon balm to add some taste. The can was just on the top shelf. She stretched her fingers up and knocked it to one side, trying to move it closer to the edge, but she was too short.

Pushing her tired limbs to obey, she dragged a chair over to the shelf. She braced herself on the counter and pulled herself up onto the chair, wobbling and reminding herself she shouldn't be doing this anymore. A fall would be bad and she didn't want to lie on the kitchen floor for days.

As she reached for the lemon balm her gaze landed on the jar of orange powder, pushed to the back of the highest shelf.

Onawa hadn't gone into detail, but she gave the powder to Rachel after hearing stories of her enemies. Rachel hadn't asked questions, just put the herbs away.

Did the orange powder cause death? Or was Onawa just out to make someone suffer terrible diarrhea? Rachel put the jar on the counter, next to the lemon balm and climbed off the chair.

There were ways to escape thoughts that gave no peace. If every morning was to be filled with pain and every night filled with nightmares, what kind of existence was that?

Rachel picked up the jar and walked to the window. The orange powder was bright with tiny flecks of something dark. She opened it and sniffed gently. Was this the odor of death?

Twisting the cap back on the jar, she set it on the window sill. A day could be bad and the next could make everything seem much better.

Rachel made her tea and sat at the table. The medallion lay in the basket with coupons and mail. She picked it up and turned it to the light to look at the design.

How old this was. One of the originals, her mother had told her. There weren't many left. Most of the families had lost them over time, and new versions hung from many necks. No, that wasn't true. Seven men at the meeting and only one wearing a medallion. The sign of the Brotherhood was tucked away in drawers or forgotten in a pocket.

What about Gabriella's claim that her medallion was magic and took her into the past? There was no way she could have known about all those people in such detail, was there?

Rachel rose and went to her desk. She bent low and reached to the back of the file drawer, pulling out a large envelope and returned to the table.

She spread the photos out, stopping to look at the young Jonas, the staunch Hernan and the unsmiling Francesca, the school house, Jonas and Carmencita standing proud in front. But this isn't what she was after.

She unfolded the brittle paper with care. Jonas had told her this family tree was passed down, but incomplete. She had sat with him, pen in hand, filling in the blanks he could remember.

When Jonas died Rachel had searched his house. She found this envelope, with the family tree and the photos revealing his true heritage. Her name was printed across the front. No note or instructions accompanied it, but she knew what Jonas wanted. She was to be the keeper of his secret.

This was the only copy. Gabriella could not have known about Consuela or the nearly complete extinction of the Martinez family during Popé's revolt. She could not have known about the love between Alejandro and Francesca. There was no one else alive who knew those things.

Rachel picked up the medallion and squeezed it. She slipped it around her neck.

"Take me. Please take me to my Alejandro. I don't have long."

Sixty-three
Gabriella
Saturday, June 14 to Sunday, June 15

I should have slept soundly that night, exhausted from the hours of searching, knowing that Maura was safe at home. If only the pillow hadn't been so lumpy, or the weather so hot, or the coyotes so loud.

If only I knew where Shannon was sleeping.

How harshly I had judged Maura's mother. As if parenting an active four year old was easy, could always turn out fine if a mother worked hard enough, had enough vigilance.

Or if a father covered all his bases, made her pray and pray so that God or Jesus or someone watched over her when he couldn't.

This judgement of mine, pushing forward without all the facts, without trying to see things from another perspective. Was that why New Mexico had sent these dreams? So that I would actually be somewhere—even someone—else? Outside my own narrow gaze?

What about judging myself? I was every bit as harsh, as ignorant, as I was with others. Didn't I owe myself some empathy?

I finally fell asleep at dawn, just after the day grew light.

My dreamless sleep was interrupted by the sound of voices. Who was here? Shannon? Or the police?

I was surprised to see James Patton. This really was a small town if the judge came over when a prisoner went missing.

I brushed the hair out of my eyes and pulled my sweatshirt closed over the ratty t-shirt I had slept in. "Look, I don't know where she is. She's scared and I made her leave. There was a missing child, it was the only way. We needed help. It's really all my fault."

He shook his head and reached out his hand. "It's okay. I'm here to thank you for what you did. I can't thank you enough."

"What I did?"

"You found Maura."

This visit was political. He needed to get in good with me—the current local hero.

"Bones found her."

At the sound of her name, my dog sat beside me with her nose pressed against my leg.

"I don't know if anyone bothered to tell you the history of our grandfathers."

"Great-grandfathers. I know about it."

"I'm glad you let all those bad feelings slide and found my granddaughter."

Granddaughter?

I was speechless.

James Patton looked at me. "I thought you knew. Grace is my daughter."

"Grace?" How could my mother be his daughter?

"Maura's mother, the woman you helped yesterday."

Suddenly the picture came into focus. The land next door. The Smith ranch it might be called, but Grace Patton, who just happened to share my mother's name, lived there.

"Do you own that property? The ranch?"

"I deeded it to Grace and Jack."

James was wearing the bolo again, and I looked at the turquoise rather than his face. "Why weren't you there? Looking for Maura?" I blurted.

"I was in Denver. I flew back as soon as I heard."

I nodded, ready for this man to leave my property. I might have saved his granddaughter, but that didn't change how I felt about him. Especially since my own daughter was running from him. "I'm happy that Maura is safe."

"Ella, I want to help you find Shannon. She won't go to jail. You don't need to worry about that."

I thought about how she would react if I sent out a search party. I pictured the people of Tierra Amarilla as they had been yesterday, gathered together with a master plan for finding a lost daughter. Only this time they wouldn't be searching the vast desert and mountain terrain. They would be walking building to building, knocking on doors where gang members lived. "Have you seen this girl?"

She would be scared if she knew people were looking. I might never find her if it sent her deeper into hiding. No, this time my daughter had to find her own way home.

✡ ✡ ✡

Sitting on the porch, staring at Los Brazos, I felt deserted by everyone, even the cliff. Real people and dream ancestors. They had all failed me. I twirled the medallion in my fingers, the image of my mother's bruised face as clear as if she sat with me. Of course the land was cursed, terribly cursed. Shannon and I needed to get away from here. I would go to Patton and ask him, beg him to let us go back to California. He owed me, didn't he?

I heard the sound of my car, and Bones stood, tail wagging.

When Shannon came up on to the porch, exhaustion nearly brought me back to angry mother mode. Then I remembered how worried I had been for the missing Maura. I remembered Grace's tears of joy when she held her baby in her arms.

"Mom, I'm so scared."

"I know, baby. Don't worry. Judge Patton came out. You're not going to jail."

"Did they find her, the little girl?"

"Yes. I know this sounds like a soap opera, but she's Judge Patton's granddaughter."

She sat and twisted her hair. The ankle monitor blinked, the red light flashing off the pale cholla.

"I'm glad you came back." I reached for her hand.

She jumped up and threw her arms around me. All the years of anger and frustration slipped away as I hugged my child.

"Mom, I'm so sorry, I'm so sorry."

In that moment, feeling Shannon move from a brush with adult intimacy to the basic need of wanting her mother's comfort—my comfort—I saw my daughter. She made her choices based on her needs. She escaped the "shoulds" that imprisoned me. Shannon took the good with the bad, experiencing it all—sorrow, joy, fear, novelty —to the highest level. Nothing was dampened or suppressed with her. She never had preconceived ideas of how something was going to turn out and so she escaped the heavy black cloud of worry that hung over my head.

"It's okay, Shannon. Really, it's all fine."

"No. It's not." She pressed her face into my shoulder. "It's Rachel, Mom. Rachel is dead."

Sixty-five
Gabriella
Monday, June 16

We buried Rachel next to her husband, which was also next to the church. It was what she wanted, Fred told me. But I couldn't help but think she would have been happy up on the hill with Francesca and Jonas.

I cried when John McDaniel and Carl Trujillo shoveled the dirt onto her wooden coffin. Not only because Rachel was gone, but because I hadn't told her my dream about her son. Fred was wrong —she would have wanted to know that Alejandro had died keeping his promise. Not murdered by the rebels, not deserting his wife and child, not leaving without saying goodbye to his parents. I was a mother. I knew what it was like to lose your child. Even for a night.

"It's okay, Mom." Shannon held my hand as we watched mourners toss flowers onto the grave. The tradition in T.A. was to wait until the coffin was covered, leaving the flowers like a blanket on top of the earth. The whole town turned out to say good-bye to Rachel, so the pile of blossoms spread until it seemed she was ready for the Rose Bowl parade.

I looked down at my daughter's ankle, where the monitor continued to blink red. No one had come to reset it or to haul her off to jail.

I wiped the tears with my sleeve. "I know, Sweetie. I felt like I just got to know her, maybe even trust her, and there was so much she could have told us."

"I know what you mean, Mom. That's why I went there. She would have protected me, but..." Shannon closed her eyes and shook her head. "I never thought I'd see a dead person."

"I'm sure she just slipped away. Old people, they've had their lives so it's not so tragic. I'm sorry you had to see it."

Tough Martinez women don't cry, but I was glad when Shannon let her tears join mine. We stood in the church yard long after everyone had moved across the gravel parking lot to the parish hall for coffee and refreshments.

✡ ✡ ✡

When John McDaniel came out on Monday morning my first thought was that he was here to take Shannon to jail. Sure, James Patton had assured me she wouldn't go, but weren't all Pattons my enemies? Why should I believe him?

"Charges are dropped. I can take that monitor off her now."

I didn't know what to ask. *Just be thankful and shut up.*

"Got notified in this morning's email. Probably not enough evidence."

Shannon sat on the edge of the porch and held out her ankle. "What about Raymundo?"

Leave it, leave it, who cares about him? "Shannon, let's just count our blessings, Judge Patton took care of things."

John McDaniel looked at me, eyebrows bunched, and shook his head. What was he trying to say?

"So we don't have to go back to the courthouse or sign anything?"

"Nope," he tucked the black box under his arm. "This won't be on her record either."

I hadn't even considered that possibility.

John walked to his patrol car and opened the trunk. He placed the ankle bracelet and the monitor inside, then pulled out a large envelope.

"This is for you."

The envelope said "Rachel" in faded writing.

"What's this?" I asked the sheriff.

"It was on the table. We looked inside and we figured it belongs to you."

✡ ✡ ✡

I tipped the contents of the envelope out onto the table. Photos, papers, a pressed flower, a zip bag—hopefully this was tea and not something else—and a small stone.

I recognized the very round piece of turquoise, the surface dull, but smooth beneath my fingertips. I had last seen this in Rique's hand. He pulled it out of his pocket often, turning it over and over between his thumb and fingers. How had it come to be here?

The envelope contained photos of people I recognized. Francesca and Hernan standing in front of what could only be the house I had visited in my dreams. A young Jonas, wearing a suit, with a smile on his face, the medallion visible around his neck as he held up some sort of certificate. A group of boys standing in front of a barn—the school, I guessed.

Shannon unfolded the brittle piece of paper.

"Careful. That looks pretty old."

"I am being careful." She smoothed it and I scooted closer so that we could look at it together.

A family tree. It was marked in different penmanship, some entries in pencil, some in ink, lots of question marks, as if passed down through the generations and blanks filled in here and there.

"Look Mom. Here's Grandpa." She ran her finger across the names. "And look at these, the other names are here. We can tell who was who."

Yehayachin Galit Marciano was written in ballpoint ink, just below Jonas's name. Definitely added later.

I worked my way back in time.

Fadrique, b. 1668, d. 1721. Thirty-two plus twenty-one, fifty-three. Rique hadn't died as a boy. The rest of the family was gone, all in 1680. Consuela died then too. They must have returned to Taos, in spite of the warnings. But Rique, he had fallen in the river, I saw it. I didn't save him.

Somehow he had lived. And the Martinez family had lived.

I pointed to Consuela's name. "She was a native as well. We have some Tewa blood."

Shannon wrinkled her nose. "How do you know that?"

Once again I contemplated the wisdom of sharing my strange dreams with anyone. It would be nice if Shannon could gain the knowledge I had learned from the actions of our ancestors. "It's a long story. One that will be perfect for our drive back to California." I traced my finger further up the page.

Romero Martín de Serrano. He was married to Gabriella. My mind swam. Was this me? Or had the medallion felt it was convenient to put me in the soul of my namesake ancestor? She was born in 1585, hundreds of years ago. She had died in 1650 and Romero had died in 1645. Wasn't that a long time to live in those times?

Francisco Martín de Serrano. 1451. This was my family, my ancestors, hundreds of years worth.

"We are Jewish, aren't we?" Shannon picked up the photo of Jonas. "What should we do?"

"I've been thinking about it. There's a synagogue, well, probably more than one, in Oakland. I'm thinking about checking it out. Do you want to go?"

"We're going home?"

"The sooner the better. Tomorrow?"

"What about selling this place?"

"Mark can take care of it. I don't need to be here. I'll give him power of attorney."

"Yeah, Mom. I do want to go, to the synagogue, I mean. And home. But what about Grandma?"

"We'll have to talk to her." I hadn't told Shannon about my vision. That would be between my mother and me. Bringing it up might not be the right thing, such a painful memory. Somehow I wanted to comfort my mother, but I didn't know how. I would never know how my father had figured out he was Jewish, but he hadn't wanted to face it. I wouldn't make that same mistake.

Sixty-six
Gabriella
Wednesday, June 16

"**M**om, we have to stop by Three Ravens on our way out. We can't leave without saying goodbye to Nathan."

"True. Can you help me with this ice chest?" Adding another person and all this extra stuff to a small car was a challenge.

We both heard the truck and turned. A yellow tow truck.

"Uh oh." Shannon grabbed my arm. "What do you want to do?"

"I don't know. Go in the house?"

"Don't hide from him, Mom. Tell him to leave."

Andy blocked the car with the truck and I felt my blood pressure rise.

"So it's true. You're leaving."

"We are. You need to move your truck."

He glanced back, then stepped closer. "Please let me explain."

"No." I tightened my fists, flashing back to the broken chair leg.

"I never meant it the way you think. He's my father, Ella. He was going to give me the land. I thought you might stay if I could offer you that."

What was he talking about?

"I don't know what you're saying, but it doesn't matter. We have a lot to do and I want you to leave."

"James is my father."

"James Patton?"

Andy nodded.

The blood rushed from my head and I reached for something to hold myself up, only there wasn't anything. Andy stepped forward and grabbed my arm.

I pulled away and sank to the dirt, pushing my head down between my knees.

"Mom!" Shannon rushed to me, glaring at Andy. "What did you do to her?"

I raised my head. He stepped away and held his hands in the air, shaking his head.

"It's okay, I'm just a little faint." I pushed the last of the unexpected emotion away and looked up at Andy. "Go away, just go away."

His face crumpled. "Please Ella, I can't leave like this. I never meant to hurt you." Tears filled his eyes.

The last vestiges of Old-Ella stepped in to comfort him. "Don't blame—"

I'd like to say that New-Ella sprang to the rescue. That my time alone had led to tremendous personal growth, and I no longer could be swept up by obligation to others, that I was strong, self-confident and told him to get a grip. New-Ella was there, struggling to make her appearance, but before she could save the day, Shannon jumped up and faced Andy.

"Give me a break," she said. "She asked you to leave, now go."

"I have to explain, please just let me explain."

Explain. There was always an explanation, wasn't there? But maybe I needed to hear this. I struggled to my feet. "It's okay, Shannon."

"Ella, I didn't know he was my father, not until I was older. My mother, she got pregnant and left. I didn't want to tell you until you could see that I'm only a Patton by accident. I'm not like them. I'm not at war with the Martinez family. When I heard he wanted to buy this property, make his parcel go all the way to the bluffs, I knew he would get what he wanted. He always does. Just because he's my father doesn't mean I agree with him."

"How long have you known?"

Andy looked down. "Since March."

"The whole time?"

"I talked to him, Ella. He doesn't listen to me, not really. I couldn't stop him from buying the land, but I convinced him to let me live here. He owes me something. He wasn't ever a father to me, wouldn't even admit he was my father until I threatened DNA testing. He had this old note from Rueben, a promissory note to my great-grandfather, Raymond. Rueben must have borrowed against the land or something. It wasn't going to make a difference, but I thought if I could delay things, maybe my father would listen to me, and you might see…"

"I might see what?"

"What we have is good, Ella. We could live here. Do you remember my dream?"

His dream? I didn't remember Andy ever telling me about dreams. "No."

"Not a dream like yours, a plan for the future. The dream of building a small house, on a rise, windows looking out at Los Brazos. I can do that for us. Can't you be with me?"

This was the question I had asked myself for two months. Being with Andy felt right—most of the time. He was kind, not mean. He helped other people and he helped me. But my marriage had felt okay too. Okay wasn't good enough any more.

Andy had lied. He had tried to take my property out from under me with this strange justification that he should have it, not me. Some emotional battle with his father had made its way into our relationship. He might say he only wanted to delay things, but what did that really mean? That he would sell me on his ideas without ever letting me in on his plan?

"I'm sorry, Andy. I know you think this is because you… betrayed me, but it's not that. I understand, I think I understand." That was as close as I could get. "But I'm not in love with you. It won't work, no matter what."

"I love you, Ella. Please don't make up your mind right now. Please think about it."

The good things he had done resurfaced. As I wavered, unable to reply, something came to me. Patton was Andy's father. "Thanks for getting Shannon's charges dropped."

"The charges dropped?" He looked down at Shannon's ankle. "I didn't get them dropped."

Maybe James Patton had followed up on his promise without Andy's influence. But what about John McDaniel's raised eyebrows when I told Shannon it had been Patton? Oh well, it didn't matter now, I was not going to trust a Patton ever again. At least I knew the Brotherhood wasn't involved in trying to take this land. Rachel, Fred, Alaura, and Nathan really were my friends. Mark could sell Patton the land or keep it or donate it for a park. I needed the money, but the curse of the Martinez land was not going to follow me.

"Andy, I'm going back to California."

Sixty-seven
Gabriella
Wednesday, June 16

We finished loading the car and drove to Three Ravens. The medallion was tucked inside my duffle, along with the photos, the turquoise stone and the family tree. I wondered if the magic would travel to California.

Shannon was chatting with the barristas, saying her goodbyes, and I went out back to find Nathan. He was sanding a beautiful inlaid cajón.

"You leaving now?"

I'd miss the small town telegraph service. "Yep. Just stopped to say goodbye. And thanks."

"I'm glad you came by. I have something for you." He took off his gloves and motioned me inside.

I hadn't been in this part of the building. It was his workshop, crowded with stacks of wood, cans of finish, a table saw and drills and sanders and shelves filled with partially completed drums. He picked up a small drum.

It was beautiful. The skin was held tight over the ends by leather traces, and the body of the drum was some sort of wood, the grain folded into twisting patterns. Painted on the top were three ravens, the beak of each touching the tail of the next, forming a circle of birds. Nathan handed it to me.

"It's so beautiful. I…" My throat tightened. "Thank you. This means a lot."

Nathan nodded and picked up a large drum. "Are you ready to be healed?"

"What?"

"Sometimes people don't think about what it means to begin the journey to being healed."

"How mystical. Of course, I want to heal."

"Ella, just listen for a minute. To heal is to change. And to change is to give up the defense mechanisms you've been using for a long time."

"Okay, Mr. Psychology. I get it. I'm ready to do that."

"To be vulnerable?"

I stopped. That word. Seemed to me I was terribly vulnerable and that was the problem. New-Ella was trying to be strong.

Nathan continued. "It's not easy. To expose your belly. To be ready to hurt and to cry and to face the reality of things."

"I... I..." Be hurt? I was hurting at every level.

"Shhh. You don't have to answer or justify or anything. I can tell what you're thinking. You have been hurt, but you fight it, Ella. This is about letting the past be the past, letting it find its way and spiral through what needs to be gone through. Just listen."

Nathan began to whistle softly. It wasn't like any sound I had every heard. Not like a bird and not like a train.

As he whistled, he started to drum. It was slow and rhythmic, as soft as a breeze and as ghostly as a flickering fire.

He reached out and touched my hand and I followed his lead, striking the smooth surface of the little drum in time with him. I felt my mind wander through the blue mist of the world around me. The tension dissolved like mixing sugar into tea, swirling and floating. I didn't guide it, I didn't think, I didn't stress about New-Ella or Old-Ella or getting on the road, or being prepared or planning or family members or lovers or loneliness. There was time for all that later.

Right now, I just was.

After

I walked down the familiar dusty road and saw the house. The adobe was solid and the wooden roof glowed in the morning sun. Roses grew along the small wooden fence surrounding the yard. A young woman swept the porch.

"*Hola,*" she called. "Are you here for the service?"

I didn't answer right away. *Why must you always take me back to a death?* I squeezed the heavy medallion dangling around my neck. "*Si,*" I called back. "*Me llamo Gabriella Martinez.*"

"Are you a granddaughter?" She squinted and stared at me.

"I don't know. Who died?"

The young woman frowned and stepped off the porch. "Jonas Martinez. Who did you say you were?"

"Gabriella. *Jonas esta mi bisabuelo. Quien es?* Who are you?"

The young woman smiled. "I am a friend of your great-grandfather. I am Rachel García Maria de la Rodrigo. I was just going to make some tea. Would you like some?"

Acknowledgements

Special thanks to everyone who made this story possible:

•My draft readers Marlene Koons, Delynn Tjoelker, Chris Phipps, Joli Roberts, Gloria Beverage and Shirley Peterson.

•My editor (and teacher) Susan Rushton, for her sense of style and acceptance of my lack of style.

•*Gracias* to the entire Whitson family for their knowledge of Spanish.

•Jennifer DuBois, for lessons on story arcs and unreliable narrators.

•The people of Tierra Amarilla, including my wonderful cousins, Doreen and Manuel, and all those who put up with my visits to Three Ravens Coffee House and my endless questions about life in Northern New Mexico and especially Paul Namkung for introducing me to all those folks and letting me use Three Ravens as a place for Ella to hang out.

•Road Scholar, especially Karen Long and Norma Libman and all my new Jewish friends, who took the time to teach me the real story, especially Sy and Marlie Zucher, for welcoming me into their home and teaching me the art of Jewish dinner conversations, Ann and Fred Letzer, for listening to all my questions, Chani Oppenheim, for my introduction to the UC Davis group.

•Jhoz Singer for reading my "Jewish" passages and pointing me in the right direction.

•The various critique groups who gave input along the way: Writers of the Storm and the Sierra Writers critique group.

•Once again, a special thanks to Leslie Batz and Dan Wentworth for giving me a space in the yurt to write (and re-write) and to Kim and Laura Glassco, who sponsored my writing time in their Dutch Flat historic cottage.

•My husband, Dan, for soothing my shattered nerves when the writing wasn't going well, and convincing me this is the right thing to do.

•And tons and tons of thanks to my parents, Robert and Roberta Martinez, for carrying on the art of family story telling and to my children, my sisters, my aunts and uncles and all the wonderful, eccentric, crazy members of my clan.

•Thanks to anyone I have left off this list, it has been a long process and my mind wanders.

Notes

Depression: I know that major depression is a serious problem for many people and that one can't "fake" their way out of major depression or postpartum depression. I believe in appropriate medical intervention for depression. That said—I also believe that meditation and mind/body interventions are highly effective treatments. I do believe that one can use mental interventions to change body chemicals, feelings, emotional reactions and more.

The use of the word *almah*. This is not a Spanish word, but a Hebrew one, referring to a "maiden" or young un-married girl who has not yet had a child.

Historical Fiction:

I have played with facts. A lot. Timelines in a work of fiction are tricky. I changed the past and I changed current events. I added characters to New Mexico history. As far as I know there was never a secret Brotherhood in Tierra Amarilla. I am not Jewish (although it is highly likely I am a descendant of a crypto-Jew), I am not Catholic and I am not Presbyterian, so please excuse any errors I have made in representing the traditions and rituals of the various religions.

The history of the Crypto-Jew is fascinating. I hope that the story will inspire you to read more about it. Below are some of the wonderful books and resources available on this topic and New Mexico in general.

To The End of the Earth, by Stanley Hordes
The Wandering Gene and the Indian Princess: Race, Religion and DNA by Jeff Wheelwright
    A Nation of Shepherds (A Novel) by Donald Lucero
    Hidden Heritage, the Legacy of the Crypto-Jews by Janet Liebman Jacobs
    Rio Arriba A New Mexico County by Robert J. Tórrez and Robert Trap
    A History of the Jews in New Mexico by Henry J. Tobias
    The Adobe Kingdom, New Mexico 1598-1958 by Donald L Lucero
    But Time and Chance: The story of Padre Martinez of Taos 1793-1867 by Fray Angelico Chavez

About the Author:

Robin Martinez Rice writes for fun and to tell the stories that haunt her dreams, swarm through her head daily, and crop up in conversations. She lives in Northern California, but takes frequent extended road trips to gather more fodder for tales.

Please visit her website for book club guides, blogs and adventures.
www.robinmartinezrice.com
PO Box 5818
Auburn, CA 95604-5818

Also by Robin Martinez Rice:

Imperfecta: In 1923 fourteen-year-old Perfecta Trujillo rebels against the strict Catholic standards of her New Mexico village. She won't be perfect anymore. She doesn't agree that laughing, dancing and having fun are sins. But even Perfecta knows that falling in love with a Presbyterian is a sin.
How will Perfecta make her way in this less-than-perfect world?

Sisters in Pieces: Meet Miriam, Callie and Phoebe Foster. Three sisters who haven't spoken in years. When Miriam accuses her younger sister, Phoebe, of killing their mother, the battle is on.
Sisters in Pieces, twenty tales of life, love, murder and intestinal distress, will bring the Foster sisters together once again.

Tales of the Elemental Goddesses: Rosarita is tired of all these religious wars, politics, and manipulative newscasts. She creates her own religion. One in which ALL the goddesses and saints and holy ones and powerful ones and fairies and anyone else you believe in work together to save the earth.

Back cover photo of Robin Martinez Rice courtesy of Sandra Bruce.

20618651R00293

Made in the USA
Middletown, DE
03 June 2015